Running Out of Time

Kyona Jiles

Kyona Jiles

Blysster Press

Email the author at kyonajiles@yahoo.com
www.kyonajiles.com
www.facebook.com/KyonaJiles
www.twitter.com/KyonaJiles

"Running Out Of Time" Printing History
Blysster Press paperback edition

Blysster Press

A new kind of publisher for a new kind of world.

Printed in the United States of America
www.blysster.com

Acknowledgments

As always, I couldn't do this without the people who go over my drafts. Kara, Jo, Erin, Carla, Danyelle: personal editors extraordinaire!! Special thanks to Charity and Clyde for your hours of hard work and devotion.
Any mistakes are all mine. . .

To my teaching buddy and friend, Shannon, who put up with my wild imagination and random Russian and murder comments. Now on to more vampires. Long live Zoe!

Charity, you are amazing. You give writers a chance to shine and you always put yourself last. Stop it!!

Kelly, thank you for sharing your family, friendship, and love with me. Forever.

For Jan Wood

You touched the lives
of so many people.
You reminded me,
and everyone you met,
that we can do anything.
We love you and miss you.

Books from
Blysster Press
by
Kyona Jiles

Vampire Shadower Series:

First Death

Running Series:

Outrunning The Hunter

Running Out of Time

1

Langley, Virginia – September

Jon's fist slammed into the side of Elana's head. She knew he pulled the punch even though her cheek went instantly numb and pain spiked into her eye. He hadn't broken skin anywhere on her body in the week and a half they'd been training. Bruises, though? Oh, she had bruises on top of bruises.

"Damn it, Elana!" Jon stepped back and dropped his head. "I telegraphed that shot from a mile away. You should have blocked it or at least ducked!"

He was barely winded and when he lifted his eyes to hers, Elana saw anger. This was the most emotion she'd seen him show since meeting him three weeks earlier.

"I'm sorry," she said as she put her hand to her face, wincing.

She traced her fingers over her cheek. This bruise was going to match the one on her thigh from yesterday's kick boxing debacle. What a joke. She wasn't cut out for field work.

"That's going to bruise. Let's take a break and put some ice on it."

Jon walked through the archway of the training room,

his anger disappearing behind the mask of stone he always wore. He grabbed two bottles of water from the refrigerator and tossed one to Elana.

AJ stopped punching his boxing bag and shouted to Jon. "Hey, Matthews, beating up on women, again?" He laughed when Jon turned to glare at him.

AJ was one of the few people who knew Jon's real name and what he was capable of. A few months back, he had helped Jon track down a Chicago Mob boss and one of his lackeys, who had been a leak in the FBI. AJ hadn't actually been in the building when Jon 'disposed of' the leak, although AJ knew the outcome.

AJ was the only person in Langley who felt comfortable trying to joke around with Jon.

"Hey, Elana, why don't you come train with someone who won't rattle your cage? I'll take it easy on you and even take you out for dinner and drinks after." AJ sauntered to where Elana stood holding the cold bottle to her cheek.

"She doesn't need someone who takes it easy on her, Jensen. She needs someone to push her to be the best she can," Jon growled.

He took the bottle from Elana, handed her an icepack, took the lid off the water, and handed it back. "Drink."

"Shit, Jon. You can train her without beating the hell out of her."

"Would you like it if I didn't spar all out with you?"

"Fuck, no!" AJ said.

"I'm not going to treat her any differently just because she's a woman," Jon said.

Elana glanced between the two men, watching their exchange with curiosity. AJ was only a few inches shorter than Jon. Where AJ had dark eyes and hair, Jon had light brown hair and blue eyes. They were both stunningly gorgeous. AJ exuded charm and an easygoing attitude whereas Jon was as charming as a pillar of concrete.

She smiled at AJ. "How about if I continue to let Jon beat the hell out of me, but I take you up on dinner?"

Before AJ could answer, Jon cut in. "You don't have time for that. We have a mission to prepare for. Grab your stuff. We're going to train where you won't be so distracted."

AJ laughed, punching Jon on the shoulder. "Whatever. You just want her all to yourself."

Jon didn't waste time with a response. He walked to the bench holding his gym bag and tank top. As Jon slipped the tank over his head, AJ mouthed the words "I'll call you" to Elana. She nodded and grabbed her bag.

"Where are we going?" she asked as Jon opened the door to his SUV in the parking garage of the CIA.

"Your place. I got you a boxing bag and mini-fridge for your spare room."

"How do you know I have a spare room?"

He started the engine and turned to her. "I know more about you than you think."

They drove in silence for a few miles as Elana adjusted her long, dark hair in the ponytail it was falling out of. She pondered his words.

"Tell me."

Jon glanced at her.

"What more do you know about me?" she asked.

"Elana Estefania Miller. Thirty-one years old. Five foot, nine inches tall. One hundred thirty pounds, clothing size four." He smiled. "Bra thirty-two C."

Elana stared at him through her sunglasses then pushed them on her head. "Measurements are not tough to guess."

Jon stopped for a red light. What poured out of his mouth made Elana feel light-headed.

"Elana Estefania Jefferies-Miller. Mother, Estefania 'Stefanie' Jefferies-Miller, deceased. Father, General Joseph Miller. Your father legally changed your last name when you were ten and a half, dropping the Jefferies, after your mother's funeral. Drunk driving. She's buried in Iowa, on her family plot."

Elana stared in stunned silence.

"Rumor is your father never really recovered from her alcohol-induced death. Seems he didn't want you around much after that. I hear you look a lot like her. Didn't he send you to Paris for school? Ballet?"

The light changed to green. "I also hear you became quite the accomplished dancer. You were asked to join a traveling troupe that's well known in Europe. You chose to come to Langley, Virginia and start working for the CIA as a lowly file clerk."

Elana pulled her glasses down and stared out the window. She pretended what he was saying didn't mean anything. She'd be damned if he'd see her cry. How was she ever going to be a good agent if she couldn't control her emotions? How could she fight for her country when she couldn't stand up for herself?

"Are you here to prove to General Daddy you're nothing like your mother? Or to yourself?" Jon pulled into a parking space at her condo.

She stared out the window for a few heartbeats then turned to the man who had the power to rip her carefully constructed world apart.

"I would appreciate," she began in a trembling voice, "if you would stay out of my personal life." Her voice gained a little more strength. "I'm only going to work with you because I have to."

Hoping her weak knees would support her, Elana stepped out. She shut the door a little harder than she would under normal circumstances and walked with her head held high. She didn't care if he followed her or not. With the way he came at her from left field? Preferably not.

Jon watched Elana walk up the stairs to her second floor condo. He was such an ass. He'd meant to politely ask

her about her past, maybe share a little about his family in
Montana. He'd been making all kinds of mistakes since this
summer. Being around his brother, Michael, and Michael's
wife, Kamielle, had turned Jon's world upside down.

The bachelor, who always wanted to live alone and be
alone, suddenly found himself wanting things he couldn't
have. He'd been attracted to Elana from the first moment
he'd seen her. He was fighting it. The best way to push her
away would be to convince her he was a worthless son of a
bitch. Looked like he was off to a good start.

Why had she joined the CIA? She wore her emotions
on her sleeve. If Deputy Director Kimball kept her as a field
agent, anyone with connections was going to find out her
daddy was a Three-Star General. That would make her
valuable for ransoms. It made her a liability.

Jon didn't like caring about her feelings. He didn't like
caring about anything. During the summer he'd come to
some realizations about his life: it kind of sucked. His brother
had found happiness with a beautiful, amazing woman. Shit,
Jon was jealous.

If he planned to survive this mission, help Elana
survive, and be at the family ranch for Christmas, he needed
to pull his whiny ass together. Emotions got people killed. He
was not going to be one of those people. And he would not
let Elana be one, either.

Jon jogged up the stairs. He knocked. "Elana, I'm
trying to teach you a valuable lesson. You need to learn how
to compartmentalize and shut down your emotions."

The dead-bolt lock clicked.

"Think of how you feel right now. You need to learn to
channel your anger, fear, and sadness into something else.
Something more deadly. Let's spar. I'll show you how good
you can be." Jon leaned his forehead against the door in a
moment of relaxation.

He wasn't one to explain himself. This was Kamielle's

fault. His sister-in-law was trying to get him in touch with his 'feelings'.

It was time to get Elana ready for the big bad world of CIA tricks. She needed to keep her feelings in check and figure out Jon wasn't worth spitting on. He'd be a good partner, but that was it. The only way to get her to work the way he needed was to continue acting like a world class asshole. It wasn't too hard for him to pull off.

He needed privacy for them to finish this conversation. It took him seven seconds to jimmy the door handle lock and six to do the deadbolt.

Elana stood on the other side of the door, eyes wide.

"Listen, girl, I've about had it with your shit."

"What? My shit? What did I do?" Elana asked.

He pulled his tank top out of his shorts and ripped it over his head.

She stared for a moment at the puffy, pink scar on his abdomen. She'd wondered more than once where it had come from yet never felt comfortable enough to ask. Finally, her brain kicked in and she realized Jon was undressing in her living room.

"What are you doing?"

"We're going to get to know each other a little better and do what we should have done from the beginning. I know a lot more about you than you do me. We're going to spar. For every point you score, you get to ask me a question. For every point I score, I get to ask you a question. Answers have to be honest and immediate." He started to circle her.

"What are you talking about?"

Elana couldn't grasp what was going on. The man who hardly talked had said more to her in the last twenty minutes than he'd said in almost a month.

"You heard me. I don't like to repeat myself." Jon lunged.

They landed in a heap next to her coffee table with Jon

straddling her waist, holding her arms above her head.

"Point for me," he said. "First question. Why ballet?"

Elana blinked rapidly. "What are you doing?"

"Answer the question. Those are the rules. If you manage to score a point, you can ask me something."

She realized this was the only way she could train and learn about the infamous Jon Matthews. She closed her eyes, centering herself. It was something she was learning in Yoga. Finding her Chi or some shit like that.

"Ballet is a way to express yourself with your body when you're no good at expressing yourself with words." She opened her eyes.

He tilted his head and released her arms. She took advantage and bucked her hips, attempting to send him over her head. He countered and leaned back. It was exactly what she wanted him to do. When his shoulders were by her knees, she used her legs to pull him down to the floor by his upper body. She had incredibly strong legs after years of dancing. Even Jon, muscular and trained, couldn't get up because of the awkward angle.

"Point for you," he panted.

"What's your real name?"

Jon spun his body, forcing her over to her stomach. He grabbed her right foot and locked in a heel hook. Elana's muffled sob was stopped by the carpet.

He looked over his shoulder. "We're changing to 'yes' and 'no' questions."

"That's not fair!" She strained to free her foot. "You can't change the rules in the middle of the game!"

He released her and jumped up. She flipped herself to her back and scissored her legs at his. Jon jumped in the air as Elana anticipated. She kicked out with her right leg and hit him in the side of the knee.

"Point for me. I get two questions because you cheated on the last one. Is Jon your real first name?"

"Yes."

"Is Matthews your real last name?"

"You already know the answer to that. Of course not." He backed outside the range of her lethal feet.

Elana stood slowly, testing the weight on her foot after that heel hook. She toed off her shoes and pulled off her shirt so she was in spandex shorts and a sports bra. While he stared, she kicked and hit him on the side of the face.

"Point. Do you like to look at me barely dressed?" She crouched, grinning.

"You definitely distract me."

"That wasn't a yes or no answer. Are you changing the rules again?"

"Yes, I like to look at barely dressed women. No, I'm not changing the rules again."

He rubbed his cheek. She'd gotten in a nice shot. Good thing she'd taken off those tennis shoes otherwise he'd be missing some skin.

Jon kicked out and Elana blocked the shot from hitting her stomach. He countered quickly with an uppercut to her jaw. She staggered backward, more than a little dazed. He straightened and held his hand out.

"I'm—"

"Don't you dare apologize for hitting me," she wiped blood from her lower lip. "What's your question?"

"Have you always wanted to work for the CIA?" Jon moved back to his fighting stance.

"No." Her answer was fast and harsh. Interesting.

Elana went down on one knee as Jon's foot sailed over her head. She pulled her punch to his crotch so she wouldn't injure him permanently, although still made contact. He winced and jumped back.

"My point. Do you hate me?" She didn't breathe as she waited.

"Hate? No. Why would I hate you?"

He knew he'd been a jerk for three weeks and he'd probably crossed the line today by bringing up her mother, except he didn't think he'd been that bad.

"Just answer yes or no. Stick to the rules you made."

He took advantage of her locked posture, sweeping his leg and taking her down at the knees. She landed on her coffee table, the wood splintering.

"Have I really been that awful?"

"Is that your point question?" She glared.

He nodded.

"Yes, you've been that awful."

They went on sparring for another twenty minutes. She kept up with him, but he was better. He averaged two questions to every one of hers. They both began to loosen up and the questions became a little more fun. *Do you have any pets? Do you like living in Virginia? Do you hate Kimball? Do you like ice cream?*

It wasn't until Elana was straddling Jon's midsection with his arms pinned under her knees that he got uncomfortable.

"Have you ever slept with someone while on a mission?" She was breathing deeply and had cuts on her from the wood of the table, sweat stinging the wounds.

He went still. "What?"

"You heard me. I don't like to repeat myself."

"We're done." He sat up and Elana fell off. She lay on the floor looking at the ceiling.

"I find it interesting when you don't like the way things are going, you just change the rules of the game."

Jon stood over her. "Life is not a game. What I do is direct things where I want them to go. If you don't like it, tough shit. Go shower. I'm going to hang up the boxing bag." He walked toward the spare bedroom.

"You don't get to boss me around in my own house you jackass. If I take a shower it's because I want to, not because you told me to!" The man was so infuriating. Finally feeling like she had the guts, Elana said, "And keep out of my personal life. Don't bring up my family. Ever."

Jon nodded once and walked into the spare room. She got mad at herself for feeling elated about a silly little nod. Like it was some kind of acceptance from a legend.

And when had he put the boxing bag and mini-fridge in her house and why hadn't she noticed?

Elana stomped through her bedroom to the master bathroom. Even though she was acting like a child, she didn't care. She wasn't ready to be a field agent and she wasn't in Jon Matthews's league. Or whatever the hell his name was.

2

Elana spent twenty minutes in the shower enjoying the hot water. Maybe if she stayed in long enough, he'd leave. Yeah, sure, like she'd get that lucky.

Damn man, thinking he knew her better than she knew herself. Dressed in a new set of workout clothes, this time with a shirt, Elana went to her spare bedroom. She felt more calm and relaxed after a shower.

She watched as Jon tightened the nut on the lag bolt he'd put through her ceiling. Without much effort, he lifted the heavy, red punching bag and hung it from the bolt. He had used the spare bathroom and showered. His military haircut barely looked different. But he was missing the layer of sweat and the splinters from the coffee table.

Elana glanced over her shoulder to the living room. The broken table was gone, all the debris picked up. Wow, he was efficient.

She turned back to say thank you. What came out instead was, "You're buying me a new coffee table, jerk." Hmm, maybe she wasn't as calm and relaxed as she originally thought.

Jon smiled. Damn that smile. He probably got bad girls across the world to do whatever he wanted with that smile. Why did she care so much about what he did with women?

First the question about sleeping with someone on the job, now this.

Jon punched the red bag. "I should have started here. You weren't ready for sparring before you got a feeling for hitting something."

"I've hit things before. I had to go through The Farm like any other recruit. I've done hand-to-hand training, range practice, and linguistics."

"You know enough about hand-to-hand you don't hurt your partner," he said. "AJ was partially right. I don't need to be beating the shit out of you until you're ready. But I meant what I said about treating you like any other agent."

"Well, of course I want you to treat me like any other agent. That's why I'm here," Elana said.

"No, you're here because one or both of us pissed someone off. I figure you're the lamb led to slaughter."

"What does that mean?"

"It means you've been a fucking desk jockey for the last six years. You've never been promoted to anything dangerous. You went on two recon missions a month ago to interpret and did it from the luxury of a hotel room. You should still be at a desk job. Instead, Kimball puts you with me. You know how many partners I've been through in the last fifteen years? You're lucky number thirteen."

"What happened to them?" Elana asked.

"Four were killed. They were good men. Five disappeared. I figure they got in over their heads somewhere and were disposed of."

Elana put her hand to her throat. "The other three?"

"I killed them myself." He walked until he had her backed against the wall.

"Wh— Why?" She put her palms flat against the wall. Jon was trying to scare her. She just didn't know why.

"Because."

"That's not an answer." She met his steely eyes.

Jon smiled again except this time didn't look boyishly handsome. He looked like the trained operative he was. He leaned in and she moved her head, smacking it on the wall.

"You better get used to me being close to you, Lana. Don't blow my cover. I killed one of those partners for blowing my cover. I killed another for trying to sell me out." He put his mouth in close to her ear. "Actually I killed two for trying to sell me out."

He was pinning her to the wall with his hips and legs.

"I'd never blow your cover or sell you out," she closed her eyes and absorbed his closeness and heat. She almost whimpered.

The man hardly ever smiled, was a bully, and was trying to scare her. Yet, if he even nodded his head toward her in invitation, she'd probably tumble into bed with him in a heartbeat. She told herself it was because she hadn't had a lover in the last decade.

He continued. "I suppose, in a way, I killed all three for trying to sell me out. The last one was a woman. I'm pretty sure the Deputy Director sent her as a distraction. She distracted me all right. Distracted my dick right up to the moment she was about to kill me."

Elana sucked in a startled breath. "Your partner tried to kill you after having sex with you?"

"Oh, baby, months of sex. I even started thinking I could fall in love. I'll never make that mistake again."

He grabbed both Elana's arms and slid them up the wall until he could clasp her wrists in one of his hands. With his free hand, he traced the light bruise he'd put on her cheek. She shivered under his touch.

"So which one are you, Lana?" he stretched out the syllables of his nickname for her. It sounded like lay-nuh. "A distraction sent by Kimball? A real agent? Or a disposable asset Kimball's using to get me out of my job?"

"I'm a real agent." She licked her lips and looked into

his eyes without flinching.

"I can feel your heartbeat in your wrists. Did you know before lie detector tests, people could tell if someone was lying by feeling their pulse?"

"I'm not lying," she said through clinched teeth.

"Then, what are you? Scared?" He pushed his body into hers. "Turned on?"

This time, Elana whimpered, yet she never turned her face or closed her eyes. She was getting ready to answer. She wasn't sure what she was going to say, though.

He let go and stepped back. "Not bad, Agent."

She blinked rapidly. "What?"

"You passed my second test. You didn't break under pressure and didn't freak out when I told you I'd killed three of my partners."

"You mean, you made it all up?" Anger replaced confusion.

"No. Everything I told you happened."

"If that was the second test, what was the first?" She took a step toward him.

"You didn't cry when I punched you at the gym." He walked out of the room.

Elana grabbed the first thing she could reach, a water bottle, and hurled it at his retreating back. "You bastard!" she yelled.

How did he reduce her to this? She never yelled at people or called them names.

Jon was back, pinning her to the wall. "Why am I a bastard?"

"You can't just play with my emotions!"

"I can and I will. If you're going to be a good agent you need to become a robot. Show all human emotions but don't feel them. Those twelve partners before you? They killed themselves. I don't care who actually pulled the trigger. They were either too soft or too stupid. I don't want you to kill yourself.

"So quit acting like a girl and act like a CIA agent. I won't die because of you and I won't watch you die. I'll be back tomorrow. Be ready to spar hand to hand. No more point system and no more going easy on you. And you aren't going to be pulling any punches either." He walked out, slamming the front door.

Jon stood outside Elana's door. Jesus, why was he being such a dick? He was attracted and blaming it on her. Hell, she probably didn't even like him. That would be better.

Suddenly he was looking for a fight; a real fight. He didn't care who it was with, either. He almost wished he was back in Kalispell so he and Michael could rough it up.

By the time he was in the driver's seat, Jon was on the phone with AJ. Sparring was only fun if your opponent knew how dirty you fought.

When she knew Jon was gone and not coming back, Elana slid her body down the wall and dropped her head into her hands. Part of her knew he was right. She was too emotional, always had been. That was why the General had sent her to school in Paris. She wouldn't let her mother's death go.

For over an hour, Elana sat on the floor, reliving her childhood in flashes. She was ten when her mother died. The General had come to her on that bleak October morning and Elana knew something bad had happened. General Joseph Miller had looked forlorn, an emotion she'd never seen on the hard man's face.

He'd dropped to his knees and held her as she screamed and cried. The rest was kind of a blur. She remembered getting on an airplane. Her mother's funeral in Iowa. Rain, wind. She sat on the cold, metal folding chair next to her father. Stefanie's parents had died before Elana was born. There was no one but her only child and devastated husband to mourn her death.

Kids at school and people her father worked with whispered about sex, drugs, and alcohol. What a bad woman she had been. Elana loved her mother and wanted to know if what the people were saying was true. Her father never answered. Not at the funeral and not for the next four years.

Finally, when Elana was fifteen, she found the newspaper articles. A sordid tale of partying, drugs, and alcohol. Her mother had not been a good person. She'd killed a couple walking on the street before she'd wrapped her car around a telephone pole.

Unable to handle the information, Elana rebelled. She started drinking, partying. Her career military, single father hadn't known how to control a teenage girl.

The General sent her to Paris.

She'd already been dancing, except Paris offered so much more than American ballet schools ever could. Luckily she didn't self-destruct in Europe. Elana threw herself into school and dance, talked to her father once a week on the phone but never flew home to visit him. She spent almost ten years in Europe.

She learned and studied languages which got her noticed by the CIA. She couldn't dance forever and the thought of traveling, doing good for her country, making her father proud, was something that appealed to her. Then she was in. The man who recruited her had told her to pack her bags and report to Virginia for training and testing.

For six years, she'd worked a desk in Virginia. Records. She was good at her job, rarely missed a day of work, and constantly asked to be moved to the field.

Two months ago, newly appointed Deputy Director Kimball had called Elana to his office and given her the words she'd been waiting for. Field Missions. The first two had been easy. Cushy hotel rooms, room service, using the pool, exercise room, and spa.

Then Kimball had mentioned Russia. The 'with Jon

Matthews' part was the only thing she hadn't counted on. Why had she been paired with him? Did Kimball want them to fail as Jon had said? Elana didn't know what to think about anything anymore.

She knew she wasn't going to give up. She was going to do what she'd wanted to do since she was little. She was going to finally make her father proud. She was going to make the world a better place. No, she hadn't always wanted to be a CIA agent. She wanted to be a dancer. Sometimes life gave you lemons. What was that old saying? 'When life gives you lemons, make lemonade'.

Elana laughed as she started throwing punches at the red bag.

"Screw lemonade. I'm going to need vodka. Lots of expensive Russian vodka."

3

Not knowing when they would leave the country was the worst part for Elana. The best part was every day she got a little more comfortable in her new skin as a spy. She was also getting more comfortable around Jon.

The days rolled into weeks and went by in a blur as Jon and Elana trained without taking a single day off. They worked on their cover story and acted in character as much as possible. He was Jon Matthews, illegal arms dealer, and she was Elana Smith, dumb girlfriend.

The constant physical training had caused Elana to lose what little fat she had on her body and build up muscle. She was in even better shape than when she'd been dancing. She could handle guns and knives like she'd been doing it for years, and could speak seven foreign languages and dialects, mostly European. Very handy when on your way to Russia.

It was strange to spend such a huge amount of time with one person and never feel like you were friends. Since Jon taught her to spend over fifteen hours a day in character, their relationship was superficial. He treated her like a girlfriend who was only good for decoration and sex. They didn't have sex, but in public he touched and kissed her. It was unnerving; more than she wanted to admit. She wanted to push it behind closed doors and see if she could seduce him. She changed her mind because she wouldn't know how to seduce him if there were a manual.

No, they weren't friends, but they worked damn well together. The bottom line was to get the job done.

Elana had become so immersed in character, she hadn't spoken to her dad and she never made it on the date with AJ. Then AJ had been sent to South America on his own mission and she hadn't thought much about anything else.

Jon and Elana's assignment was to find out who was feeding the Russian Mafia information about different government agencies from around the world. The key to the puzzle lay with a family who had worked its way back into the ranks. The brothers they were investigating were Mikhail and Boris Novlak. For the last six weeks, one or both of the brothers had been out of the country. Now they were home and it was time to move in.

The fact this was only her third field assignment sat heavily on Elana's shoulders. All she'd done was watch surveillance tapes and translate. Jon's snarky comment about her sitting around in a nice hotel room was true. She hadn't even been out of North America, for crap's sake, and now she was going to be acting like some whore in Russia. How was that going to help Jon? Who did she think she was kidding; she couldn't do this.

"I can't do this," Elana blurted her taboo thoughts then froze.

Jon was watching a small group of men load a private jet with their clothes and weapons.

"Don't do this to me. We trained hard. And well. You're as ready as you're going to be. We have a job to do."

Jon was already dressed in character while she had opted to change on the jet. His crew cut and square jaw made him look like a really big Marine. The image was ruined if you looked below his neck because the silk suit he wore didn't make him look like a soldier. Except she knew he was. He'd been in the Special Forces right out of high school. That was all any of the agents at the CIA knew about him. She wished she knew more than the stupid 'yes and no' questions he'd answered for her. Something more than the information that had been in the reports of his missions.

Elana assessed his blue eyes and chiseled cheekbones, floored again at just how handsome he was. He had the broad shoulders of a football player. The small scar through his right eyebrow added to his sex appeal. Not that she thought that he was sexy.

I don't think he's sexy. I don't, I don't, I won't.

"Quit acting like a girl, Elana, and get your ass on this jet. We've spent almost eight weeks getting ready for this mission. That's way more time than most agents get. You're ready." He took her hand and pulled her up the steps.

The jet was amazing. Like the inside of a luxury travel trailer. Jon walked to the bar and pulled out a bottle of single malt scotch. What was he doing?

He grabbed two glasses, pouring three fingers of scotch in each. He placed the bottle in a bucket of ice.

"I'm not drinking that," Elana said.

"Yes, you are."

"It's barely nine in the morning!"

"C'mon, Lana," he said.

She snatched the drink from his hand.

As the jet taxied down the runway in preparation for takeoff, Jon raised his glass. "To a safe, successful mission."

Elana lifted her glass. "I'll drink to that." She tipped it back and chugged.

Jon had taken one sip. He raised an eyebrow.

"What? I don't like the taste."

"Fine liquor is meant to be savored. Just like a fine woman."

"Well, I wouldn't know about either one. There's no such thing as fine liquor. There's probably no such thing as a fine woman or man." She put down her glass and closed her eyes. She needed to relax before she freaked out again.

Jon watched her while he sipped. At first, she was breathing methodically, almost as though she were counting her breaths. Then, her body relaxed and her breathing evened out. She was asleep within fifteen minutes. Probably because of the three fingers of scotch flowing through her veins.

Her dark hair was up in a ponytail and her face was free of makeup, making her look much younger than her thirty-one years. She was the opposite of any agent he had ever worked with. They had all been hardened. Lana still exuded innocence. If she could ever learn to school her emotions, she'd be one of the best undercover agents in the business. Almost as good as him.

He enjoyed the comfort of watching her sleep. Jon was usually only this relaxed when he was around his family. Not all of their training had been acting. He enjoyed getting to pet and kiss her in public; pretend she was his. He liked seeing her laugh and liked buying her pretty things.

Was this how Michael had felt with Kamielle at the beginning of their relationship? Hell, they were still kind of at the beginning of their relationship. Michael and Kamielle had been married at the end of July in a small ceremony in Las Vegas. What should have been cheesy had been perfect and beautiful.

Jon was glad his little brother had finally found happiness. He deserved it. So did Kamielle. The woman had been through more in the last year than most people dealt with in an entire lifetime.

That thought had him getting out his phone and texting Michael and Kamielle. *'in air. will chk in soon. luv.'* Short and to the point. That was Jon.

He reached for the bottle of scotch. The woman across the small aisle from him was causing his drinking to escalate. He didn't feel like thinking of that right now, so he added another splash to his glass and put the bottle back. He reclined his seat slightly and closed his eyes.

They had a lot of groundwork to lay when they arrived in Moscow. Jon was positive this op would be over in four weeks at the most. He and Elana were going to spend the first week in Moscow then head to St. Petersburg to see what business was like there.

As his mind worked, he sipped his scotch.

The Novlak brothers were running guns, drugs, and prostitutes. They had a lucrative business supplying Europe, Asia, the Middle East, and the United States with all three. Finding out who their middle men were was going to be tough. You didn't waltz up to members of the Russian Mafia and ask who they hung out with. Jon was going to have to work his way into the group.

The only way to do that would be supplying them with guns. That was the part of the job he hated. There was always someone higher up who needed to be brought down.

It was going to be interesting to see how his little Lana handled real field work. She'd done well in preparation for the mission. He could tell she was scared, but only because he'd studied her when she wasn't looking. When she was nervous, she chewed on her lower lip or twirled her hair. Hopefully she didn't play poker because the girl didn't have the face for it, at least, not yet.

Jon allowed himself a few more moments of pondering the puzzle that was Elana. He finished his drink and closed his eyes again. This time, he dozed until the plane hit some turbulence.

Elana mumbled something in her sleep then came awake with a start. "Where are we?"

"Calm down, we've only been in the air a few hours."

She released her seat belt and stood. Jon watched through slitted eyes as she stretched like a cat and almost touched the ceiling. Then she bent over and palmed her hands on the floor.

Jon cursed under his breath, grabbed the damn bottle of scotch, and stood. He brushed the curve of her hip with his knuckles as he passed. Elana stood quickly as though she'd been burned.

The sexual tension between them was palpable as Jon grabbed a new glass and poured himself a generous shot. "You should change," he said before slamming back the liquor.

"What's the matter with you?" she asked, walking down the short hallway toward the area with the king size bed and the closet with their clothes.

He dropped his chin to his chest. "Let's not do this right now."

She slid open the closet door and pulled out a hot pink, one piece tank dress. As she looked at the dress, something in her became emboldened.

"No. Let's do this right now. You feel it too."

Jon's head snapped up and he turned to look at her. "Feel what?" He didn't even know why he asked.

"Don't pull that shit with me, super spy," she said. "This crazy, stupid, totally inappropriate attraction."

"I don't know what you're talking about. I think you're starting to confuse reality with the mission."

"Really?" She pulled her shirt over her head.

He almost stopped breathing.

She released the zipper on the side of her slacks and let them pool at her feet. She watched his eyes widen slightly and then track down her body. She was wearing white lingerie. An almost see-through lace bra and matching thong panties. She turned her back and shimmied into the dress.

"You're playing with fire, baby girl," Jon whispered.

"I've wanted to play with fire for over a month now except I haven't had the guts." She kept her back to him proving she still didn't have the guts. But, boy, did she have the ass.

His feet propelled him toward her without his brain registering it. Suddenly he was standing behind her. Not touching her skin, he took out her ponytail, moved the curtain of hair from her back and let it fall over her shoulder.

Elana froze. She'd never expected him to do anything with her bold move. Now what? She could feel the heat from his body against her back even though he wasn't making contact. She felt his breath on her neck and tensed so much she thought she might shatter if he touched her.

There were no words for the effect on her body when his lips touched the curve of her shoulder. Light kisses rained up her neck to her ear.

"Lana. Lana. Lana. Your timing couldn't be worse. Now I do think you were sent as a distraction."

"Jon, I—" he cut her off with a quick bite.

"Don't," he said, putting his hands on her hips.

She tried to turn but he wouldn't let her.

"If we weren't getting ready for one of the most important missions of both our lives, I'd throw you down on this bed and show you fire. I'd fuck you for a week straight just to see if I could get you out of my system. I should have done it a month ago."

His hands tightened on her hips and he pulled her so the back of her slammed into the front of him. The very hard front of him. Elana tried to say his name except it wouldn't come out. There was no air in her lungs.

"But you're not the kind of girl for no strings, Lana. You're not supposed to be here. You deserve romance and love. A husband and kids. When this is over, you need to go back to your desk job. Hell, you need to go back to Paris and dance. I know you want to.

"We're not here to play house, we're here to do a goddamn job. So, I'm going to keep my dick in my pants, you're going to keep that sweet ass in those tiny little panties, and we're going to get this job done. Do you understand me?" He was breathing so hard, her hair moved with every word he said into her neck.

She wanted so badly to turn around and kiss him. Kiss him until he shut up. What did he know about what she wanted or needed?

He gripped her hips so tightly Elana was sure she'd have bruises. Then he stepped back and practically shoved her away.

She turned carefully and took in the sight of him. It was the most emotion she'd ever seen. He looked right at her, chest heaving with the force of his breathing. His entire body was tense, coiled, like he'd strike out if anything moved.

"It would have been good," she whispered.

"Yeah, it would have. But that's not why we're here." He turned. "Stay in here until we land."

Jon slid the door to the bedroom closed and went back to his seat, trying to clear the smell and feel of Elana's body from his senses. Work. Thinking of work would get him back on track.

He pictured the Novlak brothers. It was a simple trace up the chain. Would it lead him where he thought it would? Could he keep his hands off Elana? What was he going to learn, if anything, about how Deputy Director Kimball was connected to the Russian Mafia?

What was the worst that could happen?

His mind drifted to the feel of Elana's skin under his lips and the sound of her sighs. What was the worst that could happen? This was going to be a fucking mess of the highest degree.

4

Moscow, Russia – October

When the plane landed, Jon didn't talk to Elana. They had a limo set up to deliver them to the hotel with their luggage. Jon pointed at the limo then walked back to the jet. She sat in the quietness until he joined her half an hour later.

"We'll spend a week here and then we'll head to St. Petersburg. My contacts don't think the brothers are in Moscow. We'll throw around some money and see what happens."

"What do we do if they don't take the bait?"

"They'll take the bait. The bad guys always take the bait," he said. "So do the good guys."

"You didn't take the bait," she said. "What does that make you?"

Jon looked out the window. "Either really smart or really dumb. I'll let you know when I figure it out."

"Jon," she tried one last time.

"This is why the General sent you to Paris, wasn't it? You just don't know when to let anything go."

"It's exactly why he sent me to Paris."

"Didn't learn your lesson, did you?"

"You can't send me to Paris," she countered.

"Anything between us is a bad idea."

"Fine."

She sat back. She'd just wait until this stupid mission was over. As soon as they were back on American soil, she was going to jump him and wasn't going to take no for an answer.

He looked into her eyes. Almost like he was trying to read her thoughts. His habit of staring was disconcerting.

"We have a mission to do and I will not endanger one of us because of personal issues. Let. It. Go."

"Fine," she said again, crossing her arms. Although it wasn't fine. It sucked.

The ride to the hotel was grueling. Jon did his best to ignore the sexual tension, but it was difficult when the woman looked so damn good. The pink dress, that looked more like saran wrap, barely covered anything when she sat down. Add high heels lacing halfway up her legs with matching pink ribbon and she looked like a damned lollipop or cotton candy. Either way, he wanted a bite. He wanted a bite so damn bad his jaw ached. She smelled like candy, too.

Son of a motherfuckin' bitch. How in the world did he plan to survive the next few weeks?

Jon slipped his sunglasses on to hide his gaze. She had a Marilyn Monroe thing going, having hid her glossy black hair under a wig. He had the urge to ask her if she'd sit on his lap and sing "Happy Birthday, Mr. President". Maybe he needed more scotch.

They made it to the hotel without talking and Jon forced himself to breathe normally. He had to get his head on straight. He couldn't risk their lives over sex. He could do this, he had to.

There are a few different ways to get noticed by the Mafia, no matter what country you're in. Throwing around your money in a questionable manner is a great start.

As their bags were being unloaded at a hotel that resembled the Venetian in Las Vegas, Jon asked the bellhop where they could acquire some female escorts for the evening. The boy blushed and asked how many.

Elana said, "Ten to start with." Then she smashed her perfect breasts into Jon's arm and licked his neck. Within minutes, the manager of the hotel arrived and had them moved to a five bedroom suite in a private area of the hotel.

It really did look like the Venetian. The Novlaks were trying to bring their version of the United States to Moscow. Not many people who lived in the area could afford to stay there. It was rumored various political leaders, sanctioned and unsanctioned, from different countries had been meeting here since its doors had opened three months ago.

Indoor waterfalls and miles of winding canals with gondola rides greeted the couple as they strolled through the doors. Jon asked about several illegal activities, such as gambling and street drugs, to go with his extreme request for the prostitutes.

Elana spent five minutes throwing a tantrum about how she wanted men sent to their room, too.

Within one hour, there was a drunken, drug induced orgy going on in their suite. They moved through the rooms, making sure they were seen and appearing to participate, but never actually doing so.

By the time Jon secured them in a suite across the hall, Elana was exhausted and euphoric.

"This is amazing!" she said as she pulled off her wig and shook out her hair.

He tried remembering his first real mission and couldn't recall ever being so excited over the job. It was work and that was all. He couldn't remember the last time he'd thought of it as more than a responsibility either. Seeing it through Elana's eyes reminded him why he'd started working for the CIA in the first place. The excitement, getting to spend money that wasn't yours, living in a movie set every day.

And killing the bad guys. He really liked that part.

"I mean, I've never seen so many disgusting things in my life, but I felt safe with you, and everyone was sucking up to us because they knew it was our money giving them this hedonistic evening." She walked to one of the bathrooms and closed the door halfway.

He watched her in the mirror. She shimmied out of the cotton candy saran wrap and unlaced her heels. She talked nonstop and Jon wondered if she was ever going to run out of steam. Then she unhooked her bra and he must have made a sound because she stopped mid-sentence and met his lust-filled eyes in the mirror. Her hands shot up to cup her bare breasts and Jon groaned.

"I, uh, need to take a shower." She slammed the door.

He needed to get a grip. Still.

Thirty minutes later, she had composed herself enough to go back out and be in the same room with him. She'd been going on and on about everything she'd seen and done since they got to the hotel and hadn't been paying attention to the fact she was practically naked and in a room with a man that made her hotter than a raging forest fire.

Wearing the hotel bathrobe and ignoring what happened earlier, because she was getting good at that, Elana went to the room service tray that had been delivered while she was in the shower. She snacked while wandering around the smaller suite. The other shower was running and she tried not to picture Jon. Naked and wet.

It was close to midnight and she couldn't believe she hadn't crashed from jet lag or the time change. She was too jacked up and excited about finally being on a real mission.

Wearing his hotel bathrobe, Jon appeared from the other bathroom in a haze of steam.

"I can't believe you're not dead on your feet."

"I was just thinking the same thing," she said. "I'm too excited. I know it's dangerous, but this is so much better than sitting at my desk logging travel files and expense reports."

"I could never be anywhere but the field."

Jon pulled out their laptop and booted up the secure internet connection and encryption programs.

Elana jumped on one of the rare glimpses into his life. "What's your favorite part?"

"This." He waved his hand around the room. "I love going so many places in the world. My brother used to work for the FBI and he never left the states."

"You have a brother?" she said. "We've been partners for over two months and you're just now telling me you have a brother?"

"You never asked," Jon said.

"What else don't I know about you?"

"A lot, I'm sure."

Taking advantage of his mood, Elana forged on. "Do you have any other siblings?"

"I have a sister named Julie who is married to a great guy and has great kids."

He was an uncle. The most imposing man she'd ever met had family. He was human.

"Wow, I can't believe we've never shared anything personal with each other. Those yes and no questions from before don't count. Shouldn't partners be best friends?" She sat, food forgotten.

"Sometimes it's possible to get too close," he said.

"Why?"

"When your emotions get involved you can lose your edge. I don't need to know anything personal about you."

"You know plenty of personal things about me. You know more about my past than I do," she said.

"I know what I read. I don't know how you feel about any of it. And I don't want to know. That crosses my line."

And just like that, the moment she thought they were having was broken.

Jon turned away because he couldn't handle the defeat

in her eyes. He wasn't going to fall into her trap. She was sweet and good and shouldn't be working with him. The sooner she realized it, the better. He gave his full attention to the computer.

After a few clicks he said, "I've got some information on the Novlaks."

Elana tried to seem interested. His ability to change topics and shut off his emotions was giving her a headache.

"What?" she managed to ask.

"Seems their drug connection is Enrique Juarez. Makes a lot more sense as to how they've been getting by customs."

Enrique was a high level drug cartel leader from Peru.

"Who's getting you this information?"

"AJ. I pulled some strings to have him sent to South America." An evil smile tilted his lips. "Not only did it get him out of our hair, it gets us some intel we need."

"Out of our hair?" she asked confused.

"I was tired of him hanging around the gym while we were working."

"If I didn't know better, I'd think you were jealous. But that can't be true. I'm sure jealousy is an emotion you don't have."

He grunted.

Elana was tired. Following Jon's train of thought and dealing with his mixed messages exhausted her. Add in the jet ride, orgy next door, lack of sleep, and she was done.

"Not only do the Novlaks have their mitts in drugs, guns, and prostitution, it seems they have a stranglehold on the country's gambling and alcohol production. These boys have been busy."

Elana went to get ready for bed. As much as she wanted to sleep in her Iowa Hawkeyes jersey and a pair of shorts, she had to pack like the girlfriend of an arms dealer for when someone searched their luggage.

Her silk nightie was midnight blue with black scalloped

edges. It barely made it to her thighs and the spaghetti straps holding it up looked like they'd snap if Jon breathed on them. She was just going to walk right past him and go to one of the other rooms when she heard something that stopped her.

"Holy shit, Jon, you lucky fucking bastard. I'm stuck in the fucking jungle and you're in a hotel room with her. Not fair, man, not fair."

The devil on her shoulder made her go stand behind Jon at the computer.

"AJ. How are you?"

The video connection was pristine and AJ looked as handsome as ever. Maybe a little sweaty from the jungle he mentioned, but he pulled off rumpled almost as well as Jon.

"Better, darling. I will have happy, happy dreams now that I've seen you in that outfit. Whatcha guys doing?" AJ waggled his eyes suggestively.

"Working," Jon said. "Is there a reason for this?"

"Jeez. Lighten up. You're in a hotel room with Elana," AJ said. "I think things could be worse. You're not crawling around this hole. I planted some information about you that should trickle to Enrique in a day or two. The usual stories. What a great customer you are and how you've never had a complaint with your products."

"Thanks." Jon went to cut the connection.

"How about Elana and I take over communications. I'd rather look at her hot bod than your ugly mug. Night, sweetie." AJ blew Elana a kiss right before Jon slammed the laptop closed.

"Damn man doesn't know when to be serious."

"He's a hell of a lot easier to talk to than you."

"I'm not here for you to talk to. I'm here to do a job."

"So you keep saying," she said. "Are you trying to remind me or yourself?" She stomped to her room and slammed the door.

Jon moved mechanically through the other rooms in

their suite, setting up scrambling devices so when the Novlaks figured out what room they were in, they couldn't spy on the couple. The larger suite with all the prostitutes was surely bugged. If anyone asked why they weren't sleeping in it, Jon had the perfect justification. It was being used.

He tried to ignore the way Elana had looked in that damn excuse for a nightgown and how her lotion had smelled. He really tried to ignore how AJ's comments pissed him off. He was acting like a damn jealous woman.

It didn't make sense and he didn't like it.

5

Elana woke to the sound of loud voices and the vibration of a text on her phone. She palmed the pistol under her pillow while she evaluated the threat outside her door. There was a combination of Russian and English. Jon's voice was calm and steady so she checked the text instead of busting into the living room with her gun drawn.

'showtime... dont change clothes... remember ur mine... ignore the others and hang on me... ur going to b fine'.

Elana took a deep breath, deleted the text, and got ready. She put on the blonde wig, fluffed it up, and arranged her cleavage in the silk nightie. For added effect, she put a black sleep mask on top of her head. The butterflies in her stomach told her this was so much more than the translation missions. This was life and death. One wrong move and she could get them killed.

Before she let herself think about it too much, she pushed her chest out, whipped open the bedroom door, and runway walked into the living room. Her eyes never left Jon as she strutted to him.

In her peripheral vision, she spied two armed guards inside the main door, both toting automatic machine guns. The bellhop from the night before stood cowering against the far wall and a large man with a shaved head and prison tattoos was arguing with Jon in Russian. She recognized him as Gregor Malstanski, a Polish refugee who was now the head of security for the Novlak brothers.

Conversation stopped and all eyes tracked Elana. Goosebumps rose on her skin.

"Jon, Pookie," she said, "you guys' loud voices woke me up. You told me to gets lots of sleep so's we could party again."

"Not now, Lana," Jon said angrily as he reached out and pulled her roughly to him. With his chin, he nodded toward the Pole. "Can't you see I'm a little busy?"

Elana turned scared, round eyes to the other men in the room as though just noticing they were there. She let out a strangled peep and tried to hide behind Jon's big body.

"Nuh uh, lover," Jon turned her so the men had an uncompromised view of her barely dressed body. "You obviously wanted all these men to see you, so, let them look."

Elena pretended to struggle as four sets of lust-filled eyes savored everything below her neck. Even the cowering bellhop wasn't oblivious.

"This," Jon finally said to Gregor, "Is why I didn't sleep next door with all the others. My flavor of the month doesn't understand I'm the only one who gets to partake in activities. The drugs and alcohol started flowing last night and she opened her thighs for the first man that crooked his finger. So I put her in here and went back to enjoy the party."

Elana stiffened. Obviously the Novlaks head of security was questioning why Jon and Elana had gotten a different room. Had Jon really gone back to the party? Did she care if he had? Unfortunately, yes.

Gregor visibly relaxed at Jon's explanation. He reached a meaty, tattooed hand out and tried to touch Elana's hair. Jon pulled her just out of reach.

Gregor never took his eyes off her breasts. "Give me one night with this flimsy American and I will teach her to never disobey you. She needs to be broken and taught how to treat a man."

Elana shivered at the look in Gregor's eyes and the tone of his voice. They knew from research he was heavily into the BDSM scene. However, Gregor didn't know what a safe word was. More than one woman had been sent to the Novlaks' private physician and two, that Elana knew of, had died from their injuries.

"Over my dead body," Jon growled. "I handled the situation. I'm not handing her over to you since the entire problem with her is she can't keep her hands to herself. Besides, she'd probably enjoy being beaten into submission."

Jon gripped her chin in one hand and ran his other down the front of Elana's body. One of the men guarding the door let out a heavy breath and Gregor narrowed his eyes.

"Now, are we going to talk pussy or are we going to talk business?" Jon shoved Elana roughly away.

The sudden push caused her to stumble and fall to the carpet. She hissed as her knees hit. She felt the nightie ride up above her hips and figured the men were enjoying the view of her backside.

"Damn it, Lana. Could you for once not wave it around like you're selling it?" Jon demanded.

He walked over and ripped her to her feet. While leaning over to make it look like he was reprimanding her, he whispered in her ear, "You did great, honey."

His out of character concern caused Elana to stumble.

When they reached the door to her room, Jon said, "I expect you showered and dressed when my meeting is over. You've got thirty minutes." He pushed her in and slammed the door.

Elana's heart was beating so fast, she expected the men to hear it in the other room. She'd done it! She'd played a part and held her ground.

Not wasting a moment, she locked the doors and got in the shower. Thirty-two minutes later, she stepped out of the bedroom in four-inch, black stiletto knee boots and a canary yellow dress. Almost her whole wardrobe consisted of the skin-tight tank dresses. They were the opposite of fashion sense and showed off her body the best.

Jon was the only one in the room and his eyes narrowed slightly.

"Are you okay?" he asked as he surveyed her body.

She had a small bruise on her arm from where he'd held her earlier. Her knees showed a slight red from rug-burn.

"I'm fine." She felt like she was trying to soothe a caged animal. "Why the sudden concern?"

"I don't like the way Gregor looks at you. That man is dangerous. I can't believe he showed up this morning. The head of Novlak security should have better things to do than check on two Americans who just arrived."

"Yeah, I thought that, too. Prostitutes and drugs shouldn't have put us on their radar so quickly. And what was with the poor bellhop?"

Elana walked to the table to pick through the assortment of breakfast food.

"Gregor brought him up so I couldn't deny we'd slept here last night. He bought my story, though. I didn't expect them to be checking on us yet. I figured we'd have to play it up a few more days."

"Did you really go back over to the other suite last night?" she asked.

"Yeah. I found a room with three passed out women and one man. I sat in the chair for about forty minutes and then came out, making sure I left the bedroom door open so the guards could see them."

"There were guards next door?"

"When someone throws an orgy, look for the people not participating. They're probably sent to watch and report."

"I'm not ready for field work, am I?" She turned to stare out the window.

"Lana," he said, "it takes time to figure all this out."

"You were right from the beginning. I am the lamb led to slaughter. What was Kimball thinking, pairing up a super agent and a newbie?"

"I'm not a super agent and you are no longer a newbie as of last night. You played your part just as well as a seasoned agent. Quit second-guessing everything and follow my lead. You'll be doing this like a pro in no time. Now, for business."

Jon guided her to a chair and made her eat while he went over the plan for the day. Gregor would more than likely have a tail on them so Jon wanted to do some shopping and meet up with a few shady contacts in the open to make some arms deals. If the Novlak brothers wanted to see what Jon could do, they were in for a show.

Bundled in her fur coat, Elana sprinted to the limo. Once inside she sat almost on top of the heater. Every store they stopped at, she moaned about going out in the cold, but then acted like she didn't have a care in the world and wasn't freezing in the twenty degree weather.

Jon took her to three jewelry stores and bought her a watch, diamond earrings, and a ruby choker. At lunch, he made a gun sale to a man that smelled like cabbage. Elana pretended she didn't know what was going on while she sat in Jon's lap and he fed her.

Gregor's tail wasn't conspicuous. Elana picked it up at the second jewelry store. After lunch, they went back to the hotel. She wanted to warm up and get out of the hooker dress and boots.

It was a successful day.

They spent the rest of the afternoon in the room doing more research and checking in with AJ. Jon knew it was driving Gregor crazy that he didn't know what was going on. Jon had swept the room for bugs and removed all the ones planted while they'd been out in the morning.

For two more days, they did almost the same thing.

Finally, they got the break they needed. When Jon was getting ready for bed on the fourth night, the room phone rang. Elana was in the living room with her gun drawn before the third ring was complete. When she realized it was just the phone, she looked a little sheepish, flipped the safety, and waited for Jon to answer.

A brief conversation in Russian followed.

"Who was that?" Elana asked, all traces of tiredness gone from her body.

"That, my dear, was the sound of the bad guys taking the bait. I've been invited to St. Petersburg to meet with Boris Novlak."

6

St. Petersburg, Russia – Two days later

"Take your clothes off!" Jon growled.

The words Elana had been wanting to hear for weeks took her off guard since this wasn't the situation she wanted to hear them in.

"Excuse me?" She glared.

"You heard me. These men are waiting for a stripper and a good show. I suggest you start shaking your ass to keep them happy or they're going to kill us. Right after they torture us then rape you while making me watch." Jon's voice dropped to a deadly murmur. "I am not going to watch them rape you."

"If I didn't know you hated me so much, I'd think you cared." She peeled the camisole over her head and the blonde wig came off next. Both were stuffed in her bag.

Jon stared at her back, emotionless. He was worried about her going out on stage. This overprotective streak he'd developed wasn't good.

Elana grabbed a red body corset from a rack.

It was like all of her clothing decisions were to get a rise out of him. Literally. Antagonizing Jon had become her favorite thing to do on this mission.

Russia was supposed to be in economic ruin, but

someone had put a lot of money into the dance hall and outfits that went with it. It didn't matter there were people starving and freezing in the streets as long as the members of the Russian Mafia were satisfied.

The smell of sausage permeated the entire place mixed with the sweet smell of alcohol and the tang of body odor. Throw in the expensive caviar they were eating and it was a regular party. Elana was sick with the way this country operated. So she tried to quit thinking about where she was and concentrated on why. And trying to breathe through her mouth so she didn't throw up from the smells.

She had Jon help her lace the corset then she attached black garters to the bottoms that were supposed to cover her unmentionables. Her front was covered, barely, and her butt had a g-string thing going on. Great. She shifted her breasts so they were almost ready to pop out of the corset.

"What if they don't like my dancing?"

Jon continued to watch her back. "No one here is going to notice anything except you when they see that outfit. You could just stand there and they're going to like it."

He looked down the short hallway that led to the dance stage and eyed the leather couch, stripper pole, and furry handcuffs that hung from a padded wall directly in front of the tables below the stage. It reminded him of the stage in a high school gymnasium. Without the handcuffs and stripper pole, of course.

Elana turned. She was twisting her hair into a loose bun on top of her head.

"Hand me those lace-up boots."

Jon stared. Standing in front of him was the same woman who'd tried to seduce him on the jet a week ago. She tied him in knots like no one ever had.

His cell rang as he handed Elana the black leather boots. They laced up the front to her knees and had four-inch stiletto heels.

He looked away, answering his phone in Russian. Elana listened as she put on a black silk jacket over the corset. She would never admit it to Jon, but she was scared to death. This wasn't like the ballet dancing she was used to. She'd never danced for men who were drinking too much and would attack her in a second if they thought they could get away with it.

Elana jumped as Jon's warm hand closed on her shoulder. She was so caught up in not passing out she hadn't realized he was done with the call.

"That was Enrique. He's sitting at a table with Boris and they want to know when I'll be at the club. They said there is a new girl coming on and they want me to have a piece of the action." His eyes narrowed. "They're talking about you."

"Excellent. I'll go out on stage while you slip around front. This is what we needed. They trust you enough to let you into their inner circle. I don't look anything like I usually do. They won't know it's me even though they've had Gregor taking surveillance photos."

He knew she was right.

"No matter what you think of me, I will not let any man out there hurt you." He put both hands on her shoulders and gave a reassuring squeeze.

"I know you won't." She gave him a quick kiss on the cheek and turned to walk into the makeup room.

He gazed after her for a moment then snuck out the back door so he could join the bad boys who were going to watch Elana dance.

In the makeup room, Elana applied a thick layer of bright red lipstick and too much black eyeliner. She figured she could give the boys one hell of a show. Taking a deep breath, she walked to the stage as the music started and the lights dimmed.

Jon entered through the front doors just as the lights

went down. Gregor escorted him to a table up front then disappeared into the shadows. Enrique and Boris clapped him on the back as they stood to shake hands.

Boris slobbered a little as he lifted a shot glass. His English was okay, but even more broken than usual when he was drunk.

"My new friend! They have found replacement woman for missing dancer. She is beautiful, my boys tell me!"

Jon hoped Boris's boys hadn't seen him with Elana. "I know you only have the best, Boris." Jon smiled and lifted his own shot. Before tipping it back he proposed a toast to his new 'friends'. "Here's to good business yet to come."

Enrique grunted in approval as he and Boris took what appeared to be their eighth shot each.

The music picked up to a fiery tempo. The woman swaying to the beat held all their attention. The lights shining on stage went right through the black jacket Elana had put over the red corset. Every man there was treated to a tempting view of cleavage through silk.

Catcalls and lewd comments were spewed at the stage in slurred Russian and some Spanish. She understood it all but kept her head high, pretending not to hear. As she crossed the stage with the sexiest strut and sway that Jon had ever seen, Enrique and Boris began to pound on the table.

"I tell you she was pretty, yes?" Boris smiled and took another shot of vodka. "I could show pretty woman good time. I invite her for us tonight. We all have her!"

Jon bit back the rage welling up inside him. It didn't matter Elana wouldn't want to be a part of it. Boris got what he wanted, when he wanted it.

Jon watched Elana slide onto the leather couch and spin around so her legs were draped over the back and her head hung to the floor. She put her hands on her thighs and spread her legs apart so her ankles touched each arm rest on the couch. It was a perfect side split and the men went crazy.

Jon remembered how flexible she was. He'd followed her to a ballet studio when he'd found out Director Kimball was pairing him up with a newbie. It had been pure torture watching Elana bend and stretch in a one piece spandex suit.

Then he'd met her and the torture had intensified. Practicing hand-to-hand combat, helping her get better with guns and knives, watching her try on clothes. It had taken all of Jon's self-control to ignore her curves and scent. None of that held a candle to what she was wearing and doing now.

His self control was quickly deteriorating the more time he spent with her. He couldn't believe he'd made it this long. Maybe he should just give in tonight and give them what they both wanted and needed. It could be a celebration for accomplishing the first part of their mission. Jon smiled a predatory grin. What would his Lana do if he took her up on her continuous offer? Would she run and hide or go for it? He couldn't wait to find out.

After doing a few more shows of flexibility on the couch, Elana rolled off the arm and removed the silk jacket at the same time. She didn't even need to take off all her clothes. The boots, garters, and corset were enough to get the imaginations going. She spun on the stripper pole, landing on her feet as a big Russian man put his hands on her waist. He pulled her back toward him and Elana wondered what she was going to do now.

Screaming was at the top of her list of possible actions until she remembered the dancers here were also prostitutes so she was supposed to be used to this type of behavior from the crowd. Out of the corner of her eye she saw Jon shoot to his feet. Grabbing a scarf hanging from the pole, she wrapped it around the man's wrists and led him to the furry handcuffs on the wall.

Jon sat down when he realized she had everything under control. As she secured the handcuffs on the big guy, another pair of hands ran up the outside of her thighs and tried to release her garters. She swatted playfully at the hands and wrapped the scarf around the new man's head.

He was from Peru and part of the group Enrique had brought. She pushed the boy off the stage and the crowd erupted into laughter. The young man, only eighteen or nineteen, blew her a kiss and returned to his seat.

The next thing Elana knew, Jon was on stage, had a scarf wrapped around her butt, and was pulling her toward him. When they were chest to chest he leaned down to nibble on her ear. At least that's what it looked like to the crowd.

"I think it's time to end your little dance number," Jon said. "And where in the *hell* did you learn to dance like this?"

"I haven't always worked for the CIA, remember?" she said licking the side of his face.

By this time, the crowd was pounding on the tables and stomping. He had to get Elana off stage.

"Hold on. We're going to give them a show and get you out of having to tie up any more men from the audience." Before the sentence was finished, he lifted her so she was level with his waist. "Wrap your legs around me and pretend like you're enjoying it."

She wrapped her legs around his hips and locked her ankles together. There wasn't much pretending happening for her right at the moment. He effortlessly held her by keeping his left arm securely under her butt, his right hand in her hair.

"I've got to kiss you, Lana." Lips smashed to hers.

The vodka tasted good on his lips. She realized this kiss was part of a show and she shouldn't be enjoying it so much.

He slid his tongue into her mouth and rocked her harder against him. She felt the hard bulge rubbing against all the right places of her body. No one in the audience could see his hard-on, so maybe he wasn't pretending either?

"Sweet Jesus, lady, the things you do to me."

Jon nipped at her bottom lip then started sucking and biting. Every man in the room stood and thunderous applause shook the small club. The crowd thought they were having sex. Hooked together, rocking against each other to the sounds of clapping and pounding, they lost track of time.

Reluctantly, Jon started walking off stage.

He whispered into her hair as Enrique and Boris approached, "No matter what happens in the next few months, remember I will never betray you. Go home and tell them I'll be in touch. This is no place for you to be."

Tears stung Elana's eyes. He didn't think she could handle the act anymore. He thought she wasn't good enough. Well, fine. She'd leave his ass in Russia to deal with the Mafia.

Her legs detached from around his waist and she slid down his body. He cursed under his breath at the painful erection that wouldn't be getting release any time soon.

"I'm going to distract these two creeps long enough for you to sneak away."

Jon covered up their talking by pushing her into a dark corner and caressing her through the corset. She closed her eyes and moaned at the feelings shooting through her over-sensitized body.

"I can't get enough of you," he said into her mouth as he kissed her again.

Elana struggled to make sense of what was going on. A week ago he'd rejected everything she'd offered. Enrique and Boris appeared to be within earshot. Had Jon said his last sentence just loud enough for them to hear?

"Comrade," Boris took a step over and wrapped a strand of Elana's hair around his pinky finger. "Get her wet enough for the three of us but let's take her home first."

"She's almost ready," Jon said, licking his tongue over Elana's lips. "She just needs to go get her bag. It has the essential items for a night with three men."

This was when she was supposed to sneak away. A new dancer moved to the stage and the loud music gave cover for their muted whispers.

"Please, let me stay with you and finish the mission," she begged.

"If you don't leave right now, you're going to be expected to sleep with those two. Go now while you have a chance. They trust me. We're going to go to one of the warehouses tomorrow to start business. I'll be stateside in a month. I promised my family I'd be home for Christmas."

"Be careful." Tears rolled down Elana's cheeks. Jon wiped them away with his thumbs as he cradled her face in his large hands. "Contact me as soon as you get back?"

"I will Lana. Remember what I said about never betraying you." He started to walk away then turned back toward her as though coming to some kind of troubling decision. "My last name is Carter."

He kissed her roughly one more time then turned her toward the dressing room. Elana had an ache in her gut making her wonder if she'd ever see Jon Carter again.

7

The hotel room was so dark. Elana sat on the bed with Jon's pillow clutched to her face for almost five minutes. She breathed in his scent, allowing herself tears of anger and fear.

"What the fuck am I supposed to do?" She stood and hurled the pillow at the wall.

When it didn't give her any feeling of satisfaction, she went for items with more substance. The bedside lamps made a comforting crash as they shattered. The TV screen sounded like bells as it exploded with the impact of a drinking glass. The pictures on the wall came down next and by the time she was done her hands were bleeding.

She put a trench coat on over the stripper clothes and, in almost a dream state, made her way to the secure hanger where their jet and pilot were.

The flight home was a physical and emotional roller coaster of pain. She threw up three times that she remembered and woke on the floor in the main cabin when the jet touched down.

It was four a.m. in Langley, Virginia; almost a full twenty-four hours from when she'd left Jon.

Elana's head and heart hurt. *What could I have done differently?*

It was hopeless. She'd committed the CIA cardinal sin: she'd left her partner alone on a mission. Yes, he'd forced her.

In a way. She could have refused to leave. Jon was always about the job and never would have compromised the mission to argue with her.

As she was descending the ladder to meet Kimball on the tarmac, her cell phone vibrated. She'd left Jon several text and voice mail messages. So many she'd lost count.

The text made Elana's heart swell: *'glad yr ok. be safe. don't trust anyone. i'll be in touch. give att file to dir dikwad. he'll owe u. luv jon'.*

Elana knew she shouldn't read too much into the message, yet it still made her glow.

"What the hell are you smiling about?" Deputy Director Kimball barked from the landing strip.

His suit was wrinkled, what little hair he had left was mussed, and he had dark circles under his eyes. The normally sour looking man looked even worse. That was hard to do when you were five foot four, weighed just over three hundred pounds, and had a fat little pig face. Director Dickwad. . . Elana was going to have to start using that. Fit the man perfectly.

Kimball dragged her to the office, peppering her with questions she didn't have answers to. She downloaded the video file from her phone. It showed Boris bartering for weapons with Jon and drugs with Enrique.

Kimball made her write a full report before she could leave the office. Elana was too tired to argue. She cataloged the week of work she and Jon had done. All the contacts they had made, transactions witnessed, key players who hadn't been identified before, and even the two-bit dealers who had shown themselves.

Six grueling hours later, she dragged herself into her condo. She spent the weekend dreaming about being with Jon in Russia. She didn't get much sleep.

Monday morning, Elana went to the office expecting to find Jon waiting for her. He wasn't there. Kimball told her to get ready for her next field assignment.

By the end of the week, she quit asking Kimball if he'd heard from Jon. The man was definitely going to be referred to as Director Dickwad.

AJ was still on his mission in South America so she couldn't confide in him or ask his advice. They hadn't spent much time together, mostly because Jon wouldn't let them, but he seemed like a good guy. Jon had told her not to trust anyone. Did he mean AJ, too?

For two weeks Elana sent messages to Jon's email, cell phone, and left him voice mails.

He never responded.

November brought rain, the occasional snow flurry, and depression.

Kimball sent Elana on four back-to-back missions. She was flying all over the world from one place to the next. Everywhere but close to Russia.

She had secured a black market nuclear bomb in Iran. She helped break up an underground internal organ smuggling operation run by some Chinese doctors. She'd assisted in the rescue of the kidnapped child of a Brazilian Diplomat. She had also recovered the hard drive of a murdered Norwegian scientist who had been working on artificial intelligence.

Common sense dictated she should have botched all four missions since her mind was only on Jon. However, it seemed she'd learned, already, to fully compartmentalize and make herself automatic in the job.

Every day she could, Elana would call or email Kimball to see if he'd heard from Jon. Kimball had specifically told her to quit trying to contact Jon so she wouldn't blow his cover. She figured that would be okay because he would be back any day now.

Really, any day. He had to be.
There was no other possibility.

Christmas and New Year's came and went. Her father
had been sent to Taiwan for a meeting with the Taiwanese
military so she had no family to visit and no real friends to
spend time with. All her energy was going into secretly
finding Jon.

She started trying to track down the family members he
had mentioned. Were they real? Was there anyone he was
close to?

Elana kept hitting dead ends. And the more dead ends
she hit, the more she began to second-guess herself.

It didn't help that Kimball continued to keep her on a
schedule of one to two missions a week. This was eons away
from the data gathering and filing her career had started with.
She assisted in more missions with foreign governments to
recover guns, drugs, documents, stolen artwork, and black
market items.

Had she not been so depressed, she would have been
enjoying herself. She imagined what she and Jon would do on
each mission.

It was almost like Russia had never really happened;
that it was all in her mind.

Somewhere in her brain, Elana knew these actions and
this attitude weren't healthy. She just couldn't seem to make
herself care.

The end of winter brought rain and new growth;
March came in with a bang. Elana didn't even notice. She had
become the emotionless robot Jon thought was a good agent.

She had proven herself capable. No one blamed her for
leaving her missing partner in Russia; no one except her.

Saying she had thrown herself into her work was an understatement. If Jon came home he might not have recognized her.

She'd cut her hair so it barely brushed her shoulders. She'd lost weight. Her constant missions and lack of sleep were taking their toll. She was a walking zombie and hid it well. Her mind was always on her missions and Jon.

Her father didn't seem to notice the changes in his only child. He'd spent almost a month in Taiwan and when he returned, he'd called to check in. He hadn't seen her since she'd gotten back from Russia.

Feeling more alone than ever, Elana kept working.

It was all she could do.

Finally, some life was breathed into her when she found an online newspaper article about the death of a Chicago Mob Boss. The words 'FBI Agent Michael Carter' jumped out from the screen.

The CIA had more efficient search engines for name and facial recognition. However, Elana couldn't risk using company time or resources to search for Jon or his brother.

If she didn't think Kimball was watching her every move, she may have flown to Montana to track down Michael Carter.

She placed phone calls, sent emails, and even talked to Michael's old partner, Tony Medina, on the phone. The man hadn't volunteered much information. Just told her Michael was hard to get a hold of. Well, no shit, she had figured that one out for herself.

She never was able to speak to Michael Carter. It was as though he was being purposefully evasive and Elana couldn't figure out why.

The only good thing of the whole situation was she was developing just as ruthless a reputation as Jon Matthews.

Too bad he wasn't around so she could rub it in.

8

March

"I've seriously had enough of this shit!" AJ slid his body between Elana and the boxing bag she was attacking in the gym. He ducked as she punched toward his head.

"Leave me alone, AJ."

He grabbed her taped fist in his larger hand. She looked at their hands and then into his face. Her glare scared him. Where was the timid woman from this fall? AJ had been back on American soil for a week. He couldn't believe the rumors flying about Jon Matthews. For a group of spies who were supposed to be the most secretive on the planet, the people who worked the office in Langley sure gossiped like a bunch of old church ladies.

"I'm not going to leave you alone. You don't talk to people, you don't go on dates. The only thing you do is run to every little mission Kimball sends you on."

"How do you know what I've been doing? You've been in Brazil for the last three months."

Elana ripped her hand from his grasp and turned to go to the women's locker room. She grabbed her water bottle and towel from the floor. She drank down half the water and was almost to the locker room when AJ caught up.

"Checking up on me, Lana?"

He sounded so much like Jon, she stopped suddenly. Her voice was low as she vented her pent-up rage on him. "Don't you ever call me that!"

AJ almost ran into her back. He swerved around her and blocked the entrance to the locker room. "What in the hell is the matter with you? What happened over there?"

Having someone ask her what was going on was such a relief. She'd been completely alone for so many months. Elana had felt a connection with Jon, except now, didn't even know if it had been real. She was starved for human companionship. AJ had seemed like someone who could become a friend back in October. Could he be a friend now?

"Kimball can't know," she whispered.

AJ looked around. "Can't know what?"

"That I'm talking to you. He forbid me from discussing Jon or anything dealing with the mission."

"What?" AJ said.

His dark hair hadn't been cut in the months he'd been away and it would have brushed his shoulders if he hadn't had it pulled back in a ponytail.

"You need a haircut," Elana blurted.

"Will you get your mind on track? Did you say Kimball 'forbid' you from talking to anyone? What about the shrink?"

"Huh?" She was having trouble concentrating.

"The shrink? The company psychiatrist? It's SOP to debrief with a head shrinker if a mission goes bad."

Cramps assailed Elana's stomach at AJ's words. She'd left Jon alone in St. Petersburg. No, he'd sent her away. She bent over, bracing her hands on her knees.

"Lana, are you okay?" AJ put his hand on her shoulder.

"I told you not to call me that," she huffed. She was going to be sick. She tried to muscle past him but his grip held. It made fire rip down her arm. "Oh!" She flinched away and almost fell on the floor.

"What's wrong? What's going on?"

"I'm going to be sick." She dropped to one knee, covering her mouth.

AJ threw her arm over his shoulder He whisked her into the single room, wheelchair accessible bathroom between the two locker rooms. He barely got her knelt in front of the toilet when she started to heave.

Elana was mortified, but her body hurt so bad she didn't care. What the hell was wrong with her? Did she have food poisoning? She couldn't, she hadn't eaten in almost two days. Had she contracted some kind of disease while she'd been in Thailand earlier in the week?

"Thailand," she rasped.

"You've been in Thailand?"

She nodded. Then her stomach cramped again. She puked the small amount of water she'd drunk mixed with bile until there was nothing left to throw up. Finally, all she could do was dry heave.

"Oh, fuck," AJ said.

Elana had her arm and head rested on the toilet seat and could barely move. She heard rustling and then the sounds of AJ's cell phone permeated her slow brain. She found herself feeling like she wasn't in her body; almost like she was listening from above.

"Tippi. Hi honey, it's AJ. . . I've been good, but I'm not making a social call. I have a problem. . . yeah. . . no, no. I'm fine. . . yeah. Remember that new poison we were talking about before I had to ship out to Brazil?. . . Yeah, I know you weren't supposed to tell me. . . I haven't told anyone. . . it's fine. . . Did you get it functional?. . . Great job, hon, I'm proud of your hard work. But the problem is I think my friend's been poisoned with it. Do you have the antidote?"

AJ listened to Tippi explode as his worst suspicions were confirmed. The vomit in the toilet hadn't been yellow with bile, but purple tinted, almost lavender, and mixed with blood. Elana had been poisoned by a drug being developed by the CIA.

As he tried to calm Tippi, he asked her where they could meet because her lab in the building was not safe. They agreed on her place as soon as he could get there. What he needed to do in order to flush Elana's stomach was not going to be fun.

Elana drifted in and out of consciousness until she felt hands touch her shoulders.

"Hurts," she managed to say.

"I know. You've been poisoned. What have you eaten or drunk in the last hour?"

"No food," she rasped. Her throat felt like she'd swallowed glass shards. "Water bottle."

"Did you bring it from home or get it here?"

"Here."

"Okay, this part's not going to feel good. I have to make you drink some more water then you have to throw it up." His voice was apologetic. She didn't respond. "Lana, did you hear me."

"Oh, Jon," she whimpered.

AJ didn't know if she thought he was Jon or if she was praying for Jon. He knew Jon called her Lana; that's why he'd started to do it. If she thought he was Jon, he'd use it to his advantage. He lifted her limp body to the sink and turned on the cold water. It was awkward as hell, but he braced her body in the circle of his arms, put her head down by the sink and cupped the water in his hands.

"Lana, quit acting like a fucking girl and drink the damn water."

She shook in his embrace yet managed to drink the water cupped in his hands. He made her drink and drink and drink. Elana swatted at his hands to try and get him to stop, but he wouldn't. In her weakened state it wasn't like she could hurt him. Finally, she she started to throw up again.

They repeated the torture until all she was throwing up was clean water mixed with blood; no more lavender tint. Ten minutes of pure hell.

"You did great," AJ said as he backed toward the door and lowered them both to the bathroom floor.

Elana was practically in his lap. They were both soaking wet from her slapping at his hands and water that hadn't made it in her mouth. AJ stroked her hair.

"He made me leave," her voice was toast. AJ wouldn't have heard her if she hadn't had her nose buried in his throat.

"I'm sure he did." AJ wasn't sure of anything, yet if he could get her to talk, maybe he could find out what was going on.

"Dancing. My cleavage was there. Guys were looking. Like I was food. Was gross. Jon said they'd rape me. Told me to run. Left him alone. Could be dead. I left him alone." She tried to cry but there were no tears.

Dancing? Cleavage? What the hell was she talking about? The poison had to be making her delusional.

"We'll talk about it later." He dropped a chaste kiss to the top of her head. "After I know what's going on, we'll go get him."

AJ loved everything about women: their smell, taste, skin, touch, voice. It might have been a little chauvinistic, yet he wasn't like Jon. AJ didn't think women could do as well in the field. Well, maybe that wasn't quite true. He knew they could, he just didn't think they should. He wanted to protect women and be their hero.

Elana started to say something else when pounding on the bathroom door stopped her. Someone tried the handle.

"Jensen, Miller!" Kimball's nasally voice.

"Can you make it up on your own?" AJ whispered.

"To get away. From that man. I can." She moved to her knees and dropped her head as a wave of dizziness assaulted her.

AJ flushed the toilet three times and rinsed the sink. He spilled more water on the floor to wash the purple vomit down the drain.

"Open this damn door! What are you two doing in there?" Kimball was impatient. AJ found that interesting.

AJ helped Elana to her feet and put a strong arm around her waist. "Don't say a word, I've got this."

AJ pulled open the door to Kimball on his cell phone, "Find that damn janitor and tell him to get here with his keys. I need in— never mind." Kimball disconnected the call. "What in the hell have you two been doing in there?"

"Well, sir, Elana and I went out for Greek last night and I think she got food poisoning. Since I'm the one who took her, I figured I should take care of her." AJ flashed his 'eat shit and die smile'.

"You didn't go—" Kimball started to say. Then he stopped and stared between AJ and Elana. "Fraternizing between employees is not allowed."

AJ found Kimball's stopped sentence even more interesting. Was Elana being followed?

"Oh, that's not true and you know it, sir. Fraternizing between Handlers and Assets is not allowed."

"You'd know, wouldn't you?" Kimball snarled.

Kimball sounded jealous. AJ had worked his way through quite a few of the female employees in the offices. Most worked at desks or had lab jobs, like Tippi. He wouldn't really call them relationships, but the women and AJ were always happy and sexually satisfied. They knew he traveled; most found his job exciting and brave. They also knew not to get too attached.

Elana started to move and AJ thought she was going to fall. He tightened his grip until he realized she was reaching to grab the workout towel she'd dropped earlier.

She stood on her own and AJ's appreciation for women agents grew. She'd just thrown her guts up, after being poisoned, and she was almost able to stand on her own.

Elana put the towel to her face and leaned into AJ. "My water bottle's gone."

She was one smart cookie. Even in her whacked out state, she'd realized AJ had asked her where she'd gotten the water bottle.

"Time to get you home, honey," AJ said as he tried to maneuver around Director Dickwad. The nickname from Jon fit more and more every day.

"Jensen, wheels up in three hours. You're going to Botswana. Miller, wheels up in four hours. You're going somewhere else."

"Where?" AJ asked.

"None of your damn business." Kimball turned and marched out of the fitness center.

Every eye followed his movements until he was through the doors. Then all those eyes came back to AJ and Elana.

The Deputy Director of the CIA was about as subtle and sneaky as a herd of elephants. It was completely obvious he'd put a tail on Elana and he didn't want AJ and Elana anywhere near each other. But why?

"Fucking rat bastard," Elana mumbled. "I really hate that man."

"You and me both, sweetheart," AJ agreed.

"What do you think happened to my water bottle?" she asked as they shuffled to the door, everyone staring.

"Director Dickwad did something with it."

Elana tried to laugh and it came out a garbled moan. Her insides felt like someone had chewed her up and spit her out.

"He poisoned me, didn't he?"

"I think so. But don't you go throwing around accusations like that. We need to find out from Tippi how dangerous this stuff actually is."

"Who the hell is Tippi and what kind of name is that?"

"Tippi is the head of the Biological Toxins Research and Development lab. It's a nickname."

"Are you taking me to one of your girlfriends?" Elana sounded disgusted.

"Tippi is not my girlfriend. We went on some dates and had a good time," AJ said. Actually they'd gone on quite a few dates. Although he didn't have time to ponder that right now.

"Yeah, I bet you had a good time."

"You're just jealous I've been laid lately and you haven't."

Elana was quiet as they made it to the doors and away from prying eyes.

"Holy shit. You and Jon?"

"That's none of your business. But, no. He turned me down." She stopped.

"He turned you down? Is the man blind? If you came on to me, I wouldn't turn you down!"

Elana tried to smile. "You're just attempting to make me feel better. I look like walking death and I just threw up."

"Well, I meant if you'd come on to me a few months ago. But if you're Jon's, then I'll keep my hands off."

"I'm not Jon's," she said.

"He sent you home. He wanted to protect you. That means something."

"Yeah. Too bad I don't know what."

9

Tippi Aldridge lived in the Hidden Lakes Country Club. Working for Biological R&D with the CIA paid damn well. She owned a split level home that felt like a mausoleum. It had four bedrooms, three bathrooms, a family room and living room, along with a two car garage. It was almost four thousand square feet of emptiness.

She'd had it professionally decorated and any of the rooms could have graced the cover of a home or architectural magazine. Her mother thought she could have owned a better house. There was a six bedroom, five thousand square foot home on the same block. Why couldn't Tippi have bought that one? Mom hadn't complimented on the beauty of Tippi's new place. Oh, no. Not Teresa Aldridge. She'd found every little thing that was wrong with Tippi's house. Nitpicked until Tippi wanted to cry.

Nothing was ever good enough for Teresa. Didn't matter that Tippi had grown up with old, dirty clothes and sometimes went without meals. Teresa never did anything wrong and Tippi never did anything right.

Tippi had graduated at the top of her class from Johns Hopkins Medical School and gotten a job that most people would kill for, literally. She wore designer clothes, kept herself in perfect shape, never broke any laws, and led a staid life, all to try and make her mother proud. And so far, nothing seemed to work. The only thing that made Teresa remotely happy was the monthly check Tippi deposited into her mother's bank account. How was that for buying love?

Tippi sighed as AJ pulled his Jaguar into her driveway. It had been over an hour since he'd called her. She'd left work five minutes after hanging up the phone. Can anyone say "Jump? Okay, how high?"

She opened the empty garage bay and AJ pulled in.

He was a magnet and she was metal shavings. He could have treated her like crap and she'd still do anything he asked. Except he didn't treat her like crap. He was sweet, caring, brought her flowers when they went out, and always paid for whatever they did. Dinner, movies, museums, art shows. And the sex had been off the charts fabulous.

There was a woman in his car. Tippi had assumed AJ's poisoned friend was a man. But, of course, it was a woman. Did AJ even make male friends? Women gravitated toward him. Tippi tried to shake off the jealousy she felt. She didn't have a claim on AJ. No one did.

He folded his large frame out of the dark green car. She loved his Jag. It was definitely a step up from her economical Camry. Not that she couldn't afford a Jag, she just tried to save her money.

The woman appeared unconscious. Tippi's medical training overrode her jealousy. "Get her in the spare room, I have the IV drip ready."

"Thanks, Tippi, I really appreciate this." He came around the front of the car and gave her a swift kiss on the lips. She was momentarily taken aback. Would he kiss her if the woman in his car was one of his girlfriends?

"What happened?" she asked as AJ went to the passenger side and opened the door. He reached over the unconscious woman and unbuckled her seat belt. As he pulled her out of the car, she started to moan.

"Well," he began as he lifted the woman gently in his arms and shut the car door with his hip. "I think someone poisoned her water. Elana was working out pretty heavily and I stopped her. She drank some water and about one minute later she wasn't making much sense. Then she told me she was gonna get sick. It wasn't until she was puking purple that I realized she'd been poisoned."

"Elana? Is this Elana Miller?"

"I just told you she had purple puke and all you care about is her name?"

"Oh, yeah, I'm sorry. I, just, well, she's become something of a legend because of how quickly she's worked her way up the ranks. That and the fact she went on a mission with Jon Matthews and came back without him. I'm just shocked. What are you doing with her?" Tippi was talking a mile a minute while leading AJ into the kitchen and upstairs.

He'd been in her house before, just in the dark. Six dates together, two of which had landed him back here in her bed. Then AJ'd been sent to Brazil right after New Year's and he hadn't talked to her since.

He stopped walking when he realized the mission to Brazil had come from Kimball right after AJ had left three messages on Elana's voice mail that he wanted to see her.

But that was a problem for another day.

"I said, what are you doing with her? I didn't know you knew Elana Miller?" Tippi stopped walking and turned.

"Are you jealous?" AJ wasn't trying to be mean. He'd never understood jealousy. Probably because he'd never had anything worth being jealous over.

"I'm sorry. I'm not your girlfriend and I don't have any claim on you." She started walking back up the stairs.

AJ stared at her back, confused. Finally, he shook his head and followed.

"Put her on the bed and I'll get the IV going." Tippi ushered AJ into a room two doors down from her own.

He was distracted, remembering the huge four-poster bed in Tippi's room and how he'd tied her hands to one of the columns with his tie. He smiled.

"AJ, put her on the bed."

Tippi sounded upset and AJ was disgusted with himself. He needed to make sure Elana was okay and he was distracted by sex with Tippi. The fabulous Tippi. Who looked like she wanted to rip his face off.

"What?" he asked.

"Can you quit daydreaming about her long enough to save her life?"

"Daydreaming about who?"

Tippi motioned to his arms.

"I'm not daydreaming about Elana," he protested.

"Well you're holding on to her tight enough and you won't put her down. What else do you expect me to think?" Tippi stared at him. She held an alcohol swab in one hand and tourniquet and catheter in the other.

AJ put Elana on the bed and brushed the hair back from her face. He straightened her limbs so she looked comfortable and finally Tippi pushed him out of the way so she could get to work.

Tippi put the tourniquet above Elana's right elbow and cleaned the top of Elana's hand with the alcohol swab. Then she inserted the cath, attached the lock and syringe, and removed the tourniquet. After flushing the new line with saline, Tippi taped everything to Elana's hand and got the IV ready. When the IV was attached and the nutrients were making their way into Elana's blood to help hydrate her, Tippi took a deep breath and turned to AJ.

"Now, tell me what's going on."

"I honestly don't know," AJ said. "I'm not dating Elana and you shouldn't be acting jealous."

Tippi stared at him. "Get over yourself. I want to know what's going on with Elana. How was she poisoned with my

R&D project?"

AJ almost laughed. He was a mess. Since he'd left Tippi's bed three months ago and been in Brazil, he'd been celibate. All by choice. He'd had plenty of beautiful, Brazilian women come on to him, yet he hadn't been interested.

And he just figured out the reason was standing in front of him. Five foot six inches of blonde hair, blue eyes, toned, tanned skin, and sex appeal. But she didn't know she had sex appeal and that's what attracted him the most.

They'd met between his missions to Peru and Brazil. How he had missed such a beautiful woman at work was beyond him. They'd been getting coffee at the cafeteria and ordered the same drink. It had led to an hour of chatting and dinner that night.

He knew she'd worked for Research and Development for almost four years, lived in a house that resembled something that should be on display, not lived in, and was much more warm and friendly than her outer facade let on.

He hadn't seen her since their sixth date, the second time he'd been in her bed, and they'd been talking about work. Her eyes had positively glowed when she told him about her projects. He couldn't bear to tell her all the science talk made his head want to explode. It was enough to just hear her voice while she talked about science. Naked.

"Remember my last night here?"

"Yes," she said faintly.

"Well, I remembered you telling me about a clear, liquid poison you'd developed. How it wasn't really a poison, it was just something you could put on food or in a drink to make someone sick enough to believe they had food poisoning. You said it was almost ready except for a few small side effects. One of which being that it turned the victim's vomit purplish. Another being that it made their skin sensitive to touch and any doctor worth their salt would know it was a poison and not food poisoning."

Tippi stared at him with her mouth hanging open. He'd just repeated their conversation, almost word for word. She'd thought he was bored by her work and wouldn't remember any of what she'd said. He'd been in a post-coital haze, so Tippi hadn't thought he'd even been awake. She'd needed someone to talk to about it since just that morning was when she'd realized the purple vomit factor.

"I knew it wasn't supposed to be deadly," AJ went on. "I figured since Elana hasn't been eating or sleeping, her immune system is shot and I think she got a bigger dose than she should have. It affected her more intensely." Almost to himself, AJ said, "I wish I had time to review the security tapes from the fitness center and find out where that water bottle went."

AJ smiled and walked toward Tippi.

"What are you doing?" she asked as she backed up.

"You told me the sex-induced endorphin rush you get from being with me made your brain work better. Maybe we should give you an endorphin rush."

"Sex? You want to have sex? With me? Now?" Her mouth opened and closed.

"Why do you sound so surprised?" He kept advancing on her. "How long will Elana be out?"

"Not long. I didn't give her a sedative. Her body will wake up when it's ready. Why hasn't she been eating or sleeping?"

"Oh no you don't. You're not going to change the subject that easily." AJ reached out, snagged her arm, and ripped her toward him. "I only have a couple of hours and I want to spend as much time with you as I can. In bed and naked."

"A couple of hours?" Tippi's voice was weak and so was her body. All rational thought seemed to fly out of her mind when he touched her. As AJ kissed a trail from her neck to her lips, she asked, "Why do you only have a couple of hours? Do you have to go somewhere?"

AJ loved how breathless she sounded. Loved how her skin tasted. He was all kinds of bastard to do this, but if he could have her just once before Kimball sent him off, then it was worth it.

"I have to go on another mission. Director Dickwad is trying to keep me away from Elana so we can't find Jon. Bastard is sending me to fucking Botswana. Can you believe that shit? Botswana." He nibbled her ear.

Tippi knew she should be offended. She hadn't heard from him in three months and now he wanted sex and was going to leave again for who knew how long. She couldn't bring herself to care. Every time she was with AJ she felt like a woman. A living, breathing, hot-blooded woman who wasn't wanted by other scientists because of her brain or by her mother for her money.

"I shouldn't let you do this," she tried to protest as AJ swung her up in his arms.

"Yeah, I'm kind of taking advantage of you. But you need to take pity on me because I haven't had sex in three months. Some hottie has me thinking only of her." His admission slipped out easily, yet before either of them could think about it too much, they'd reached her bedroom.

For an hour, AJ drove Tippi crazy and showed her things about her body she didn't even know. She reveled in what he did to her, in his skill. The only man she'd been with before AJ had been a friend from college who had spent three minutes in her bed. One of those minutes had been spent putting on and then removing the condom. Tippi hadn't known sex could be like this. Playful, dark, and emotional all at once.

AJ tried not to think too much about how he was getting addicted to the sounds Tippi made when he pushed into her. Or the way she pulled his hair and the whimpers she made when he nibbled on her clit and lapped with his tongue.

It wasn't until after his third time of taking her that AJ tried to close his eyes and relax. Jeez, he'd been an animal.

"Don't you dare say you're sorry," Tippi said as the shadows of the setting sun filtered through her curtains.

"You read minds, now?" AJ asked amused.

"The night we came home from the art gallery, the first night we were together, you were romantic and slow and we only made love once. Then you went home. Three days later, when you brought me home from the movie, we made love again. You were still romantic and slow, except there was an edge to it. You tied my arms." She blushed and her voice got quieter. "I realize now it was because you were getting ready to go on a mission. That was the night you left for Brazil." Realizing she sounded like a high school girl reciting from her diary, she stopped talking.

"No, tell me," AJ encouraged her. He rolled to his side and pulled her toward him. Her bare breasts rubbed against his chest and she sucked in a breath. Unbelievably, AJ's cock responded and grew until Tippi could feel it throbbing against her thigh. Her eyes widened.

"Hold that thought," AJ laughed. "It seems the body is willing, but I really want to hear what you have to say. I'm not going to ravish you like an animal again."

Tippi hid her face in his neck and whispered, "But I want you to."

AJ's cock bounced against her leg with her admission. He'd been trying to be suave and romantic because that's the kind of woman she was. Maybe he'd been wrong. He thought about how he'd tied her that night before Brazil. Thought about how her nipples had pebbled and the light sheen of sweat had dotted her skin. How could he have missed that? Probably because his mind had already been on the mission.

"What changed tonight? What made you let loose?"

AJ could barely hear her. He understood her need for privacy but he wanted to turn on all the lights and make her look at him; really look at him. And admit all her deepest, darkest fantasies.

"What changed tonight?" He echoed. "Well, I haven't had sex since that night with you. Who knows how long I'll be in Botswana. Mostly it was your trust. I called you and needed help. You didn't ask why, you didn't question what I wanted. You dropped everything and helped me. You didn't accuse me of being the one to poison Elana even though I know your project is top secret and you haven't told anyone."

"Of course you didn't poison her." She pulled her head back and looked at him. "You're a good man and you wouldn't poison anyone. You wouldn't steal from me, either."

Her immediate response had him grinning like an idiot. AJ rubbed his hand over her cheek and then fisted it lightly in her hair.

Between biting kisses he explained, "I work in a job full of lies. Anyone else would have been suspicious and assumed I'd used the information you told me. That's why tonight is different. I realized how special you are. And I let go with you the way I've never let go with another woman."

He rolled her to her back so he could hold her head in his hands. Their bodies aligned and her wet, swollen folds teased him. "I want you like I've never wanted anyone."

He was getting ready to kiss her again when a scream pierced the air.

"Elana," they said at the same time.

AJ jumped up, grabbed his gun, threw open the bedroom door, and ran down the hallway.

10

Tippi stared at his bare ass, then collected her wits. "AJ, you're naked. Get back here!"

She wrapped the sheet around herself, grabbed a throw from the chair, and followed him down the hallway.

Elana lay on the floor of the spare bedroom, sobbing. She'd ripped out the IV and her hand was bleeding all over Tippi's white carpet.

"Elana, it's okay." AJ said. He put down his gun and was trying to get her attention. "Pull it together."

She sat up and took in her surroundings. "Where am I?" Her voice was still brittle.

"We're at a friend's house."

Elana noticed AJ's nakedness and then saw Tippi standing in the doorway wrapped in a sheet. "What kind of friend? And, seriously, Jensen? I was dying and you thought you'd stop and get a little?"

Elana could feel her strength coming back. She noticed the IV stand and her bleeding hand. She wrapped it up in the bottom of her shirt.

"It wasn't like that," Tippi said. "You weren't dying. I know it felt like it, but since you vomited up all the poison and AJ got you here quickly, you're going to be fine."

Tippi secured the sheet more tightly around her, then tossed AJ the small throw blanket.

"Cover yourself. Elana's had enough of a shock today without seeing your, well, your man parts."

"My man parts," AJ parroted. "You're just so damn cute." He held the blanket in front of him. "You fix her IV and I'll go get dressed." He kissed Tippi on the nose and walked out.

Elana and Tippi both stared at his bare backside.

"That man has one fine ass," Tippi said on a sigh. Then she clapped her hand over her mouth and blushed.

Elana tried to laugh and ended up coughing instead. "Maybe someone should tell me what's going on." She held out the hand that wasn't bleeding. "I'm Elana Miller."

"Tippi Aldridge. I'm friends with AJ, but I also work with you at The Agency."

Elana raised a brow as Tippi gathered some items, squatted next to her, and started to clean her hand.

"Well, I'm not an agent like you two, but I work in the Biological Weapons Research and Development science lab. It's my concoction, for lack of a better word, that you were poisoned with."

Elana stilled.

"I didn't poison you," Tippi hurried on. "You were given one of my experiments. No one is supposed to know about it and it hasn't been cleared for use."

"So I really was poisoned," Elana said.

"Yeah. We were right," AJ said from the door. He'd put his shorts and shirt back on. "Tippi, should Elana stay hooked to the IV?"

"It would be a really good idea. Especially if you're supposed to leave again in a few hours. I'd also like to check your vitals, if you don't mind."

Elana nodded and climbed back on the bed. Tippi found a new vein and ran the IV.

"I'll be right back. I want to get dressed and get my stethoscope." Tippi hurried from the room.

AJ sat on the bed.

"I was hoping it was all a poison-induced nightmare. You're really going to Botswana?" Elana asked.

"Yep. That jackass has it in for me now, too. Kimball hasn't liked Jon since Kimball was appointed Deputy Director. Seems everyone Jon gets close to becomes a target."

"I wonder where he's sending me this time?" Elana closed her eyes. "Do you trust this Tippi girl? And I mean with our secrets, not just enough to fuck her."

"You didn't used to be so crude," AJ said.

"I didn't used to be a real agent. Jon and everything that's happened has changed me."

"What happened over there, Elana?" AJ asked. Kimball's actions didn't make sense. Why hadn't she been allowed to talk to the psychiatrist? Why hadn't Jon come back?

"I started to fall in love and Jon doesn't do that. I think when he decided I was in the way, he sent me home."

"Fall in love? Agents don't fall in love. It doesn't happen. We can't risk our emotions like that."

Tippi chose that moment to walk in the room. The look on her face was one Elana knew well. Tippi thought she was in love with AJ.

"Well, AJ," Elana said, "we don't get to choose who we fall in love with. It happens." She gave a reassuring smile to Tippi. "Hit me, doc, apparently I'm off to another hole-in-the-wall country when we're done here."

Tippi started checking Elana's vitals.

"Tell me more," AJ prompted. "You said something about dancing when you were delirious."

"The night I left, I had to pretend to be a stripper and Boris and Enrique expected me to go back and sleep with them. Jon told me I wasn't going to do that and he couldn't let them kill me. So he sent me home."

"He was protecting you." Protecting a woman, AJ

could understand. Falling in love with one, he couldn't.

"But I had a job to do, dammit!" Elana said.

"That's enough, guys." Tippi put her stethoscope around her neck. "The more you argue, the more Elana's heart rate spikes. You need to relax before you go on another mission. I'll make some dinner."

"Thanks, Tippi," AJ said absently as she left the room. "Why was the Russia mission so important to him?" he asked as soon as Tippi was gone.

"I don't know. Wasn't it just another mission?"

"You don't know?" AJ said.

"Know what?"

"Kimball tried to get three different agents to go with Jon to Russia. He flat refused every one of them. Then Kimball said you and Jon caved. Didn't even put up a fight."

"He didn't tell me," she whispered.

"He wanted you in Russia but then he sent you away. It doesn't make sense."

For about five minutes they discussed different ways to get a hold of each other and AJ shared some of his more important contacts from around the world. People Elana would be able to trust if she needed help.

"I meant it when I said you needed a haircut. You look like a girl," Elana laughed.

"Yeah, I just haven't had time. Now I'm going to fucking Botswana."

"You really hate that place, huh?" she asked.

"Well, yeah. First of all, it's in the middle of nowhere. It's not like it's a vacation hotspot. Second, I got shot there a year ago and I'm pretty sure Kimball knows that. It's got to be why he's sending me there now. He's pissed. By the way, did you hear me tell him I took you out for Greek and you had food poisoning?"

"No. I was really out of it."

"Well, he started to say we hadn't been out and then

stopped. I think he's been having you followed."

"I figured. Pretty sure he's tapped my phones, too. I bought a disposable cell but I don't have any way to get the number to Jon. I've been trying to find his brother."

"He told you about his brother?" AJ said.

"I know. I couldn't believe he had a brother either. Wait, you already knew about his brother, didn't you? Do you know his last name?"

AJ stared blankly.

"Carter," she said.

He smiled. "Well, well, well. Looks like our Jonny-boy likes us both more than he'd ever admit. He's shared a few personal tidbits with the two of us. I know you probably need that IV in a whole lot longer than the almost two hours it's been there, but we need to get you cleaned up so you can get your go bag and be ready to head out."

AJ jogged downstairs and found Tippi tossing a green salad and frying a few chicken breasts. He smiled at the domesticity of it then got her to go up and take care of Elana while he set the table.

When Tippi came downstairs, he moved behind her, nuzzling her neck. "You smell good."

"Thank you, I think."

"I wish I could stay. I haven't gotten my fill of you."

She shivered.

"Oh, Tippi, the things I want to do to you." He quit nibbling her neck. "What's your real name?"

"What?"

"What's your real name?"

"Tippi?"

"It's not a nickname?"

"No, why?"

"I just assumed it was a nickname," he said.

"Tippi is already bad enough. I couldn't imagine what it would possibly be short for. My mom was trying to convince a rich socialite I was his illegitimate child. She thought Tippi sounded like a name someone rich would name their kid. I think it sounds like the name you'd give a pet poodle."

AJ opened his mouth and Elana laughed as she came down the stairs.

"You're no one's pet poodle, Tippi, although I have to agree with you," she said.

"When you get back from wherever you're going, would you like to get together for coffee, Elana?" Tippi thought she'd regret the invitation as soon as it was out of her mouth, but she didn't. It would be nice to have a friend.

"I have a more hectic schedule than AJ, but I'd like that. And thank you for taking care of me. Although I hope I never get poisoned by one of your concoctions ever again."

"Me either. I need to see if anyone checked out a sample and how much is missing."

"No!" AJ and Elana said at the same time.

"What? Why not? This is my job and my reputation we're talking about. I need to find out how someone got something out of my lab without me knowing."

"Let it go," AJ said.

"No!"

"Tippi," Elana soothed. "What AJ is trying to say is if you go snooping around, you might get dragged into whatever this mess is. It all started with Jon and it's trickled down to AJ and me. We don't want you to get involved or get hurt."

AJ was gripping the dining room chair so hard Elana thought he might break the wood.

"This is my life," Tippi said. "Someone stole from me. Stole something that isn't supposed to be deadly or used on our own people." Her eyes clouded with tears.

Before Elana could say anything, AJ was by Tippi's side. "Honey, you didn't have anything to do with this. Your beautiful brain does wonderful work. You had nothing to do with Elana getting sick. Now, let's eat this great dinner you prepared."

He'd successfully distracted her. "I don't think I'd call it a great dinner. Anyone can make salad and chicken."

"I can't boil water," Elana said. "This is much better than what I've been eating for the last few weeks."

"Which would be nothing," AJ agreed.

Happy to have the attention off her, Tippi watched the two friends interact.

"I've been a little frickin' busy and stressed out," Elana snapped.

"You could have come to me," AJ said.

"You've been in South America and Kimball keeps me on a short leash."

"I know and that bothers me. Why the sudden interest in a former desk jockey? What makes you so important?"

"I think I should be offended," Elana said to Tippi. Suddenly Elana realized she was having a fun, social conversation that wasn't for her job and wasn't a lie.

"I think you should be, too," Tippi agreed laughing.

They ate, engaging in friendly banter with AJ doing an excellent job of keeping both ladies in a good mood. His motto was you never knew what tomorrow would bring so you sure as hell better enjoy today.

After another thirty minutes, Elana stood and stretched her sore muscles.

"You have to leave, don't you?" Tippi finally said.

"Yeah. I don't need Kimball any more pissed off."

"Neither do I," added Elana. "I'll just wait in the car. Take your time saying goodbye." She made it to the door to the garage and turned back around. "By 'take your time', I don't mean too much time, okay, Jensen?"

"Yeah, yeah," he said without looking at her.

When he heard the door close, AJ grabbed Tippi and kissed her with a wealth of passion and emotion he didn't know he'd been holding back.

Finally, he pulled away and they were both a little breathless. "Get me a notepad and pen and stay out of arms reach before I forget I have to leave."

Tippi grabbed a pad and pen from the counter in the kitchen. AJ wrote down two numbers. "This one is my personal cell through the Agency. Call if you want to talk. I can't always check it, especially in Botswana, but I will call you back as soon as I can.

"This one," he said, pointing to the second number, "is in case you have an immediate emergency."

"Why would I have an emergency? And why would I call you?"

AJ wasn't sure what to say. He was worried about her and he wanted to be the one she called if she needed something. Did he tell her that?

"I want you to know you can call me if you need me."

"Okay. The same goes for you. I'm either at work or home, I don't do much else. You won't be here to take me out, so I won't be going out." She blushed and grabbed the notepad. "I know you already have my cell and home number, but this is for the office." She scribbled the number down and they stood and stared at each other.

"Tippi, I know I have no right to ask you this, but, will you wait for me to come back? I'd really like to spend some more time with you?"

"I'll wait. I knew I'd wait for you the first time you touched me. Now go and save the world and be safe. I will be here when you get back."

She kissed him again and pushed him toward the door before she did something stupid like throw herself at his feet and beg to have his children.

Tippi opened the garage door and he backed out. She closed the garage door, shut and locked the other doors, and turned out the lights. She listened to the echo of her breathing as she went upstairs. She made it all the way to her bed before she threw herself down and broke into tears.

In his car, AJ and Elana tried, once again, to brainstorm how to get to St. Petersburg and pick up Jon's trail.

The best they could come up with was to try and keep in touch over their missions until they had a lag. It wasn't much of a plan but it was something.

AJ waited while Elana grabbed her go bag from her condo. She waited while he did the same at his house. They were pulling into the CIA parking garage when AJ's phone started to ring.

"Bastard wasn't kidding when he said three hours." AJ let it go to voice mail just to piss Kimball off.

They took the elevator to his floor and strolled into his office. The look on Kimball's face said it all. He hadn't expected Elana to be walking, let alone looking normal.

"Miller, I see you're better. Food poisoning through your system?"

"Yes sir. I'm harder to take down than that."

The veiled threat hung between them.

"You two have become quite chummy," Kimball nodded his head to AJ.

"Always good to have friends, sir," Elana said with the same lack of emotion.

"Jensen, go report and get your papers."

AJ waited a moment then hugged Elana. "Be safe," he whispered into her hair.

"You too," she said.

Then she was alone with Kimball and getting information for the retrieval of a kidnapped rich socialite in Paris.

It was almost like the beginning of the day hadn't happened.

11

One week later

Tippi and Elana sat at the coffee shop in the CIA building. Elana had a black eye but her skin color was good and her face didn't look as haggard. The doctor in Tippi noted Elana didn't look as sickly as she had a week ago.

"Have you been eating?" Tippi asked around a sip of her blended coffee drink.

"Yes, mom," Elana said with a roll of her eyes. "I've even started having protein shakes in the mornings when I'm in a place I can make them. You were right about me having more energy during the day."

Four days earlier, Elana had called Tippi out of the blue. It had shocked Tippi so much she resorted to her typical medical babbling and asked Elana what she'd been eating and how she'd been feeling. Tippi had been mortified until Elana laughed and explained she had called to see if her new friend was as wonderful as she remembered.

It was like a bond had been forged. An instant friendship between two women who had never really been very good at making friends.

"Have you heard from AJ?" Elana asked.

"Why would I hear from AJ?" Tippi said with a snort.

"He kinda whirlwinds into my life and bed when he happens to be in town. It's not like we chat on the phone every day."

"I haven't heard from him either," Elana said. "I have no idea how we're going to get together and find Jon."

Tippi looked at the people milling in the coffee shop. "Should we be talking about this here?" she whispered.

"Probably not," Elana said easily with another drink of coffee. "I figure Kimball knows my every move right now anyway. The only place I know isn't bugged is my house because I sweep it every night."

"Sweep?" Tippi asked confused.

"Check for bugs?" Elana said.

"Bugs?" Tippi's voice squeaked.

"Do you watch spy movies? Read techno-thrillers?"

"No, why?"

"AJ's right, you are too cute." Elana laughed at Tippi's naiveté. It was refreshing. "Bugs are listening devices and sweeping for bugs means I'm checking for listening devices and disposing of them if I find any."

"Wow. It's like spies have their own language,"

"How did you get a job working for the CIA?" Elana asked. "And I'm not trying to be rude. You're just so much different than any of the other people who work here."

"All I've ever cared about is science," Tippi said with a smile. "I want to make the world a better place and the CIA offered me the best arrangement. They promised my work would help our county and never be used for malevolence." She frowned and looked at her plastic cup. "That's why I'm so upset about you being poisoned by X-232."

"X-232?" Elana asked. "Is that the name of the purple vomit poison of death?"

"It wouldn't have killed you," Tippi said. "But, yes, that's its lab name. Experiment two hundred thirty-two."

"Just don't start asking questions about it. AJ and I already explained why."

Tippi took the domed lid off her drink and started wiping away the whipped cream, licking it off her finger. She wouldn't meet Elana's eyes.

"What have you done?" Elana asked.

"I haven't really done anything," Tippi hedged.

"Tippi," she said with a hint of heat in her voice.

"I was very discreet. I have every right to look over the logs of my research." Tippi sat up straighter.

"AJ's going to be so pissed," Elana said.

"Well, AJ's not here, is he?" Tippi finally looked at her. "Just because you two deal with death every day doesn't mean I'm going to get attacked for doing my job."

"We want you to keep doing your job. We don't want you looking into how I was poisoned with your experiment. We probably shouldn't even be seen together. Just promise me you won't start asking questions."

Tippi wouldn't look at her again.

"Now what?" Elana asked in exasperation.

"When I checked the lab after you and AJ left, I verified a vial of my experiment was missing from the cooler. I asked my assistant, Marcus, about it and he had no idea a vial of X-232 was missing because none of the other employees are allowed to access my work without me. My passkey is supposed to be the only one that will open that part of the lab." Tippi finished off the whipped cream and then took a sip of her drink. "I put in a request to Tech to have the security footage sent to me."

Fear laced up Elana's spine. After months of not feeling anything but regret and coldness, it was a shock to know she cared about a woman she hardly knew.

"I want to know who was in my lab," Tippi said.

"We told you to drop it."

"What would you tell me if I asked, no told, you and AJ to let this whole Jon Matthews business go? Wouldn't you tell me to shut the hell up? Wouldn't you tell me he's your friend, and this is your job, and this is about doing what's best for your country?" Tippi huffed and sat back in her seat. She ran a hand through her hair then wrapped both around her cup, as though she needed something to do with her hands.

Elana stared at her, knowing Tippi was right.

Anger tinted Tippi's voice as she continued. "I know you would. I can see it on your face. What makes you guys better than me? What makes your work more important than mine? I bet almost every biological agent AJ and Jon have used over the last four years has been of my making. I bet I've saved more lives than the two of them combined!" As though suddenly realizing where they were, Tippi smacked her hand over her mouth.

"You're right," Elana said, "not the time or place. You're also right about finding out who took your X-555, or whatever, vial. And, for the record, I don't think we're better than you. Your work saves lives."

Tippi's eyes widened slightly.

"Yes, I'm agreeing with you. AJ will have my ass for this, but I don't care right now. The stipulation is you're going to get a top of the line alarm system installed in that house of yours, you're going to get a concealed weapons permit and a gun, and you're going to take some self-defense classes." When Tippi opened her mouth, Elana cut her off. "I will not back down on those. If you're going to look into this, you're not going to be defenseless. You're smart and you know what we do is dangerous."

Tippi nodded. Seemed she was out of steam and still couldn't believe she'd stood up to a CIA agent.

"Let's go." Elana stood and Tippi followed.

The tail Kimball had on Elana could have had a neon sign. Elana gave him a finger wave as she and Tippi walked by and he dropped down to pretend to tie his shoe. Moron.

"Do you know him?" Tippi asked, almost running in her heels to keep up with Elana's trek to the parking garage.

"He's one of the tails Kimball has on me."

"Tails?" Tippi asked.

"Tail me? Follow me?"

"You're going to need to write all this down," Tippi said in exasperation. "I can't keep up with your slang."

Elana laughed as she got in her Jeep Wrangler.

"Where are we going?" Tippi asked as she climbed in the passenger seat.

"To get going on the list of things I'm making you do before I have to leave again. We're going to start at the courthouse to get you a concealed weapons permit. While you're filling out the paperwork, that's simple, by the way, because you already have CIA clearance, I'm going to call and set up for the alarm system to be installed in your house. Do you care how much it costs?"

She had a deer in the headlights look.

"Tippi, I'm not kidding about any of this. How much are you willing to spend on an alarm system?"

"I don't care how much it costs. Get the top of the line. Whatever you or AJ would get if money wasn't an obstacle." Her voice was quiet.

"Are you sure? Good security systems are expensive."

"Yes."

Tippi was starting to sound more sure of her answers. If AJ and Elana thought she needed these things, she'd get them. Well, Elana thought she needed them. She never really knew what AJ was thinking. Unless it was about sex.

Tippi stared out the window and tried to focus on the signs of spring. It wasn't working. Elana seemed to understand Tippi's need for silence because she turned on the radio and they listened to country music without saying a word while Elana drove to the courthouse.

When would AJ call? Would he call? Feeling like a fool, Tippi closed her eyes and tried to think about what she was getting ready to do. Get a gun? Take self-defense courses?

Could she do this?

Her mother's voice floated through her mind. *"You've never been good enough. If you had been perfect, your daddy would have claimed us and I'd have enough money to buy the things I need."*

Tippi snorted, then put her hand over her mouth and shot panicked eyes to Elana.

"Care to share?" Elana asked.

Tippi shook her head, hand still on her mouth.

"We need to work on your poker face, girl," she said.

"Why?" Tippi asked as she moved her hand.

"You're like an open book. When you're embarrassed, you cover your mouth and blush."

Tippi blushed, proving Elana's point.

Elana laughed as she pulled into a parking spot at the courthouse. Her tail parked across the street and she eyed him in the rear view mirror.

"Is that the guy you said was your tail?"

Elana opened her mouth then closed it.

"I may not understand what you guys are talking about the first time, but after that," she shrugged, "I don't forget."

"Yeah, that's my tail. He was new last night. Second one this week. They're idiots. Six months ago, I never would have been able to pick him up because I wouldn't have paid attention. Now? Now I think everyone is tailing me." Elana shook her head. "Jon made me paranoid."

"Maybe that's good in your line of work?" Tippi wanted this look into Elana and AJ's world.

"I suppose."

After a short, uncomfortable silence, Tippi opened the door. "Well, I guess I need to get in there and do this."

Elana got out. "I'll take you in and make phone calls while I wait."

Two hours later, Tippi's application for her concealed weapons permit was processed, the alarm company was going to be doing their installation the next day, and Elana was driving them to a hole-in-the-wall gym.

"Why have we been driving in circles and on side roads for the last ten minutes?" Tippi asked.

"Been losing my tail," Elana smiled. "I really like this gym and I don't want Kimball giving Chin-hwa any trouble."

Tippi looked over her shoulder. "I haven't seen him behind us since McFarland Street."

Elana smiled. "Good job, Tip, I spotted him once after that, but you're right."

Tippi bloomed under Elana's praise then felt silly for caring so much about what Elana thought.

Elana drove by the Taekwondo studio and parked two blocks down. As they walked to the building, Tippi thought it looked like it should be condemned. Blue paint was peeling from the bricks, the sign was crooked and chipped, and one of the panes of glass was replaced with a piece of plywood.

"I know it looks bad, but Chin is amazing." Elana pushed open the door to mirrored walls and matted floors.

"I trust your judgment."

Tippi's total confidence shook Elana. She was so used to being alone. She'd allowed herself to become tied to Jon and now Tippi and AJ. It was unnerving.

Shaking it off, Elana bowed to the Korean man who came to meet them at the door. Tippi followed Elana's lead and also bowed. Then she stood silently as Elana spoke in a language Tippi didn't know.

Chin-hwa was a good-looking, middle aged man who had lived in the U.S. for fifteen years. Elana had discovered his facility right before going to Russia and came in every day she was in town, which had been less and less over the months.

Chin switched to English and assessed Tippi. He ran his hands down her arms and cupped her elbows and then wrists. "You are strong, already. That is good," he said.

"I work out at the gym in our building and jog in my

neighborhood."

"No more working out at CIA. You come here every day." He smiled to reveal perfect teeth and released her.

Tippi couldn't help but smile back. "Can I start tomorrow?" she asked. "I already did my regular workout this morning."

"This isn't for working out, this is to learn Taekwondo. Self defense," Chin said. "You both come back in one hour."

He shooed them out the door.

"He's a little pushy, isn't he?" Tippi asked.

"I'm used to it, but, yeah," Elana agreed. "It's what makes him such a great master."

They walked to the jeep.

"I think we'll start shooting practice tomorrow on the range at work," Elana said. "I don't have an assignment until late next week, so that gives us time to work on your shooting and self-defense. We'll get you in a routine before I leave."

As Elana started the car, Tippi put her hand on Elana's arm. She looked up in surprise.

"I don't have many friends. Thank you for helping me be safe," Tippi said.

"I think any woman should know self-defense and at least be aware of gun safety. I hate encouraging you to put yourself in danger by looking into your missing experiment. But, you're going to look into it anyway, so I'm going to help you. I don't have many friends either." Elana held up one finger. "I guess you." she held up a second finger. "And I suppose AJ is a friend. Two. Not much."

"What about Jon?" Tippi asked. "He must be a good friend if you and AJ want to go to Russia and rescue him."

Elana forced out a laugh. "Jon doesn't have friends. He also doesn't need rescuing."

"Then why are you going to try and find him?" Tippi didn't understand.

"I don't really know." Elana closed her eyes briefly.

"Maybe to yell at him."

"I don't think you'll yell at him," Tippi said quietly.

"I have no idea what I'm going to say or do."

"Do whatever your heart tells you."

"My heart? I don't know if I even have a heart anymore. It doesn't feel like it. I can't afford to have a heart. Especially where Jon is concerned."

Tippi didn't know what to say; didn't know if there was anything to say. So she shrugged. Taking a leap of faith, she finally said, "Do what I do with AJ. Go day to day and enjoy what time you can with him."

"I'll have to find him first."

"Well, until then, let's teach me to take care of myself. We better go get some workout clothes," Tippi said.

"You can take care of yourself," Elana said.

"How much time do you want me to spend at the shooting range and Taekwondo studio?" Tippi asked.

"As much time as you're willing. You should go to both places as often as you can. The only way to get comfortable is practice."

"Okay."

"Really? You're just going to drop everything and do this?" Elana sounded doubtful.

"I don't have a life," Tippi said. "I figure you're the expert."

"Remember to keep things at work as quiet as possible. I don't want you inviting trouble. I just want you prepared in case it pops up."

"Sure. It's going to be nothing, you'll see," Tippi tried to reassure her. "I mean, really? What's the worst that could happen?"

Famous last words.

12

April

Another three weeks. Sometimes Elana couldn't keep track of her days. When she wasn't on missions for Kimball she was working with Tippi. When she wasn't with Tippi she was searching for Jon. She talked to her dad once. What a life.

It had been six months since she'd left Russia. Where was Jon? He'd promised to be home in time for Christmas. It was way past Christmas.

"For whatever the hell your promises mean," Elana muttered as she logged on to her computer.

The cubicles surrounding hers were mostly empty. It was six-thirty in the morning. The few people at work were down attacking the coffee machine and visiting with one another.

None of them talked to Elana. She had nothing in common with these people. They had families, dogs, and white picket fences; the pictures on their desks proved it. Elana looked at her desk. There wasn't a single picture, plant, or personal item.

For almost two hours, Elana did her customary internet searches to see if anything exciting had been happening in Moscow or St. Petersburg with the Novlak brothers. Besides the usual social pictures, there was nothing. She did paperwork for the mission she'd been on and sent Tippi a text to remind her they were working with Chin at five p.m.

The email program dinged to let Elana know she had a new message. She clicked on it as her phone rang. She answered the phone as she skimmed the email. Kimball wanted to meet with her as soon as possible.

"Hello?" she said absently.

"Director Kimball wants you to come to his office," Maryanne, Kimball's assistant, said.

"Yeah, I just got the email, too," Elana rolled her eyes. "Let the Deputy Director know I'll be there as soon as I finish this report."

Elana was hanging up the phone as she heard Maryanne say, "He wants you here now."

No sooner had she hung up, it rang again.

"I said I'll be there," she snarled.

"Well, Ms. Miller, you are a ball of fire, just like my brother said you would be."

Elana gripped the phone. "Brother? Michael Carter?"

She braced herself for whatever the call would reveal. She'd been trying to track down this man for the last five months. Was he calling with bad news? Any news?

"Yes, ma'am. Michael Carter."

"You've spoken with him? Where is he? What did he say?" Elana couldn't hide her concern or impatience.

"I've talked to him twice since you came back without him. I've tried to contact him every single day for the last four months. The only proof he's not dead is his answering service is still accepting messages. And if you'd quit harassing me, I'd have more time to search for him," Michael said.

Elana made a sound of protest but he cut her off.

"Wait. It was a warranted harassment. You were right when you thought he was in trouble. What have you heard from that side of the government?"

"Absolutely nothing. At first, they acted like everything

was all fine and told me he could handle himself. Then, three months ago, they quit mentioning him and I was told not to ask again or I'd be reprimanded." She let out a frustrated breath. "He told me he'd be back in two months. It's been six. The CIA acts like he doesn't even exist. Either that or they think he's—" Dead. She couldn't finish the sentence.

"They think he's gone rogue," Michael said.

"They what?" Elana sprang to her feet sending the rolling chair crashing into the side of her desk. Heads popped up from behind cubicles like ground squirrels.

"He took a month mission and never checked back in. He sent his partner home early and disappeared. They think he turned," Michael said.

"You don't believe this, do you?" she asked.

"Of course not."

"Then what's going on?"

"I'm not sure," he said. "He told me he had a lead on something huge and wasn't willing to risk anyone until he had the evidence he needed. That's why he sent you away."

"He sent me away because he didn't like me. He was upset I was partnered with him and he didn't think I could handle staying. So he patted me on the head and sent me home like a good little girl." Elana sat back down.

The light on her phone blinked showing she was getting another call. It was probably Maryanne. Two more emails popped up telling her to report to Kimball's office.

"He did like you. The only reason he got you out was so you would be safe. When he contacted me about your mission, he explained the situation wasn't safe for you anymore. If he hadn't cared, he would have let you get raped or killed and written it off as collateral damage."

"He told you about our mission?"

"Jon and I tell each other everything. It doesn't matter now. You have a meeting to get to and I have a package to deliver to you. Don't open it unless you're alone. I want—"

"How do you know I have a meeting?"

"Deputy Director Kimball is waiting to talk to you. He's going to introduce you to Pete Campbell. I had a few favors owed to me and I called them in. I found out about you and your next mission."

"You ran a check on me?"

"We're talking about my brother here, lady. I wanted to find out if you were on the level. I have the same trust issues as Jon." Michael said. This woman was just as his brother described her; hard and soft at the same time.

"What did you find out from this little background check?" Elana bit out.

"That you're already earning a rep as the best field agent in the CIA, besides my brother, of course, and you're one hell of a language expert. I also hear you're becoming adept with weapons and you can be a master of disguise when you need to be. Now, go put all those skills to use and save my brother's ass. I want him home soon because he's going to be an uncle again.

"This line is secure and I've scrambled the call so you may have to explain who you were talking to. Don't trust anyone and be prepared for anything. Good luck."

Michael hung up and left Elana staring at the phone.

Don't trust anyone. Those words again. Elana wished she had AJ around to talk to.

She walked down the hallway to Kimball's office. It was hard to concentrate on Director Dickwad while the phone call with Michael kept replaying itself in her head.

"Agent Miller, how nice of you to join us." Kimball glared at her. "This is Pete Campbell. He's going to be your new partner on this latest assignment." Kimball sat in his big leather chair behind a monstrosity of a desk.

A young man in a suit sat in one of the hard plastic chairs in front of Kimball's desk. Elana glared at the young agent as she crossed her arms. It was obvious he was wet behind the ears.

"Where do you pick these kids up, riding skateboards in grocery store parking lots?"

The boy stood, offering his hand. Elana didn't take it.

"Ma'am, I can understand how you would be intimidated by a younger agent, but I assure you I'm not out to get your job. I just want to learn from the best."

He had a slight southern accent, bright red hair, and freckles across his nose and cheeks. Freckles. He looked like an oversized version of Opie Taylor. Could this get any worse? Her question was immediately answered.

"You can choose to take this assignment and new partner. Or you can go back to your records keeping desk job and not go on another field assignment. Ever. Again." Kimball's tone made Elana's body rigid.

Would it be bad to punch your boss?

"Talk, I'm listening," she said through clenched teeth.

"Six months ago you came back from a mission. It's incomplete. I want you to go back to Russia next week with Agent Campbell and finish it. That will give you time to brief him so he's up to speed. There are a few differences from the first mission, though." A malicious smile curved over Kimball's round face.

"You are to terminate Boris and Mikhail Novlak along with Enrique Juarez. You are also to remove their business partner who is helping them evade us. His name is Jon Jacobs."

Elana tried not to let any hint of emotion play across her face. She knew Kimball was talking about Jon. Her Jon.

"You have two weeks from the time you arrive to complete the mission." He glared at Elana before she turned. "You better kill all four of them. If you don't, don't bother coming back."

She opened the door, waited for Pete to walk through, and slammed it.

Pete followed Elana to her cubicle. She shut off her computer and wrote her address on a slip of paper. He fidgeted next to her, obviously unsure of what to do or say. He followed her wordlessly to the elevator.

While they were in the elevator, Elana finally spoke. "I'm going to run some errands, Petey. I suggest you get your field gear together and meet me at my condo in two hours." She handed him the paper. "We're going to get to know each other inside and out before we get on that jet in a week." She eyed him. "How many field assignments have you been on?"

"Well," Pete puffed his chest out. What was he, like sixteen? "I was part of a drug bust in Mexico last week."

"How many field missions, Pete?" Her patience was wearing thin, but she was trying not to lose it with the kid. It wasn't his fault Kimball was an asshole.

"One." He lowered his head.

"Kimball must hate you more than he hates me." And Jon, she thought. Pete looked at her with question in his eyes.

"He sent me to Russia for the first time when it was only my third field assignment. He hated me then, too." She smiled. "Meet me in two hours."

Elana stepped off the elevator and waited until Pete was out the front doors. Then she went in search of Tippi. It would have been funny that she sought the other woman's companionship if there had been any way to find humor in the current situation.

Tippi was hard at work in her lab wearing the customary white lab coat and safety glasses with her hair in a bun. Elana knocked on the glass wall. Tippi didn't notice.

Tippi's assistant, Marcus, waved and walked over to let Elana in. He was a handsome, African-American grad student who worshiped the ground Tippi walked on.

"Agent Miller, Dr. Aldridge didn't tell me you were coming." Marcus smiled a big cheesy grin.

Elana had been in Tippi's lab a grand total of four

times and Marcus acted like she'd been there hundreds. He was big on procedure and refused to call her Elana.

"Marcus, good to see you again. Dr. Aldridge didn't know I was coming. Is she busy?" Elana lifted her chin to where Tippi stood over vials of different colored liquids, her head now buried in a microscope.

"She's just comparing some strains of Ebola. She'll be done in a moment."

"Oh. Okay." Nothing like Ebola to momentarily take her mind off the assignment from hell.

She waited while Marcus droned on about different types of biological agents and how they could be used for biological warfare. He gushed about how much he admired Dr. Aldridge for spending the majority of her time working on antidotes that we would hopefully never need.

It took everything Elana had to not yell at Tippi to hurry up.

After what felt like an hour, only four minutes according to Elana's watch, Tippi stood and removed her glasses. Realizing Elana was there, she smiled.

"Mr. Mann, record your results while Agent Miller and I are in my office. Remember to take your time. I'll be looking for mistakes."

"Yes, Doctor," Marcus said.

"What's wrong?" Tippi asked as soon as they were in her office with the door closed.

"What do you mean?" Elana hedged.

"Don't pull that with me. I know something's wrong. Your eyes are slightly dilated and you're clenching and unclenching your left hand."

Elana put her left hand in her jacket pocket.

"I have a medical degree and three doctorate degrees, two of which are in psychology and physiology. I can read you."

"Well that's disturbing, considering I'm supposed to be

such a great spy."

"I've spent a tremendous amount of time with you over the last month. I'm your friend. Tell me what's wrong."

Elana told Tippi about Kimball sending her to Russia with Pete. She didn't mention the assassination part, but she said she was going to try and find Jon while she was there.

Tippi listened with wide, frightened eyes. She knew this was a big deal because they'd talked about how Kimball hadn't allowed Elana even close to Moscow or St. Petersburg since she'd gotten back.

"Why the sudden change?" Tippi asked.

"I don't know. I need to get a hold of AJ, though. Let him know I'm going to Russia. Do you have a different number than I do for contacting him?"

"Maybe." Tippi grabbed her phone and showed Elana the two numbers she had. "I've left him some messages but he hasn't called back."

"Don't worry, Tippi, he's probably just in the field. He'll call you when he can," Elana said.

"I know. So, when do you leave?"

"A week. But I'm going to have to spend all my time with the new agent they're sending with me. I have to cancel our dinner and workout plans. I'll try to see you at least once before I fly out, but I can't guarantee anything." Elana turned to leave.

"Be careful. I'll miss you." Tippi practically threw herself into Elana's arms and gave her a huge hug. When she pulled back, tears were in her eyes.

"I'll be back in a couple weeks. Hopefully with Jon."

"Okay," Tippi hiccuped.

"I'll call you," Elana said and slipped from Tippi's lab before the ice around her heart melted any further.

This feeling stuff was going to hurt her if she wasn't careful.

13

Elana drove to her condo with her mind moving in a hundred different directions. What had Michael Carter meant when he said he had a package to deliver to her? Did Jon know Elana was coming to find him? What was he going to do when he saw her? What was she going to do? Who was Pete Campbell and why had Kimball paired him with her? And where was AJ? She could really use his help about now.

Too many questions and not even a direction to go to find the answers.

She took a moment to sit with her eyes closed when she pulled into the parking lot at her condo. After a few deep breaths, she jumped out of her Wrangler and ran up the steps. She had told Pete not to come for two hours so she could buy herself an hour alone. She needed to be in her own space and have time to think things through before Pete showed up. While she'd managed to become the robot Jon wanted her turned into, she still couldn't hold her emotions together when it involved anything dealing with him.

When Elana opened the door to her condo she noticed two things at once. There was a large manila envelope sitting on her kitchen table and her alarm was shut off. She drew her Beretta from the shoulder holster and made a sweep of her home. Nothing was trashed or moved and every room and closet were intruder-free.

Holstering her weapon, she went back to the mysterious envelope. There was a note.

Here is the package I promised you. Take good care of it and yourself. I expect you to bring my brother home safe and sound. Sorry about shutting off the alarm. I only work with the best.

MC

At least one question had been answered.

Elana wondered who Jon's brother had sent to break into her home and how they knew about the alarm. She dismissed the thought quickly. How did Michael Carter expect her to bring Jon home when she was supposed to kill him? Carter knew about the meeting, he must have known about the orders. How did he think she was going to get Jon back in the country?

She grabbed a pair of gloves made from a Teflon-like substance and slowly opened the envelope. She was pretty sure she could trust Carter, but she had trusted his brother and look where that had gotten her. Angry, alone, depressed, and robotic. Just to name a few.

The gloves were one of many toys Jon had given her while they had been training. They fit like a second skin so she could use them in the coldest of temperatures or while diffusing a bomb and they didn't add excess bulk. Then there was the added bonus of not leaving fingerprints.

The envelope contained thirteen photos of different men. As Elana stared closely at each one, she felt the hair on the back of her neck stand up. They were all black and white and looked like surveillance photos. It was as though she recognized each man but couldn't place from where. The back of every photo had a name scribbled on it; names she recognized but had never seen faces to go with. They were all assassins. Hit men.

Finally, she came to a photo with nothing written on the back. She turned it over. Jon Carter. The photos fluttered to the floor as Elana realized what she was looking at. Michael had sent her all of Jon's aliases. He was a hired assassin. A hired assassin for every corrupt government agency in the world – including the United States.

Just when things looked to be complex and completely overwhelming, they turned downright impossible.

"What the hell have you gotten yourself into, Jon? Shit, what have you gotten me into?" The questions echoed in the silence.

Elana slid down the dining room wall until she was sitting on the floor with her knees drawn to her chest. It reminded her of sitting in her spare bedroom months earlier when she'd begun training with Jon. She peeled off the gloves and threw them across the room.

Resting her forehead on her knees, she counted to ten. Then she counted to twenty. When she realized counting wasn't going to calm her, she decided to do something that always helped her think. Since she couldn't go work out with Chin and Tippi, she'd settle for the next best thing.

Elana changed into workout clothes. She'd kept the room Jon had created. Six months of being beaten had turned the boxing bag to a dirty red, duct-taped mess.

Over an hour later, the doorbell chimed. Elana grabbed her third bottle of water and snatched a towel off the handle of the spare room door. Wiping the sweat out of her eyes, she made her way to the front door.

The peep-hole showed a face full of her new partner, Opie. She opened the door. "I think we're going to have to be a couple for our cover."

Pete stared at her. Elana's hair was slicked back and sweat ran in rivulets down her face and body. In a sports bra and spandex shorts, she was a teenage fantasy. Pete hadn't been a teenager all that long ago.

"If we're going to pretend to be lovers, you can't look at me like that." She shut the door.

"Lovers?" Pete said.

"Lovers," she said with the hint of a smile.

"Look at you like what?" He still hadn't met her eyes. It seemed that her sports bra was quite interesting.

"Looking at me like you've never seen a naked woman. Shit, you've seen a naked woman before, right?" She walked over and lifted his chin so he was looking in her eyes.

"I'm scared," he whispered.

"So am I," she admitted.

"You don't look scared."

"That's part of a cover, Petey my boy. You will learn how to do it."

Elana spun in a tight circle and nailed Pete in the face with a flying backfist. He dropped to his knees and clutched his bleeding nose.

Hell. He might even be greener than she was before Jon got a hold of her. He hadn't even seen it coming.

"You need to always be on the defensive. Rule one. We don't have much time to train and get you comfortable around me. We leave in seven days. Let's get started."

Pete's bloody nose took a few minutes to clean up then Elana had him change clothes. She walked him though a few basic hand-to-hand moves and set him to work on the boxing bag.

The boy had no muscle and lacked coordination. If they lived through this mission it was going to be a miracle.

"How old are you?" Elana said as she watched him bounce around the boxing bag.

"Twenty-two," he mumbled.

He stood tall, still three inches shorter than her, and flipped an orange curl from his eyes. He looked like a high school student just waiting to be stuffed in a locker or garbage can. Definitely greener than she had ever been.

"Pete, if rule one is to be on the defensive then rule two for you is to exude confidence. It's like you have a 'kick me' sign on your back. You have to stand up straight and make eye contact. The people we're going to be around will kill you without thinking twice."

She went to a wall safe and pulled out a stack of cash.

"Go get a haircut," she said. "Military short to hide your orange curls. Go to Sweeny's Tailor shop on 5th Avenue and tell them I sent you. You need at least four tailored suits. Sweeny will know how to make you look bulkier than you are." Pete took the money. "Practice walking with your head up. Make eye contact with everyone on the street. And clean the blood off your face before you go."

He left five minutes later with a look of panic in his eyes.

Once she was showered, dressed, and as close to relaxed as she was going to get, Elana brewed some tea and pulled out her laptop.

This mission was going to be the hardest thing she'd done in her life. Keep Opie from getting killed, watch her own back, and rescue Jon. Impossible times three.

According to her South American contacts, thank you AJ, Boris and Mikhail had been looking for a new drug supplier.

Maybe the best way to get Pete noticed would be to have him pose as a drug dealer. She sent a secure email to Kimball asking for background to be built for Pete. She put her request for both of them to be drug dealers. She didn't want to go in as another bimbo girlfriend.

Elana was making her second cup of tea when the computer chimed that she had a message. It had been ten minutes since she'd emailed Kimball. He couldn't be getting back to her already. She hoped the message was from AJ.

It was Kimball. She frowned. He had to have been sitting on his computer to get back to her so quickly. There were attachments with the message. He already had their backgrounds built. A sliver of unease trailed over Elana. Kimball was never this hands-on with missions. Usually he had his assistant get Elana information or let Elana set up her own backgrounds. Why was he being so involved?

Nothing about this was right.

Pete was going to be posing as a Russian drug dealer who had been living stateside to make money from U.S. high schools. And, of course, Elana was going to be his bimbo girlfriend. Kimball had no imagination.

Pete's cover was that he'd grown up in Kazan, a small city southeast of Moscow. He'd been through the foster system and had a rap sheet that included various drug convictions and a murder charge that hadn't stuck. If Pete was a murderer, Elana was the tooth fairy.

What a horrible background.

She accessed Pete's personnel file. Maybe he'd be able to pull off more than she thought. His psych eval was good and his IQ was off the charts. If he was as smart as he appeared on paper, maybe she'd be able to teach him some things after all. But even if he could fool the Russians into believing he was one of their own, he still didn't have the mannerisms of a criminal. He exuded the innocence Elana figured she'd once had.

Her innocent nature had been destroyed over the last six months. She had one week to turn Opie Taylor into a badass.

Corrupting Opie Taylor had to be a sin. She was so going to hell.

14

St. Petersburg, Russia – April

Six months of hell.

Jon stared in the mirror and almost didn't recognize himself. His normally short hair was below his ears. Streaks of blonde and brown he hadn't known were there made him look like an actor or a model. He snarled at his reflection.

Jon Jacobs was a bad man. He'd been Jon Jacobs for so long he almost couldn't remember what it was like to be Jon Carter. He'd missed Christmas. Julie and Kamielle were going to be so pissed at him. If he made it back alive.

There was a knock on the bathroom door. "Jonny?" A feminine and heavily accented Russian voice asked.

He lowered his head and sighed, "I'll be out in a minute, Talia."

The woman was a poor substitute for the one Jon really wanted. But the one he wanted was safe and sound in Virginia last he checked. It was her fault he was stuck in Russia and getting lost in Jon Jacobs. Who was he kidding? It was his fault. Fifteen years with The Agency and he'd never slipped up or made a mistake. Never. He slammed his palm on the counter.

Since the day he'd followed Elana Miller to her ballet class almost a year ago, he'd been making all kinds of stupid mistakes. Black mark after black mark on his perfect record.

Hopefully he wouldn't pay with anyone's life.

Jon opened the bathroom door and stared around the plush room. He'd been a 'guest' in the Novlak mansion since the night he'd sent Elana away. Part of him wondered if he should have kept her with him. But every time he watched another woman get raped or another person get killed, he knew he'd done the right thing by sending her to safety.

The room Jon was in looked like the honeymoon suite of a lavish hotel. It was also bugged and Jon hadn't been able to place a secure contact to his brother in over four months. If he didn't figure out how to get a hold of him, Michael might come to Russia, guns blazing, to try and save Jon's ass.

Talia walked backward and lowered herself to the bed. Her dark hair pooled behind her naked body as she moved her arms and legs up like she was posing for a Penthouse photo shoot.

Jon barely glanced her way as he walked to the closet at the far end of the room. "I have a meeting, Talia."

He chose a short-sleeved, button-up shirt from the closet and slid it on. Natalia huffed like a spoiled child and stomped to him. She pulled out a pair of slacks that matched his shirt.

"Jonny," she purred, "you not touched me in almost week. What wrong?" She rubbed her chest against his arm.

"I'm sorry. I've got a lot on my mind." He took the slacks, kissed the end of her nose, spun her around, and slipped one of the shirts from the closet on her.

He lightly pushed her toward the door. "When this deal is complete, we'll take a trip, just you and me."

Natalia deserved a second chance. She was nineteen, maybe twenty, and worked as a maid in the mansion. She'd been delivered to his room the second night he'd been there.

He wasn't proud of the relationship that had been going on for the last six months. He'd slept with her only so the Novlak brothers wouldn't get suspicious. Illegal arms dealers didn't turn down free sex.

Yeah right, he slept with her because he had to. That would almost be funny if his life weren't in danger.

The longer he played the part of Jon Jacobs, the closer he came to forgetting who he really was. Once a week, he'd let his iron control slip, drink half a bottle of fine Russian vodka, and he'd lose himself in the pleasures of Natalia's body. Only he pretended it was Elana. How more fucked up could this get?

Jon left the room. He didn't even bother to lock it anymore; someone searched it at least once a day. He needed to get into the city and try to make contact with Michael.

Jon missed his brother and Kamielle. He missed his sister and his nieces and nephews. Hell, he even missed AJ. He'd always taken his family and few friends for granted. He knew he could see them whenever he wanted. He'd had tough missions, long missions. But he'd never gotten in this deep.

He missed Elana. What would she think of what he was doing? What would she think if she knew what kind of man he really was?

A plan began to form in Jon's head. Along with his plan, another thought played itself over in his head for the millionth time.

He had to get out of here before he lost himself completely.

Somewhere in *Fucking* Botswana – April

AJ grumbled as he swatted at another fly. He *really* hated this place. The Kalahari Desert spread out in front of him. At least if he had been farther north, there would have been the river to offer some cooler temperatures. But nooo. He had to be in the middle of the desert. He was tracking diamond smugglers and wished he was in Langley.

With Tippi.

In Tippi's bed.

In Tippi.

He closed his eyes and allowed a moment to think of her blue eyes, blonde hair, and creamy body. It had been five weeks since he'd left her house. Five weeks of celibacy. It was like the last time he'd been away from her and hadn't had sex for three months. Three months! That had to be a record since he'd lost his virginity in the backseat of his mom's car at fifteen.

He hadn't called Tippi. When he was with her, she was all he wanted. But when he went back out in the field, he convinced himself he wasn't good enough for her and she deserved better than to sit around and wait for him. But wasn't that what he'd asked her to do?

She'd left him one message a week. She didn't call every day and harass him. She never begged him to call and she hadn't cried. A few times he'd heard her voice crack then she'd quickly get off the phone. He still had all five messages and he listened to them every day. Then he dreamed about her. He felt pathetic.

The number he had for Jon didn't work any more and the messages he'd left for Elana had gone unanswered. If anything, he should call Tippi just to find out what was going on with Elana. Yeah. Then he could see how Tippi was. But only because he was checking on Elana.

AJ rolled his eyes and let out a breath. "You're acting like a girl," he muttered.

It was a good thing he was alone in the desert.

He watched the caravan of cars and trucks work their way over the winding sand road to a factory that was literally in the middle of nowhere. He'd been able to piece together that the diamond smuggling ring took the gems from the mines to one of six factories spread out over the desert.

It was from here AJ wasn't sure how they were processing the diamonds and getting them out of the country. He looked through the scope on his sniper rifle and tried to make out the faces driving the vehicles four hundred yards below him.

Swatting at another fly and unable to concentrate, AJ sat up and pulled his secure phone out of his pack.

"Just call her. Tell her you got her messages and appreciate she's been calling." He blew out a frustrated breath and cursed his trembling hand. Why was he having so much trouble talking to a woman? When had the tides shifted?

He knew right when it had been. He'd been totally in lust with her before. But he started feeling more when he'd watched Tippi take care of Elana with such methodical care. Then they'd gone to her room and she admitted she wanted him to be a little rough with her in bed. The fact she was so honest and said she'd wait for him.

One little woman had rocked the foundation of his world and scared the shit out of him. Now he didn't know how to talk to her like an adult. What was wrong with him?

He hit the speed-dial button before he could change his mind.

She picked up after two rings, sounding breathless.

"AJ? Is it really you?"

Why was she breathless? Was there someone with her? Was she in bed with some other man?

"What's going on?" AJ demanded.

"What do you mean?" Tippi asked. "Where are you?"

"I'm asking the questions. Why did you answer the phone so fast? Why are you out of breath?"

He sounded crazy and he didn't care. He wished he was in Virginia so he could rip the dick off whatever man had thought it was okay to touch his woman.

She was silent for a beat and then, "You're upset because I answered the phone too fast? You think I'm out of breath? What in the world are you talking about? What's the matter with you? Are you okay?"

"Who's with you, Tippi?"

"No one's with me. It's the middle of the night. Wait. You think there's someone here with me? In bed?" Her voice rose an octave. "You haven't returned a single one of my calls in five weeks. You don't get to ask if someone's in my bed!"

What the hell did that mean? "Just tell me," he said.

"AJ Jensen," Tippi said. "Quit being a jackass. There is no one in my bed but me. I told you I'd wait for you and I meant it. What in the world is the matter with you?"

Her upset tone finally registered through AJ's thick skull. He stared at the vehicles still driving to the factory. Taking a few deep breaths of the oppressive desert air, he got himself under control.

"Wow, Tip, I'm sorry. I am being a jackass. I'm proud of you for standing up to me. I don't think you've done that before."

"Elana's teaching me to be more assertive."

"It's working," AJ chuckled. Wait. "You've been with Elana? I figured she was out of the country because she hasn't returned my calls."

"You haven't called her," Tippi said. "She's been trying to get a hold of you for weeks."

"No, I've been trying to get a hold of her," AJ countered. "I've left her messages."

"Did you leave me messages, too?" Tippi asked.

"Um. . . " Busted. AJ took another deep breath. "About that. I haven't called you, no."

"I see," Tippi said. But she didn't see. She didn't understand why he hadn't returned her calls.

"Listen, you know my job is stressful. I can't talk to you every day."

"I haven't asked you to talk to me every day. I thought at least once in the last five weeks would be fine." She was getting upset again.

"I'm calling now, aren't I?" AJ demanded. This is why he didn't do relationships. Women got clingy and demanding.

"And the first thing out of your mouth was an insult to me. You know I don't sleep around. There hasn't been anyone in my bed but you."

She hated how her voice shook and how he made her feel so vulnerable. She wanted to hit something. Elana was rubbing off on her.

"I need to talk to Elana. Do you know where she is?"

"Training a new partner. Kimball is sending her and this new kid to Russia tomorrow. That's why she's been trying to get a hold of you. She wanted to know if there was any way you could meet her in Moscow or St. Petersburg."

"How do you know all this?"

"Elana and I are friends. We talk to each other. Now, why haven't you returned her calls?" She wanted to ask, 'And why haven't you called me?'

"I'm telling you, I haven't gotten a single message from her and I've been leaving her messages," he said again. Then almost to himself, "I wonder if Kimball has somehow been able to intercept our messages."

"It's possible," Tippi said slowly, "If he has the right computer equipment and has been monitoring her phones. He's had a tail on her almost nonstop so it wouldn't surprise me if he was messing with her phone."

"How do you know about tails and monitoring phone calls? What's she been teaching you?"

AJ didn't like that Tippi knew so much about his world. He liked his secrets and he liked her being oblivious because it was safer that way. Safer for him or her, he wasn't sure.

"She's been teaching me to take care of myself and be a strong woman."

"I don't like it," he said.

"I don't care what you think right now. In fact I'm

really upset with you." Tippi started to cry and hated herself for it. "I've missed you, I've thought about you every day. I left you messages. I am not some piece of ass you can take advantage of. Give me your message for Elana and then don't call me again. Don't crawl to my door when you come back home." She bit her fist to keep from sobbing.

When he didn't respond, she couldn't hold the sob back. He was supposed to apologize and tell her he couldn't live without her, not ignore her. So much for the romantic outburst she wanted from him.

AJ felt the hot muzzle of the pistol push against the soft spot behind his ear. He'd been so engrossed in talking to Tippi he hadn't noticed the caravan of vehicles had stopped. They'd probably caught a reflection off his scope since he'd been waving the thing around like a damn flag.

The man with the gun spoke English and had a deep voice. "You should not have loud arguments on the phone when you are supposed to be working. Tell the woman goodbye so she does not have to hear you die."

AJ closed his eyes.

Tippi heard every word the man said and screamed, "AJ, oh God, AJ! What's going on? Are you okay? I'm sorry. I'm sorry I said all that! I love—" The sound of the gunshot caused her to drop her cell and when she picked it up from the folds of her comforter, the line was dead.

She was absolutely afraid AJ was, too.

15

During the week, Elana quizzed Pete about illegal drugs in between his language lessons. She brushed him up on his Russian history, language, and accent when he spoke in English. Luckily, his IQ was as high as his file claimed. The downfall was major book smarts but not a single social skill.

Pete had a photographic memory. Once he saw or heard something, it stuck with him forever. Another mark against his social skills. He was the smartest person she'd ever met besides Tippi. It seemed against the odds she would meet two geniuses. One quickly becoming her good friend and the other she hoped she wouldn't get killed for working with her.

Not that it would ever happen, but Elana wondered what children from Tippi and Pete would turn out like. Brilliant, since they were both too smart for their own good. Gorgeous, since Tippi was. Of course if Pete even looked at Tippi, AJ'd snap him like a twig. Elana smiled for the first time in days.

They were one day away from leaving for Russia and Elana figured Pete was as ready to go as he would ever be.

"We need to go shopping," Elana grunted as she slammed her palm into Pete's solar plexus. He let out a whoosh of air.

"How can you hold a conversation while you beat the crud out of me?" Pete asked, dodging Elana's fist as it went flying toward his head. He stepped back and put his hands up. "Please, can we take a break?"

"You have to quit saying things like 'crud' and 'please'. I've never met a drug dealer who talked like that." Elana grabbed two bottles of water and tossed one to Pete.

Every night, Elana worked with him on his fighting skills for at least four hours. He'd done basic self defense at The Farm and worked out on a regular basis to try and build some muscle tone. It wasn't working. Pete looked like he should be sitting behind a desk in some office going over computer files instead of preparing to be a drug dealer.

Elana was ready to go. No matter what Kimball had ordered her to do, she wanted to find Jon and figure out what the hell was going on. She would not kill him. She couldn't. If he had gone rogue, as the Government suspected and Elana wouldn't believe, she still couldn't kill him.

She'd had to kill a few people over the last six months, but it had all been in self-defense. Their faces still haunted her dreams. She didn't know if she could kill the Novlak brothers and Enrique. It would be an execution. They were scum, she knew that, but she wasn't a murderer.

Elana had, at first, wanted to join the CIA to prove to her father she was responsible. Filing and submitting reports had given her a sense of making a difference in the world. Working for her country and saving lives.

Then she'd met Jon and he'd changed her perspective on a lot of things. There were horrible people in the world who deserved to die. He did his job without question. And now it seemed that he was a hired assassin. What did those pictures from his brother mean? Did Jon really get paid by other governments to kill people? Why had Michael shared that information with her?

Jon had trained Elana as she was training Pete now. Jon had taught her how to school her emotions and how to stay in character. He had made her feel things for him. Of course, he didn't feel anything for her; it was all part of the cover. She didn't want Pete getting confused.

"Follow me, Petey. You are going to be comfortable around me if it kills you. You need to learn to relax. Pretend for a moment that we're in a room at the hotel we'll be staying at."

She walked to her bedroom and pulled off her sports bra with her back to him. He spewed water all over the floor and began to choke.

"That's what I'm talking about. You can't act like you've never seen me naked."

"But I haven't seen you naked!" he said coughing.

"We need to change that now."

She turned and he dropped his water bottle as she unlaced her shoes.

"You can look at my boobs every once in a while, but you still have to make eye contact. Think of it as if the woman you just had sex with climbed out of bed and is going to take a shower. It's no big deal she's walking around naked. Pete, eye contact, remember?" Elana slid her gym shorts down her legs. The black thong she wore barely concealed what Pete was looking at.

"Uhh. Eye contact. Sex. Uhh. Shower. Got it."

"Oh, Pete. Listen up. Look at me, not what's behind my underwear. Not my chest, either. They're called boobs, get used to it. Okay, eyes. Do you want to be a field agent?"

"Yes. More than anything." He finally looked at her.

"Then quit acting like a choir boy and act like a CIA Agent. We're going to do everything together but have sex. I am going to hang on your arm in some skimpy ass clothes, lick the side of your face, rub against you, and we're going to be sharing a room for two weeks. There are going to be women throwing themselves at you. Feel free to fuck them if you want. What an agent does on a deep cover mission is their choice. Just don't blow our cover."

She tried to shock him on purpose. The people they were going to be with would be saying and doing worse.

"I wouldn't sleep with someone I didn't know!"

"Neither would I. But you might find yourself close in order to be convincing." Elana thought back to the hallway of the strip club with Jon.

Pete seemed to remember Elana was nearly naked. His ears turned as red as his face and redder than his hair.

"Get dressed. We're going out," she said.

She fixed her wig, going with a sleek red one that fell almost to the middle of her back. Her dress was something close to a Pretty Woman look. It had two pieces, barely, held up by gold rings on the sides of her ribs.

Pete had black colored contacts, dark brown hair dye, a dark goatee, and a well cut suit. He didn't look anything like Opie Taylor now.

Elana drove them to the train station.

"Let's go hit some clubs and get you a little more practice. You need it. The more time you pretend to be Shane the Russian, the better."

They spent six hours out on the town club hopping. Pete pretended to be Russian the whole time. His accent slipped every once in a while, but he did well overall. Elana wished they had more time to get him ready.

Just after midnight, they caught the train back to Elana's jeep. She'd kept her phone off because she didn't need any other possible distractions for Pete.

Now she had four frantic voice mails and numerous text messages from Tippi. She couldn't even understand some of them because Tippi's voice was so frenzied. The point was the same: I need to talk to you.

Elana had warned Tippi about leaving messages with too much information in case Elana wasn't the one who got it. The last text had more detail: 'AJ finally called. Need to talk to you asap. As in NOW. Need you!'

The fear Elana always felt for Tippi made her slam her door a little too hard.

"I need to make a quick stop before we go back to my condo. We're leaving in six hours from Camp Lejune. You can sleep on the flight."

"Okay," Pete said, looking at her funny.

She had reservations about taking him to Tippi's house, but she needed to know why Tippi was so freaked out and what AJ had to say. She didn't want to do that over the phone. Pete could stay in the car.

Elana raced to Tippi's and pulled to the curb a block from the house. She pulled off her wig and quickly ran her fingers through her hair.

"Stay here. I'll be back in ten."

"Where are we?" Pete asked looking around. "Do you know someone who lives here? Don't some famous people live here? At least some really rich people?" He acted too much like a little kid.

"I said. I'll be back. In ten." She slammed the door.

She jogged carefully in her heels across the street and down to Tippi's house. She went around back and through the fence that surrounded the yard. She stepped onto the porch and watched through the sliding glass door as Tippi paced in her kitchen, gripping her cell phone.

Elana rapped her knuckles on the glass, causing Tippi to scream and throw her phone in the air. It flew into the living room and bounced off the couch then to the floor.

One hand over her mouth, she ran to the sliding glass door. "Oh, Lord, you scared me!" Tippi threw her arms around Elana. She was shaking.

"What's wrong?" Elana held Tippi at arm's length. She'd been crying. Her nose and eyes were puffy and red.

"AJ's dead," she said sobbing.

"Dead?" Elana whispered. AJ couldn't be dead. "Why do you think he's dead?"

Tippi started to cry harder. "I should have." Sob. "Told him." Sob. "How much." Sob. "He meant." Sob. "To me." Ragged breath. "I should have—"

"Tippi!" Elana grabbed her by the shoulders and shook her. "Pull yourself together and tell me what happened."

Elana took her to the living room and picked up the cell phone. She handed it to Tippi and gently pushed her to sit on the couch. She held the phone tightly in both hands as shudders wracked her body.

Elana waited until Tippi seemed to have regained control then encouraged her to talk with a pat to the knee.

"I was asleep and had my phone next to my pillow," Tippi took a trembling breath. "It rang and the screen showed it was the special number AJ gave me."

"Okay," Elana prompted.

"When I answered, I was kind of breathless because I couldn't believe he was finally calling." She smiled lightly through her tears. "He accused me of having a man in my bed." She dropped her head and said to herself, "Like I'd want any other man." She wiped her eyes and nose with the back of her hand.

"What else happened?" Elana said.

"We argued and I told him he was a jackass. He kind of apologized and told me he couldn't believe I stood up to him. I told him you were teaching me to be more assertive," Tippi laughed and it sounded dry and hollow. "As soon as he realized we'd been spending time together, he wanted to know why you hadn't returned his calls."

Elana wrinkled her forehead in confusion. "Haven't returned his calls? I haven't gotten any calls."

"That's what I told him," Tippi said. "He said he's been calling you. I said you've been calling him. He thinks Kimball's somehow keeping your calls from each other. That's crazy, isn't it?"

"Anything is possible. Someone has been keeping us

from talking to each other." Elana took Tippi's hand. "Tell me the rest. Tell me why you think he's dead."

Tippi opened her mouth but nothing came out. More tears rolled down her cheeks. Finally she spoke. "He wanted to know what you've been doing. I told him you were training a new partner and had to go back to Russia. That you wanted to figure out how to meet up with him. Then, after he told me he didn't like my new attitude, I told him he could kiss my ass and not call me again or come to my house. He was silent and then I heard a voice, not AJ's, say that he shouldn't have loud arguments when he was supposed to be working."

She choked on another sob. "Then the guy told AJ to hang up. So. . . so. . . so I wouldn't have to hear him die." Tippi's voice became so quiet, Elana had to lean close. "I heard a gunshot and— Oh, Elana, a gunshot." She was trembling again. "Then the line went dead."

Elana pictured the scene in her head. The fact the man spoke to AJ before he shot him could have given AJ enough time to get the drop on the killer.

"How long ago was this?"

Tippi's trembling hands fumbled with the phone. She touched the screen and huffed in annoyance when the shaking caused her to press the wrong buttons two different times. Finally she was able to pull up the call log. The call had taken place at 12:06 a.m. and lasted four minutes and twenty-six seconds. It was almost one.

"Did you try to call him back?"

"Of course I did! Then I tried to call you. Then I tried to call him. I did that four times. Every time I called either of you, it rang once and went straight to voice mail."

"That's because my phone was off. He probably shut his phone off, too. He could have been the one that fired off the shot and he's fine."

"Then why hasn't he called?" pleaded Tippi, more tears bubbling to the surface.

"I don't know. Maybe he can't. Obviously he was caught unaware. He may need to get to a secure location before he can contact you again."

Elana got up and grabbed a pen and pad from the kitchen counter. She wrote down what she knew of her and Pete's itinerary for the next few days.

"When he calls back, give him this information if I haven't."

"You're so sure he'll call back?" Tippi seemed to be relaxing because Elana was calm.

"It's AJ. He's been in tougher situations." Elana took Tippi's hand again. "He's fine. You'll see."

"Okay. If you say so." That was all Tippi needed. Elana's steady reassurances. She pulled her hand free of Elana's grip, stood, and started pacing again.

She stopped suddenly and gaped. "What are you wearing?"

"I was out."

"Out?" Tippi said dubiously. "You don't go out. And the few times you have, you didn't dress like. . . like. . ."

"Like a 'ho'?" Elana almost laughed.

"Well. It is a little risqué."

Now Elana did laugh. Tippi was smart, beautiful, had the worst mother in the world, but wouldn't say a bad thing about anyone.

"I was kind of working. Breaking in the new partner."

"'The best way to become the part is to practice the part.' You told me that once." Tippi recited.

"He's got a lot of work before he's great, but I don't have time to teach him. It's going to be sink or swim."

"You'll be fine." Now it was Tippi's turn to reassure Elana. "You're cool and calculated under stress. Nothing bothers you or ruffles your feathers."

If only that were completely true, Elana thought. This mission was doing more than ruffling her feathers. It was ripping them out and tossing them to the wind.

A sound from the front door had Elana shooting off the couch. She retrieved a small stiletto blade strapped to her hip under the dress. She waved Tippi away and mouthed, "Get behind the couch."

Without making a sound, Elana slipped off her heels and pushed them out of the way. She crouched low and went to the front door.

Tippi stood frozen in the middle of her living room with one hand gripping her cell, the other over her mouth.

Tippi had reached her quota of stressful things for the night. Elana waved her knife in Tippi's general direction and it made her jump into action. Tippi finally dropped to the floor and scrambled behind the couch.

The front door handle rattled. Elana heard the sound of metal scraping. She waited patiently, her body pressed against the wall behind the door, while whoever was out there picked the lock.

Tippi poked her head out and shook her phone at Elana. She whispered, "911?"

Elana shook her head, waving Tippi back.

It took over sixty seconds for the lock to click.

Amateur.

The door swung open slowly. Elana relaxed her muscles for a split second before she lunged at the intruder.

A howl of pain filled the air as Elana jumped the unknown assailant. She flipped him to his stomach, held the stiletto to his throat, and gripped his two hands at the small of his back.

She kicked the door closed and sat on his back. "Seriously, Pete? Sixty seconds to pick a lock?"

Just to prove a point, Elana let the blade of her knife barely cut his skin before she took it from his throat.

"Yeah?" he choked out with the side of his face buried in the plush carpet, "At least I managed to figure out which house you went into."

Elana used the back of Pete's head to push herself up. He grunted and rolled over on his back, rubbing his neck. "You didn't have to cut me."

"Yes, I did." She went to the door and relocked it then put her shoes back on. "I told you to wait in the car."

"You were gone for nine minutes. I got worried."

"I told you I would be back in ten."

She didn't want Pete to know anything about her personal life. What little bit of one she had.

"You wouldn't have been back in ten. You're still here." Pete picked himself off the floor and glared at Elana.

Tippi made a sound as she popped up from behind the couch.

Pete stared at her.

"Who is this?" Tippi demanded. "Why are you talking like you know who he is instead of calling the police?" She was waving her cell phone around again.

"This is my new partner. We're leaving." Elana ushered Pete toward the sliding glass door.

"You can't just leave!" Tippi protested. "We weren't done talking. Also, you need to introduce us and your partner needs a band-aid for his neck. Or something."

"No, I don't need to introduce you and he damn sure doesn't need a band-aid. I'll be in touch."

"Come on," Pete pleaded. "Just introduce us. I don't know anything about you. Is this your sister? Your friend? Shouldn't partners know each other?"

Elana was instantly catapulted back to a similar conversation with Jon. Such a trick question. She didn't trust Pete enough to let him know about her.

"Partners don't need to know personal information. Partners need to know they can rely on each other. You ignored me. That's not trustworthy. Now let's go."

"Can I at least use the bathroom first?" Pete asked.

He was acting like a little kid again and it was pissing her off.

"No," Elana said at the same time Tippi said, "Of course."

The two women stared at each other for a moment.

"What's it going to hurt to let him use the bathroom?" Tippi asked as she pointed to the half bath just off the living room.

"We need to leave," Elana said as Pete walked to the bathroom and closed the door.

She could have pulled him out of there, but what would that prove? It wasn't like Tippi was in danger from Pete. Elana just didn't want him here.

"Is that really your new partner?" Tippi whispered. When Elana merely nodded, Tippi continued. "He isn't very big. Or very old. I can pick a lock faster than he can."

Elana opened her mouth to ask how Tippi knew how to pick a lock and stopped. Of course Tippi knew how to pick a lock. She probably knew how to hotwire a car, too. Her brain worked so much differently than anyone else Elana knew. If Tippi wanted to know something, she read about it, practiced, and she could do it.

"Wow. Now I know why you said 'sink or swim'. You're going to need luck."

"Yeah." Elana gave Tippi a one-armed hug. "Set your house alarm. It should have been on when I got here."

"I know. I shut it off when I was calling and texting you to come over."

"Don't ever do that. You leave it on until you know who's at your door."

"Okay, sorry."

"He'll call, Tippi. You'll see him soon."

Pete popped out of the bathroom. "Who'll call?"

Elana closed her eyes. "We're leaving."

"Jeez, you're in a bad mood." He put his hand out.

"I'm Pete Campbell, Elana's new partner."

Tippi shook his hand. "I'm Tippi—"

"Bye." Elana cut her off before she could get out her last name. Damn normal people and their social niceties.

Elana pushed Pete out the door after telling Tippi to set her alarm again. The pair made their way to Elana's jeep.

"She seemed nice," Pete said.

"Don't tell anyone we were here and don't ask me about her," Elana said without looking at him.

"Can I just ask one thing?" When Elana ignored him, Pete continued. "Is Tippi her nickname? Because I can't see anyone naming their child that. Maybe a poodle, but not a child."

Elana almost smiled.

16

Jacksonville, North Carolina – Camp Lejune

Getting only four hours of sleep hadn't improved Elana's mood. Pete was still pissing her off.

He stared at the huge plane and gulped. "I thought we were flying on a jet."

She glared at him in disbelief. "You're afraid to fly."

"I've learned to handle myself in jets. I can pretend I'm riding in a car. That thing is noisy, doesn't have real seats, and you feel every dip and movement."

They were catching a ride with the Marines on a Bell-Boeing V-22 Osprey. It was a beauty, too. With a box-like fuselage and rotating engine pods set at the wingtips, it resembled a giant helicopter with wings. Since the wings were set above the fuselage, instead of coming out of the sides, it was actually able to take off and land like a helicopter. But that's where the similarity to a helicopter ended.

Once airborne, the engines rotated and the aircraft converted to a turboprop airplane capable of high-speed, high-altitude flight. It was just over fifty feet long and its max speed was almost 320 mph. Yeah, baby. Elana stared with appreciation. It was the perfect flying machine.

But Pete was right. It wasn't designed for comfort, it was designed for duty. They were catching a ride to the

Ukraine. Kiev to be exact. That's where they'd get on the plush jet that would fly them into Moscow, Russia.

As they walked across the tarmac Elana said, "Don't say a word to the Marines. The less they know, the better."

She handed the classified documents to the man who met them at the rear of the plane.

"Ma'am," he said.

"Sergeant. Just hitching a ride."

The marine opened the sealed folder and saw the documents had been signed by the Deputy Director of the CIA and the Vice-President of the United States. There were no names given to the 'secret cargo', just orders to let them off at the secure runway in the Ukraine. Every few months, Sgt. Jackson got orders like this.

"Yes, ma'am, although it will be a shame to not get to know you better." He grinned and winked.

She looked good in military Battle Dress Uniform, BDUs. The camouflage did something for her hair and figure. Of course, Jackson was career military so he thought camo looked good on just about everything.

"Nice try, Sergeant," her lips curved slightly. "Lead the way, we have work to do." She waved her hand.

She watched Pete square his shoulders and gather his courage. His BDUs were too big and hung off his small frame. He looked like a boy playing dress-up in his dad's Army clothes.

"Come on, Shane," she said over her shoulder as she followed Sgt. Jackson to the transport.

"Right behind you, Ellie," Pete called in his slight Russian accent, trying to get himself into character.

Sixteen hours later, the Osprey touched down smoothly in the Ukraine. To Pete's credit, he'd only thrown up twice. The twenty marines on the plane had started to raz him, but a sharp word from Sgt. Jackson shut them up.

Elana had power-napped and tried to get Pete to do the

same. They sat side by side, strapped in from above with harnesses. The hard seats were uncomfortable. Elana had shown Pete how to secure his head to the harness with a bandana so he could sleep without his head whipping from side to side. As soon as he was secure, he was out like a light.

Upon landing, Sgt. Jackson produced a card with a ten digit number. "We'll be back this way in two weeks, ma'am. This is the sat phone number. Call it if you need an early or alternate pick-up location."

Elana looked at the card then nodded her head to Pete. Jackson held the card out and Pete read the numbers.

"Thanks, Jackson. We won't need an alternate pick-up. See you in two weeks."

"Don't you want the card?" Jackson said.

"Can't take it with us, Sergeant, you know how top-secret missions are. Besides, he has the number." She tapped Pete's forehead and he smiled, finally feeling useful.

"Your call-in name is Elana," Jackson said as she and Pete turned to walk to the airport.

"Really?" Elana said without turning. He was more connected than she thought.

"Really," Jackson answered with a slight chuckle. "I hope you won't need it, though."

"Oh, I hope so, too."

"AJ said you had black hair," Jackson said.

Elana turned, but didn't remove her sunglasses. "AJ hasn't seen me in a while. How is he?"

Crazy, sneaky, hopefully alive, bastard.

"Wanted you to know we've got your back," Jackson winked. "I've got your front, too, if you need it."

"Is he your brother? You both know how to make a girl feel special."

Their banter confused him, but Pete wisely kept his mouth shut.

"Brother in arms, ma'am. Absolutely nothing is to

happen to you while you're with me."

"Did you talk to him this morning?" Elana held her breath.

"Yes ma'am. Told me to tell you he's harder to kill than some people assume."

"Good to know, Marine." After a salute, she turned.

She needed to talk to Tippi and find out if AJ had contacted her, too.

"Aren't you worried he knows your name?" Pete asked.

"Nope, what can it hurt? Ellie and Elana are close. Ellie could be short for Elana. Besides, if things go bad, he'll be the one to save our asses."

"Yeah, Ellie and Elana are close. El-lie. E-lay-nuh." Sometimes Pete was such a dumb ass.

They snuck in a side entrance of the small airport to find the utility closet where their baggage was supposed to be stashed. Elana quickly located four large Coach suitcases filled with clothes, weapons, and drugs. Just enough to keep her and Pete's cover intact.

Still in the utility closet, they both quickly changed clothes. Nothing too flashy. Just casual business attire so they would blend in with other people in the airport.

They waited an hour for the jet. Elana spoke quickly and quietly on the walk across the tarmac. "It's time to quit acting like Pete and start acting like a drug lord with a Russian accent. Shane doesn't ask questions, he gives orders. From this point forward, we're in character. You never know when a room is bugged or someone is listening."

Pete whispered, "Do you think the jet is bugged?"

"Maybe. You're going to act like it is." She adjusted her sunglasses and pretended to fix her hair. She shed Elana like a snakeskin and swayed on board with Pete behind her. Time for the show to begin.

"Have our bags brought on board." Pete waved his arm at one of the men. "This does not concern you, woman. Go change." Pete barked at her in his Shane persona. "You will also get me a drink."

The captain and co-pilot quietly introduced themselves. The co-pilot directed the landing crew to bring the luggage on board. Elana stood to the side while her luggage was set on the bed. When the man was gone, she pulled out her phone and texted Tippi.

She said AJ was alive and she wouldn't be in contact for at least a week. Hopefully that would keep Tippi in a good mood. The girl was in so deep with AJ it wasn't funny. Reminded Elana of herself six months ago.

She pulled a neon green mini skirt from one of the suitcases. They had an excellent array of clothing. At least Director Dickwad had gotten something right. She chose a skin tight babydoll shirt with bright blue and neon green lightning strikes on it. Last was a pair of green sling backs with a three inch heel. Pete was going to hate how tall they made her.

She fluffed her wig, added some lipstick and checked herself in the mirror. She looked a little like 'Barbie dressed as Marilyn Monroe dressed as a slut for Halloween'. Perfect.

When she stepped out of the bedroom, three sets of male eyes locked on her.

"Shane-baby? How 'bout if I make us both a martini?" She added just a hint of bimbo-breathiness to her voice. She could be a phone sex operator. "Captains? Could I mix you up a little something?"

"Ellie, think for a moment about what you just asked." Pete grabbed her chin. "Do you really think we want our pilots to drink?"

"Ow, Shane, honey, you're hurting me."

"Well then, do not act so stupid." He let her go. "It is good thing you are good lay or you would not even be here."

Elana mixed the drinks while the Captains got ready for the flight. She handed Pete his drink then tipped hers back in one swallow.

She sat in a plush seat, put her head back, and tried to relax. She quickly fell asleep to the rocking motion of the plane. A few moments turned into almost two hours.

Elana came awake with a start and had to orient herself. The descent of the plane and the vivid dreams had woken her. The dream memories had been so real she had to re-familiarize herself with the surroundings of the jet. Pete was sleeping across from her in one of the reclining chairs.

Of course, she'd dreamed of Jon.

After months of being away from him and slowly separating her emotions, Elana wasn't sure what was real and what was fantasy.

The first thing she was going to do when she found Jon was ask him what the hell was going on. No. First she was going to slap him upside the head. Then she was going to ask him what the hell was going on. Then she was going to kiss him and walk away. Let him see what it felt like.

Yeah right. She wasn't going to be able to do any of those things. She was going to be so happy to see him, she'd probably cry like a girl and piss him off. Wouldn't that just be perfect? She'd become an agent similar to him and he was the one person who could make her rock hard exterior crumble.

As the jet bounced on the runway, Pete came awake with a start. He took a few breaths and glanced at Elana.

"Did you enjoy your nap, my dear?"

"I sure did, Shane-baby. Sorry we couldn't be part of the mile high club this trip." She giggled. The jet belonged to the Novlak brothers. Elana would guarantee it was bugged.

They taxied onto the runway and she looked out. They were being waited for by some military jeeps and a Mercedes SUV with tinted windows. They were in Moscow and had to be driven north to St. Petersburg.

The co-pilot entered the cabin. "I am Petrov. I will be your driver and bodyguard."

Pete looked at Elana quickly then back at Petrov. "That will not be necessary. I can take care of both of us."

"Nyet." Petrov said.

Pete looked again to Elana.

"Whatever, baby, I don't mind another man along." She blew a kiss to Petrov and stepped down the stairs into the cold.

"No, I disagree," Pete let his Russian accent become more obvious, as though his anger made it harder for him to concentrate on English. "We will be taken to train station and given first class accommodations to St. Petersburg. Boris and Mikhail say nothing about having babysitter. They are lucky I do not get back on jet and fly to Kazakhstan to do business."

Pete was really getting into this. Maybe they were going to be okay.

"I am very sorry, sir," Petrov bent at the waist. "I mean no disrespect. I have my orders. We drive."

Petrov snapped his fingers at one of the military men. Pete and Elana stood and watched as their bags were unloaded. It was odd how well they were being taken care of. Yes, 'Shane' was going to be a major asset if things worked out. But he hadn't even been introduced to the Novlak brothers yet. They usually only spent this much money and energy on their well-known associates.

Something wasn't right. Elana hoped she could piece it together quickly. She had a bad feeling.

17

St. Petersburg, Russia

Boris was the party animal, Mikhail was the brains.

For the first time in three weeks, Jon was invited back to Mikhail's private study to drink vodka, smoke cigars, and discuss business. They'd, of course, had numerous business meetings and attended parties over the last six months. However, Jon was only invited to meet with Mikhail alone about twice a month.

Mikhail, hating all things American that couldn't make him money, didn't like Jon's name and had taken to calling him Nikoli after the night in the strip club. One more way to assert his authority.

"My attention has been shown, Nikoli, our friend in CIA sends another, how you say, asset. He will be called Shane Gunther but real name is Pete Campbell." Mikhail thoughtfully stroked his mustache. "I must get this right. He drug dealer pretending to be CIA pretending to be drug dealer. Our friend Kimball is nothing if inventive."

"Our friend Kimball is nothing. You should let me go back to the states and make him disappear." Jon tried, again, to get out from under the damn thumb of the Novlaks. Except he couldn't leave yet because he didn't have the information he needed.

"Oh, no no, friend. I need you here take care of our problems. You become most useful inside agent I employ."

Jon took a drink of vodka and a strong pull on his cigar. So this is what his life had been reduced to. Pretending to be rogue in order to bring down the Deputy Director of the CIA. He was getting in too deep and knew it. He was on the payroll of Novlak Industries, met with all their foreign arms traders, and brought weapons into the former Soviet Socialist Republic. Oh yeah, let's not forget he killed their competition. The only saving grace for Jon was that he'd be killing the competition anyway if he was still legit on the books with the CIA. Maybe he wouldn't rot in the deepest pits of hell.

The problem was if he didn't prove Kimball was a lying, traitorous bastard, Jon was going to look like the traitor.

"What does Enrique think about this? You bringing in another drug lord, an American at that?"

"That is beauty part. Shane-Pete is no pretending to be American. Kimball has make him Russian. Papers will show he is long lost nephew from sister. I do not have sister!" Mikhail slapped Jon on the back and laughed heartily. "I love how you American change history with paper."

Jon tried to say something and Mikhail cut him off with a wave of his hand. "Enrique is business man. He will want more access to get drugs in United States. He gets percents of what we make. He like the money. More money come from American high schools."

Taking a pull from his own cigar and a shot of vodka, Mikhail set down his empty glass and stood. He walked to his desk and grabbed a folder.

"Shane has brought woman with him. Kimball not come out and say what her role is. There is no way she is agent. Woman with body like that cannot have brain. But, if she agent, maybe dirty agent, there are possibility. Kimball sure to let know they both disposable."

Mikhail tossed the folder to the table in front of Jon and some photos fanned out. This Pete guy looked like a kid. Jon leaned forward to look more closely. The one with the woman was partially covered. Jon saw long, lean legs encased in green heels. He ran his fingers up the legs until he pushed the other photos out of the way. The woman was dressed skimpily and had short, blonde hair. She wore large sunglasses and her head was turned to the side.

The instant hardening of Jon's dick had him picking up the photo and staring at Elana Miller. "What's her name?" he managed without losing it.

"Yes, fabulous, is she? I might able convince her stay with me at mansion. What she doing with boy like that when she could have man?" Mikhail laughed and drank more vodka. "Her name Ellie Shepard. Do you recognize?"

"No. And that worries me. What if Kimball is lying about her?" Jon set the photo back on the table and hid all his questions about why Elana was here under the mask he always wore. "I think you should let me be alone with her when they arrive. I'll find out what she really knows."

"Oh, no, I think no, Nikoli. She spend few moments alone with you and she not want to come to my bed. Natalia has barely left you room. I decide who get Ellie Shepard."

"If she turns out to be against you, can I have her?"

"Oh, I love your ability to dispose of problem, Nikoli. Yes, you have leftovers if woman turn out to be trouble." Mikhail sat back and sipped his alcohol.

Boris, Enrique, Gregor, and a few other men strode into the study. The others began discussing more business and soon their exchange turned to women and sex. Conversations Jon never participated in.

Jon knew how Mikhail and the men treated woman. It was one of the other reasons he'd kept Talia in his bed. The girl didn't deserve the beatings that were often dished out during sex. He hoped leftovers weren't what Elana became.

Jon had been able to keep tabs on Elana for the first two months just like he'd been able to keep in contact with Michael. He knew Kimball had been sending her on numerous missions and very few brought her to Northern Europe. If she would have been anywhere near him, Jon would have figured how to get to her.

In the deepest depths of his soul, Jon knew she wasn't a dirty agent. He just wished he knew something concrete and helpful.

Every CIA agent had contacts all over the world. You had to be able to drop into a location and get current information when you needed it. The problem was trusting the people who were your contacts. Most weren't government agents; they were criminals of some caliber. If you went to them with something they could make money from, they'd sell you out in a nanosecond.

Jon hadn't been able to get in contact with AJ, either. It was like Kimball knew the only two people Jon wanted to talk to and he was keeping them out of reach. At least Kimball didn't know about Jon's family in Montana.

Jon's European contacts were afraid of the Novlak Empire. In the beginning, he'd been able to use his questions to say he was flushing out everyone against the Novlaks. The problem was, the few people he found who were willing to help him bring down Mikhail and Boris always ended up dead. Somehow, the Novlaks were always one step ahead.

The bugged room wasn't it; Jon never conducted business at the mansion. He usually had to take Talia to one of the cities for shopping and then meet up with people while she was occupied spending his money.

Jon was used to working alone, he reveled in it. Alone meant no collateral damage. Over the summer when he'd been with Michael and Kamielle bringing down a mob boss, Jon had never felt such fear. The possibility of something happening to his brother or his brother's beautiful lover, who was now his wife, made Jon's stomach tighten in fear.

He felt he'd made rookie mistakes while working with Michael. He absentmindedly brushed his hand over the scar above his eye to remind him what working with others brought him. Lack of concentration and usually some of his blood spilled. And little Elana blew his concentration all to hell and back.

Jon needed to know what was going on. Was Pete Campbell a lackey for Kimball? Would Pete kill Elana? Jon knew Pete would sure as hell try to kill him. Was Elana Pete's lover? Jon's hands clenched at the thought. Would she do whatever it took to get a mission done? How good would she be at keeping her cover?

And, as always, Jon had to watch his back around everyone. There was a bounty on his head for his supposed betrayal to his country. Any second-rate, American from any alphabet soup agency would shoot Jon first and ask questions later. Not to mention every half-rate thug in Europe who would become a 'legend' for bringing down the Novlaks' new hired gun. Most Novlak assassins didn't live three months. Jon had already made it a full six and was still going strong.

He had to keep Elana safe, keep Pete from trying to kill him, and bring down the Novlak Empire so he could go home and flush out Kimball. Easy.

Sure.

Jon excused himself from the muted conversations around him. He was going to have to find a way to get Elana alone. He wondered what she'd do when she saw him. He hid a grin behind his glass of vodka as he pushed through the big mahogany doors. Hopefully he could get her to repeat the dance number from the club.

That worked for him last time.

Langley, Virginia

Tippi was sure someone was following her. She turned her car down random streets on her way home, the way Elana had taught her.

The text from Elana came through an hour earlier. The relief at knowing AJ was alive was staggering. She didn't question Elana could be wrong. If Elana said AJ was fine then he was.

After driving around aimlessly for almost fifteen minutes, Tippi made her way home. She didn't see the headlights anymore and breathed a sigh of relief. Her hands were shaking when she pressed the button for the automatic garage door and pulled her car in.

After locking up the garage, she keyed the alarm code and rested her head against the door. She felt boneless. AJ was alive. But was he okay? Where was he? When was he going to call again? Didn't he care enough about her to call?

Tears pooled in Tippi's eyes as she put her purse and keys in their place. She'd worked late because she didn't want to be at home. Her feet and back hurt and she was hungry. But who rushed home to a cold, dark, empty house? Not her.

Doing something out of character, Tippi went to her fridge and pulled out one of the beers she kept for AJ.

How pathetic. If she ever had a drink, she drank wine and never more than a glass. She didn't like the feeling of being out of control. Once in college she'd had two glasses of wine in about a half an hour and the 'buzzed' feeling was one she never wanted to repeat.

The dark, imported beer had to be opened with a bottle opener and Tippi rummaged in a drawer until she found it. Popping the top she tipped back the bottle and drank it as fast as she could.

She didn't like the taste of beer and wasn't sure why she was even drinking it. A sad, silly way to feel closer to AJ. She grimaced at the hoppy taste when she wiped her mouth with the back of her hand. Suddenly, she let out a very unladylike burp. Giggling, she covered her mouth and mumbled "Excuse me," to the empty room.

Glancing at the clock, she saw it was after ten. The pizza place AJ always ordered from stopped delivering at nine-thirty, so no pizza for dinner.

Tippi threw away the bottle and rummaged in her fridge. For some reason, another beer beckoned her. She popped the top and found a bag of tortilla chips.

Walking up the stairs to her room, she stumbled slightly and giggled again.

"Wow, beer is much more potent than wine," she declared to her bedroom.

A trail of clothes landed on the floor with chip crumbs as Tippi made her way to the shower. She turned on the stereo in her bathroom and changed it from her usual classical station to "Hot Hits".

Lady Gaga's 'Born This Way' was about halfway through and Tippi turned it up and sang along to every other word while she finished stripping and climbed in the shower.

Marcus often listened to loud, fast music at work when Tippi wasn't in the office. She kind of liked it but didn't want to admit it to anyone. What would people think if they knew she liked popular music?

She scrubbed off the day and enjoyed hot water on her sore lower back. As she got out of the shower a song started that she really liked but would never tell anyone. It was called 'S&M'. How decadent. A song about sex and submission.

The stereo went louder as Tippi danced naked to the strong beat of the song and finished off the second beer. Feeling like a nice glass of red wine, she slipped on her silk Kimono robe she always wore when AJ would come over then skipped and stumbled down her stairs.

It took her three tries to open the bottle of wine

because she couldn't quite get the bottle opener lined up with the cork. This made her giggle, too. She sloshed a large amount into a glass and saluted the darkness of her backyard.

"Well, AJ. I think you're alive. I think I'm in love with you." She took a large swallow of wine. "I'm worried about Elana. I know someone has been stealing from my lab but I don't know who." Another large swallow of wine. "Are you ever going to come back? And if you do, then what?"

Finishing the wine, it occurred to Tippi she didn't feel well. She set the glass down and thought about what she'd done. Two beers and a glass of wine in thirty minutes was not a good plan for a woman who didn't drink.

The room tilted slightly. "Oh, I shouldn't have drunk that much," she mumbled to the floor as the sounds of the stereo blasting from upstairs continued to thump.

Then she heard a different noise behind her.

"You can keep dancing, drinking, and singing. Don't stop on my account."

The voice sucked the breath from Tippi's lungs.

Without thinking about what she was doing, she grabbed the wine and hurled the bottle like a shot put at the shadow in the corner of her living room. She fell from the momentum, and too much alcohol, hitting her head on the corner of the coffee table.

As her vision wavered in and out she registered the thudding sound the bottle made as it hit the floor and the grunt of the man.

There was a man in her house.

She tried to get up but her body wouldn't work right. Her head hurt.

"I was told you weren't going to be a problem," the man said as he came toward her.

Tippi didn't say a word. She tried to concentrate on his big body as he got closer. She kicked out at his groin when he was next to her. He grunted again and dropped to his knees with his face contorted in pain. He looked like Mr. Clean. A black, on steroids version of Mr. Clean.

Tippi squeaked out a scream and tried to scramble away from him. His hand clamped around her ankle. She felt the rug-burn on her cheek as the giant man dragged her flailing legs back toward him.

She was going to die before she told AJ she loved him. That was the first thought that went through her mind. The next was she couldn't believe the coroner was going to tell people she was drunk when he gave the autopsy results.

18

St. Petersburg, Russia

Elana tried to sleep but Petrov kept putting his hand on her leg. She was smashed uncomfortably between him and Pete. Finally, she pushed herself against Pete and stared out the window of the SUV.

The ride was flat, but picturesque. There were signs of the Communist times: abandoned buildings with "Power to the People" spray painted on them. The further they got from Moscow, the nicer the landscape became. There were small homes with decorations in the windows, farms, trees, and green grass fields. If she hadn't been on such a screwed up mission, she would have enjoyed the scenery.

They arrived at the nicest hotel in St. Petersburg well after midnight. It was owned by Boris and Mikhail.

She was so tired, she didn't even undress. Elana dropped to the bed, gun tucked under her pillow. Pete went to the couch and soon they were both asleep.

Knocking on the door at noon woke Elana. She glanced at the clock, hardly believing she'd slept for so long.

Pete staggered to the door and pulled it open before she could stop him.

Petrov stood on the other side. He looked at Elana on the bed and then to Pete's blanket and pillow on the couch.

Question was in his eyes.

"What do you want?" Pete said.

"You will attend a party tonight," Petrov said in Russian. "Mikhail says to be there by four. You will need to dress appropriately."

"Okay," Pete said and closed the door.

He turned to Elana and opened his mouth.

She held up her hand, nodding her head at the bathroom door. "C'mon, Shane."

She grabbed him by the arm and dragged him into the bathroom. She turned on the faucets in both sinks and then the shower. "Stay here. Don't talk." She walked back in the room and turned on the radio to Russian Folk music.

"The room is probably bugged. This should give us some cover."

"What are we going to say when someone asks why I slept on the couch and not with you?"

"Stay in here. We'll put on a show for the listening devices so they won't question why you slept on the couch."

It was time to work. She shut off the water in the bathrooms and morphed to Ellie.

"Shane-baby, let's have some fun." She walked to the bed and made some rather bored sex noises. Pete wrinkled his nose at her.

"Maybe we should take this back to the shower." Pete turned the water back on and shut the door. "What were you doing?"

"I told you we were putting on a show."

"Could you have sounded any more bored?"

"Probably," she said.

Pete glared at her, then smiled.

He went out and bounced on the bed making obscene noises. Elana had to keep from laughing.

They spent a few hours watching TV and pretending to have sex.

Finally it was time to get ready.

Elana pulled a dress from the garment bag and fingered the delicate fabric. She pulled a small lingerie bag from a zippered pocket.

They went to the bathroom and turned on the water.

"Should you wear a bra with that dress? Or even underwear?" Pete whispered.

The back of the dress had an oval cut out that showed all of Elana's back and dipped down just to the dimples above her ass.

"It's a special bra." She held it up to show him. "This strap goes around my neck like a halter top where the dress is. The sides at the cups are adhesive and stick to my skin."

She dangled the underwear from her finger. The strings were so thin, Pete thought of dental floss.

"The bra has a knife strap hidden in it," she pointed to the halter part and a thin knife. "And I have a guillotine wire where the underwire of the bra would be."

Pete quickly dressed in his suit.

"Ellie and Shane from here on out, okay?" Elana said.

"Okay. Ellie and Shane. I can do this. I swear I can."

"Show me." She gently pushed him out the door.

As they rode the elevator, Elana took deep breaths and tried to still her shaking hands. Jon was here, she knew he had to be. What was she going to do when she saw him for the first time in six months? Would she be able to keep her emotions in check? Hell, what was he going to do when he saw her? Would he be happy? Angry? Surprised? Would he show any emotion at all?

"Please don't let me screw this up," she whispered as Pete stepped out of the elevator.

They walked slowly until the noise of the party drew them in. They stood at the top of the steps to the Grand Ballroom. There were at least thirty crystal chandeliers lighting the room in muted gold. Everyone was dressed to show their status. The only thing that kept Pete from looking like a high school freshman who brought a hooker to prom was the dark contacts, slicked back hair, and fitted suit.

Every couple they passed stared. The men with longing and the women with distaste and envy. The white and gold skin-tight dress that left nothing to the imagination was probably the reason. Not to mention her four inch, stiletto, fuck-me heels making her legs look like they went on forever.

Russian military men in uniform offered her a bow and tried to kiss her hand. Some she let, some she didn't. Elana maneuvered them next to Mikhail Novlak. He, of course, took her hand, holding it to his mouth longer than necessary. Pete swore the man's tongue swept out like a reptile's and licked Elana's fingers.

She laughed and patted Mikhail on the cheek. He beamed like a boy.

"At last, I get touching beautiful Ellie. Pictures do no justice of your beauty, my dear."

Pete cleared his throat and stepped next to her. "Mr. Novlak, thank you for the invitation to your wonderful hotel. The room is fabulous."

Mikhail still had not let go of Elana's hand. He was absently rubbing each of her fingers. And he was enjoying the up and down motion way too much.

Boris sided up to them, wedging himself between Elana and Pete so she was sandwiched between the brothers. While trying to keep from being felt up, she listened to the conversation and eyed both men.

If they hadn't been drug, prostitute, and arms dealers, they might have been attractive. The Novlaks had come about their reputation the old fashioned way: by beating the shit out of, or just killing, anyone who stood in their path. Boris was in his mid-forties and Mikhail was in his late forties. Their father had been killed fifteen years earlier and was rumored to have started the illegal business dealings.

Both brothers had dark eyes. Boris had the build of a wrestler, a shaved head, dark, thick eyebrows, and a dark goatee. Mikhail looked like a boxer with military short hair that was starting to gray at the temples. He sported a very 80's mustache only Tom Selleck could pull off.

Boris pushed the front of his body into the back of Elana's and the action pushed her closer to Mikhail. Her height and heels put her boobs almost even with Mikhail's face. The man actually leaned up and sniffed her. *Sniffed* her. Then that reptilian tongue shot out and licked her neck.

It took everything Elana had to not flinch, move, or take him down. If the lure of sex would get them to the mansion, she would pretend to like it. Even though she'd probably have to throw up and take like ten showers later to get the men's thoughts off her body.

Mikhail lifted his head and his black eyes were swimming with lust. "I do not like taste of lotion. You will change that."

Elana nodded and feigned speechlessness. She didn't trust her voice to not betray her loathing. She wondered when Pete would step in as Shane.

"There is someone I want you meet. He demand see you, talk to you, touch you tonight. I promise him one dance. I make him watch us together to add his need."

Elana's heart rate picked up. It had to be Jon. Who else would want to see her?

She smiled at Mikhail, batting her eyelashes. "I will dance with anyone you wish. As long as I get to dance with you the most." She kissed his cheek and tried to turn to Pete.

Mikhail gripped her upper arm so hard, she winced. "I know you dance with me."

"That's enough," Pete said. He grabbed her other arm. "She will dance when I say she can. And right now, she's going to dance with me. When you are ready to talk with your brain and not dick, come find me."

Pete pulled her to the dance floor. "That man is slime," he said as he hauled her into his embrace.

"The job," she reminded him, scanning the room.

"I didn't forget. The real Pete would have pulled you away when snake boy started licking your fingers. I figured Shane would draw the line at Mikhail handing you out like a hooker."

"You're right," she said. If Shane didn't care about Ellie's well-being a little bit, he wouldn't have brought her on a drug deal to another country.

A hand settled on Elana's hip and Pete's eyes widened as he looked at whoever was touching her. He let go and took a step back.

Bracing herself, she plastered on a smile and turned.

It wasn't Jon.

Enrique Juarez yanked Elana into his body. "My darling," he said in his rich, South American accent, "I have been waiting to dance with you all evening."

Elana realized Enrique had a different feel to him than when she'd been here in October. A lot could happen in half a year. She was a walking testament to that. Enrique had the air of a man who was in control; a man who got what he wanted. She could see in his eyes he wanted her.

She put Ellie into full effect. Enrique would take her back to the mansion. "Are you the mysterious man Mikhail was trying to make jealous?" She smashed her breasts against his chest.

"One of many, I am sure." Only the barest hint of satisfaction entered Enrique's eyes.

"Now that you have me, what are you going to do with me?"

"Dance."

Enrique had charisma, good looks, and money. He was also a drug runner and probably a murderer. The way he gripped Elana's hips made her think he wouldn't be shy about forcing a woman to do what he wanted.

The Mambo started and Elana enjoyed the few minutes of being able to dance. Enrique was an exceptional dancer. She was better, though, and he knew it. When the music stopped, many people from the crowd applauded and Elana looked around to find Mikhail and Pete glowering at her. Boris was grinning like an idiot and walking toward them.

"Where on earth did you learn to dance like that?" Enrique asked. "I didn't think a young woman without even a high school education would know any traditional dances."

Kimball hadn't put professional dance training in Elana's dossier cover story. She thought quickly as Boris came to her and pulled her into his arms for a Waltz.

"When you spend so much time with rich men who want a pretty woman on their arm, you learn what you need to. I have many other talents as well."

Boris grunted his approval but Enrique eyed her with suspicion.

"You come back to mansion and show us some of talents," Boris said.

The man was a deplorable dancer and his breath stunk. Elana did her best to make it through the song.

As Boris and Elana danced, Pete and Mikhail spoke.

"I brought Ellie for amusement. My amusement. We have business to conduct." Pete took a cigar from a tray carried by a scantily clad waitress.

"Business. Yes," agreed Mikhail. He put a cigar in his mouth and waited for Pete to light it for him. "Tell me, Shane, is lovely Ellie as good in bed as she looks?"

Pete waited to answer as he lit his own cigar. "Better."

"I thought this. We will go back to mansion and let Enrique spend time with her while we discuss business. Then I spend time with her and you and Enrique finish up details."

"I just told you she's here for me." Pete tried to give his best menacing stare. Mikhail didn't even look at him.

"You in my country now and you do as I wish."

Pete got a bad feeling. "Mikhail,"

"Should you not call me Uncle Mikhail?"

Novlak finally looked at him and what Pete saw was not good. There was a smile on the cold man's face. "Kimball said you nephew. Family stick together and share."

"Kimball?" Pete asked with what little breath he could pull into his lungs. What in the hell was going on? Kimball never mentioned he'd been speaking to the Novlaks.

"Do not play dumb, boy. I tired of all stupid pretend. I have business to conduct and I not want play games. I want know how else CIA help me. Kimball say you will help. All you have done is pretend and slobber over whore. So you know, our rooms have video and sound. You room was interesting since you arrive."

Mikhail turned to one of his bodyguards. "Juan, have the cars pulled around. We go back to mansion."

The band finished playing the waltz and Boris walked Elana back to the others. Pete stood rigidly, fear etched on his face. Enrique stood on one side of him, Mikhail on the other.

"Shane, honey, what's wrong?"

"Do you not mean Pete?" Mikhail asked.

"What are you talking about?" Elana didn't break stride or waiver. Her instincts and training screamed at her. Don't Break Cover was Jon's rule. She was sticking to it no matter what.

"What's going on Shane?"

"It seems Uncle Mikhail has been in contact with someone in the U.S. named Kimball. This Mr. Kimball wanted Uncle Mikhail to remind me family shares."

Elana widened her eyes like the bimbo girlfriend of a drug lord. "Shares? What does that mean? Uncle Mikhail? I didn't know he was your uncle. Is he old enough to be your uncle? And who is Mr. Kimball?" She hoped she sounded convincing enough to pull them through this because Pete was losing his grip fast.

Mikhail's hand shot out and slapped her. "You need to learn place, girl. No one give permission to ask question."

Elana put her head in her hands and tried to muster up silent tears. She wasn't sure even her acting was going to be that good. What she really wanted to do was take Mikhail down and crush his windpipe with her fuck me stiletto heels.

"She does not work with you?" Mikhail asked Pete.

"Work with me? What are you talking about?"

Good boy, Elana thought to herself. You can do this.

"I tire of these games. The cars are ready."

Elana felt a hand grip her hip on one side and her forearm on the other. Enrique had a death grip as he marched her back up the sweeping staircase. Pete was flanked by Mikhail and Boris. Boris kept trying to ask questions but Mikhail would not let him talk in such a public place.

"Juan and I ride with boy in front car. Boris, you and Enrique ride with woman. Do not break skin." It looked like Mikhail was talking to Enrique when he issued that order.

Mikhail forced Pete into a black SUV as Elana was hefted into another. She quickly decided Boris would be her saving grace. He'd been drinking all night and had also been doing some drugs. He was infatuated with her and wouldn't let Enrique beat her or rape her. At least she hoped not.

The SUV seats had been changed so they were like the inside of a limo. One bench seat was against the front driver and passenger seat and the other bench had been spaced back and faced forward so Elana could see out the windshield. The SUV in front drove away.

She tried to pull from Enrique and go to Boris.

"What's going on? Why did your brother seem so mad? I didn't do anything to upset him, did I?" She batted her eyelashes, opening her eyes wide.

"I know not what goes on. Mikhail may be upset about business."

"You say you do not know what the issue is?" Enrique asked in her ear. Goosebumps rose on her skin.

"No. Why did Mikhail call Shane Pete?"

"We will know soon enough," Enrique snarled.

That's what Elana was afraid of.

She launched herself across the small space and into Boris's lap. When Enrique tried to pull her away, Boris stopped him.

"She is just poor frightened woman in middle of something she not understand. Much like my little Natalia. Leave her be. I comfort her."

Elana hoped she made it to the mansion fully clothed as Boris's hand settled firmly on her butt and began to rub.

19

Langley, Virginia

Tippi kicked her feet back at the man who was going to kill her. She may have been drunk and possibly have a concussion from hitting her head on the coffee table, but she was not going down without a fight. If she was going to die she had nothing to lose.

Her fight or flight instincts were muddled from the alcohol. When she normally would have rolled to her back to see her opponent, she just stayed on her stomach, clawing at the carpet and kicking blindly.

She made contact with his body a few times and it felt like kicking a brick wall. Finally she rolled to her back and kicked him in the jaw. He released her ankle and she scrambled to the kitchen on her hands and knees. She started pulling out pots and pans, anything in the lower cupboards, and began hurling them toward the living room.

Not a stealthy or well-thought out plan, but she was doing something.

"Damn it, Miss Aldridge," came when a muffin tin slid across the floor back at her. "Quit trying to maim me with kitchen gadgets and listen."

Tippi threw a Pyrex dish toward the voice. Something hit the floor and shattered.

"Ouch! Tippi, knock it the hell off! AJ said you were docile. Fat lot of shit that boy knows."

"AJ?" Tippi pulled herself up with the counter and looked into the living room.

The man was standing next to her couch. He had a bloody nose and there were various pots and pans strewn all over the living room. One of her lamps was broken.

"Who are you and how do you know AJ?"

"I guess I should have started with that instead of my little quip earlier. AJ didn't tell me you would try and kick my ass. He said you'd scream like a girl and while you were trying to dial 911 I could take your phone and talk to you."

"I'd scream like a girl? That's what he thought?" Her headache and possible concussion were forgotten as she stumbled to the man. Her head barely reached his chest when she stood in front of him.

Swinging out, she slapped his shoulder. "When did you talk to that jerk? He better hope he's really hurt or I'm going to hurt him!" She slapped the giant again.

He stared at her like she was a bug he might smash.

"Ouch," she said, cradling her hand. "What are you? Like nine feet tall and 400 pounds?" Obviously alcohol turned off her brain-to-mouth filter.

"I'm Eli. We've wasted enough time. AJ's stashed nearby and I need you to get all your medical supplies and come with me."

"Medical supplies? He's hurt? Why did you waste all this time?" Tippi stared at Eli with wide, blue eyes.

AJ hadn't been wrong when he'd said she was model-material. He'd been dead wrong when he'd said she was defenseless. If she hadn't forgotten to set her house alarm, it would have taken Eli a lot longer to get in. An alarm AJ hadn't mentioned. She also would have hurt him with some of those kicks if the alcohol hadn't dulled her senses.

Eli had handled things wrong.

AJ made him think Tippi was like most of the women Eli'd had to relocate in the past. Crying, whining, defenseless, rich socialites. The name didn't help. However, she was far from crying and whining.

"You were on the phone with him when he got shot. You know he's hurt."

"I thought he was dead," Tippi said. "And, what's going on? Why are you in my house? How did you get in? How do I know I can trust you? Who are you?"

Eli wondered how she would have handled the situation if alcohol wasn't involved. Would she continue to have a conversation with a stranger in her living room?

"Here's the quick version because I've already wasted enough time. AJ was shot in Botswana. I happened to be in the area and brought him to the states. He told me the only people he trusts are you, Elana Miller, and Jon Matthews. Elana went wheels-up to Russia and Jon's MIA. So here I am collecting you.

"AJ said you could trust me. That if I told you to bring some ties for his wrists you'd understand what that meant and would know I talked to him. I didn't have a clue until I heard you belting out S&M. Now I get it."

"If I weren't slightly under the influence of alcohol, I'd be very offended by your comment!" She glared.

"Slightly under the influence of alcohol? I've never seen anyone get drunk from two beers and a glass of wine. Also, you might want to, uh," he nodded down and she finally noticed her thrashing had caused the robe to open. She ripped the sides together and retied the sash.

"Go get dressed so we can go to AJ and you can stitch him up."

The adrenaline of the last ten minutes quickly cleared Tippi's brain. She ran upstairs to put on clothes. She pulled out a bag, threw in another change of clothes, and a pair of shorts and a shirt AJ had left at her house. She grabbed a medical bag, hoping she'd have what she needed. If it was bad, she was going to make him go to the hospital. She'd thought he was dead. She wasn't going to let him die.

After putting her hair up, shutting off the stereo, and slipping on shoes, Tippi bounced back down the stairs.

"I'm ready." It had been only five minutes and Eli seemed a little shocked.

Shaking his head, he nodded to the alarm pad by the back door. "Set your alarm before we leave. And get your cell phone. AJ's got destroyed and he said he needs yours since it's encrypted."

"The alarm," Tippi said as she skidded to a halt. Eli ran into her back and almost knocked her over. As he steadied her she turned. "That's how you got in. I forgot to set the alarm. Stupid, stupid, stupid."

"Don't be too hard on yourself. You almost kicked my ass." He smiled and Tippi thought he looked like Mr. Clean again. He even had a little hoop earring.

"Almost only counts in horseshoes and hand grenades. Elana told me that. She also told me to never forget about the alarm."

"Well, it's done. Let's go."

Tippi followed Eli down the alley behind her house. He had hefted both bags over his shoulders and taken off without letting her argue. They reached a large black SUV in a matter of minutes. Eli opened the back, set the bags in, and then opened the passenger door for Tippi.

She wondered what the evening was going to bring. She knew part of her should be scared, yet all she could muster was happiness at seeing AJ. And some anger for sending this big brute to 'kidnap' her.

"How long were you in my house?" Tippi demanded once Eli was driving.

"Well. I watched you come home. I waited a few minutes and came in when you went upstairs. I noticed the empty beer bottle and saw it was still cold.

"Then I heard the music and shower. You came down and had more alcohol. I thought you were just tipsy. I kinda figured you'd laugh at me, not throw the bottle at my head." Eli rubbed a hand over his bald head.

"You deserved that. You shouldn't have scared me. I swear, you, AJ, and Elana need to learn how to use doorbells and doors like normal people. I wasn't completely drunk."

Eli flashed a lopsided grin in the glow of the streetlights. "Sure you weren't. I'll admit I screwed up. That wasn't the best way to get your attention. My mouth has gotten me into trouble more than once. I'm sorry, okay?"

She was debating whether or not to forgive him when he pulled up to a chain link fence around a building that looked like it was abandoned.

"This is where you left AJ?" she said. "There are probably rats in there! Is there even electricity and running water? He better not get an infection due to your negligence."

"Wow. First of all, it's got water, electricity, bedrooms, bathrooms, and a kitchen. It just looks awful from the outside. Second of all, he already has an infection. He was shot in the middle of the desert and only had the mediocre medical attention I could get him."

"How bad is the infection?" Tippi asked as she climbed out then grabbed her bags. She didn't know where the door to the building was or how to get in once she found it. She didn't care. AJ was in there and he needed her. For once, AJ needed her.

Eli rolled down the window. "Slow down, Florence Nightingale. I've got alarm systems. I don't need you setting them off and making AJ think he has to fall out of bed and save the world. Get back in so I can open the gate and we can park out of sight."

Tippi impatiently climbed back in, placing one bag at her feet and one on her lap. Eli pushed a button on the center console of the SUV and the gate slid open. He drove around back and pulled into what was once an underground parking garage. Now it was just crumbled concrete, cracked bricks, and filled with garbage.

Without talking, Eli took the bags and led a tense Tippi to a door. He entered a code and they went through and walked down a long hallway until they came to another keypad. An elevator made noise and the door opened.

Tippi hesitated. She no longer felt the least bit under the influence of alcohol. She'd run blindly out of her house with a man who had attacked her and she hadn't even remembered to bring her pistol. Elana would be so angry if she knew how badly Tippi had screwed up tonight. Maybe she wasn't doing as good a job as she thought at taking care of herself. Eli could have killed her. He still could.

As though sensing her thoughts, he waved a hand toward the open elevator door. "If I was planning on hurting you, I would have done so by now. Four floors up you'll see AJ and know I'm telling the truth."

"Fine. Take me to him." Hoping she wasn't the biggest fool on the planet, she stepped into the elevator and watched Eli squeeze in after her. She hadn't been kidding when she'd asked how big he was. He had to be close to seven feet tall. She stared at his head that didn't look all that far from the ceiling of the elevator.

"Six eleven," Eli said without looking at her as the elevator began moving.

"What?" Tippi asked confused.

"I'm six foot eleven. Not nine feet tall."

"Oh," Tippi mumbled, embarrassed.

She couldn't believe her behavior over the last hour. She'd had too much alcohol, rocked out to questionable music, and had a fight with a strange man. Not only that, she'd left her house in shambles to go somewhere with a stranger in the middle of the night. She was a much different person than she'd been a few months ago.

The elevator doors opened to a modest looking apartment. There were two large couches, a couple of recliners and an open kitchen. Tippi saw five different doors as she scanned the room for AJ.

"Four doors are rooms, one is a bathroom. The main bedroom," he nodded his head at a closed door, "has its own bathroom. That's where I put AJ."

Tippi practically ran to the door. When she reached for the doorknob she hesitated, hand shaking.

"Don't chicken out now," Eli said.

Tippi walked in. There was a small lamp next to a king bed holding an unmoving body.

"AJ?" Tippi whispered.

The lamp was on low so when she got closer, she could see AJ's dark head on the pillow. He was lying on his back and his right shoulder was bandaged with a dirty rag. There was blood seeping through.

Eli dropped the bags on the floor behind her. It made her jump.

"Sorry," he mumbled. "I know it's bad, but he seems to be doing better. He's been running a fever."

"When was his bandage changed?" she asked, grabbing a chair from the corner of the room then opening her medical bag.

"I put it on yesterday morning."

"It hasn't been changed in over twenty-four hours?" she demanded angrily. "No wonder he's running a fever. Get me some bottled water, an icepack or a bag of ice, and clean sheets for this bed."

AJ was sweating and rivulets of mud covered his body. He had a fine coating of sand on his skin.

"You're going to help me put him in the bathtub and then you're going to change the sheets."

Eli looked like he was going to argue and Tippi

narrowed her eyes. "You brought me here to help. You're going to do what I say."

He shrugged and left the room.

The first thing she did was pull off the nasty bandage. She almost gagged as she stared at the ragged, bleeding wound on his shoulder. It looked like hamburger. What in the world had he been shot with? The good thing was the wound was still oozing blood. That meant some of the bacteria had been pushed out. However, AJ hadn't moved or made a sound. That worried her.

She stared at his pale face and pushed back some hair. "I'm here now. I'll take care of you."

Eli cleared his throat from behind her.

She had him put the items on the small table next to the bed. "Go start the bathtub. Make it lukewarm. We don't want to shock his system."

While Eli puttered in the bathroom, Tippi cleaned the wound with bottled water then alcohol. AJ moved his head slightly when she gave him a shot of antibiotics and a shot for pain. She had never been more thankful for all her degrees. Now they weren't wall decoration. She had knowledge to save the life of the man she loved.

Carefully she cut what was left of his shirt off his body. Then she undid the button and zipper on his cargo pants.

Eli came back. "I'll put him in the bathtub and take him out, but you need to leave his underwear on. I draw the line at bathing with a naked dude." He smiled.

"Sissy," she said.

She didn't try to say anything else, knowing if she did she wouldn't be able to hold back the sobs.

Eli carefully placed AJ in the bathtub. Tippi put a towel on the back of the tub for his head. It was a utilitarian tub, so there wasn't a lot of room for his large frame. The minute his body was in the water, it turned sickening shades of brown from the blood and dirt.

"I'll change the sheets and make us some dinner. Let me know if you need anything," Eli said and left.

Using a washcloth and soap, Tippi cleaned AJ's body and wound the best she could. She was glad he was passed out because his shoulder had to hurt. After twenty minutes and draining the bathtub twice to put in fresh water, AJ started to wake.

He moved slowly at first then his body stiffened.

"It's okay, AJ. I'm here," Tippi said quietly. "Eli brought me to you."

He slowly opened one eye, then the other. He moaned when he tried to lift his arm to touch her face.

"No, no," she soothed, taking his hand and keeping it on the edge of the tub. "You need to just lay here. I'll have Eli help me get you out of the tub. I'll get you stitched and bandaged up."

AJ stared at her. "Are you really here?" His voice was scratchy and low.

"I'm really here."

"Maybe I'm dead and you're my angel."

"You're not dead and I'm nobody's angel." She turned her head to reach for the bar of soap.

"You're my ang—" he stopped.

"What?" she asked, thinking maybe he'd hurt himself.

AJ sat up, groaning.

"What are you doing? Lay back down until Eli comes in to help. Eli!" she called.

"What in the fuck happened to you?"

"What?" she asked.

Eli rushed in.

"Who did that to her? Did you do that?" AJ demanded as he tried to get himself out of the tub.

"Do what?" Tippi and Eli asked at the same time.

"Have you looked in a mirror?" AJ bit out as he flipped

the bathtub drain. Maybe he'd be able to stand if he wasn't in a tub full of water.

Tippi looked in the mirror and sucked in her breath. There was dried blood on the left side of her face and she had red marks on the right side. Carpet burn.

"It was an accident," she tried to explain. "It happened when I fell and hit my head on the coffee table. The red marks are carpet burns from when Eli pulled me across the carpet."

AJ bellowed like a bull, charging out of the bathtub. "I told you not to hurt or scare her!" AJ yelled. "I can't believe you hurt her!" He swung his good arm at Eli.

"Knock it off, man," Eli countered. "She attacked me first. Your girl isn't defenseless like you think."

"So you threw her into the coffee table and dragged her across the floor?" AJ swung again.

"AJ, stop! That's not what happened! Calm down! Your feet are wet and you're going to—"

Tippi didn't get to say fall before AJ's feet went out from under him. His head hit the tiled floor with a sickening thump.

"Dear lord," Tippi shrieked as she dropped to the floor next to AJ.

The dumb man had knocked himself out cold and his shoulder was bleeding again.

20

St. Petersburg, Russia

The SUVs skidded to a stop. Jon sat in the study sipping the endless glass of scotch. It was a nice change from vodka. Mikhail hadn't wanted him to attend the hotel party and Jon knew why. Pete and Elana were there and Mikhail didn't want 'Nikoli' anywhere near Ellie.

Jon wondered if Pete and Elana knew just how deep they'd gotten themselves. Kimball had delivered them to the bowels of hell and hadn't even thought twice about it.

Trying to decide the best way to go about meeting Ellie, Jon looked out the window just as the back door of the first SUV opened and a body tumbled out. The door of the second SUV flew open and a streak of white ran to the body.

Elana.

Jon didn't need to see her face to know it was her. Her wig was mussed and her dress looked crooked, yet she didn't appear to be harmed. She was yelling at Mikhail, but Jon couldn't make out her words.

Mikhail's hand shot out and slapped her hard across the face and Jon's hand clenched around his glass. He couldn't go running out to defend her. It didn't fit with his normal attitude of not giving a shit. But he honestly wasn't sure what he was going to do if they really hurt her.

Agents knew they could be tortured. Would be if they stuck with the job long enough. Jon knew he'd only be able to watch a little bit of torture when it came to her. He would not be able to watch her be raped. He didn't care if he sealed their death sentences.

Jon had been tortured. He'd watched one of his partners tortured and killed. Thought for sure he was going to be next before a squad of SEALs came in and rescued him in Thailand. He'd made his peace with death a long time ago. People died in his line of work. He had no illusions he was going to live to be ninety. Some days he wondered if he'd live to see forty. He knew he was going to die in the field.

Little Miss Lana had been getting in the way of his job since the moment he'd laid eyes on her. Was she going to be the death of them both?

Elana stared at Pete's bruised and bloody face as she laid her hand on her own warming cheek. Mikhail slapped like some people punched. It didn't help she hadn't been expecting it. One minute he seemed refined and polished, the next he looked like he'd rip your heart out and feed it to you. It was a scary thing to see your death in someone's eyes.

"Jesus Fucking Christ, Mikhail! What in the hell's gotten into you?" Pete could barely see through his right eye, but he hadn't missed the slap. "I told you in the truck she doesn't know anything about any mission and she doesn't know Kimball. I brought her in for fun since I didn't want to come to this godforsaken country to begin with."

Pete managed to get to his hands and knees. He spit blood and wiggled his tooth with his tongue. Juan and Mikhail hit like world class boxers. He was so screwed.

"You see, Shane, your stories not make sense. Kimball tell me you have information about newest drug routes. You no offer any kind of device for me to use on computer. You come to hotel and want to wait to meet. You want to relax.

"You show up here and think you can play when work

is to be done. You are also, what is good American word? Pussy. If one hit me, I hit back. You take hit after hit and sit like pussy."

What had Kimball done? It was obvious Pete had taken an upper body beating on the ride over. Why hadn't he even tried to fight back? Elana shook with fear.

"How's it my fault Kimball is a lying scumbag? I have the drug info but Ellie is not a CIA agent. Look at her! You ever seen a CIA agent who looked like that? And I didn't want to hit you back because I'm your guest." Pete tried to make eye contact with Elana. Was anyone buying his lies?

Juan kicked Pete hard in the ribs and Pete felt them break. Juan had seemed the least imposing, quiet, small, and dressed in a plain suit. Apparently he was also their torture specialist.

Pete's breaths bubbled from his throat and he felt Elana drop to the ground next to him.

"Ellie, no, stay back," Pete wheezed.

He tried to move to his knees again and Juan kicked him in the head. Pete went face down into the paved driveway knocking into Elana.

"Stop it!" she screamed at the two men. "Stop it! What's going on, Shane? Oh my god, what's going on?"

Elana wrapped herself over Pete. She didn't know if she could protect him from more blows or not. How could they get out of this? She'd never been involved in anything this dangerous. She'd always followed someone else's lead. Pete's lead was apparently to give up.

Pete tried to lift his head but the pain was too much. He threw up and the loose tooth came out.

"They know—" he said as Elana said, "Shh, don't talk."

"Get up, dog," Mikhail ordered. He grabbed Pete by the collar and hauled him to his knees. "Unless you want to watch lovely Ellie gutted like fish in driveway, you walk to house."

Pete struggled to get his legs under him. There was no way he could stand up, not with the excruciating pain in his side. Elana tried to help, but Enrique dragged her away. He pulled her against the front of his body and wrapped one arm around her waist and the other around her shoulder and neck.

As he forced her to watch Pete, tears were streaming silently from her face and the slimy bastard licked them off one side.

"Get. Your hands. Off. My woman," Pete snarled.

He spit blood bubbles with each word and they slid down his chin. As far as menacing went, he couldn't really pull it off in his condition.

"Your woman?" Enrique laughed. "She stopped being your woman the minute you set foot in our country. Kimball made it very clear Ellie was a gift for all of us."

"This isn't. . . your country. . . you South American. . . spick," Pete managed before Mikhail kneed him in the ribs.

Elana stilled against Enrique. More references to Kimball. He was dirty. Kimball had to be the reason so many missions in Europe had failed. No one had been able to keep any kind of evidence on the Novlak brothers or Enrique for their crimes. They were all in bed.

Kimball had set Jon up to take the fall, making the evidence look like Jon was rogue and working with the Novlaks. Elana cursed her damn need to always push and find out what she wanted. No one could save her now. Kimball was disposing of loose ends. Kimball knew she wouldn't stop looking for Jon.

It was all a bogus mission to have Elana disappear like Jon. Pete was just another pawn. They would both die and no one would know where or why.

Elana struggled weakly against Enrique. She knew plenty of ways to break his hold, but then he'd know she wasn't some bimbo. The question was how long did she play the part of Ellie? Pete wasn't even trying to defend himself.

Maybe it was time to quit pretending. If they were going to die, Elana wanted them to know she wasn't some flake. Then again, Jon had taught her to stay in cover until your heart stopped beating. You never knew how many other people's lives you might put in danger by giving away your real identity.

"Let's move them to the basement so I can do this the right way." Juan's quiet voice floated over them.

"Leave Ellie out of this and I'll tell you whatever you want to know." Pete stood as much as he could and met Elana's eyes.

"No," she whispered.

Enrique reached between his body and Elana's back to pull something from his pocket. Light reflected off metal as Enrique pushed the tip of a knife into Elana's face. He wasn't gentle and blood slowly trickled down her cheek.

"Is name really Pete?" Mikhail asked, his eyes on Elana.

"Yes," Pete said slowly. Maybe he could save her.

"What is role at CIA?"

"Damn it, get out of the driveway before some paparazzi freak with a camera gets a load of what's going on!" someone yelled before Pete could answer.

That voice. Elana thought she recognized that voice.

"Ah, Nikoli, the fun is begin. I glad you come play."

"Just get in here."

Elana tried to turn and see who was talking. It didn't matter Mikhail had called the man Nikoli. It sounded like Jon. The voice she'd needed to hear for six months.

Juan came to her with a syringe in his hand. She knew they weren't going to kill her yet, but she didn't want to be incapacitated. They could do whatever they wanted to her if she was unconscious.

"No," Elana screamed. She rammed her head back and felt the crunch of Enrique's nose just as Juan stabbed the needle into her arm. She was out in less than twenty seconds.

"Puta," Enrique yelled as he dropped her.

It took everything Jon had to not pick her up and run.

"You'd think you guys never do this," Jon said. "What the fuck are you thinking? Pulling this shit in your driveway?"

Enrique was getting ready to kick Elana in the head when Jon pushed him off balance. "I didn't think even you would kick someone when they were down."

Enrique raised his fists and moved toward Jon when Mikhail's voice boomed across the driveway. "As much as hate to admit, Nikoli right. We should have in basement. Enrique, be cleaned and join us. Juan, prepare room. Boris, sober up so you understand what goes on. Nikoli?"

Jon met his gaze with what he hoped was disinterest.

"You will help take pigs to basement."

Jon went for Elana and Mikhail clucked his tongue. "No, no. You do not carry little slut. You get Pete."

Mikhail signaled one of the front door guards.

Jon resisted the urge to grab Elana anyway. He went to Pete's heaving form. The boy was trying his best to make it back to his feet. Pissed they had all been put in this situation, Jon yanked Pete up by his arm ignoring his whimpers and indrawn breath.

As the guard hefted Elana over his shoulder in a fireman's carry, Mikhail, Enrique, Boris, and Juan went into the house. The guard followed with Elana.

Jon whispered, "Do you know who I am?"

Pete nodded.

"Are you here as Kimball's bitch?"

Pete shook his head and spit up more blood.

"Don't lie to me you little sack of shit!" Jon hissed through unmoving lips.

"Not lying. . . thought I could. . . trust Kimball. Sent us. . . real mission. . . I thought."

Pete moaned as Jon dragged him through the doors.

Juan was already moving down the narrow stairs to the basement. Mikhail was right behind him. Enrique cursed in Spanish while holding a handkerchief over his nose. He went to the kitchen.

Boris stood stupidly in the middle of the main entrance watching everyone.

"Coffee, Boris," Mikhail yelled from the stairs.

Boris followed Enrique.

The remaining guard closed the front door and the other walked to the stairs with Elana. Jon was torn between not letting her out of his sight and staying back a few extra seconds so he could grill Pete. Talking to Pete won out.

As they reached the top of the staircase Jon ripped away his arm so Pete didn't have any balance. He tripped down three stairs before Jon grabbed him again.

"Walk slowly," Jon whispered.

After moving down a few more steps Jon turned so he could see up and down the rounded staircase. He knew their voices would echo so he leaned in close. Pete had to have a punctured lung. The blood bubbling from his lips wasn't just from losing a tooth.

"I want you to nod yes or no. No talking. Do you understand?" Jon said in Pete's ear.

Pete nodded, trying to regulate his breathing.

"Do they know you're CIA?"

Pete nodded again.

"Do they know Elana is?"

He shook his head.

"Is this your first undercover mission?"

He waited a heartbeat then nodded, acting like he was going to speak. Jon stopped him.

"I'm sure Kimball had you in the field before this, but no missions like this."

Pete nodded.

Boris's slurring voice came from the top of the stairs.

He was asking someone why Ellie had been taken to the basement and not the bedrooms. Juan replied something about a lying whore being taught a lesson. Jon knew he only had moments.

"Have you ever been tortured?"

Pete's eyes widened and he barely moved his head no.

"It's going to get ugly. If it comes to the point it doesn't look like you're going to survive, do you want me to end it?"

Pete stared at Jon in confusion.

"Do you want me to end it? End you?"

Finally Pete caught on. He closed his eyes and his lips moved with no sound.

"Damn it, kid!" Jon fought to keep his voice low and started moving Pete down the stairs. "Do you want me to put you out of your misery so the pain ends?"

"Yes," Pete whispered slowly, as though coming to terms with his mortality. "Just make. . . sure. . . Elana. . . lives."

The heavy footsteps of Boris and Enrique started down the concrete stairs. By the time they reached the bottom, Elana had been strapped to a wooden chair that resembled an old fashioned electric chair.

There were leather straps holding her ankles and wrists in place. Her head drooped as much as a strap around her neck would allow. Jon wondered how long the drugs would keep her out.

Juan motioned for Jon to put Pete on the far wall so Pete and Elana would be able to see each other across the ten foot span. Close enough to see the pain but not close enough to do anything about it.

It was like being in the dungeon of a medieval castle. Mikhail had a regular torture room set up for Juan to play in. Jon had been down here many times and it chilled his blood to see Elana in this environment.

Pete's suit jacket, shirt, shoes, and socks were stripped off. His arms were cuffed above his head to keep him off balance and eventually pull his shoulders out of the sockets. He made small noises as Juan secured him, but it seemed the beating and Jon's talk had taken all his energy. He hung by his wrists with his head down. If it hadn't been for his labored breathing, Jon might have thought he was already dead.

The room was temperature controlled and Juan went to the thermostat to drop it down to fifty-five degrees. The cold would make Elana wake sooner.

From previous occasions, Jon expected they would leave the room for at least an hour to drink and smoke and let the fear work up the prisoners.

"Now we wait," Mikhail laughed.

Yep. Predictable.

Pete watched everyone leave as cold air began to blow.

Then the lights went out.

Blackness like he'd never known surrounded him.

21

Langley, Virginia

After staring in shock at AJ's outburst and subsequent head bashing, Tippi shook it off and had Eli carry AJ back to the bed. She put towels under his upper body to keep blood from getting on the clean sheets.

AJ had a goose egg on the back of his head, but luckily, he wasn't bleeding. She couldn't believe he'd attacked Eli.

"Is there anything I can do?" Eli asked.

"After I stitch him up, I'm going to need your help wrapping his shoulder."

"Just tell me what you need," he said quietly.

Tippi turned. "AJ is an ass and he's not thinking clearly. I know you didn't hurt or scare me on purpose. Geez. You keep acting all timid and I'm going to think you're just a big teddy bear."

Eli regarded her silently but didn't smile.

"Fine," she said. "Let's get him cleaned up."

They worked in silence for twenty minutes while she washed sand, dead insects, and dried blood from the wound. She applied iodine, stitched up what she could, and put ointment on every surface of his shoulder. After it was bandaged, they wrapped his arm to his waist so he wouldn't be able to lift it and she gave him another small dose of antibiotics and pain meds.

When they were done, Eli went to the kitchen to stir the soup he had simmering on the stove. Tippi went to the bathroom to wash up and clean the blood off her face.

AJ had overreacted. She washed the dried blood away and there was only a small cut above her eye. She quickly put ointment and a band-aid on her temple. There wasn't anything she could do about the carpet burn. It would probably be gone by morning.

Morning. Tippi looked at the time on her cell phone. It was a little after midnight. She was having trouble remembering what day it was so she double-checked her phone again. She didn't know if she should try to contact Elana or not. She'd wait and see what AJ thought.

Walking back to the bedroom, Tippi looked at AJ and her heart skipped a beat. What kind of life did he live? She knew he worked a dangerous job, but she'd never seen anyone hurt like this before. She'd never seen AJ without his confident attitude. It reminded her that he could die. She couldn't afford to have her heart hurt like that. Maybe she should just walk away before she fell completely in love.

She snorted. Too late.

In the living room, Tippi saw Eli had put a steaming bowl of food at the bar. Her stomach growled.

"It's just canned soup, but I figured you'd be hungry after the night you've had."

"That was very thoughtful of you," Tippi said. "Now I *know* you're a big teddy bear."

He finally smiled. "Don't tell anyone. My badass reputation will be ruined."

She took a sip of soup. It tasted heavenly. Eli stood on the other side of the bar watching her. Then he slid some crackers over.

"Who has to think you're a badass?" she asked while

crumbling crackers in her soup.

"I'm a U.S. Marshal. I work with the relocation program."

"I hope you make better home visits with the people you relocate than you did with me," she joked.

"Yeah, I usually do. I don't always have to sneak into people's houses in the middle of the night. They know I'm coming or they meet me at my office."

"Where is your office? Here in Virginia?"

"Nope. I work out of Arizona."

Tippi stopped eating. "What were you doing in Botswana and how do you know AJ?"

"Stories for another time, my dear. I have to go back. Give me your cell so I can program my number in. AJ knows all the security codes for the building, so don't try to leave until he wakes up."

Tippi slowly handed over her cell. "So I'm going to be stuck here?"

"AJ wanted you with him. I didn't expect him to knock himself out. You're stuck until he wakes up. I also figure it'll be better if I'm gone when he comes to. Don't want him to hurt himself again trying to kick my ass."

Eli handed back her phone and walked to the door.

"Wait," Tippi said frantically. "What am I supposed to do here? I need to be at work in seven hours."

"That's for you and AJ to figure out. It was nice to meet you, Tippi. Good luck."

And Eli was gone.

Tippi stared at the closed door and felt a sense of dread when the green light by the handle switched to blinking red. She was locked in an abandoned building with an injured man. With no car. How the hell was she going to get to work?

She wanted AJ to go to a hospital to have his injuries checked out. If he didn't wake up soon he could have a concussion. There could be torn muscles in his shoulder that needed repair. She wasn't a surgeon.

She put her head in her hands and rested her elbows on the bar. The soup curdled in her stomach. Tears, along with panic, took over. She stayed like that for a few minutes until she got herself under control. Finally relaxing as much as she could, she cleaned the kitchen.

Not knowing what else to do, Tippi peeked into each of the other rooms. They were plain, with single beds and small dressers. She wondered if this was one of the houses Eli brought relocated people. She wasn't even sure she knew what a U.S. Marshal did. And why had a U.S. Marshal from Arizona been in Botswana?

It crossed her mind to lay down on one of the small beds, but the lure of AJ was too much. She took his temperature and noted it had gone down one degree but was still too high.

She slipped off her shoes, jeans, and sweatshirt, then crawled into the other side of the bed in her tank top and underwear. AJ was under the sheet so Tippi slid over until her body made contact with his hot one.

She set her phone alarm to go off at six so she could call Marcus and let him know she'd be in late or maybe not at all. Snuggling up to AJ, Tippi closed her eyes and tried to forget loving him would be impossible. She would just continue to take what moments she could.

She slept fitfully, dreaming of AJ in a bathtub of blood and the sounds of gunfire.

Movement and groans pulled her from the dream. It had been so real Tippi stared at his thrashing body for a moment before reality set in.

"AJ, stop," she said quietly, putting her hands on his warm face. "You're going to hurt yourself."

His movements stilled slightly and his eyes twitched behind closed lids. Tippi muttered soothing nonsense until his body stilled. She scooted up in the bed and reached for her cell phone. It was only two in the morning.

Cradling his head against her chest, she stroked his hair. She stayed like that for a long time and was just falling back asleep when AJ's rough voice broke through the silence.

"Your soft hands and soft pillows are doing wonders for my headache."

Tippi, momentarily startled, jerked away and AJ's head slid from her 'soft pillows'.

"Ouch," he complained.

"AJ," Tippi sat up on her knees and flipped on the bedside lamp. "Are you okay?"

"Damn," AJ mumbled, "can you turn the light off? It hurts my head."

"No, I can't turn the light off. I need to have you talk to me so I can make sure you don't have a concussion. Then we need to take you to a hospital."

"Slow down, beautiful." He struggled to piece together the jumbled thoughts and pictures in his mind.

He wasn't in Botswana. He remembered getting shot by that prick who'd snuck up on him. That prick had AJ's knife buried in his face. That's the only reason AJ wasn't dead. The man had cursed as he covered his bleeding face with one hand while AJ ripped his shotgun out of his other. AJ hadn't had the strength to shoot the man as he ran away.

He remembered making the call to Eli to save his sorry ass. Then he'd hunkered down, waiting for the team to appear that would be sent to kill him. In the three hours he'd waited for Eli, AJ had wrapped his bleeding shoulder the best he could and tried like hell to not pass out.

When Eli showed with the chopper, AJ had made a fool of himself going on and on about getting him back to Langley and one of his friends. He'd thought briefly he was going to die. Had he told Eli anything embarrassing?

Eli. That bastard had hurt Tippi. AJ sat up so quickly he hit his nose on Tippi's chin. Stars peppered his vision as he flopped back on the bed and covered his face. He heard Tippi's sharp intake of breath and whispered curse.

"Damn, sorry baby," he mumbled through his hand.

"Will you lie down and stay still?" she said.

"No, I need to make sure you're okay."

"Make sure I'm okay?" she said disbelievingly. "I'm not the one who was shot and knocked myself out on the bathroom floor!"

"It's my job to take care of you," AJ said, then was hit by the ramifications of his words.

Tippi stared at him. "No it's not," she whispered.

AJ didn't know what to say so he rolled from the bed, staggered his way into the bathroom and slammed the door.

Washington D.C.

CIA Deputy Director Max Kimball stared at the locked, metal case in the passenger seat of his car. The bio-weapons samples were going to make him rich. Had already made him rich. But there was no such thing as too much money.

He wondered if Pete and Elana were dead yet. Pete was disposable, but he felt a little remorse over Elana. She would have been a good agent to have on his side. Kimball had made a major miscalculation with Jon Matthews. Everyone was corruptible in some way; Kimball just hadn't found Jon's weakness. He wasn't quite ready to expose Jon to the Novlaks. Jon had been killing the competition and keeping the Novlaks in business, which kept Kimball in business.

Kimball didn't know why Jon was still in Europe and hadn't tried to clear his name. Maybe Mikhail had turned Jon and the rumors Kimball started were true. That would make things easier. Then when Kimball killed Jon, it would be for his job and he'd get a commendation for flushing out a traitor.

Lights flashed in a room on the top floor of the building Kimball was parked beside. He hefted the case and entered the building. His contact was waiting for him just like the times before.

"I need to make sure the vials are inside and your money will be transferred." The man had a Russian accent but his English was better than Mikhail's.

Kimball didn't say a word. He liked the power it gave him to act like he was better than the man who always took the cases from him. He didn't know the man's name and, as far as he knew, the man didn't know his.

After a quick inspection of the five vials, the man pulled out his phone. He looked at Kimball. "A half-million each, just like before. Mr. Novlak wants to know when you will have the new vials; the ones you have been bragging about."

"I'll let him know when our R&D Team has perfected it. Tell him those vials will be one million each."

The man nodded and pressed another button on his phone. Kimball received the notification on his phone almost immediately that he had a deposit in his account. Two point five million for about an hour of time. Not bad.

22

Novlak Mansion, St. Petersburg

Mikhail surveyed the few items Elana and Pete had with them. Pete's wallet and Elana's small clutch with some money and a cell phone were all they had. Mikhail had sent two of his men to the hotel to get their luggage and check the room to see if anything had been hidden.

Juan sat in the corner. "The boy will break, of that there is no question. You just need to let me know what you want."

Juan's English was much better than Mikhail, Boris, and Enrique's. Jon had learned Juan was a graduate of a U.S. University. Unfortunately he'd earned a medical degree to help with his interrogation and torture techniques.

"And the woman?" asked Gregor from the doorway. Jon had been hoping Gregor wouldn't show. Gregor was the only one who had been close enough to Elana six months ago to possibly recognize her.

"The woman is mystery," Mikhail said thoughtfully. "She has not act like agent. She does not look like any agent I have seen. She will make me much money if she is just a regular woman."

"I want her," Gregor demanded.

"I've got first dibs," Jon said carefully. Gregor would be

suspicious if Jon seemed too anxious. He never wanted women that came up from the basement.

"I said you could have if she was dirty agent," Mikhail said with a laugh.

"I thought more about it and I'd rather have her if she's not an agent. She'll be less likely to try and kill me."

Mikhail looked thoughtfully from Gregor to Jon. "I did promise Nikoli, Gregor. He never ask for anyone. He has Natalia for months; how bore. Nikoli get Ellie first. You can have when he tires of her."

Jon let out his breath and took a drink. Gregor glared at him and stormed from the room.

He wasn't sure what he would have done if Mikhail had handed her over to Gregor first. He was pretty sure he'd have to kill Gregor and get the hell out of dodge with Elana. That would change the game too early. Jon was going to have to keep an eye on Gregor.

"Who will be in the basement with Juan?" Jon asked.

"Me," demanded Enrique with a nasally voice. The blood was gone, but his nose was broken.

"Maybe you should get your nose looked at first," Jon said.

He didn't really want Enrique in the basement. Juan, despite his sadistic ways was at least methodical. He was doing a job. Enrique was emotional. He would probably walk down and break Elana's nose just for payback.

"I am tired of you, American." Enrique looked at Mikhail. "Why do you keep this pig around?"

"Because he useful," Mikhail said. "I not completely trust Kimball. Nikoli, however, has been loyal for last six months."

Enrique cursed in Spanish and walked out.

"You know how to clear room," Boris laughed. "I wish not to partake now. I need find Natalia."

Once Boris left, Juan, Mikhail, Jon, and one guard,

Petrov, remained.

"It has been half of hour. Let us go see if Pete can breathe and Ellie is awake. I look forward to time to come." Mikhail stood.

He was more antsy than usual, Jon noted. Unless there was something very important to learn, Mikhail was never in a hurry.

Juan led the way back to the basement. Petrov brought up the end. Mikhail rarely went anywhere without someone who could take a bullet for him.

Pete looked up when the large door swung open, blinking his eyes rapidly. He was gripping the chains connecting the shackles to his wrists. He found it took the stress off his shoulders if he held on with his hands. The stretching movement was killing his ribs and he was unable to take any breaths that weren't laced with fire. He'd been trying to get Elana to respond to him. She hadn't made a sound the entire time they'd been downstairs.

Pete was ready to give up and beg Jon Matthews to kill him. How pathetic.

"You have anything to say, Pete?" Mikhail asked as he sat in a large padded chair at the base of the stairs.

Juan walked to where Pete hung and examined the bruises forming on his side and chest.

"I will move you to a laying position next. Your lungs will fill with blood and fluid. You will almost drown. Then I will put you back here." Juan's detachment made the whole situation surreal to Pete.

Still he said nothing.

Juan jabbed two fingers into Pete's windpipe. Struggling for breath with a punctured lung and broken ribs was nearly impossible. Now it was. Pete tried to scream, choked on a blood bubble caught in his throat, then started gagging.

When his breath came back, his breathing was labored and made gurgling sounds like a water fountain.

Juan went to Elana. "I know you are awake, señorita, I can see the goose bumps on your skin."

He ran a finger down her arm and she couldn't prevent her recoil. Still, she did not raise her head.

"I will enjoy breaking you," Juan whispered.

She finally looked up. Juan blocked her view of Pete and she didn't know if she wanted to see him considering the sounds he was making. Juan moved behind her to let her look. Pete was pale and stretched in a Y against the wall. The side of his chest was bruised and his face was bloody. His breathing was back under control, yet he wasn't moving. He had to be in excruciating pain.

"Shane," she tried to say but her voice was too gravely from the drugs and the strap at her throat.

"My dear, do not keep up with game. We know he Pete, remember?" Mikhail said from behind her.

"I know him as Shane," she whispered.

"Shane, Pete," Mikhail crooned. "Does not matter. We see how much you know soon. Juan. Water."

Jon winced. Petrov rolled out the hose, handing it to Juan. Bigger than a garden hose but smaller than a fire hose, Juan directed the nozzle toward Pete. He nodded. A heavy stream of water was directed at Pete's chest and the pressure was enough to make his body sway as it pummeled his broken ribs.

"Stop!" Elana yelled.

Juan turned the hose on her. Luckily the chair was anchored to the floor. The water whipped her head back as she sputtered, trying to breathe. Juan kept it pointed at her face. Pete made a sound and the hose went back to him.

The games had begun.

It didn't take Pete and Elana long to figure out whoever made noise got the hose until the next person made noise. For ten full minutes they battled over each other with grunts, cries, and finally verbal insults at Juan. They were trying to protect the other from the debilitating spray of water. All they were getting for their efforts were wet, cold, and almost drowned.

"Enough!" Mikhail finally said. "This not fun. They keep try save each other." He turned. "Nikoli, get Enrique."

Jon knew better than to hesitate. The nurse they kept at the mansion had finished giving Enrique pain pills and had put bandages across the bridge of his nose. His eyes were already starting to blacken.

"Finally," Enrique bragged as he pushed aside the nurse and quickly walked to the basement.

When they got back downstairs, Pete was strapped down to a table. He was already having difficulty breathing as the fluids pooled in his punctured lung.

Elana struggled in her chair. "What's going on? What did he do? He's been spoiling me. Let me go! I just thought I was getting a vacation, money, and some pretty clothes."

"Sure you did," mumbled Enrique as he moved in front of her. "Do you see my nose, bitch?" Before Elana could think of a response, Enrique punched her. Her eyes watered and blood began to flow from her nostril.

He pulled out the knife he kept in his jacket. Starting at the dress slit on her thigh, he sliced the flimsy material like it was made of spider webs. The sharp tip of the knife left a small, bloody trail up Elana's stomach and chest as the dress peeled open like a zipper. Jon moved behind Elana to make sure Enrique didn't slide the knife into her stomach. He could see what was going on, but she still didn't know he was there.

As she squeezed her arms next to her ribs Jon noticed a small blade tucked in a sheath on her bra. Pretending to fondle her, Jon slid his hands over her breasts and up her sides.

Palming the knife he looked at Juan and pitched his voice low, "Good idea. Look what the water did to her bra and underwear."

As Enrique's eyes traveled to Elana's crotch, Jon slid his hands away and put the stiletto in his own pocket.

Elana waited for whoever was behind her to either give up the knife or stab her, yet nothing happened. Was someone trying to help her?

Pete made more gurgling noises.

"I can make the pain stop," Juan said. "All you have to do is explain why you did not give us the information Kimball said you would have. I will put a tube in your chest and relieve the pressure and pain."

Pete closed his eyes.

Mikhail moved to where Pete lay. "And explain why you pretend have sex at my hotel. Jump on bed and make noises. Kimball say you were seasoned, would know how to operate. You like small boy and cannot handle little pain."

Mikhail pulled a hammer off a tray under the table.

Elana made a sound and Enrique grabbed her by the hair, stretching her neck as much as he could.

"Kim. . . ball. . . can't trust," Pete wheezed.

The table titled up and Pete visibly relaxed as air came easier. Mikhail didn't let him enjoy it. He grabbed Pete's right hand and slammed the hammer down on his little finger. Pete howled in pain and Elana screamed. Enrique pulled harder on her hair and the pins holding her wig in place slipped.

"Well isn't this interesting," Enrique said as he ripped the blonde wig off Elana's head, tearing out some strands of her dark hair. "If you are not agent, why do you need a wig?"

"Not that it's any of your business, prick, but he's paying me good money. He wants to fuck a blonde, he gets one."

Enrique slapped her and leaned down. "I like women with dark hair," he said, rancid breath blowing over her face.

Looking away, Elana pleaded to Mikhail, "Please, tell me why you are doing this."

"I not like traitors or liars. You both lie," Mikhail said.

Juan moved away from Pete to stand in front of Elana. Enrique watched with excited eyes.

Juan took two pieces of her shredded dress. He gripped Elana's jaw and stuffed the fabric into her mouth despite her attempts to break from his hold. The sound of ripping duct tape filled the basement. Elana whimpered as Juan secured her mouth. Then he moved to Pete and repeated the process.

"Let's leave them in the cold, dark silence for a bit longer," Juan said as he put the roll of tape down.

Mikhail laughed as they herded an angry Enrique up the stairs.

"I want to make sure her nose is broken," Enrique said.

"Even if it is not, she's going to have trouble breathing. They are both going to have trouble. You know this will help us get answers."

Enrique continued to complain as everyone went up the stairs.

Pete turned frightened, pained eyes to Elana. She made a show of breathing deeply through her nose and moving her fingers, trying to show Pete he needed to relax.

The lights went out and they both whimpered. It wasn't too dark until the door at the top of the steps slammed shut.

Elana had never been in the middle of so much blackness. During the night, your eyes eventually adjust and you can pick up shadows and shapes. There wasn't a speck of light in the basement so there was nothing for their eyes to adjust to.

Elana fought the need to hyperventilate. She wasn't scared of the dark; she was scared of being out of control. The darkness was consuming. She could hear Pete thrashing. The fabric taped in her mouth kept her from reassuring him and it was hard to breathe. If her nose wasn't broken she was lucky.

She knew it was part of the interrogation; to keep them

scared, cold, and hungry. She never thought the darkness would bother her. It was like being blind. Knowing your eyes were open but not being able to see anything. She would clench her eyes closed for a few seconds then open them wide. Hoping that, just once, she'd be able to see something.

23

Pete struggled not to panic. It was getting harder and harder to breathe. He almost hoped he'd die before they came back. But then Elana would be alone. Well, not alone. She had Jon Matthews, a real spy. How in the world had Pete thought he was prepared for this mission? He'd never imagined pain like this. Nothing about working for the CIA or training with Elana had prepared him at all.

He couldn't hear anything over the pounding of his heart or his own ragged breathing. He wished he could do something, anything. He started counting to sixty to distract himself and see how many minutes passed.

It didn't help. He counted two minutes, but couldn't get over the fact no one had asked him anything important. How had they known his real name? What in the world could he possibly have in his brain that would gain them anything? Mikhail said their hotel room had video and audio. He'd seen them pretending to have sex. They had also said something about not giving the information Kimball said they would. Kimball hadn't told him the Novlak brothers would know he was a spy.

Pete knew what would distract his mind from the pain. He used his photographic memory to replay his conversations with Kimball like the slides of a movie through his mind.

Deputy Director Kimball's office was quiet and dark the evening Pete met Elana for the first time. When Pete arrived, Kimball's secretary had already gone home for the day and the office door was open a few inches. Pete nervously stepped toward the door and knocked lightly.

"Come in, Campbell," Kimball said, startling him.

"Sir," Pete began, "I received your message to come here after meeting with Ms. Miller."

"What did you think of her?" Kimball raised his eyebrows.

Pete frowned. "Sir?"

"Did she come onto you? Rub those tits in your face? Flaunt what you can't have? I see she made you get a haircut. Makes you look more like Matthews." Kimball didn't sound happy about that.

"Sir?" Pete repeated. He didn't know how else to respond. This was a side of the Deputy Director he'd never seen.

"Answer me, damn it!" Kimball smacked his hands on the desk.

Pete struggled to keep his composure and recall the question. "She was dressed in workout clothes when I arrived: sports bra and shorts. She told me we were going to pretend to be lovers while on assignment."

"I knew that bitch would come on to you," Kimball turned his back and looked out his window. "She sleeps with everyone, Campbell. Is sleeping her way to the top. You'll be another rung in her ladder; mark my words. Play her game, get close. Do whatever it takes. She needs to rely on you."

Pete was more confused. Finally Kimball turned around. He seemed to have his temper under control.

"Here's how it's going to be, kid. You are going to get in her head. Her last partner, Jon Matthews, is a traitor. He's working with the Novlaks and who knows who else. He's going by the name Jon Jacobs. Miller is the only person to ever get close to Matthews and live to tell about it. We're going to use her to find him."

"How do you know Jon Matthews is a traitor?" Pete asked.

"If you want to continue working in the field as an agent, you will not question what I tell you. I am the Deputy Director of the CIA!

My word is golden; I am like talking to God! Boy, if you know what's good for you, you'll follow orders like an agent is supposed to!" Little bubbles of spit were forming in the corners of Kimball's mouth.

"I'm sorry, sir," Pete dropped his head.

Kimball pulled out a photo. There were many people in the picture and Pete recognized some of them.

"Matthews is the one taking the briefcase of money from the Ukrainian arms dealer. You know the Novlak brothers. That is Gregor, one of their enforcers. Enrique is the drug man. You'll be working with him. Drug dealer will be your cover."

Pete stared at the photo. He hoped he was going to be able to be a part of this world.

"More than likely, Elana will have you with her at all times as you prepare to leave. That's why I made the timeline so short. When I paired her with Matthews, I had to give them months so he would become comfortable around her. Elana will take you under her wing because you're new and unimposing."

Pete didn't know if he should be offended or not.

Kimball continued, "Your job is to bring home Jon Matthews dead or alive. I'll make you Deputy Director Aide upon your return."

Noise distracted Pete from his memories as he struggled to breathe through his nose. Kimball had made it seem so easy. Like Pete would just walk up to Jon and escort him back to the states. How could he have been so stupid?

The noises came again. It was Elana tapping her foot on the concrete floor.

Tap. Tap. Tap.

Pete repeated it. Elana paused then did it again. He responded with the same amount of taps. She hit the floor multiple times, almost like applause. How long had she been trying to get his attention?

He knew he could be here for hours. Not knowing what Elana was trying to communicate with him, he went back to distracting himself from the pain. His mind went to the last meeting with Kimball.

"She sleep with you yet?"

It was two in the morning. Pete was exhausted after being with Elana in character all night and then being at Tippi's house. That had been a mystery. But no time to think about it now.

They were in the parking lot of a 7-11. Kimball always began his clandestine meetings the same way. Asking if Elana had slept with him. Pete almost wanted to say yes just to see what Kimball would do.

"No, sir. And I don't think she's going to."

Kimball made a rude noise. "What did you do tonight?"

Pete was momentarily distracted by the quick change.

"We spent the evening going to clubs and staying in character," Pete paused. He had already decided he wasn't going to tell Kimball about Tippi. Elana appeared to be honest with Pete all week. Kimball seemed to always be leaving out details. Even if she had been evasive tonight at Tippi's, Pete couldn't really blame her. It seemed as if he'd invaded the one personal connection Elana had.

"She dropped me off at home, I contacted you, and now I need to get a few hours of sleep before we go to Camp Lejune and fly out."

Kimball smiled, "You're going to be a star here, Pete. You'll forever be known as the man who brought in one of the biggest traitors and rogue agents in the history of our agency. Go get him, boy!"

Wow. He was dumber than a box of rocks and Kimball was a piece of work. The only thing nagging at Pete was wanting to know what Kimball had planned from the beginning. Obviously failure. Complete and utter failure. What did Kimball gain by having Pete and Elana dead? Pete wondered if he'd ever get to find out.

He tapped his foot three times and waited for Elana to respond. The ache in his chest and ribs had become a continuous body pain. He couldn't pinpoint any one spot, he just felt the pain thump in time with his heart. His breathing was labored. He'd read about body trauma but was quickly learning reading a book didn't make him an expert.

He wasn't feeling as smart as he thought he was.

Back upstairs, two men delivered Pete and Elana's bags from the hotel. Juan and Enrique methodically pulled out every piece of clothing, ripped out the seams and stitches of the luggage, and ran bug-checking devices over all of it.

They hit the jackpot when they found the satellite phone tucked in the bottom of Pete's suitcase. Jon hoped to hell the ingoing and outgoing texts and numbers had been cleared. He got lucky with that part. He also got lucky when speed dial '1' was for Ellie and not Elana.

Mikhail pressed number one and the phone from Elana's purse rang.

Mikhail stopped the call. "Maybe Pete brought her to distract us. Maybe she is plain woman but Kimball want me to think she dangerous."

"You can't believe anything Kimball says and does. I told you that," Jon said. "I still think you should let me kill him."

"If I let you kill, who will deliver shipments? Yet, I begin to think Kimball just sent these two so I kill. The story he give is obvious not same he give Pete."

"He sent the kid in to fail. What does that tell you?" Jon didn't wait for a reply. "He wants the boy dead and is using you for his wet work. We should keep them both alive to find out why Kimball wants him dead. Maybe we can use it for leverage."

Jon was grasping at straws. He was working hard to seem like it was all a power play. What he was really doing was keeping Elana alive.

"Kimball tell me Pete will be another asset. We find out what he can give. If not useful we killing him and ship off Ellie. I will enjoy this."

Juan made them wait another hour before going back to the basement. Enrique, bored, had taken a woman to his room. His attention span was like a teenager's, luckily for Jon.

Juan, Mikhail, Boris, Gregor, Jon, and Petrov went downstairs.

When the lights came on, Elana dropped her head and closed her eyes. Pete didn't move. He didn't appear to be breathing.

Juan went to Pete.

"He will die if I do not put in a tube and inflate his lung. Do you wish him to die now or do you want him to live long enough to ask him questions?"

Mikhail paused a moment before saying, "Keep alive. For now."

Juan moved to his instrument tray and pulled out a scalpel and rubber tubing. Without prep, Juan felt for the spaces between Pete's ribs. He inserted the scalpel quickly and Pete's cry of pain was muffled by the gag.

Elana watched with wide, horrified eyes.

Juan slid the tubing into the slit in Pete's chest and secured it with medical tape. His breathing was better, but the wound was leaking blood. Juan pulled off the duct tape. Pete was too weak to spit out the fabric balled in his mouth. Juan muttered in Spanish and ripped it out with the tip of the scalpel, nicking Pete's lip in the process.

Pete took small breaths.

"We'll keep you comfortable. The woman, however, will suffer for your lies." Juan turned.

Jon stiffened as Elana cried silent tears. Juan moved to Elana and ripped off the duct tape. She worked her mouth then spit out the fabric.

"I'm just here for fun. I don't know anything." The tears flowed down her cheeks.

Jon watched the by-play between Elana and Pete. She said the words while looking at Pete. It was a silent message to keep cover no matter what they did to her.

Pete struggled against the table he was strapped to.

"Mikhail, I don't know what you want. Ellie is my piece of ass for this trip. I brought her along because she's dumb and hot. Just put her on a plane home and leave her out of this."

And there was the mistake Jon had been waiting for. If Pete really didn't care about 'Ellie' he would have been indifferent about her safety. His request to send her home would be their downfall. Juan and Mikhail now knew Pete wanted her safe. They would use it to their advantage.

How long would Pete be able to watch her tortured? How long would Jon be able to watch? Jon hoped they were all strong enough to get through the next few hours.

Juan smiled and spoke to Gregor. "Bring the bed."

Gregor dragged in a metal bed frame from a darkened corner of the basement. He quickly unstrapped Elana from the wooden chair. She struggled until he grabbed a handful of hair and whispered against the side of her face.

"I can strap you to a metal bed or I can strap you to a real bed. Juan and I have different ideas of torture. You fight too much and Mikhail will let me be the one to break you."

She went rigid and turned her head when he licked at and then bit her ear.

Jon stiffened slightly, looking sideways at Mikhail. Mikhail nodded his assent. Gregor would get Elana. Shit.

She barely moved as they secured her to the frame using handcuffs on her wrists and ankles. She may as well have been naked for the lack of covering her bra and underwear gave. That was the least of her worries.

She kept eye contact with Pete the whole time. If he gave up her cover they were both dead. She ignored Gregor's wandering hands, tuned out the other men standing in the shadows, and hoped her acting ability could withstand the pain to come.

She sucked in her breath and began to sob when Gregor and Juan rolled over a cart with switches, gauges, and jumper cables attached to it.

"Shane!" she screamed. "What are they going to do to me? Tell them I'm your girlfriend! Tell them not to hurt me!"

Elana walked a tightrope of fear. She had to be scared; not hard to do because she was. But she also had to keep up 'Ellie and Shane'.

"Oh, God, Shane!"

Juan was enjoying her fear. Torturing the innocent was always so much fun because they couldn't tell you anything to stop the pain and they knew it.

As Juan hooked the jumper cables to the bottom of the bed frame, he turned to Pete. "Did Deputy Director Kimball of the CIA send you to us?"

"Yes," Pete said. "But Ellie is not an agent."

Juan turned one knob and a small volt of electricity shot through Elana's body. She gritted her teeth. It was like touching an electric fence.

"You will only give me answers to the questions I ask," Juan warned.

"Okay, okay," Pete pleaded. "I just don't want you to hurt my girlfriend!"

"So she is your girlfriend now? Not just a fun piece of ass?" Boris was finally sober enough to understand what was going on.

Pete looked wildly from Juan to Elana and then to Boris. "She's innocent, that's all I mean."

"No one who comes to my country with CIA is innocent. What is mission?" Mikhail demanded.

Pete's eyes widened and he couldn't help but looking at Elana again. He was back to being Opie Taylor. He didn't know what to say. His pain-muddled mind couldn't produce a reasonable lie. Hell, he couldn't even think of a bad lie.

Gregor stepped over to Elana and tried to put a thick piece of rubber tubing in her mouth. She refused to open. He leaned down and kissed the edge of her lips. His tongue came out and traced the seam of her closed mouth. She shuddered.

"If you like your tongue, you will bite down on this. Electricity causes your muscles to spasm."

Elana opened her eyes wide as Gregor pulled back. He put the piece of rubber up to her mouth and she bit down just before the shock waves started.

Her back bowed as much as the cuffs would allow as the electrical current ripped through her body.

The pain was so intense she couldn't breathe or scream.

24

Langley, Virginia

Tippi stared at the door to the bathroom. What in the hell just happened? His job to take care of her? If only. It wasn't a declaration of love, but it was something, wasn't it? She decided to give him some time. Then she'd let him know she didn't expect anything from him.

AJ stayed in the bathroom for five minutes. He wanted to pace but was too weak so he sat on the edge of the bathtub holding his head in his hand. What was wrong with him? Did he want to take care of Tippi?

He snapped his head up. Did he? He didn't know. She was the first person he'd thought of when that prick had pushed the gun barrel against his head. He'd thought Tippi was saying she loved him when he dropped his phone. It had filled him with elation before his mind had reminded him he was about to die.

Didn't books and movies say people had epiphanies right before they died? Shouldn't there have been some kind of bright light and a picture flash before his eyes of he and Tippi married with a dog, cat, white-picket fence, and two-point-five kids? If so, he was screwed. The only thing on his mind had been survival.

What did he know about love? Not a damn thing. His dad had left before he was born and his mom had done the best she could raising three kids of a half-Asian father. Southern California hadn't been kind to multi-racial kids. AJ's two sisters looked Asian; beautiful and exotic. AJ thought his skin was muddy: not dark, not white.

Fights had been a common part of his life. He'd stuck up for his mom, sisters, and himself growing up.

His mom never married. His sisters each had three kids a piece, all from different men. Neither of them was with the guys who had fathered their children. What he knew about families could fit in a peanut shell.

AJ had gotten the hell out of the city as soon as he could. Barely graduating from high school, he'd joined the Army and hadn't looked back. He sent his mom and sisters money, but he hadn't seen them in years. Hadn't even met a couple of his nieces and nephews.

What did he know about love and family? Not jack-diddly-shit.

A knock on the door startled him.

"AJ?" Tippi's voice was husky.

Even half dead with a headache that could bring down an elephant, it turned him on. He closed his eyes. He didn't know about love, but he knew about lust. He shuffled to the bathroom door.

"I'm sorry—" they said to each other at the same time.

"What do you have to be sorry for?" he asked.

She took his hand and pulled him toward the bed. "Let's not talk about it. Pretend it didn't happen. I don't expect anything from you. Let me take care of you because I can. I'm a doctor. That's why I'm taking care of you."

AJ stopped. Isn't this what he'd always wanted? A woman who didn't want to make things difficult?

"That's the only reason you're taking care of me?" he demanded before he thought. Damn mouth was going to get him in trouble. Why couldn't he just shut up and leave well enough alone?

"Please, AJ? Not now. Let's just take the moments we get. I'm taking care of you because I can." And I need to, she added silently to herself.

"You can take care of me all right," he said, putting her hand on his crotch. His underwear did little to hide his growing erection.

Tippi's eyes widened. "How can you— I mean, how is it possible—"

"That I'm hard as a fucking rock and want to nail you six ways to Sunday?" He was angry. Angry at the world for not giving him a fair break as a kid. Angry at life for not showing him his epiphany of love when he was about to die. Angry at Tippi for being so goddamned irresistible.

She continued to stare at him as he bullied her to the bed. His head hurt, his shoulder ached, and his dick throbbed. He couldn't do anything about his head or shoulder, but he could try and get Tippi to do something about his dick.

"Absolutely not!" She finally managed to get the words out. "What is wrong with you?"

"What's wrong with me is I haven't had sex since the last time I was with you."

"You, you, ass!"

She had better names to call him but couldn't bring herself to say them out loud. Once again, AJ made her lose her temper. No one made her lose her temper, not even her mother.

AJ smiled a predatory grin.

"No," Tippi said.

"I don't want sex," he reasoned.

She looked momentarily shocked. "You don't?"

"Well, depends. Does oral sex count?"

She considered hitting him on the head or the

shoulder; something to cause him pain. Instead she stormed from the room.

She went to the kitchen and started looking through cupboards. She wasn't looking for anything in particular, but she looked loudly. Pans crashed, cupboard doors and drawers slammed.

She didn't realize she was crying until AJ cleared his throat and she spun to glare at him.

"Hey," AJ was scared by the look on her face. "I'm, uh, sorry," he said. "I'm an ass."

"Yes, you are," she said, wiping her eyes with the tips of her fingers.

AJ waited hesitantly for her to continue.

"Don't think for a minute I'm going to tell you it's okay and don't worry about it. I thought you were dead! Earlier tonight I thought I was going to die before I realized Eli wasn't sent to kill me!

"I had to see you in the worst possible shape, clean and stitch you up, and you're being the biggest asshole in the world! In the universe!" By the time she finished her tirade she was crying again.

AJ hadn't even considered what she'd been through tonight in order to get to him. Eli was intimidating to people who knew he was a U.S. Marshal. He couldn't imagine the fear someone as sweet as Tippi would have felt finding the hulking brute in her house.

He carefully stepped toward her with his good hand up in a non-threatening gesture. "Come lay on the bed with me and tell me what's been going on for the last month."

She eyed him warily, "I don't have the energy, nor the inclination, to play your games or deal with your mood swings, AJ."

"I'm not playing games, I promise," he soothed. "I just want to hold you and hear your voice."

He didn't deny the mood swings. She shook his world

up and down like the sand in an hour glass. He felt bi-polar.

What she should have done was demanded he let her out of the prison of a safe-house and tell him where he could stick his not-really-apology. What she did was let him lead her back to the damn bedroom and arrange them both on the bed so she was cradled in his good arm.

Weak. She was so weak when it came to him.

There was silence for endless minutes until she thought he'd fallen asleep. When she went to move, he tightened his hold.

"I really want to know what you've been doing for the last five weeks."

She sighed and snuggled back into him, enjoying the comfort of not being alone. Even if it made her weak.

"Elana took me to her Taekwondo master and I've been working with him almost since you left."

She waited for the explosion.

His muscles tensed briefly then he asked, "Why does Elana think you need Taekwondo? Is it for a new workout?"

"No. It's for fighting." Now she was purposely goading him. Wanting him to get mean so she could demand to leave.

"Fighting?" he asked carefully. "Any particular reason a scientist needs fighting skills?"

"Elana thinks I'm capable and I can take care of myself." It was easy to say because she didn't have to look in his eyes. "She knows I could be in danger—"

AJ tensed more. "Why in the *fuck* would you be in danger?" he demanded in a quiet, level voice.

It was now or never. He'd either treat her like a competent, capable woman or a dim-witted moron.

"I looked into the vial of X-232 that was stolen from my lab and used to poison Elana."

AJ carefully removed his arm from under Tippi's head and slowly scooted up the bed until his back was propped against the headboard. He grimaced in pain as he tried to adjust his upper body.

"Can I get some more drugs before we continue this discussion?" he asked in the same quiet voice.

His face was a mask of stone and she now knew what Elana meant about having a poker face. She couldn't read AJ's thoughts at all. Was he angry? Indifferent?

She warily moved from the bed and went to her bag. "Do you want an injection or pills?" What a strange turn in the conversation.

"Injections work faster, right?"

"Yes," she nodded.

"Give me a shot. I need the pain meds in my system as soon as possible," he said through clenched teeth.

She quickly swabbed the vial with an alcohol pad and did the same to his arm. She injected the drugs. He sat against the headboard, eyes closed, while she put things away and went to the bathroom to wash her hands.

Seeing her reflection was strange. She looked like a different person. Her hair was tangled around her head, there was a band-aid on her temple, and her cheek was bruised. Her face was pale and there were dark circles under her eyes. She couldn't go to work like this; she'd scare Marcus.

She went back to the bedroom and noted AJ still had his eyes closed. She should have had him lay down before she gave him the pain meds so he'd be more comfortable.

She sent a quick text message to Marcus saying she wouldn't be to work because she was sick. She looked up into AJ's piercing dark eyes. He wasn't asleep or relaxed.

"Who was that to?"

"My assistant, letting him know I won't be to work."

AJ nodded. "Can you sit in the chair and," he paused as if searching for the right words, "explain to me what's been going on?"

She was shocked at his civility. She hadn't expected to really tell him about her missing work, she thought they were going to fight.

"Um, okay."

She put a chair about five feet from the bed. AJ raised his brows.

"What?" she asked.

"Please move it right next to the bed so I can look at your face. I need to be able to see and touch you but I don't think you should be on the bed with me."

"Okay," Tippi said again slowly.

She was used to him being intense during sex, like when he'd tied her to the bed. Having all that concentration directed at her when they weren't having sex was unnerving.

She started at the beginning and went over meeting Elana for coffee and trying to get her to take better care of herself. AJ's features softened as she talked about the friendship she'd forged with Elana. She explained about the missing vial of poison and how Elana wanted her to be safe since AJ and Elana were never around for very long. He grudgingly agreed Elana was right and Tippi almost fell out of her chair.

By the time she finished telling him about her new security system, what she'd learned from Taekwondo, and shooting guns, he was staring at her like he'd never seen her before.

"Please say something," Tippi pleaded. She was used to his outbursts, not his silence.

"I don't know what to say," AJ finally said. "I thought I could protect you by keeping you in a bubble of happiness. Elana knew that wasn't right. It should have been me doing those things for and with you."

Of all the responses Tippi expected, that wasn't the one. She gaped at him.

"Did you really attack Eli?"

She nodded.

"That would have been a sight. He wasn't prepared for

an alarm or a fight." He smiled at the thought.

"No, he wasn't," she smiled back. Then she glared. "He scared the living hell out of me. I really thought he was going to kill me."

"Why?"

"What? What do you mean why?" she said.

"Why would you think someone would kill you?"

"There was a huge man in my living room! What else would I think? You and Elana have me so freaked out about looking into the stealing of vials from my lab."

"Wait. Stealing of vials? More than one?"

"Yes. Marcus, my assistant, and I started marking the vials. We used pen that can only be seen with a black light. Over the past three weeks, four vials have been removed and replaced with fakes. Who knows how many before that." She was getting angry all over again. Thinking about someone stealing her work, and the implications, made her sick.

"The tech department sent me video footage of the door to the vault where the samples are stored. The video has been looped so we can't see who accessed the keypad. I even had it dusted for fingerprints and there aren't any besides mine."

"Who knows the samples are missing? Who did you tell? What's missing?" AJ's heart was pounding. What had she done?

"Calm down. Marcus and I know, Elana knows, and now you. Besides X-232, there are four samples of different biological weapons missing. Anthrax, Ebola, a type of bubonic plague, and then an unnamed agent I call X-100."

"What is it?" AJ demanded.

"It's a fungus that destroys any plant which uses photosynthesis. That means every plant."

"What? Why?" he asked in horror.

"I was told there's been talk someone is trying to develop a fungus that will destroy plants. That means no crops, no vegetation. Whatever country can produce crops after world-wide failure would become the richest; have import and export control. They'd be in control of the world. I was asked to make it first so if another country develops the bio-weapon, we'll have something to counter the attack."

"Unless someone steals it. Then you won't have the counter agent."

"Of course I do." Tippi tapped her temple.

She didn't realize it, but she'd painted a giant target on her back. By creating the counter agent she'd actually created the fungus. She'd created a weapon of mass destruction and didn't know it because she didn't think like that.

AJ waited, willing her to figure it out. As though she could read his mind, it slowly dawned on her.

"Oh my. I created a. . . created a. . . kill. . . " she started to hyperventilate.

"Breathe, baby. I'm not going to let anything happen to you. How much sick leave and vacation do you have?"

"Um, I don't know the exact number of hours." She tried to think about something other than the destruction of the crops of the world.

"AJ?" She looked at him with scared, teary eyes. "What have I done?"

He pulled her to him on the bed, back in the crook of his arm. He kissed the top of her head. "You didn't do anything. After you relax, you're going to put in for a vacation. As many days as you can be gone. Tell work you're going to Tahiti."

"We're going to Tahiti?" she asked, confused.

"No. You're going to tell work that. We're going underground."

"Underground?"

He closed his eyes. She so wasn't a part of his world.

"We're going to hide out for a while. You're going to get me every piece of information about X-100. All your notes from work, all your computer documents, all the brilliance in that beautiful brain of yours. I want to know everything: who your boss is, who told you to make it, where you heard the chatter about the initial idea. Everything. You are not going to be out of my sight."

"But, you're still hurt," she tried to argue, yet her body was already relaxing.

"Good thing I have my own personal doctor then, huh?" He squeezed her shoulder and kissed the top of her head again.

He wished he had the strength to make love to her. He needed to feel her goodness and her heat. To know she was safe. He couldn't believe someone hadn't tried to kill her or kidnap her yet.

Was it love if you put your life on the line and risked committing treason to keep someone safe?

Nah. It was just duty.

25

Novlak Mansion

While going through training at The Farm, recruits were subjected to various forms of torture. You can't just read about pain; you have to experience it. After only hours in the Novlak basement, Elana experienced more pain than she'd ever thought possible.

The feeling of electricity ripping through her body was so intense her muscles still jumped and spasmed even after Juan turned the electricity off. Every electric attack felt like an eternity. The heat ripped through her body four separate times. She couldn't gauge how much time passed with each shock or how much time was spent between. All she could do was regulate her breathing the best she could and keep her teeth on the rubber tubing.

The fifth time the electricity hit she bit through the tubing and started to choke. Blessedly, the surge stopped. She tried to spit out the pieces, but only managed to roll them out with her tongue. Gregor's face wavered above hers. Bright lights danced in front of her eyes as her vision faded in and out. It felt like she had the worst sunburn in the world. The scent of singed hair and burnt flesh filled her nose and she thought she might throw up.

"Stop!" Pete yelled. "My mission was to come here and gain your trust so we could find out who your drugs are being sent to. Kimball didn't tell me you would know I was an agent. This is only my first real assignment!"

Pete wanted them to quit torturing Elana. He would do what he could to keep her cover intact since he knew his was already blown.

"You make this too easy, puta," Juan said.

"You are no use to me," Mikhail said.

Boris stepped from the corner. "None makes sense, Mikhail. What goes on?"

"Someone has been lying to us for a long time," Jon snarled. "I told you from the moment I got here you couldn't trust Kimball."

Jon was going to skin that rat-bastard Kimball alive for sending him, Elana, and Pete to this hell-hole.

"Kill boy," Mikhail said. "Let whore sit with body until I decide what we do with her." Mikhail stomped up the steps muttering in Russian about not being able to trust Americans.

Elana broke into sobs as Juan walked to where Pete was strapped to the table.

Gregor laughed. "I know what to do with her." He slipped the key into one of the handcuffs on Elana's ankles, running his hand up her leg until he was groping her crotch.

She tried kicking but he hadn't released the cuffs yet.

Juan had been in the process of unstrapping Pete from the table. As soon as Pete was free, he charged at Gregor. Stumbling before he made it three steps, Pete started to fall and Gregor kicked him in the head.

A spray of blood flew from his mouth as he hit the concrete floor with a sickening crunch. He didn't move.

Elana was frantically calling "Shane," over and over in a broken whisper.

Jon glared at Gregor. "Mikhail did not give you permission to touch the woman."

Gregor flexed his muscles and barreled toward Jon in a rage. "I do not need permission to do things, Nikoli! I do what I want!"

Jon deflected Gregor with a quick side-step and an elbow to the back of his head. Gregor bounced to the ground much the same way Pete had. He levered himself up and shook his head. Then he made a growling sound like a wild animal.

"You will pay, American."

Elana tried to see who Gregor was talking to, but Gregor stood and blocked her view. Then she was back to worrying about Pete.

Gregor went for Jon again.

"Enough!" Juan finally yelled. "This is my basement, my work. Everyone out. I will not have something broken because you two can't think without using your dicks."

Elana whimpered. She watched through slitted, blurry eyes as Gregor stumbled up the stairs with two others trailing. She looked back to Pete and willed him to get up. Her hope deflated like a balloon.

Juan used the hose to spray down Elana and Pete, washing blood down the drain in the center of the floor.

Pete twitched.

"Shane," Elana pleaded. "Wake up."

He moaned and began crawling to her.

Juan didn't pay attention as he meticulously cleaned and straightened the basement.

Pete made it to the bed frame and managed to pull himself to his knees. His right arm hung loosely at his side, dislocated or broken from his fall. It was the same arm Mikhail had smashed with the hammer. The breathing tube in his chest was coming out. His skin was molted with bruises, scrapes, cuts, and welts. Blood ran from gashes on his face.

He used what strength he had left to propel his body into Elana's. The air whooshed out of her as his face smashed into her neck.

"I recorded. . . our conversations." Pete slobbered blood on her with each word. "Every time. . . I talked to him. . . since the fir—" a shudder ripped through his body. "First weird. . . meeting."

"Shh, don't talk. Save your energy." What weird meeting? She tried to keep an eye on Juan and soothe Pete at the same time.

"Can you get to the handcuff at my ankle?" Elana whispered. Gregor had left the key in the lock.

Pete didn't appear to hear her. He continued with the gibberish. "When get home. . . find file hidden in—" he coughed and the painful, gurgling sound made Elana gag. "Tippi," Pete said.

Elana's eyes widened. "Tippi what?" she whispered.

"Hidden in. . . Tippi. . . Use recordings. Bring down Kimball. Sorry. Got you in this."

"I think we got each other into this, Petey."

Tears leaked from Elana's eyes. How in the hell had Tippi gotten involved in this? Elana couldn't worry about it now. She was going to have to survive and get to Tippi.

Juan moved behind Pete with something in his hand. Elana stiffened and opened her eyes wide.

"Please," she begged in a whispery voice. Using every ounce of womanly charm she could gather, which wasn't much since she was half electrocuted, Elana looked directly at Juan. "Please don't kill him. I'll do anything. Anything!"

Light glinted off the pistol in Juan's hand as he put the barrel to the back of Pete's head. He didn't acknowledge her as he shoved Pete so his head rested between her head and elbow.

The sound of the gun was so sudden and loud Elana couldn't initially comprehend what happened. Chunks of brain matter, pieces of skull, and blood coated her face.

Spitting, screaming, and whipping her head from side

to side, Elana shook with terror. She couldn't hear, she could only feel.

Pete was alive and then he was dead.

The emotion Elana felt threatened to drown her. After months of being frozen inside, she didn't know what to do. She lifted her head and screamed at the ceiling. Whether she was screaming at the Novlaks or God, she didn't know.

She screamed her pain and terror until she couldn't make another sound, eyes shut, body shaking. She knew she was covered in Pete's blood and. . . other stuff. Big bad CIA agent she was, she couldn't even think about what was on her.

The pressure of Pete's body was on her arm. She wiggled until he slid to the floor in a squishy heap. Not able to handle it anymore, she turned her head to the other side and vomited.

Water slammed into her face, but she was grateful for the spray. It would wash away the evidence of Pete's death. She held her breath and moved her head back and forth in hopes of getting as much water on her as possible.

The spray stopped.

She tried to open her eyes, but couldn't make her brain relay the message.

She heard the door open, footsteps down the stairs. Two men?

"What the fuck?" a voice roared.

"Oh, Nikoli," Juan chastised, "You so worry about the little things."

"Little things? She's supposed to be my play toy! Did you shoot her?"

"She will be mine!" Gregor argued.

Rough hands removed the handcuffs at Elana's ankles and wrists. She couldn't make herself open her eyes or even struggle. Ignoring what was going on around her, she shivered.

She was lifted without care and slammed back on the

wooden chair. The straps were secured around her wrists, ankles, and throat.

Juan roughly jerked her head back. "You will not die as quickly as the boy. I will make it last for you."

She choked on a sob, still keeping her eyes tightly closed. She hoped they left her alone in the darkness so she wouldn't be able to see Pete's body.

After endless moments of hushed arguing she couldn't make out, they went upstairs. She was finally alone. She made herself open her eyes. The light was on. Squishing her eyes closed once again, Elana tried to do anything but think about what had happened. She mentally reviewed their timeline since they'd arrived. How had things gone so horribly wrong? Pete hadn't been ready for field work. Obviously Elana hadn't been able to handle this intense of a mission, either.

She worked with the facts she had. Kimball had made Pete think he was Superman. Kimball had told Mikhail Pete was an agent and would have information for them. Pete hadn't known anything about that. He would have told her, wouldn't he? It didn't matter now because Pete was dead. She could never ask him.

Dead. He was dead.

There was no doubt in her mind she would die too. Just not quickly.

Unable to think about anything else, Elana dropped her head as far as the strap would allow and sobbed.

She may have dozed or passed out. She wasn't sure which. The spray of the hose woke her and she choked on the water.

"Time to play," Gregor said in her ear as Juan and Enrique removed the straps.

They stretched her up on the same wall Pete had started this horrible torture trip with. Enrique pulled the chains higher so her feet didn't touch the ground.

"That's for breaking my nose, you bitch!"

Juan set up a fan and directed it at Elana. Within moments, shivers racked her body. More discomfort. It also spread the stench of death throughout the room

"What do you want?" she screamed.

"The truth," Juan said as Enrique said, "Your pain."

Enrique smashed her body against the wall. As much as she didn't want him near, the heat was welcome. Her body shook as Enrique fumbled for the button and zipper on his slacks.

Elana went crazy. She lifted her feet and pushed off the wall trying to knee him in the groin.

"Oh no you don't, puta." Enrique said as he tried to pin her back to the wall.

"I don't think so," Gregor said as a meaty hand grabbed Enrique by the neck. When Enrique didn't let go of her, Gregor pushed his body closer and squeezed harder.

Elana felt Enrique's erection throb against her stomach. He was getting more turned on by Gregor's roughness.

Elana looked at Gregor. "You're turning him on. I wouldn't stand so close if I were you." She'd use whatever advantage she could to keep everyone off balance. It was going to be her only chance at survival.

Gregor wrapped a second hand around Enrique's throat, choking him, muttering in Polish about sick South Americans and their penchant for nasty things.

Enrique's eyes rolled back in his head and Gregor let his body fall to the floor.

"You will soon learn when to keep your pretty mouth shut." Gregor stepped over Enrique, pinning Elana to the wall.

"How many times do I have to tell you to stay out of my basement?" Juan demanded. "You cannot have her until I am done."

Gregor glared at Juan and pushed Elana against the wall harder before walking away, almost stepping on Enrique.

Juan retrieved the hose. Elana only had a moment to register that fact before the water came on and completely soaked her.

The water woke Enrique. He sputtered and picked himself off the cold, wet concrete. He looked around and saw Gregor as he went through the door.

"I kill you, bastard!" Enrique said in Spanish as he staggered up the stairs.

Elana's teeth chattered uncontrollably as Juan hit her with another blast from the hose.

"I saved you from both men, Ellie. You should tell me some truths to balance what you owe me."

So that was why Juan was pretending to care about whether or not she was raped.

"I don't owe you shit," Elana said, spasming uncontrollably.

"Maybe we should play with the electricity again?"

"Go to hell."

"Do you work for the CIA?"

"No. I already told you that."

"Then I have no use for you. The Novlaks will have no use for you."

"I guess not," she agreed.

Juan rolled over the cart with the jumper cables and Elana kicked at him as he attached them to the chains on her arms.

"I'm not sure I believe you," said Juan.

26

For two days they kept Elana in the basement with Pete's body. She tried to look at him, but her mind couldn't comprehend his mostly headless corpse.

Juan, the sick bastard, had put a clock in the basement with her so she could tell how much time passed. The ticking of the seconds were a relentless reminder of Pete's absent heartbeat.

Petrov came down a few times a day to let her use the bathroom. She wouldn't eat or drink and only used the bathroom to spare herself any more embarrassment and comfort issues.

She hadn't spoken a word the entire time.

Juan would come down, use his knives or electricity, slap her around, then leave without asking anything except if she worked for the CIA. More techniques to break her.

Pete's blood had congealed on the floor and the smell permeating the room increased her nausea. Not that there was anything left to throw up.

During the forty-eight hours, she careened from one emotion to another. After the initial shock and pain, she'd worked hard to try and get back to her robot role. Then she'd glimpse Pete's body. That's when she'd lose her composure again. *If* she survived loomed over her head every moment they kept her in the basement.

Footsteps echoed down the stairs. Petrov or Juan?

She turned her head and visibly flinched when Enrique stopped and smiled at her. Both of his eyes were green and black from when she'd broken his nose. She could see the bruises on his neck from where Gregor had choked him. Shit, this wasn't going to be good.

"I have missed you," Enrique's slimy voice was low as he walked to her. He eyed her bloody body with more lust than anyone should have.

He walked two circles, trailing his hands on her hair, neck, and the swell of her breasts. She tried to ignore all the horrible comments he made. The promises of what he was going to do with her when she finally left the basement. Her lack of reaction was goading Enrique. He expected her to cower or beg.

She didn't break eye contact even when he punched her in the face and her head shot to the left. The strap around her neck dug in. Time to do something. She wasn't going to die here without a fight. She made fists with her secured hands and licked the blood off her lower lip. It might have been sexual if there hadn't been blood. She knew it would entice Enrique. Sure enough, he went to punch her again.

A hand shot out of the shadows over her head and squeezed Enrique's fist. Even through the ringing in her ears, she heard the bones crack. He doubled over, grasping his broken left hand. A string of garbled Spanish followed. Elana smiled despite how much her face hurt. His montage had to do with goats and the other man's mother and a bodily action you shouldn't do with goats. Or your mother.

Elana heard Mikhail laugh from the other side of her. When had two other people come down? She hadn't even noticed. Probably because she'd been so intent on ignoring Enrique. Yet one more reason she wasn't meant to be CIA.

Enrique stumbled up the stairs. When he was partway,

he turned and yelled, "You will not always be under Mikhail's protection. I'll kill you then."

"I'm not under anyone's protection, you stupid fuck."

The voice sounded so familiar.

Mikhail lit a cigar and walked behind her. She waited for the burn on her skin but, instead, the strap around her neck loosened. Until she gulped in the rotten, metallic air, Elana hadn't realized how starved for oxygen she really was.

Mikhail walked to her side and held a glass of water to her lips. When she refused to open her mouth, water ran down her face. Goosebumps rose on her flesh.

"It would do good to rinse blood off mouth."

"Why?" Her voice was hoarse from screaming when Pete had been shot. She also hadn't been able to hold back the screams when Juan had used the electricity again.

"Because my men not like taste of blood!"

He dumped the glass of water over her. Then he gripped her hair and turned her head, forcing her to look at Pete's lifeless body. She snapped her eyes closed.

"You not realize how much trouble you in. If you not agent, I have no use. You come my country for good time. You miss young lover, yes?" He laughed. "I provide new lover. Many. You will never be sad or lonely again."

Elana kept her eyes closed as Mikhail grasped her arm and turned it over so her palm was face up. She didn't so much as flinch when he took his cigar and ground it out in her hand. The sting and burn was nothing compared to the pain she'd already endured.

Pete was dead.

Jon was probably dead.

She was going to be dead soon.

Curling her hand around the cigar as best she could, she opened her eyes and finally made eye contact with Mikhail. Then she spit in his face. He slapped her exactly where Enrique had punched her. Tears stung her eyes but she refused to let them fall.

"Nikoli! You want first, you get first!"

She had forgotten about the man who had broken Enrique's hand. She jerked at the pinch of a needle between her shoulder and neck.

The man named Nikoli unstrapped her wrists and ankles from the chair, noting her skin had been rubbed raw. She barely moved when he picked her up.

"When tire of her, give to Gregor. I be in room. You know why. I not wait long." Mikhail left.

If Mikhail had seen his eyes, it would have been all over. They held the rage he had been hiding for months. Gregor would be getting her over his dead body.

When no one was within hearing distance, Jon leaned down and whispered, "Elana."

Her eyes fluttered open at the familiar voice. It had happened. She was crazy. It couldn't be him; he was dead. She forced herself to raise her head and she met the eyes that had been haunting her dreams.

Right before she lost consciousness, she whispered, "It can't be you."

The small injection had been Vitamin B1, not a sedative. She'd passed out from exhaustion. Mikhail had needed to think she was drugged. Jon carried her toward his room. Mikhail was waiting and it would raise too much suspicion if he tried to leave immediately.

Natalia waited halfway up the sweeping staircase. "What are you doing with her?"

Jon saw something in Talia's eyes that hadn't been there before. Obviously there was jealousy, but he also saw rage. She tried to touch his hair and he moved his head. He didn't have time for this shit.

"This woman needs medical attention, Talia. It would be best if you stayed away for a couple of days."

"You would choose this American whore over me?"

She followed him, whining.

"Not now, Natalia. Just go to your room."

"Maybe I will just find myself a new boy-toy to play with. You can have your whore."

"Fine with me," Jon said.

When he reached his room, he looked down at Elana. Under the bruises and cuts, her face was pale. His body tensed again as he felt the overwhelming urge to rip the head and arms off everyone who'd laid a hand on her. Most of the physical wounds were from Juan. The mental wounds were Mikhail's, Enrique's, and Gregor's doing. And Jon's. He'd mind-fucked her too.

He knew there was a camera trained on his bed. Every day he would disable it and every evening it was back. Mikhail was a voyeur and liked to watch. Jon tensed at the thought of what he was going to have to do so Mikhail could have a show. He tried to block out it was Elana in his arms and repeated his mantra in his head: "Anything to get the job done, anything to get the job done." It didn't help. He felt his stomach roll.

He tossed her on the bed. She landed with her arms and legs contorted and he quickly walked away. He went to the bathroom and started water in the tub. Making it a comfortable temperature, he let it run as he stared at the churning water.

That must be what his head and stomach looked like. That must be how indecision would appear if it had a way to materialize into a form. He stared for a full ten minutes while the tub filled. He took deep even breaths, finally shut off the water, and walked back to the bed.

Elana hadn't moved. He pulled a knife from the sheath on his ankle and used it to quickly cut the fabric of her bra and panties. He tossed the scraps toward the door and trailed the knife in a path from between her breasts down to the juncture of her thighs, tracing the small scabs from when

Juan had done the same thing. He didn't break the skin, just played into his role as cold-blooded rapist and assassin for Mikhail's camera.

Jon wouldn't forget Mikhail's camera.

He threw her over his shoulder and walked into the bathroom. He wished he could wrap her in a blanket and hold her in his arms for the next twenty-four hours.

Couldn't happen, though.

He left the door open so the camera could see the edge of the massive bathtub. As much as he wanted to walk in and close the door to keep her safe, Mikhail was expecting torture and rape to ensue. Jon had to give the illusion or Mikhail would give her to someone else. Someone who would torture and rape her for real. Probably Gregor.

He put her in the tub and watched the water turn pink from her blood and the blood of her dead partner. Jon suffered no remorse for the death of Pete. He'd almost gotten Elana killed. He deserved to die.

Jon shoved Elana's head under the water. She went down, bubbles rising from her nose and mouth. He pulled her head up and watched water run in rivulets down her face. Nothing. She didn't cough or move. He did it again. This time her body's response to lack of air kicked in. She shot up and was immediately in fight mode. She swung her hands and arms, but weakness kept her from hurting him. Her eyes weren't focused and she froze when Jon gripped both her flailing hands in his hold. His other hand grabbed her hair and made her look at his face.

She closed her eyes, opened them, and blinked rapidly. Water still ran down her face and Jon swiped his hand over her forehead, then pushed her hair back before gripping her head again.

Her lips trembled and then tears began to fall. "He's dead. Pete's dead," she said in barely a whisper.

"Yes," Jon said.

"Jon's dead," she sobbed.

Didn't she recognize him?

"Jon's dead. You're Nikoli."

"When I'm here, I'm Nikoli," he said.

"Nikoli won't be nice to me."

She closed her eyes and Jon loosened the hold on her wrists. She slipped one hand free and tried to wipe her face.

"Jon will make Nikoli be as nice as he can."

He grabbed a bar of soap from the edge of the tub and tried to hand it to her. It was incredibly weird to refer to himself as two different people, but that's what his life had become. The relief he felt was staggering. She was here. Now if Michael or AJ could show up and get them out, life would be perfect. Well, as perfect as his fucked-up life could get.

Elana tried to grip the soap but it fell in the bath. She looked down and all she could see was the pink water. She tried to bolt from the tub.

"Get me out of the blood, get me out of Pete's blood!"

She had the look of a wild animal and Jon wondered if his act as Nikoli was going to push her over the edge. He pulled her from the tub and roughly shoved her toward the shower. She fell, sprawling naked on the floor right in front of the bathroom door, in clear view of the camera. She lay for a moment, trying to keep from breaking into sobs.

She turned her head and closed her eyes. "Camera?"

"Trained on the bed and the bathroom door."

"Sound?"

"Just outside the door to the room. If we whisper, they can't hear. However, Mikhail's gotten good at reading lips." Jon had his body turned so all the camera could pick up was his back.

She started to push herself up. Her head was clearing. "This wasn't how I pictured our first meeting after all these months." She sounded lost. "I was going to show you how strong I was. How I didn't need you. What I want is to crawl into your arms and let you fix everything."

Her voice broke and she rose to a sitting position. Without meaning to, she was giving Mikhail his show. She was broken, beaten, and defeated.

Jon's breath caught. He wouldn't admit it, but he had also wondered how their first meeting would go. This wasn't it. "Elana, look at me."

She braced her body and turned her head to look over her shoulder. Welts from the metal bedsprings marred her back. Slices from Juan's knives peppered her skin in other places. Her wrists and ankles were rubbed raw and she had bruises on her neck from the straps of the chair. There were also the bruises on her face from being punched and slapped.

"I'm going to do my best to get you stuck in this room with me. They all want you, even Mikhail. But he likes to watch more than participate. Keeping you in this room will keep you alive and safe from the rest of them. Do you understand?"

She nodded and tried to stand.

Jon moved behind her, yanking her to her feet. She cried out and he put his head next to her ear. "I have to look like I'm hurting you. I'm sorry if I actually do."

He turned and bullied her to the bed, pushing her pliant body face down on the sheets.

How sick was he that the thought of finally getting to have her was making him hard? How sick was it he was finally going to have Elana and it would be on camera?

Jon once again resisted the urge to pull her into the bathroom and shut and lock the door. Mikhail and Gregor would come to the room and drag her out.

As twisted as it was, this was the only way.

Jon stripped off his shirt and went for the buckle on his belt.

27

Elana's eyes went wide as Jon slid down his zipper. She could see he was hard and he expected her to shrink back from him. Instead, her nostrils flared and she met his eyes. He didn't see fear, he saw heat. It made him harder, if that were possible.

"Jon—"

He pulled the rest of his clothes off and climbed on the bed, covering her body with his.

"Turn your head toward the windows. The camera's behind us, above the door."

The heat of his body made her groan.

Jon moved her wet hair from the back of her neck. "God, Elana, I've thought of, dreamed of nothing but you since the night at the club when you left. Can you kick your acting skills into high gear right now like you did then?"

He slid his hand down between the comforter and her wet body. She moaned and arched back. His erection bumped her ass.

"You have to fight me a little, baby girl."

"I don't want to fight you," she breathed. "I want to feel alive. I need to feel alive with you."

He bit the curve of her shoulder. "Not right now. Right now I have to be Nikoli and you have to be Ellie."

221

"I want to be Elana, I'm tired of all this." She almost lost it; her voice betrayed her emotions.

"I know, baby, I know. As soon as I can, I'll get us alone so you can be Elana again and I can be Jon. But right now, I need you to be Ellie. A broken, scared, getting attacked Ellie. I'm sorry."

He gently kissed the bite and then became Nikoli; became what the camera had to see. He gripped a handful of her hair, ripping her head back. She cried out. Turning her head so he could kiss her, he surrendered for a moment to all the fear he'd felt from the moment he'd seen her come out of the back of that SUV. From two days ago when he'd heard the gunshot, run to the basement, and seen her covered in blood. Thanked God it had been Pete's blood.

The kiss was punishing. There was no finesse, no chance for gentleness. His mouth covered hers and their teeth and lips slammed together. The hand between the bed and Elana's body drifted lower so he could brush his fingers over her. He was going to have to be rough for the camera but he'd do his best to make sure he didn't hurt her.

Elana came alive when his fingers delved into the heat of her body. She cried out again and tried to yank her head from his hand. He pushed her shoulders down so her face was shoved into the mattress.

"Kick your legs or something," he said into the wet skin of her shoulders.

He found her clit with his thumb and Elana kicked. She bucked her body and almost threw him off the bed. As his fingers pushed inside her, she tightened her muscles and they both groaned.

"Jesus, you're tight," he panted and his cock throbbed against her ass.

Elana almost screamed as his thumb brushed her clit again. A flood of wetness covered his fingers. She shuddered.

"I can't wait," Jon groaned.

As he started to slide down her body, he looked briefly at the condoms on the nightstand. He'd used one every single time with Talia.

"Birth control," he bit out. The thought of sliding into Elana's slick wet heat, skin on skin, was about to blow the top of his head off.

"Birth control implant," she said as though she was also having trouble thinking straight.

Still on their sides, he moved down her body and pulled her hips up. He took his hand and guided himself toward her wet entrance.

"Hard and fast. Not just because of the camera, but because I finally get to have you. I'm sorry if I hurt you." He'd apologized twice in the last five minutes and he never apologized to anyone.

She grunted in response and Jon gripped her hips with both hands, then slammed forward.

This time she did scream. She bit the blanket and let his body crush her farther into the bed. It hurt and it felt so damn good. She tried to block out it was a show for the camera and gave up fighting. She moved her hands behind her to grip at his back. It looked like she was clawing at him.

Jon pushed his body forward and over her. In less than a minute, he felt the tightening low in his body letting him know he wasn't going to be able to keep going for much longer. He bucked into her wildly. Her response was a low growl as she snaked her own hand down to where their bodies were joined.

What little blood was left in Jon's brain rushed to his cock when Elana's hands touched him and herself. He braced one arm on the bed to try and lever his body a little more so the camera couldn't see Elana's arm or hand. It wasn't working.

He pulled himself out of her and sat back on his knees. Elana didn't move. He grabbed a handful of her hair and wrapped his arm around her waist. It looked like he was pulling her up by her hair, but he used his other arm to support all her weight.

When her back was plastered to his front, he moved his hand from her hair and wrapped it around the front of her neck and chin, gripping her hard. He pinned her arms to her body by wrapping his arm back around her middle, her hands locked down in their laps.

Now all the camera could see was Jon's back and his punishing grip on her throat. He slammed into her with short digs that let him get some control back.

Elana was on the verge of losing consciousness. Her entire body was poised on the brink of exploding. She was alive, finally felt alive after months of being dead inside. Jon's heat made her feel whole and complete.

She didn't think about anything but the feeling of him inside her, stretching her. She moved her fingers over where their bodies were joined. Squeezing, pinching. Her mixture of light and hard touches pushed them both over the edge. She screamed and bit down on his fingers.

They fell forward, Jon still inside her. Sweat had fused their bodies together and she didn't move from the weight of his body. She still didn't move as he slid himself out of her.

Jon's breathing was harsh. As he slowly came back to earth, he registered the chill caused by Elana's wet hair and their sweat so he reached down to pull the sheet up. That's when he noticed the blood. His chest was covered and the sheets looked like he'd killed someone.

How could he have forgotten how injured she was? Sex did that to a man's brain.

Of course, Nikoli wasn't supposed to care she was almost dead. But Jon did. Even Nikoli would draw the line at this mess.

She had passed out again, he was sure of it. Her breathing was even, yet a little fast. Her body knew to be scared even when unconscious. Jon wiped the blood off his chest with one of the blankets as the phone in the room rang.

"Impressive," Mikhail's voice said as Jon put the receiver to his ear. Jon turned his head to glare at the camera. "You not even give time for fight. Much shorter time than with Talia," Mikhail goaded.

Jon grimaced and wiped more blood from his body. "Yeah, and now I have a mess. Send up one of the maids and the nurse, would you?"

Mikhail was silent for a moment. "I have business. You call servants. I look forward to next performance."

"Yeah, well, you might have to wait a day. I like them conscious."

"Pity," Mikhail said and hung up.

Jon resisted letting out a huge breath. Maybe Mikhail would leave them alone for a day and she could actually rest.

He called and requested food, a maid, and the nurse.

He walked to the bathroom. While the bathtub water was still pink, it was warm. He added some Russian soap that was like Epsom Salt and went back to get Elana. He carried her to the bathtub and put her in the water.

He didn't have everything he wanted to bring down Kimball. But with Elana alive and Pete dead, it might be enough for Elana to convince the Director of their division Kimball needed to be audited. Now that she was here, they were going to get the hell out of this hole.

Jon had a stash of money, some weapons, and a couple fake passports at the main train station. He'd only been there twice since being here and no one knew about it. He was sure he hadn't been followed when he'd taken Talia to the market.

There was a small knock on the door and two maids came in. Jon propped Elana's head on the side of the bathtub with a towel and stepped into the main room.

The women spotted the blood on the bed. Their eyes widened then they noticed Jon. He was still naked. One covered her mouth on a 'o' of surprise. The other started gathering the bloody clothes. As her hand reached out to pick up the bra, Jon stopped her. He didn't want anyone to see the knife sheath hidden in the fabric.

"Just clean up the bed," he said in Russian.

She snatched back her hand and pulled her linen cart from the hallway.

Used to Gregor, Boris, and Mikhail's sick ways, the two women stripped the bed, putting all the soiled linens into plastic bags, and making the bed up with quick efficiency. Jon pulled on a pair of boxer briefs as they worked. He caught them sneaking looks at him. One woman in fear, the other in revulsion.

When they were done, they rolled in the food cart and left. The nurse came in slowly with her medical bag. She'd never once been summoned to Jon's room.

"She's in the bathtub soaking in healing salts," Jon said in Russian.

The nurse's eyes opened wide and she acted like she was going to say something.

"Leave your medical bag. There are salves, bandages, and pain medication?"

The nurse nodded.

"I'll take care of everything."

He glanced at the clock. It was late, but not too late. Maybe he could get them about eight to ten hours alone in the room.

"Come back in the morning with more drugs."

He pushed the speechless nurse out and locked the door. He didn't know for sure if it would work, but if Mikhail saw on the cameras Elana was just bandaged and drugged, maybe he would let things go until tomorrow.

Grabbing the bag of supplies, Jon went back to the bathroom and closed the door all the way. Fuck Mikhail.

Elana hadn't moved. He was worried about her.

Worried about the woman she'd been six months ago and the woman she'd become. Elana Miller was finally a CIA agent. You could tell from how well she'd held up the last few days. But she'd still broken.

Jon turned on the shower then got another Vitamin B1 shot ready and also half a dose of morphine. He wanted Elana better, but not out of it. He gave her the injections then shot a dose and a half of morphine down the sink drain. The nurse would be reporting back to Mikhail. Jon wanted them to think Elana was so drugged they wouldn't have to worry about her.

He lifted her from the bathtub and took her to the shower. He pulled her close, trying to wake her. "Elana?"

He ran his hands down her arms looking at her cuts. Her back was a mess. The springs from the metal bed had ripped her open. He let the water from the shower wash over her. That's what brought her awake. She moaned into his neck.

"It's me," he whispered into her hair. Her body relaxed. "Say something, please." He'd been reduced to begging.

She shook her head.

"Let's get you cleaned up. I gave you a vitamin shot and some morphine." Her dark eyes met his, full of pain.

He wanted to kiss her. He wanted to kiss her because she was Elana and he was Jon and there wasn't a camera. But he didn't because she was a mess and probably scared to death.

She slowly washed her hair. He hated how short it was. He'd always wanted to know what her long, black hair would feel like trailing across his chest and stomach.

"There aren't any cameras in here. It's not much," he said. "Not that I've had privacy for the last few months."

"Why?" She turned to face him, finally asking the question she'd wanted to know for six months. The water pounded on her back and she winced.

"Let's get you cleaned up while I try to explain."

She nodded.

Jon quickly washed her blood off his body as she watched him. He wished he knew what she was thinking. After he was done, he beckoned her to him, washcloth in one hand soap in the other. She leaned heavily into his body as he washed her arms and legs.

When he passed the washcloth gently between her legs, she gasped and her arms tightened around him.

"Damn it, Elana, I'm trying to be good."

"I wish I had the dress and lingerie I had when we were on the jet."

"I wish I'd thrown you on that bed. I also wish your back didn't look like hamburger. We need to get you cleaned up. You might need stitches."

"You wish you would have thrown me on the bed? Where? The jet?"

Would things have been different if he just would have had her back at the beginning? Would his mind have been on the job instead of her safety? He didn't know and he never would. He'd never second guessed himself before he met Elana. She was his weakness and he was tired of pretending she wasn't. She'd almost died. Either one of them still could.

"Let's get you bandaged," he said again as he lifted her. She immediately wrapped her legs around his waist.

Her voice was quiet, "I wanted you. You. On the jet. On the stage of the strip club. In that hallway. Why did you send me away?" Her voice shook and she couldn't hold back the tears any more.

He made her feel complete, full. She didn't care she was probably making a fool of herself. Watching Pete die, getting tortured, had a way of making you want to know the answers to life's burning questions.

"Because I wanted you," he said.

"That doesn't make sense," she argued.

Finally, Jon kissed her like he'd been wanting to. She melted in his arms, she exploded in his arms. Just like all those months ago, he rubbed against her. But this time they were naked and it wouldn't take much for him to slip inside.

"Please," she whispered and bit his tongue.

He wished she wasn't beaten and broken. He wished they were on U.S. soil, somewhere warm.

"Ah, fuck." He gave in and slid home. Life was too short to pretend he didn't want her. She tensed around him and threw her head back. "I can't believe how tight you are."

"It's been a long, long time," she said, eyes shut as though in pain.

"How long are we talking here? Weeks? Months?"

"Try years."

Holy shit. Years? The relief at knowing she hadn't had sex with Pete made him feel boneless.

"Why? You're attractive. I'm sure you've had offers."

"Do you really want to have this conversation right now?" she asked trying to get him to move inside her.

"Yes, I do. Normal people have these conversations."

"We're not normal, Jon."

"That's right. Say my name." He slammed into her and her eyes shot open. "Know it's me." Slam. "Not, Nikoli." Slam. "Not even Jon Matthews." Slam. "Jon Carter. Say it, Elana. Say my name." Slam.

"Jon," she sobbed. "Jon Carter."

The sound of his real name on her lips did funny things to his insides.

She was going to be the death of him.

28

Elana watched as Jon dismantled the camera.

"Are you sure that's the only one?"

"I've been in Mikhail's room and seen his camera system. He has one in every bedroom."

"Sick bastard," she mumbled.

"That's only the beginning," he said as he stepped down from the chair.

He grabbed the nurse's bag and pulled out the bandaging supplies. He gave her more morphine and also some penicillin so she wouldn't develop an infection. Shower sex had not been a good idea. He had been angry with himself when he'd seen more of her blood running down the drain.

She hadn't cared and told him so. She was going to savor every minute she could. She kept expecting to wake up and be in the basement with Pete's body. Jon was the only thing keeping her from losing it completely.

She winced as he put salve on her back. He couldn't figure out how to cover all the burns so he took gauze and wrapped her upper body like a mummy. Then he wrapped it again with bandages to hold everything in place. Next he wrapped her hand where Mikhail had put out his cigar. The skin was missing in a small circle with little blisters ringing it. Jon wanted to grind a cigar into Mikhail's face.

Since she didn't have any clothes, Elana put on one of Jon's button up shirts and stood in the middle of the room as though not sure what to do next. She couldn't sit in the chair or lay on her back on the bed.

Jon propped himself against the headboard, and patted his lap. She slowly climbed on the bed and found herself lying on her stomach, head resting on his leg.

He ran his fingers through her hair as he started talking. "Four months before I ever met you, I got suspicious about why the Novlaks were on the CIA and FBI radar, blatantly breaking the law, but nothing would stick to them."

She made a non-committal sound. The drugs in her system along with the comfort of his hands were going to be her undoing.

"I started following Kimball. I had a gut feeling he was feeding them information about busts and locations."

"Was he?" she asked.

"I'm sure of it, yet I never could get any evidence."

"AJ said you turned down partners before me. Why?"

Jon looked at where his hand was tunneled in her hair. The bedside lamp gave off enough light that hints of blue played over the strands. "I knew the others were rats. They would have reported back to Kimball about everything I did. They wouldn't have been able to handle it over here."

Elana moved until she was sitting, her shoulder against the headboard. "And me? I couldn't handle it over here so you sent me home."

"Lana, I," he was at a loss. "I don't know how to explain it."

"Try. I deserve that much. Your brother said you did it to protect me. That if you hadn't cared you would have let Boris and Enrique rape me and said it was part of the job."

"You talked to Michael? He said that?"

"He said a lot of things and gave me even more pieces to your screwed up jigsaw puzzle life. I've been waiting for months to ask you why. Been waiting for months to be with you and now I can't figure out where to begin."

"When did you talk to Michael?"

"Two weeks ago?"

"Are you asking me or telling me?" Jon said.

"My days are a little messed up. I don't know how long I've been here."

He pulled her into his arms. "I know, I'm sorry. My heart damn near stopped beating when I saw you fly out of the back of that SUV."

"You've been here the whole time? You saw Pete and me when we got here? Why didn't you do something?" She tried to get out of his arms, but her body and head hurt too much to fight him.

"I couldn't just waltz out and say 'hey, let go of my CIA buddies. That's not nice to beat them up.' I did what I could. I kept Gregor away from you. I hid the knife from your bra."

"That was you?"

"Yeah."

"You did what you could? Pete is dead!" She weakly pounded on his chest. She didn't blame him for Pete's death, she just didn't have Kimball to beat on.

"That green little shit deserved to die. He could have gotten you killed."

"One mission before Kimball sent him here, Jon. One. He didn't stand a chance. It's almost as bad as when Kimball sent me here with you."

"Okay. You were right. We need to start from the very beginning before we both get more confused."

Jon spent twenty minutes telling Elana about following her to her ballet class then being in Montana with Michael and Kamielle. He told her how he'd been such a dick when they started training because he was attracted to her. Part of him didn't want to tell her, although the realistic part of him knew getting everything out in the open was the only thing that was going to get them out of Russia alive.

"Michael was telling you the truth." He finally got to what she'd wanted to know from the beginning. "I've always been about the job. You know about the people who worked with me before you. How I feel about Pete's death. I don't feel that way about you. I couldn't keep you here and hope you wouldn't get hurt. My emotions screwed everything up from the beginning. It's why I don't show them."

He'd just bared his soul. At least as much of a soul as he had remaining.

"I might need more drugs if we're going to keep this up." She tried once again to move away from him.

"Nuh uh. I just told you more than I've ever told anyone other than my brother. Spill it, baby girl. What's been going on since I sent you back? You're a different person. You're not the green agent I trained. There's something dead in your eyes I never wanted to be there. What did Kimball do when you came back alone?"

Elana found it easier to talk when she didn't have to look at him. She started with admitting the first few months were a haze. She told him about the times she thought maybe it had all been a dream. Trying to get a hold of him, Kimball sending her on multiple missions a week, the few people she'd had to kill. That one caused her to cry and Jon held her while she got herself pulled together. She was raw, mentally and physically.

She took a drink of water. "I became the robot, Jon, the robot you told me I needed to be. Kimball didn't have to tell me why I was doing something; I just did it. My reputation was getting as bad as yours. AJ got back from South America and almost didn't recognize me."

Jon tensed as Elana told him about being poisoned and meeting Tippi.

"Kimball fucking poisoned you?" he finally said.

"I just told you about things missing from an R & D

lab and all you care about is AJ and I think Kimball may have poisoned me?"

"You know, with what you've told me, what AJ and Tippi know, and what Kimball did to Pete, I think I finally have enough to bring Kimball down."

Elana sat up quickly then cried out when the action pulled at the wounds on her back.

"What?" he demanded as she tried to push away.

"When Pete knew he was—" she stopped the sob trying to emerge.

"Yeah?" he prompted.

"He told me he recorded his conversations with Kimball."

"Holy shit. The boy did something right. Where are the recordings?"

Elana's shoulders dropped. "I don't know. He said something about Tippi but it doesn't make any sense. He was only at Tippi's house once." As though realizing something else, she covered her mouth.

"Now what?" Jon asked.

"We have to get a hold of AJ. I can get us out of here."

Jon waited expectantly as Elana smiled.

"I can get us out of here! AJ told the secure transport person who I was. Sgt. Jackson of the Marines gave us his call in number in case we missed the rendezvous. What day is it?"

"Last day of the month; April 30th."

"Pete and I were supposed to be out today. Jackson is going to know something is wrong when we're not back."

Jon shook his head. "I need to secure a phone. Everything here is bugged and I haven't been able to get to my stash because I'm always followed."

Elana's face fell. "I don't have the number. Pete memorized it."

Jon was going to tell her how stupid that was then changed his mind. She didn't need any more reminders about how wrong this whole mission had been.

"You said AJ set up the contact?"

"Well the transport was set up by Kimball but the Marines on board knew AJ. At least the sergeant did."

Jon thought about how to get into town with Elana.

"I'm still confused. Why did Kimball send us here?"

"I think Kimball knew I was on to him. If he's moved from just passing along information to selling bio-toxins, he needs everyone out of the way who might be able to link him to that. Kimball figured Pete would crack and give you up and then you'd crack and give me up.

"The Novlaks get to kill three CIA agents, I go down as a traitor, and life goes on for Kimball. Except now, AJ and Tippi have been dragged into it."

"If anything happens to Tippi, I'm going to feel responsible," Elana said.

"You did the right thing by having her learn self defense and shooting. She's going to be better off because you helped her."

"If you weren't such a lone wolf, none of us would be in this mess. I know for a fact AJ would have helped you from the beginning if you had gone to him. I also know we could have done this job together if you had let me stay."

Jon glared. "I already explained why I work alone."

"That's a bunch of bullshit."

"I can't concentrate with you around!"

Elana straddled his legs and scooted until she was sitting on his lap. She wasn't wearing underwear.

"Now you're being honest. Can't concentrate is a whole lot different than being worried about me. You distract the hell out of me, too."

"I've been honest since we started talking. I'm worried about you. That's dangerous for both of us!" he said.

His penis throbbed against the heat of her.

"Dangerous was wondering about you these last six

months. Wondering if you were even alive." She reached down and gripped him through his underwear and he hissed. "I was so angry. I should thank you, though. I never would have become such a heartless bitch if it weren't for you."

Jon wasn't sure what to do. She looked predatory. Looked like he'd felt in the shower. Maybe it was time to let her be in charge.

"Michael sent me pictures of you." Elana left on Jon's shirt to cover her bandages and cuts. She wanted him to see her as sexy.

"Pictures?" He was having a hard time concentrating.

"I know what you do for a living and I still want you. Want you more than my next breath."

"He told you what I do?"

"Pay attention, Jon. I've known what a bastard you were since I met you. Michael sent me your aliases and I still wanted you. I threw myself at you on that jet. It's you I want, Jon Carter, not the job. The man."

She hoped she was finally getting through to him. She'd almost died, could still die. She wanted to feel alive.

"What if one or both of us don't survive the next few days?" Elana balanced herself on her good hand so Jon could lift his hips and slide off his underwear.

"Don't think like that," he said on autopilot.

He didn't even register he was taking off what little clothes he had on until Elana winced and closed her eyes as she settled herself back on his lap.

"Damn it, Elana. Quit distracting me with sex."

"No," she said. "We could have been amazing months ago and now you're stuck with the broken version of me."

"You'll never be broken." He leaned forward, kissing her neck. "Just slightly bruised." She smiled as he kissed her cheeks, eyes, and nose. "I wish—"

"No wishes. Just now. Just what we have. If I learned anything after you were gone it was we have to take the moments given to us. Not figure we'll do it later. There isn't always a later." She lifted her hips and Jon slid into her.

They both froze as he gripped the side of her face, waiting for her to open her eyes.

"Okay, we'll live for the moment," he said.

He did his best to make love to her, except he'd never been good at slow and sweet. Since he couldn't wrap her in his arms or change their position, he let her take control.

It was control she needed. After months of feeling like she hadn't been the one making the decisions in her life, she celebrated the power.

When it was over, she fell forward onto his chest and cried. She wept for Pete, herself, and Jon. She wept for all the decisions she'd had to make that had led her to this point. She cried because she didn't know what she was going to do when Jon wanted to send her away again.

He looked at the clock. "You need to get some sleep. I know you're hurting. I'm not sure how many hours Mikhail will put up with not having video. He knows I'm not like Gregor and I don't do the pain thing. He's going to want to start passing you around."

"Let's fucking kill them all," she said into his chest.

"You have become heartless, haven't you?"

"Anything to get the job done, right?"

Jon didn't answer because there was nothing to say.

29

The door to the room splintered with the shriek from a woman. Jon immediately put his hand out and touched Elana's thigh. She wasn't the one screaming, so what the hell was going on?

Gregor's hulking frame loomed in the doorway and the body of a naked woman was sprawled in the fragments of door littering the floor. Talia.

Jon reached for his knife and slid the small one he'd taken from Elana's sheath into her hand. The lights blared on and Jon held up his arm to block the brightness.

"Oh, how sweet. You are sleeping. I told Mikhail you wouldn't know what to do with a woman. He let me have Natalia until I get Ellie. Natalia is done. I want the other one."

Natalia looked dead. She was covered in blood and bruises, her delicate face puffy, nose broken. Jon growled and leapt from the bed, grateful he'd slid his underwear on before falling asleep.

"Get out of my fucking room!"

Gregor and Jon circled each other like the predators they were. Elana stayed motionless on the bed, knife gripped in her good hand, eyes barely open. With the camera off, she figured they only had moments until someone came to see what all the commotion was about.

Gregor made a step toward the bed and Jon countered,

238

tossing the knife to his other hand.

"You've had your fun with the American whore, let me have her now." Gregor's words were slightly slurred.

"I'm not done with her," Jon said.

"You seem to care a lot about what happens to her. Don't think I didn't notice how you were more involved than usual. I do not think you are a dirty CIA agent.

"What will happen when I demand the American? Mikhail will give me the girl, you know he will. You don't want me to have her? Why?"

Jon didn't waste time talking.

"You treat this one like the one who was with you when you first got here. The one you said you disposed of because she was no longer worth your time. Mikhail was going to give me her, too, but you knew that, didn't you?"

Elana stiffened. Mikhail had given her to Gregor six months ago? Was that why Jon had really sent her away?

"I didn't need Natalia," Gregor said.

What was with Gregor tonight? The alcohol?

"Then why did you hurt her?" Jon demanded.

"You are like, what do Americans say? White knight? You had Natalia for months. I figured she must be special and maybe you would trade."

Jon glared, knowing he was going to have to explain all this to Elana. And Natalia. He just had to get them both out of the mansion first.

There was a gun in the closet, but he'd never get to it in time. He only gave Elana the knife to use in case something happened to him. He didn't want her to be completely helpless. That spurred him to action.

He lunged at Gregor, slicing the side of his face, then jumping back. Gregor swiped a meaty hand down his cheek and when it came away bloody he grabbed one of the bedside lamps, throwing it at Jon's head.

Jon ducked as the lamp shattered against the wall.

Gregor rushed him. Jon stepped and swiped his knife hand as he went by. Gregor's howl could have woken the dead. Guards would be coming any moment.

Talia moaned and twitched on the floor. She said Jon's name. He looked down and Gregor charged him again. Picked up by the brute and slammed into the wall, Jon lost his breath and the knife. Plaster crumbled around him as he fell to the floor. Shaking his head, trying to get his bearings, Jon watched Gregor go for the blade.

Elana moved to her knees then her feet. As Gregor backed up to lunge, Elana flew from the bed, her small knife gripped in both hands. She buried it at the base of Gregor's skull and the huge man dropped to his knees, then fell to the floor almost on top of Talia.

Jon stared at Elana. She gaped at Gregor's dead body.

Doors slammed against walls and feet pounded in the hallway. Jon ripped Elana's knife from Gregor's neck and threw it under the bed. He handed her his larger knife.

"Protect yourself and Talia. Cut me if you have to."

"What goes on?" Mikhail yelled.

Elana waved the knife around like a madwoman. "Get away from us!" She crouched over Talia.

"Natalia, my Talia!" Boris was at the door, too.

"Your jackoff moron of a bodyguard did this, Mikhail! I told you he was going to go too far one day. Call the nurse while I get the knife away from the American."

"How she even get knife? Gregor is dead?" Mikhail obviously hadn't been watching Gregor's bedroom camera.

"Look at this mess!" Jon demanded. "Gregor may have killed Talia because you let her go to his bed. He threw her through my door!"

Jon moved toward the women. Elana took the opportunity to slice his arm. He backhanded her and she cried out, dropping the knife.

He picked it up and put it to her face. "Am I going to

have any trouble from you?"

She shook her head vigorously, eyes wide.

"I didn't think so. Sit here without making a sound and I might let you live."

Mikhail grunted his approval.

The next hour was a blur. Elana climbed into bed and sat with her shoulder against the headboard, watching everything. Every once in a while Jon would meet her eyes then quickly look away.

The nurse came to the room and treated Talia like spun glass. She was dressed and bandaged. Her broken nose was set and she was taken back to her room. Boris went with her. Juan and Petrov took Gregor's body. Mikhail demanded, again, to know what had happened.

Jon wrapped his own arm so the nurse wouldn't see the slice had barely broken the skin. "I had the bitch drugged so I wouldn't have to worry about her trying to sneak out, not that she's going far with the wounds she has."

Jon finished wrapping his arm and stretched it out, drawing Mikhail's attention from Elana back to him.

"I was finally getting some sleep when Gregor busted down my door using Talia as his battering ram. What the fuck were you thinking, giving him a girl like her?" Jon hoped Mikhail wouldn't want to explain himself and he'd leave.

"I did not give her. She must have gone of own will. I know not what she thinking. Probably that this was first time you send her away from your bed."

Mikhail went for Elana and Jon intercepted. He dragged her to the bathroom, shoving her in and slamming the door.

"Why don't you set up the play room, Mikhail?"

Jon referred to the sex room Mikhail had on the other side of the basement. It was just another torture room as far as Jon was concerned.

"Give me two hours to clean up, drug Ellie a bit more

so some of the fight is out of her. Bring the boys. We'll teach her what happens to bitches who play with knives."

Mikhail smiled. "Enrique be happy."

"Yeah, well, Enrique can have her. I recommend he kills her when he's done. She's not worth it."

"You should let me take now," Mikhail said.

"Nope. You know I don't do the weird shit with the other guys. I get her a few more times. Two hours."

"Would you rather be in new room?"

"I like her in the bathroom. Nowhere she can go, lots of water to wash away the blood."

"You have streak I never knew there," Mikhail said stroking his mustache.

"It never came up," Jon said.

When Jon unlocked the door, Elana was waiting on the other side with a drawer from the vanity in her hands.

"Nice weapon."

She dropped her arms and closed her eyes. "I wasn't sure who would be coming through the door."

"We need to run. I wish I could give you more time to rest."

"I'll rest when we get wherever we're going. I want out of this place."

She went to the sink to wash Gregor's blood off her hands. It wasn't bothering her as much as it should have that she'd killed Gregor. She only wished he could have seen it was her when she plunged the knife in. That would have been a nice payback.

"We're going to sneak to Talia's room and get you some clothes. We're taking Talia with us."

Elana stopped washing and stared at him. "It's going to be hard enough to sneak out of here with me and I'm a trained operative. What is she? Nineteen? Not to mention half dead. I've become the heartless bitch and now you're the charity worker? She's been in your bed for the last six months? Really? What is she, your girlfriend?"

"No! Of course not. She's a maid and they sent her to me when I got here. I couldn't turn it down. The people they work with are horrible. I had to stick to character. By keeping her with me, I kept her safe."

She raised an eyebrow. "I don't know what's worse. That you said that or that you believe it."

He didn't try to explain. He hadn't been able to protect any of the other women paraded in and out of this place. Keeping Talia safe was the only thing he could do.

He opened the bathroom door an inch and looked out. The blood and door fragments were still there. Mikhail hadn't wasted any time going down to set up the room.

He quickly dressed and put his gun and extra clothes in a duffel bag. As much as he wanted the gun on, he couldn't use it in the mansion. A gunshot would let everyone know they were trying to get away. He reached out his hand for hers. She hesitated and he turned.

"I'm going to get us out of here," he said. "I'm going to get you stateside. Then I'm going to lock you in a room with me for a week. Keep that in mind." He kissed her hard.

She nodded and put her hand in his.

Jon handed her the duffel and secured his knife. Elana noticed her shredded bra in the corner. She grabbed it. When Jon looked at her questioningly, she slid the guillotine free of the fabric and balled it in her hands.

Jon looked down the hall. He hoped like hell Mikhail was in the basement and not watching the hallway cameras.

They snuck to the east wing without incident. Just as they were getting to Talia's room, the door opened.

"I be back in a moment, dear," Boris said in Russian. He had his cell phone pressed to his chest. When Talia's door was closed he put the phone to his ear. "I will be there."

He ended the call and straightened his suit. By the erection in his pants, he'd just been told about what was going to be happening in the basement.

"I hoped that by offering you up, they'd all go down there and give us time to get away."

"I don't know if I should be flattered or sickened I'm that important to them," Elana said.

They waited until Boris was out of sight before Jon went and tried the door handle. It turned easily. He let go of Elana's hand and pushed into the room. There didn't seem to be anyone there.

"Come on. Go to the closet, get dressed, and pack clothes for both of you. You're the same size."

Elana tried not to care he knew they were the same size while she found the closet.

"Maid my ass," Elana said to the rows and rows of designer clothes.

There weren't any jeans or tennis shoes. The best she could find were some slacks and tops that cost almost as much as her monthly paychecks. She was going to need to discuss this with Jon later. Maids didn't have rooms like this. Was she Boris's mistress?

Elana dressed quickly in Talia's clothes, putting the guillotine in her pants pocket. She threw more clothes and shoes in the bag.

Jon had Talia's naked body propped up on the bed. She was completely incoherent.

"Just carry her and let's get the hell out of here," Elana said.

She was right. He grabbed a robe from the back of the door and put it on Talia. He picked her up and headed for the main door.

"I'll go first, give me the knife," Elana said, hand out.

"You have to be in pain," Jon said.

"I was in pain for four days. Now I'm just numb. The farther we get from this place, the better I'm going to feel. Give me the goddamn knife and let's go." He handed her the knife. "Which way?" she asked.

"There's always a car parked outside the kitchen. Go down the main stairs and to your left."

Elana led the way quietly down the stairs. She expected Juan, Enrique, or Petrov to jump out at them from every door and corner. Her heart pounded in her ears and she could feel the throb in her wounds. When they reached the kitchen without incident, she almost broke into tears.

Jon used his chin to point at the door exiting the kitchen. "I've never seen a guard out there, but check anyway."

"I know," Elana said as she slowly made her way to the door. Their shoes clicked on the tile floor.

She looked out the curtain. There was a black car and there didn't appear to be anyone outside.

She nodded her head and he came to the door. "It's push-button start, so we don't need keys. We'll dump it as soon as we're in town."

"Isn't there a gated entrance and guard?" Elana asked.

"Yeah. Wait here while I take care of that."

Jon put Talia in the back seat and pushed Elana into the driver's seat. He took the knife from her hands and pulled his gun from the bag.

"If I'm not back in three minutes, leave."

"No," she said.

"Yes," he argued. "All of this has been to keep you safe. I won't let you die here."

"No, all of this has been to keep us safe. I just got you. I'm not losing you."

Jon kissed her. "Three minutes, Lana."

Then he turned and jogged into the darkness.

30

Elana slammed her palms into the steering wheel, the pain reminding her neither one of them were invincible.

It had been five minutes. "Three minutes? Even the great Jon Mathews, Jacobs, Carter, whatever the hell his name is, can't get rid of an armed guard in three minutes."

What if he didn't come back after ten? Could she drive away with Talia the slut in the backseat and leave Jon?

No.

Suddenly he was standing at the driver's door glaring at her. "I thought you could tell time."

"No watch," she said as she slid gingerly over.

He started the car and drove slowly down the driveway with the lights off. When they reached the gate, he drove through, jumped out to hit the button to close it, and got back in. He drove another mile with the lights off. When they hit pavement, he turned on the headlights and slammed his foot on the gas.

They traveled at breakneck speeds for almost half an hour. It was at least an hour until dawn and no people had been on the road. They'd had to dodge the occasional squirrel, rabbit, and cow though.

"What's the plan?" Elana asked when her heart had slowed and she was sure no one was following them.

Jon glanced at the clock. "I know Mikhail won't wait a

full two hours. He left my room forty-seven minutes ago. I figure we have another forty-five until he realizes we're gone. I have a locker at the train station with a sat phone, money, and passports. I only have one female passport, though."

"Can we buy another one?"

"There's no time. I'll find somewhere to stash Talia. Maybe she has family we can get her to. I'm getting you out of this country."

"Speaking of Talia, her closet—"

"Jonny?" Talia's scared voice said from the backseat. "Jonny is that you? Where are we?"

Jon pulled the car over. "Can you drive?"

"Well, yeah, but where to?" Elana was peeved at how quickly he dropped everything for that damn girl.

He pointed to the sign up ahead. "Those are the signs directing to the train station. Just follow them." He climbed in the backseat and Elana moved behind the wheel.

She listened as they spoke in Russian. Was there somewhere in the city she could hide? Gregor was dead and would never hurt her again. When Talia asked why the American whore was driving, Elana waited, holding her breath. What was Mr. Used-to-be-coldhearted-was-now-acting-like-a-girl going to say?

"Ellie has been abused just like you, Talia. I don't like that. I decided to take you both away tonight. I'm going to put you with someone you know and trust then I'm going to take Ellie to a church."

"Was, was Mikhail wrong about you all these months? Do you still work for the CIA?" She had just the right touch of whine and sex in her voice to make Elana feel like nails were running across a chalkboard.

"I work for myself, Talia. Always have, always will."

He wasn't giving anything away to Talia. Elana wouldn't say it out loud but she was impressed with how well he came up with lies on the spot. Made her wonder how many things he'd lied to her about.

She watched in the mirror as he helped Talia dress.

They were still ten miles from the train station when Elana pulled over on a side street. "We need to ditch the car."

"What does she mean? 'Ditch?' I do not understand," Talia said in English.

"We need to switch cars."

"Where are we going?" Talia asked.

"The train station," Jon said.

He gave Talia the bag to hold and picked an ancient truck to hotwire.

Talia and Elana eyed each other while Jon got the vehicle running. Before Elana could move, Talia climbed in the middle and smashed herself next to Jon. Elana carefully climbed in the passenger seat and slammed the door. She knew her back was bleeding through the bandages and hoped the black fabric of the shirt she'd put on would keep the blood hidden.

Riding in the truck wasn't nearly as comfortable as the luxury car. Elana had to bite her tongue a few times to keep from screaming as fire shot up her back with each bump.

Talia was almost sitting in Jon's lap as he tried to maneuver the truck and shift gears. Elana wanted to cry in relief when the train station parking lot came into view. Her body hurt so badly. Why wasn't Talia in pain?

Jon parked close to the entrance, surveying the few people. The sun was coming up. They should have time to get his stash, buy three tickets, and then the women could sleep. Hopefully the train would be gone before Mikhail noticed they were not at the mansion. He had the clout to call the station and keep the train from leaving St. Petersburg.

"I have no money." Talia started to cry.

Jon put his arm around her and Elana glared at him. She rolled her eyes and turned to open the passenger door. That's when Jon saw the back of her shirt was wet.

"You're bleeding," he said.

"No I'm not," Talia said.

Jon looked at her. "Not you, Ela-Ellie."

"I'm fine," Elana said and slid out of the truck.

She grabbed the duffel and shut the door knowing Talia would get out on Jon's side. She took a moment to stretch carefully.

Her burnt hand, feet, and rest of her body seemed to be okay. Elana was almost afraid to look at her back. She could tell the bandages needed to be changed. She dug in the duffel for more penicillin. The last thing she needed was an infection. She needed to stay on the ball since Jon was so sidetracked with Talia.

"Let me help," Jon said, Talia tucked under his arm.

"We're going to attract attention if Talia and I don't walk in there under our own steam. Go get your stuff from the locker and buy the tickets while we go to the bathroom and take care of this blood."

"I do not understand," Natalia said, clinging to Jon.

"I'm getting you out of this hellhole," he explained while stroking her hair. Elana looked away. She knew he was doing it to keep Talia calm, but she didn't have to like it. "Just trust me, okay?"

"Is she CIA like they all said?"

"No. She's a woman like you who was in the wrong place at the wrong time. I'll meet you both at the gate to board the train in fifteen minutes." He kissed the top of Talia's head.

Natalia smiled. Elana wanted to slap her.

If Talia hadn't been sleeping with Jon, Elana would have been fine with his behavior. She had the potential to become a screaming mass of scared female and that was not the type of attention they needed.

Elana started making her way to the stairs that would lead them into the big building. She sensed when Talia was finally following. They went through the doors and the air was warmer than outside, causing a chill to ripple over Elana's skin. It was painful.

"I know I have been difficult," Talia said quietly, coming up next to Elana. "I am scared."

Elana looked sideways. "It's okay. I'm scared too."

"Are you one of Jonny's women?"

Elana stumbled. What to say?

"After they tortured me, and killed, my boyfriend," Elana almost choked on the words. Pete's death seemed so recent yet a hundred years ago. "Jon took me to his room. He said he wanted to keep me safe from the men. Especially Gregor."

Talia blushed and looked away. Then she gently touched her nose. "I never thought Gregor would hurt me like this. I was trying to make Jonny jealous."

The women reached the bathroom. Elana checked each of the stalls and sighed in relief when they were empty.

"Let's make sure you're doing okay, first."

"Oh, no," Talia argued. "You are hurt much more than me. I cannot give shots, but I can do bandages. Remove your shirt. Should we lock the door?"

"Yes."

Natalia locked the door as Elana removed her shirt. The blood had dried in some places and stuck to the bandages, pulling on it and, in turn, her skin. She winced.

"What caused this?" Natalia asked, horror in her eyes.

"Metal bed frame with electricity."

"You were really tortured?"

"It wasn't pretend torture," Elana said. What the hell did Natalia think went on in the basement? "They killed my boyfriend. Well, I guess he wasn't my boyfriend. He was undercover CIA and used me."

Elana teared up again. It would help her cause with Natalia, except it wouldn't do any good to start crying over

Pete. There'd be plenty of time to cry later.

Natalia didn't say a word as Elana dug in the duffel bag. She popped some pain pills, offering the bottle to Natalia. The other woman took a pill with water from the sink as Elana had.

Elana made muffled noises as Talia cleaned and bandaged her back. Not being able to rest and then riding in the car and truck had taken its toll. There were angry red marks starting to run over her shoulders and toward her arms. She had an infection.

Ignoring the pain, she had Talia grab her a new shirt from the bag. As Talia chose one, Elana remembered the amazingly stocked closet.

"You have some great clothes for a maid," Elana said.

"Oh, I am not a maid," Talia said. Then she whipped her head up and locked eyes with Elana in the mirror.

"I didn't think so," Elana said.

Talia transformed before Elana's eyes. The stoop to her shoulders was gone, her face became hard.

"Why couldn't you just leave everything alone? Better yet, why couldn't you have died in the basement with your boyfriend? Why does Jonny want you?" Talia's Russian accent was almost gone. "Daddy told me I could have Jonny. He has been mine since he got here and I will not share."

"Daddy?" Elana said.

"Yes, daddy. Boris." Shit. Elana hadn't seen that coming. "Then you show up and he's suddenly interested in the basement. Wouldn't let me sleep in his bed. He was the best sex I ever had besides Gregor."

Elana shuddered at that comparison.

Talia still had her hand in the bag. Instead of pulling out a shirt, she pulled out the gun.

"Are you even hurt?" Elana asked.

Talia put a hand to her face. "That bastard was rough last night. Things were going like usual, except he was drinking, and he hardly ever drinks. The more he drank, the more upset he got about the thought of Jonny having you. He hit me a few times and when I tried to get away, he carried me to Jon's room. That's the last thing I remember."

Elana took the opening. "I don't know what you think is going on. Jon took me to his room. There was no sex. He just wants to save the two of us."

Talia smiled. "You lie."

"No. You need to tell him you're Boris's daughter, not a maid. He'll return you to the mansion and take me to the church. Please let me get away from this place!" Elana put her scared, American acting into gear.

"I don't want you away, I want you dead."

Luckily Talia didn't appear to know how to use a gun. She was pointing it at Elana, but the safety was on. She pulled the trigger. When nothing happened she cursed in Russian.

Elana supposed she should feel lucky Talia had taken the time to help her clean up and re-bandage her back.

She kicked and knocked the gun from Talia's hands.

In a huff, Talia threw the bag at Elana's head. Were they really going to fight like girls? Elana punched Talia in the nose, causing the younger woman to cry out. She dropped to her knees clutching her bleeding face.

Elana turned to unlock the door and give Jon a piece of her mind.

"I watched him fuck you. Why did you lie to me?" Talia's voice was full of pain and anger.

Elana stopped and turned slowly. "You sit in a room with your sick uncle and watch sex tapes?"

"Maybe I should take you back to the house and make you watch the hours and hours of Jonny and me."

Elana knew Talia was trying to piss her off. Damn it, it was working.

She walked back to Talia. Suddenly she didn't care Talia was an untrained girl, she wanted to kick her ass.

When Elana was a few feet away, Talia exploded from the bathroom floor. She wasn't fighting like a girl. Elana was quickly backed against the door after a series of roundhouse kicks and punches. What the hell?

Out in the main area of the train station, Jon stared into an empty locker. Empty. His money, his weapons, his passports. Gone.

"Damn, I'm dumb," Jon said, leaning his head against the metal door. The only person he'd ever brought from the mansion had been Talia. She had sat in the car when he'd stashed his stuff in the locker. She'd stood near the pay phone the few times he had tried to reach Michael and AJ.

She was the only common denominator.

Elana was right, he did think with his dick. He just hoped he hadn't gotten Elana killed.

He slammed the locker and ran toward the bathrooms.

31

Since AJ had his phone synced through the speakers of the Jag, Tippi was hearing every horrible thing being said. To her credit, she hadn't made a sound, but there were going to be teeth marks on her fist from trying to keep silent.

"Tell me again," AJ said to Sgt. Jackson, not really wanting to hear it.

"Chatter is the Novlaks have the body of an agent. Your tasty treat, Elana, never met our rendezvous point two days ago and I didn't get a call. No one is saying if the body is male or female. How many agents you got over here?"

"Three that I know of," AJ said.

"Well, the good news is only one is dead."

Tippi made a sound and AJ rubbed her thigh.

"Jax, I'm going to call in my favor."

Aden 'Jax' Jackson sighed heavily. "Damn you, Jensen, I knew you were going to do this to me. As soon as I saw that woman's ass, I knew she was going to be trouble."

Tippi glared at AJ through her tears. That was okay with him, anger he could handle. Tears? Not so much.

"Shut up, Jax. Elana isn't mine. She's Jon Matthews's." AJ waited a beat for that information to sink in. "I'm hoping the dead agent isn't one of them."

"The Novlaks have had a new player on the team. Jon Jacobs. Is that Matthews?"

"Pretty sure," AJ said.

"Wow." The silence weighed heavily.

AJ couldn't handle it anymore. "Damn it, Jax! He's been there almost seven months and I haven't asked for you to interfere. You owe me."

"You know this will take a few days. Maybe a week."

"I'll be there as soon as I can," AJ said.

"I'll be in touch." Jax disconnected.

"What do you mean you'll be there as soon as you can? You can't go to Russia!"

Tippi had made AJ stay in the safe house for a full two days. He didn't have much mobility in his arm. She wanted him in a hospital with a surgeon checking for muscle, nerve, and tissue damage. He wouldn't do it. She had even withheld sex, telling him until she knew he was okay she wouldn't risk hurting him. He still wouldn't budge.

She was mad as hell. "Are you just going to take off and leave me here? Who's going to take care of your arm?"

"You're going with me."

"I can't go to Russia!"

"Do you have a passport?"

She nodded.

"Are you up to date on all your shots?"

She nodded again.

"Then you can go."

When she glared and opened her mouth to protest, AJ cut her off. "I feel safer having you with me and knowing what's going on. I'll just be worried about you the whole time I'm over there. Besides, you've already put in for the whole month of May for vacation." Then he threw down his last card. "And, if Elana and Jon are hurt, you can help fix them."

She crossed her arms.

"Damn it, Tippi, please!"

"Fine. But don't think you're always going to be able to fucking strong arm me into doing everything you fucking want!" The problem was it had worked so far every time.

AJ was so stunned by her cussing he almost ran off the road. She was either really pissed or just trying to see if she could get a rise out of him.

"We need to go to my house and then my lab."

AJ nodded.

AJ's headlights reflected off the windows of her house as he pulled into the driveway.

Tippi got out to open the garage door using the keypad. When the door was halfway up, she ducked down and walked under. She heard AJ yell something, but was tired of arguing with him. She went to the keypad to shut off the alarm and noticed the red light wasn't flashing to show the countdown of seconds she had left to disarm it. The red light was solid which meant the alarm was already off.

A meaty arm wrapped around her waist and something cold pressed to her temple. "Well hello, doctor. I've been waiting all day for you to get home."

Tippi swallowed a scream. Screaming wasn't going to help. She needed to be calm.

"Why didn't you pull your car in?" the man asked.

"Because she wasn't driving," AJ said from the garage door, gun in his left hand. When he'd seen legs in the garage, his heart had almost come out of his chest.

AJ knew how to shoot with both hands. He was right-handed, though, and he couldn't lift his goddamn right arm to shoot the bastard that was using Tippi as a shield. He didn't know if he felt confident enough to shoot left handed without hitting her.

The man holding Tippi cursed and his breath stunk of beer and cigarettes. She was not going to be killed by someone stinking of beer and cigarettes.

Tippi slammed her heeled foot down on the man's instep. He yelled and a loud noise sounded right next to her ear. She screamed and jammed her elbow back into his large stomach. He let out a whoosh and dropped something as he tried to run into her house. Wood splintered behind her. She dropped to the cement floor trying to crawl to AJ.

"Tippi! Tippi!" AJ was whispering.

She looked at his face. He didn't look like he was whispering. He looked like he was yelling.

"Goddamn it, Tippi, say something."

AJ was on his knees in front of her. He was holding her head and she could barely hear him. That's when she remembered the loud noise. She looked back and saw a gun on the ground. AJ's hands in her hair hurt so she swatted at him. He moved his hands to her face then her shoulders.

"Can you hear me?" he asked.

She closed her eyes and concentrated on being calm. She had a horrible buzzing in her ears, especially her right ear. That man had put a gun to her head. Her eyes shot open.

AJ ran his hands down her arms then they were back in her hair.

"What are you doing?" she asked a little too loudly.

"The gun went off," AJ said. "The fucking gun went off right by your head. I thought for sure the son of a bitch shot you. Did he shoot you?" It was like he was incapable of keeping his emotions in check when it came to her.

"I don't think so," Tippi said slowly. She put her hands over AJ's. "My ears are just ringing. I think he accidentally pulled the trigger when I stepped on his foot." She opened her eyes. "Stop moving your right arm so much. You're going to pull out your stitches."

"I'm fine," he argued. Then he kissed her. She leaned into him, wishing life were back to normal. She just wanted her life back. She dropped her head from his.

"I'm sure he's long gone by now, but I need to check things out." AJ picked up the gun the man had dropped. He checked the chamber and clip, handing it to Tippi. "Sit here and watch the door. I need to pull the car in."

"Should I touch this? Don't we need to give it to the police?"

"I'm more concerned with you being protected than fingerprints. He was wearing gloves, anyway."

He was? How did AJ notice that? Damn, she should have noticed, too.

She held the gun on the door while AJ pulled the car in. He wondered if anyone in suburbia had heard and reported two gunshots since it was the middle of the night.

Tippi was looking at her door. "Did you shoot, too?"

"Hell yes, I shot! As soon as your head was clear of his. Damn it, I was shaking so bad I missed."

She smiled. "You're not perfect, AJ."

"Yeah, well I should be when your life is on the line." He pulled his gun back out. "I want you to sit right here while I go sweep the house. I'll knock on the door before I come back out. If this door opens without knocking, put as many rounds as you can into whoever comes through."

Before she could argue, he slipped inside. She sat on the cold concrete, staring at the door for what felt like an hour. There was still a ringing in her right ear. Finally, there was knocking on the door. AJ stood there, her dark avenging angel. His face was back to being a mask.

"What?" she asked as he helped her from the floor. She looked past him into the ruins of her kitchen and living room. Her house was trashed.

Every cupboard was open, dishes and glasses broken on the counters and floors. Pictures had been ripped off walls, canvas sliced open. Holes punched in sheet rock.

AJ kept waiting for her to scream, cry, something. She stood and surveyed the destruction in total silence. It wasn't until she looked up stairs that her face showed any emotion.

"My office?"

"Same," he said.

"My bedroom?"

A small tick developed in his eye. "Seems the jerk had a little too much fun going through your bras and underwear but your clothes and shoes seem okay."

"What was he looking for?"

"My guess is as soon as you called in for vacation, whoever's been stealing from your lab panicked. They came here looking for data. And you." His eye twitched again.

"Everything's at the lab or in my head," she said, once again confirming his worst fears. The man who had been in her house hadn't been sent to kill her, he'd been sent to abduct her.

"Pack some clothes. Then we'll go to your lab."

She sucked in a breath when they reached her bedroom, but still didn't freak out. She silently went to the closet and found her big suitcase under a pile of clothes that had been ripped off the hangers. She packed clothes and then toiletries. Finally AJ couldn't handle her silence.

"Say something," he said.

She looked at him. "Like what?"

"I don't know. I expected you to go all weepy female on me. You don't seem to care he destroyed your house."

She frowned at him. "Of course I care. I don't have to cry about it, though. I've never liked this house, AJ. I'm upset someone was in my personal things. Upset a man I don't know stood in my room and touched my stuff. But everything is just that. Stuff. All those pictures downstairs can be replaced. Walls can be fixed. It's just a dumb house." She was more upset she didn't have anything personal.

"Then why do you live here?"

"Is this really the time for you to hear my life story?"

"What else do we have to do?"

"Oh, I don't know. Figure out who's stealing from my lab and save Jon and Elana's butts?"

"We're doing that. We have to talk about something while we drive around. And it's a long ass flight to Europe."

Tippi finally smiled. "You're doing it again."

"What?"

"Strong arming me to get your way."

"I'm not strong arming you. I'm participating in polite conversation."

Tippi rolled her eyes and finished putting the last item in her suitcase. AJ hefted it in his left hand. "Tell me about the house. Tell me about your mother."

They walked to the garage. She set the alarm, as silly as that seemed, as he put the suitcase in the backseat. When they were in the car, Tippi started talking.

She gave him the brief version of growing up without a father, but a number of rich stepfathers. She told him about her mother's need for money over affection. She left out how hurt she still was about her mom's lack of love.

"Your mom sounds kind of like a bitch," he said.

Tippi couldn't help it, she laughed. "Sometimes. But, you know, I never went without. The men she shacked up with or married had money. Lots of money. It was a horrible childhood, but I got a great education out of the deal."

"How many times has your mom been married?"

Tippi thought about it for a moment. "Um, seven? I didn't go to the last three because they were in other countries and I had work."

AJ stared, forehead wrinkled. The street lights let her see his expression.

"I know, right? She's not just the b-word, but maybe a little bit of an s-l-u-t."

AJ laughed because she wouldn't say bitch or slut but she'd dropped the f-bomb earlier. He was getting ready to pick on her about it when his phone rang.

"Jax. What have you got for me?"

"No intel. However, I can get you on a jet out of New York tomorrow. It will get you to London. After that, you're on your own."

"London's fine. I need two seats."

"Two?" Jax asked.

"Two. I'll email you the information as soon as I have access to an encrypted site. By the way. I need you looking into something else for me. I've got a good lead we might have stumbled onto a smuggling operation. Bioweapons. Do some discreet digging for me, would you."

Jax whistled. "When you said you were calling in your favor, you really meant it."

"You still owe me. It's a pretty big debt."

"Yeah, yeah. I'll see you in London. Bye."

"What's the debt?" Tippi asked quietly. She'd shared her secrets; he could share some of his.

"So Jax and I were on a mission about ten years ago and he's trapped by some pretty heavy fire. I killed some people, busted down a door or two, and saved his ass. Carried him five miles through the desert to get him to safety."

"Why are you calling in the favor now?"

AJ lifted her hand and kissed her fingertips. "Because, my dear, I know I need Jax's help to keep you safe."

Blood rushed to her ears and butterflies settled in her stomach. She held his hand as they drove the rest of the way in silence to the CIA building. After a brief search and declaring their weapons, the guard let them through. It had started to rain so AJ pulled as close to the doors as he could. He didn't want to go into the parking garage in case they needed a quick exit.

Tippi opened the car door. She felt like she was on the verge of a new life, something scary and exciting. She wanted her life back, but she couldn't imagine it without AJ. She shook her head. She'd always been smart, boring, Tippi Aldridge. Nothing exciting ever happened to her except the time she'd aced a molecular chemistry final.

Ever since AJ had hurricaned into her life, it had been far from boring. And, Tippi realized suddenly, she wouldn't have it any other way. Death threats, stealing from her lab. It would all be happening. Since she had AJ, everything would be fine. He'd keep her safe.

She stopped him before they entered the building and kissed him. They stood in the mist, Tippi standing on tiptoes, arms wrapped around him.

"What was that for?" he asked when she let go of his lips with her own.

"Because I can do anything when I'm with you. Because you make me feel beautiful, smart, safe, and strong."

AJ stared at her, but didn't respond. Then he turned and used his key card to let them in the building. He hoped he was able to keep her safe.

It was dark and quiet since normal office hours were over. Deeper in the building they had to go through another guard check.

Tippi's office came into view.

"Marcus is here," she said in surprise as they noticed him sitting in a chair. He didn't get up when they moved closer to the windows.

"What the fuck?" AJ said.

Marcus wasn't sitting in the chair. He was taped to it. His eyes were wide and scared. He kept staring at Tippi and AJ then down at the floor. He was trying to bounce the chair to the door and even through the duct tape covering his mouth they could see his lips moving.

The explosion blew the huge glass windows out of Tippi's lab.

AJ was thrown into the opposite wall, Tippi to the floor.

Black smoke filled the hallways as the fire alarm went off and the sprinkler system came on.

Neither one moved as the guard came running.

32

Talia screamed as she kicked Elana in the face. The contact caused her head to slam back against the bathroom door. She fought dizziness. Where had the slut queen learned to fight like this? Had to be Mikhail and Boris's doing.

Shit. Boris's daughter. How could he have let his daughter just go around sleeping with the house guests? And evil people, at that. Peace offering? Sweetening the pot? As Talia's foot came back up, Elana decided she needed to pay attention to what was going on in front of her, not why the crazy Russians were so crazy.

"You bitch. I will kill you and have Jonny."

Now it was Elana's turn to do the talking. "Oh, Talia," she goaded. "Your Jonny has been using you as a distraction. Have you noticed how much you and I look alike? He had you because he couldn't have me. I bet he drank a lot before carting you off to bed, didn't he?" Elana was making it up but knew she was right when Talia's eyes opened wide and her mouth made a little 'o' of surprise.

"What do you mean?"

"Jon and I are both CIA, Talia. Good CIA. Not two-timing like your dad and uncle think. Jon's been here making the best case ever to put them both in jail until they rot."

"You lie, again."

"You watched. Did it really look like he was raping me? Did I look like I was fighting back?" Elana couldn't remember all that had happened that first night. She knew Jon had tried to shield her body and she hadn't fought the way she would have if she had been hauled to another room.

Pounding came on the door. "Talia? Ellie? Come on, girls, we need to go." It was about time Jon showed up.

Elana went to unlock the door and Talia punched out, slamming her against it again.

"I'm going to kill you!" Talia screamed as she charged and wrapped her hands around Elana's neck.

Jon debated wasting the precious seconds to pick the lock and not make a scene or just bust the door down. He looked around. A few people milled near the ticket counter, but the early morning offered a lack of audience.

When he heard someone crash against the door again, and Talia scream something about killing, he knew his mind had been made up for him. He slammed his shoulder into the door and the flimsy lock gave easily. The door, though, was being held shut by the two women. He pushed against it again and heard Elana cry out in pain.

Elana pushed at Talia's chest to try and get away from the door slamming into her back. It opened just enough for Jon to get his head through and take in the situation before Talia slammed her back again.

Jon held the door with his weight and slipped inside. He punched Talia in the face and she let go of Elana, sliding to the floor, knocked out.

Elana coughed and sputtered as she fell. "If I hadn't been tortured almost to death, the slut queen wouldn't have been a problem. I can't believe a girl almost kicked my ass."

Jon laughed as he slid Talia's body out of the way to get to Elana. He knelt on the floor next to her. "So my locker is empty. Talia's been playing me from the beginning."

"Gee, you think?" Elana said rubbing her neck. "I can

one up you." Jon raised an eyebrow. "She's Boris's daughter."

"Whoa? Really? Shit. That's screwed up."

"I can't believe you thought she was a maid. Did you ever see her do anything in the mansion?"

Jon racked his brain. "No. I guess not."

"Men. You are so predictable. You always think with your dicks. They sent her to you hoping you'd slip up."

He shrugged.

"I can't believe you slept with her for six months."

"She looks like you," he said quietly. "I'd get drunk and pretend she was you."

Elana's eyes jumped to his. That's why Natalia had looked shocked; Elana had been right. Double damn. Not that that made it okay.

Talia screamed from the floor and kicked Jon in the head. He fell to the side and Talia went for the gun that had been knocked from her hands earlier.

Elana put her hands on her thighs to sit up and felt something in her pocket. The guillotine. She grabbed the small roll of wire and wrapped the protected ends in her hands. She was straddling Talia's back and wrapping the weapon around her neck twice before the thought had even completed. The bitch had slept with Jon, she was not going to kill him.

It didn't take long for Talia to die. The wire cut quickly, severing her trachea. Blood was coating the floor when Jon lifted Elana from Talia's body.

"You're okay, it's okay." Jon said in her ear.

Elana hadn't realized she was crying. She looked down at the dead woman. She'd killed someone else. In the span of a few hours she'd killed two people with her bare hands.

She turned to Jon. "I've become you, haven't I?"

He grabbed the duffel and fished out a shirt. He put it on her to cover the bandages that were bleeding again, then pushed her toward the door.

He grabbed the gun and unwrapped the guillotine from Talia's neck. He rinsed it in the sink and threw both weapons in the bag. He felt the reassuring sheath of his knife before he zipped the bag closed.

"Check to see if anyone's nearby," he said.

She poked her head out, not believing a single woman hadn't needed to use the bathroom. "Clear."

Jon snuck out, handing Elana the bag. He quickly went to the custodial closet next door and pulled out yellow cones and a cart, placing them in front of the women's bathroom door. He scoured the closet for anything else useful and found a length of chain and a padlock on a shelf. Using the hole in the door from the lock, he chained the door shut. Then he put a yellow cone in front of the men's bathroom door. He pulled Elana into the bathroom with him.

A man was at the urinal and he met their gazes in the mirror. Jon winked and smiled at him as he pushed Elana into a stall. The man quickly zipped, flushed, and fled the bathroom. Jon locked the door behind him.

"What are we doing?"

"I always keep more than one stash."

He picked away at a brick under the bank of sinks. When one brick was free, he pulled out five more. The mortar had been replaced with clay five months ago when he realized he couldn't make a move without the Novlaks finding out about it.

He pulled out a bag with American currency, British pounds, and Russian Rubles, passports for him and Elana, Mr. and Mrs. Smith, and another gun.

Elana took the bag and looked through. Her picture was on the Angela Smith passport. She glanced at Jon.

"I had them made when we came over," he shrugged.

"Did the passport in your locker have my picture?"

"No. That one just had a name and no picture. It was ready to be made. I didn't trust that hiding spot like this one."

Jon eyed her. "We need to get you cleaned up again."

"No. We need to get on that train."

He nodded and they left. Elana stared at the chain on the bathroom door. "Did she really deserve to die? She was a kid doing what her daddy and uncle wanted her to."

He kept walking but gripped her hand tighter. "Lana, I taught you all those months ago. It's them or you, no matter how old they are or what you think they have or haven't done. We're alive. She would have killed one or both of us."

He glanced at his watch. The train left in ten minutes. Hopefully Mikhail would wait the full two hours Jon had originally demanded.

Jon bought their tickets while Elana leaned heavily on him. She was starting to crash. Her whole body hurt, she was running a fever, and she was so tired.

Jon paid top dollar for a sleeper car. He didn't care they were taking the long train. Mikhail would expect him to take the fast train. That would be the one they would send people to check first. Jon wanted a bed and privacy. The twelve hour trip would be a godsend.

He half carried Elana, carefully maneuvering her through the aisles. He noted the phone stations that were available. How far was Mikhail's reach? If Jon called AJ or Michael, would Mikhail be able to track it? Not willing to risk his friend or brother, Jon dropped the idea. He'd call as soon as they were out of Russia. Mikhail was too powerful.

As soon as they were in their berth, he stripped her and put her face down on the bed.

"You deserve a black eye," she mumbled.

Jon glanced in the mirror. Yep, Talia's kick to his face had given him a small bruise. "Lana—"

"Just promise me you'll quit thinking with your dick," she said as he removed the blood-soaked bandages.

He kissed her neck. "I promise to only think with my dick when you're around."

"You're impossible."

"Only where you're concerned."

He filled the ice bucket with warm water and cleaned her back. It looked worse than yesterday. There was no way she was going to be able to heal if he didn't keep her prone and relaxed.

"It's infected," he said through clenched teeth.

"I noticed that earlier," she mumbled. He almost couldn't understand her.

"Sleep, Lana, I'll be here the whole time."

She didn't answer.

Jon gave her more antibiotics and pain shots. Looking at the locked door, chair propped under for extra support, he stripped and climbed on the bed with her. He allowed himself to fall into sleep.

The rocking of the train helped to keep her sleeping. Jon woke after four hours. He showered and shaved, glad to be free of the Novlak Mansion.

He knew there were going to be people waiting for them when they got to Moscow. Mikhail was going to have twelve hours to gather his forces and spread the word Jon was to be terminated on sight.

How to proceed was the question.

Jon gave Elana more shots and then climbed back in bed. She hadn't moved a muscle.

After another four hours, Jon woke her. He kissed her temple and moved her hair. "How are you doing?"

She groaned.

"I don't think you should take a shower, so I thought I could help you wash your hair and clean up a bit."

"I don't know if I can move," she admitted.

It took some time, but he helped her get to the edge of the bed. She felt like hot coals were rolling across her back.

"The drive really took its toll on you, didn't it?"

"Yeah."

"Your infection looks a little better and some of the smaller cuts are starting to scab."

"That's good." Her eyes met his. "I never in a million years expected you to be so hands on and caring."

Jon frowned.

"When I first met you, you didn't show emotion. What gives?"

"I don't know. I don't like it, but I feel responsible for making sure you're safe. I've never cared about taking care of anyone except my sister and brother. Then my sister had kids and they became part of the safety group. Then Michael married Kamielle. Then I met AJ."

"You're like the Tin Man, Jon, or the Grinch. You found your heart." She tried to smile.

"I don't like it."

"Yeah, you said that."

Elana stood and made sure she wasn't going to fall on her face before shuffling to the bathroom. She let the conversation drop. She liked the 'new' Jon, and didn't want to push it and scare him away.

He came in behind her. She had never been naked in front of a man so much and she wasn't used to it. But when she tried to cover up, Jon took the towel away.

"It's nothing I haven't seen before. Besides, you need to let your back dry out for a bit and I don't want you to make yourself bleed by rubbing material on it."

Elana let him help wash her hair and take a sponge bath. She was still having trouble putting this man in the same box with the one she'd trained with. She had a picture of Jon Matthews in her head and this wasn't it.

"That's it," she said while she was brushing her hair.

"What?" Jon asked.

He was looking at her like maybe she'd lost her mind. Considering they hadn't spoken for the last fifteen minutes, he had probably been deep in thought as well.

"You're Jon Carter."

He stared at her like she was crazier.

"Okay. You've always been Jon Matthews to me. This is the real you, isn't it? Jon Carter. Caring, loving."

"Still a highly trained killer and assassin," he said while turning his back to her.

"I wasn't questioning your manliness, I just think I understand. It's got to be hard pretending to be someone you're not."

It didn't matter anymore. She already knew who he was. "It's been hell looking at myself in the mirror for the last four months, Lana. I didn't know who I was. I didn't know if I was going to be able to come back from this one."

She moved him toward the bed. "Just lay with me and hold me. Tell me things you need to say but haven't had anyone to say them to."

"I've had plenty of conversations with you in my head. Maybe that's why I was so fucking scared when I realized you were here. I couldn't imagine the thought of you under the same roof with them. Those men are lower than the scum of the earth. I've never met two people more fucking evil than the Novlak brothers. And I've been around some really sick bastards over the last twenty years."

Elana laid down and Jon crawled in next to her.

"How long do we have?" she asked quietly.

"About four more hours until we arrive in Moscow. There's going to be people waiting for us, you know that, right?"

She nodded.

"I've got a plan, but I want you to sleep at least two more hours. You need the rest."

"I never doubted you had a plan."

"When we get to the states, I'm taking you somewhere far away from Virginia."

"After we take care of Kimball," she said.

He clenched his teeth.

"Jon, after we take care of Kimball we'll go somewhere." She tried to get up but he wouldn't let her. "You're going to try and take him down alone, aren't you? When are you going to learn you don't have to do everything alone? Damn you!"

He tried to make peace. "First I'm going to take you to the ranch so you can meet Michael, Kamielle, Julie and her family. Then I'm thinking Hawaii. Still in the States but tropical."

"Michael," she groaned into the pillow.

"I'm Jon, thank you," he said.

"No," she turned her head. "I forgot to tell you something Michael said."

"What?"

"He said I had to save your ass and bring you home because you're going to be an uncle again."

"Holy shit. I wonder if he means Kamielle and him?"

"Why is that so shocking?"

"She had an accident when she was married before. The doctors didn't think she'd be able to have kids."

"That would be wonderful if she could," Elana said. "I'll never have kids." She closed her eyes.

"I'll get you home, Lana."

She smiled. "Even if one of us dies, it's been amazing."

"Don't fucking talk like that," he said as he moved a lock of wet hair from her forehead.

"Oh, Jon, knock it off. You're the one who taught me the job means death. People like us don't live to be one hundred."

How many times had Jon said that exact same thing?

33

St. Petersburg, Russia

Boris knelt in the pool of congealed blood surrounding Talia. He cried and wailed openly while Mikhail yelled at the security guard. Petrov was taking care of bribing the police while Juan and Enrique were locating the person who could show them video footage of the station.

"What kind of place is this that you don't notice when someone is killed violently?" Mikhail demanded.

Boris wailed louder.

"Sir, the train comes in from Finland. After crossing the border and going through inspection, it is the earliest one. Most people stay on the train to sleep and only a few board. That is the slow train. The fast train leaves thirty-five minutes after that. The big crowd comes in later to board the fast train." He took a breath to say more.

Mikhail pulled out a gun. "I will find someone to do your job."

He shot the security guard in the head. Then he turned the gun on the custodian. Mikhail fired once more and the custodian's body dropped not far from the security guard.

"Call someone to clean this mess."

Mikhail gave Enrique instructions to have Talia's body taken back to the mansion. He also asked Enrique to take

Boris home as well.

"There will be payback, brother," Mikhail said.

Mikhail clenched his fists. How could he have been so wrong about Nikoli? What had been his American name? Jon Jacobs, yes, that was it. Six months. The rat-bastard had lived under his roof for six months. He had to die before he made it back to the United States. He knew too much.

While Petrov made sure the bathroom mess was taken care of, Juan took Mikhail to the control room and they looked over security footage. Since hardly anyone had been in the station, they were quickly able to locate Ellie and Talia going to the bathroom together. They watched Nikoli go to the row of rentable lockers. Mikhail had to laugh. Juan looked at him.

"When Nikoli first got here, Talia told me of him coming to the train station. She snuck in and watched as he put items in this locker. I had Gregor come get them. Money and passports, nothing to be worried about."

"Maybe you should have been worried," Juan said.

Mikhail glared. If the damn foreigners weren't so useful, he would have put bullets in their heads long ago.

The video showed Nikoli go to the women's bathroom and bust down the door. They watched him chain the door closed and drag a limping Ellie into the men's bathroom.

"Go check," Mikhail demanded of a security guard.

The man operating the video footage showed Mikhail and Juan the two buying tickets and then leaving.

"I want to know where they bought the tickets to and what train they are on!"

It took almost half an hour of precious time before someone finally worked up the courage to tell Mikhail what they learned.

Nikoli was probably Mikhail's most worthy adversary.

"Sir, the bathroom had bricks missing. Looks like some kind of hiding spot." Mikhail nodded for the man to continue. "The ticket counter shows there were ten different tickets purchased." The guard swallowed as he watched Mikhail's face turn red. "There are tickets to five different locations, sir. Three in Russia and two in Finland."

Mikhail cursed and knocked papers and computer monitors off desks. He attacked the guard who had delivered the information, beating him to a bloody pulp until Juan pulled him off.

"Get your emotions under control," Juan demanded. "You will not find Jon Jacobs and the woman this way. Call Kimball. It is time to start cleaning up and cut our losses."

Mikhail stood, chest heaving. "You do not tell me what to do!" He fingered the gun at his side.

"I have been with you for five years, Mikhail. You have never been this worked up. Admit he is smarter and better than you and move on." Juan was walking a tightrope. Mikhail's temper was unpredictable.

"He killed my niece."

Juan laughed. "A niece you treated like a whore. Boris is the only one who ever cared about Natalia and you know it. You are not angry she is dead, you are angry Jon Jacobs beat you at your own game."

"He knows too much!" Mikhail raged at the room. "He didn't steal money. He could have left any time. He's known everything about us for months. He's killed my competition. Yet he doesn't leave until the Americans show up."

"Exactly," Juan said. "The Americans. Either Jon Jacobs never was a rogue CIA agent or he's been playing both sides and when the Americans showed up, he had to leave."

"But why take Ellie?"

"Entertainment? Or she really is CIA," Juan guessed.

Mikhail pulled out his phone.

He took an hour to make several calls. Five were to small hit teams in each of the locations Nikoli had bought tickets to. They were to look for and detain the man and woman whose pictures were going to be emailed to them.

The sixth call was to Langley, Virginia.

Mikhail switched back to English since the fat man, Kimball, had never bothered to learn Russian.

"We have problem," Mikhail said when he answered.

"What? Who is this?" Since it was almost midnight in Virginia, Kimball was sleeping.

"Who this?" Mikhail demanded. "The man who hold your life and bank account in palm!"

Kimball was wide awake now. Mikhail hadn't contacted him by phone in months. Everything had been by courier so it looked like mission files were being sent to legitimate sources.

"Mr. Novlak, I'm sorry, I didn't recognize your voice." He sat up and turned on the light. "To what do I owe the pleasure?"

"No pleasure! I have many dead people! Some mine, some yours!"

Excellent. Kimball wanted Jon, Elana, and Pete dead. With them dead there would be no one left to point the finger at him. Except that bitch doctor and her grad student. But they would be out of the picture soon.

"I'm sorry. I don't understand." Kimball said.

"Your agents. Pete is dead. I decide to keep woman."

"Keep the woman? She's CIA, you idiot! You can't keep her!" Kimball felt safe a continent away from Mikhail. "What about Jon Jacobs?" Kimball asked. He'd been so sure that Elana and Pete would crack under the pressure. At least Pete. Kimball had hoped Pete would blurt out they were all there to kill the Novlaks. "Is Jon dead?"

If Mikhail could have reached through the phone to strangle the fat American he would have. "Why would I kill best inside agent? He rogue and kill for me."

Kimball tried to figure out how to keep Mikhail as an asset but get him to kill Jon. "Don't you think it's time to start over, Mikhail? Let's move on. Kill all the dirty CIA agents, Elana included."

"Elana?" Mikhail asked.

"That's Ellie's real name. Her name is Elana Miller." Kimball smiled, he had his plan. "She was there when Jon first came to Moscow. Remember the blonde he had with him everywhere? When she realized Jon was rogue, she cut and ran. Jon will want to kill her. Do it first and save us the trouble."

Mikhail sat down. They knew each other. Ellie and Nikoli, no, he needed to think of them as Elana and Jon. Gregor and Enrique had been correct when they thought something was amiss. Jon had taken an unusual interest in the woman. And Mikhail had played right into his hands.

"Why did not tell from beginning people all knew each other? Why you send agents? You hope they kill me?"

This wasn't going like Kimball had planned. None of it. They should have all been dead by now. Kimball had hoped Mikhail would have Pete and Elana killed. Jon would kill Boris and Mikhail and then someone on Mikhail's staff would have killed Jon out of revenge. It had seemed so simple when he'd planned it.

"I didn't want you dead, Mikhail, I wanted the agents who were on to us dead."

"Then why you not just do it?"

"I can't just kill the top agent in the CIA. People ask questions."

Silence.

"You need me. I have the last set of vials for your man. I'm supposed to meet him tomorrow. When you get them, you will see you need me because I have the complete formulas. My price has doubled. And you need to kill Jon and Elana. Call me when it's done." Kimball hung up knowing he'd either just done the smartest or stupidest thing in his life.

Mikhail stared at the phone. How dare the American

issue orders! He would pay! Mikhail made one last phone call.

"Ilia," he said, switching back to Russian. It would be fine with him if he never spoke another word of English in his life. "When you get my vials, kill the fat American. I do not need him. My scientists can make the compounds. And if they can't, we will use the American doctor who made them in the first place. In fact, find her. Kill the fat American and bring me the American doctor."

Washington, DC

Ilia Petranov disconnected the call with Mikhail. He was tired of being in this awful United States. He wanted to go back to Mother Russia. Wanted to be back in Moscow with his dogs in his country. It was getting tiresome and messy taking the occasional job for Mikhail. Now he was supposed to bring back the cases of bio-weapons and an American woman?

Not impossible, but not neat and tidy the way he liked.

Killing the fat American would be fun. Ilia never liked meeting with him. The man acted like he was better than Ilia. As if any American could be better than a Russian.

Ilia packed everything up and got ready. He wondered if the American had the vials yet. If he did, then Ilia could go to his house now, get the vials, and kill him. Yes, that would be much easier than waiting twenty hours to meet.

It took Ilia a few hours to clean the hotel room, wiping down every surface and changing the linens. He was careful. That was why he was still alive.

The drive to Arlington did not take long.

Kimball's house was dark. He did not have a wife or a pet, so Ilia would not have to worry about anyone else. He snuck through a window in the garage. Kimball's main car was gone. Why was he not home at three in the morning?

The alarm also was not set.

Ilia went into the house. There was a message on the answering machine.

"Sir, this is Ted from the main security office. There's been some kind of explosion in the Research and Development lab. We've called in the Director and he wanted us to call you. I'm going to try your cell."

Ilia snarled. Wasn't the Research and Development lab where Kimball had been stealing the samples from? What if the doctor he was supposed to kidnap was dead? What had the dumb fat American done now?

Ilia checked the house just to be sure Kimball wasn't there. He also looked for the briefcase with the vials, but did not find it. He went back out through the window and to his car. He drove to Langley and the CIA offices.

There were ambulances, fire trucks, and police cars blocking the main entrances. Ilia spotted Kimball's car but didn't see Kimball. A coroner's van pulled up and Ilia watched as two bodies were wheeled out and placed in the van.

He needed to find out whose bodies those were. If the doctor was dead then he needed to get the vials, kill Kimball, and finally go home.

Ilia sat in his car for over an hour watching the people scurry like rats in a maze. They helped people to ambulances, the coroner's van drove away, and finally he saw the fat American. Kimball was talking to someone in a police uniform and another man in a rumpled suit. The discussion looked heated.

Kimball pointed at one of the ambulances, yelling.

Then he stomped inside the building.

Damn. Ilia would have to wait until Kimball left the building to take care of him. He settled himself in to wait for as long as it took.

34

Langley, Virginia

Tippi felt like her body had been dragged behind a car.
She tried to open her eyes, but couldn't. Her ears were ringing
and her face was wet. She tried to lift a hand to wipe it away
but didn't know where her hand was.

What was happening? What was going on?

An explosion! She remembered going to the CIA
building with AJ and seeing Marcus duct-taped to a chair.
Marcus! Marcus was dead, he had to be. He'd been in the
middle of the explosion.

Where was AJ? She couldn't sort through the jumble in
her brain.

"Ah, hell! Damn it, Tippi! If you don't open your eyes
right now, so help me God!"

"Please stop yelling, Agent Jensen, or I'm going to ask
you to leave."

"You won't get me out of here unless I'm unconscious
or dead," AJ said.

"That can be arranged," said the other voice.

Tippi didn't know who AJ was talking to. She moved
her lips to tell him she was okay, but nothing happened.

"You touch me with that syringe and I won't be

279

responsible for my actions."

Syringe? Oh, good. Maybe it was a doctor and they could check his shoulder.

"At least wipe the blood off her face to see if she's okay," AJ demanded.

Blood? There was blood on her face? Why? Oh, that's right. The explosion.

Feeling started making its way back into her body. Her left arm ached worse than any other part.

Tippi concentrated. "A—"

"Tip, darling, I'm here."

"AJ. You okay?"

AJ wanted to laugh but was afraid he'd start to cry like a big baby. "Sure. I'm fine, honey. It's you I'm worried about."

She made a noncommittal sound and, finally, the EMT in the back of the ambulance got the IV started and began to clean all Tippi's various cuts and scrapes.

When AJ had realized Marcus was trying to signal them, he'd gone for Tippi, except the explosion happened first. He'd watched in horror as her body was hurled back and she skidded across the floor. She'd been closer to the glass walls and had been peppered with debris. While AJ had also been thrown, he'd been close enough to the main wall he hadn't really taken the brunt of the blast. It had been over in seconds. It felt like hours.

When he'd gathered her in his arms, her head had lolled to one side, blood all over her face. He was sure she was dead. Agonizing pain had ripped through his chest, but it hadn't been pain from the explosion; it had been a pain in his heart. He couldn't lose her. He couldn't.

And it was his fault she was in danger. He'd killed her. Finally he'd found her pulse. Tears had been streaming down his face but he hadn't cared. She was alive and that was all that mattered. He'd held her to his chest and tried to carry her away from the death that surrounded them.

Even when the security guard and then the Director and ambulance crews had shown up, he wouldn't let go of her. He'd carried her to the ambulance and refused to leave.

The woman finished wiping Tippi's face and she appeared to only have a few minor cuts.

"My arm."

"Which one?" AJ asked before the EMT could.

"Left."

The EMT gently probed Tippi's arm from the shoulder, working her way down. When she got to the elbow, she cried out in pain.

"It might be broken."

"Shit," Tippi said.

Now AJ did laugh. She cussed at the strangest times. "A broken arm is better than a broken neck, baby."

Tippi sighed as her arm was wrapped.

The EMT turned to AJ. "Your turn."

"Not until I know for sure she's okay."

"Your hero act. Is getting old," Tippi whispered. "You need to make sure. Your shoulder is okay."

"Shoulder?" The tech asked.

Tippi slowly told the nurse, in doctor speak AJ didn't completely understand, that he may have a torn trapezius, whatever the hell that was, and his rotator cuff needed to be checked. She explained the gunshot wound and everything she'd done to keep his arm immobile.

The EMT was asking Tippi about her medical degrees when AJ heard a familiar voice.

". . . damn woman's lab. Talk to her."

AJ poked his head out of the ambulance. Kimball was yelling at the Director and the security guard who'd called 911 and helped get them to safety.

"Why in the hell was she here in the wee hours of the morning? Why was Jensen with her? I think you need to look at them."

Kimball was trying to blame this on Tippi? Oh hell no.

AJ pulled the doors to the ambulance closed. "Fine," he said "Let's go to the hospital. Tippi may be in danger so I am with her at all times."

The tech's face softened. "In danger?"

AJ leaned over Tippi and whispered, "I think that explosion was meant for her."

"I can hear you," Tippi said, closing her eyes.

"It's up to the doctor if you get to be in the same room or not." The EMT pounded on the wall behind the driver. "Let's go." She looked back to AJ. "I'm sure you can convince whoever it is, though."

"I can be quite persuasive," he agreed.

"So can I," Tippi said, eyes still closed. "Let the woman look at your injuries on the way to the hospital or I'll tell the doctor I don't want to be anywhere near you."

"You wouldn't dare."

Tippi opened one eye, the room didn't spin as much that way. "Try me."

AJ gritted his teeth, then nodded.

Tippi smiled. AJ wasn't the only one who could manipulate the outcome of a situation. She relaxed into the gurney, listening to AJ complain and the sounds of the ambulance siren.

Everything was kind of a blur for her once they got to the hospital.

Four hours later, the sun was up and AJ and Tippi were safely tucked in a hospital room on the Air Force Base. They had guards stationed outside the door. AJ's shoulder didn't have any permanent damage, but he had needed new stitches. They'd ripped out when he'd hauled Tippi out.

Tippi's left arm was in a cast from her bicep all the way to her fingers and AJ's right arm was in a sling. It had almost killed him to be separated from her while she got x-rays and a cast and he got stitches. What a pair they made. They were alive; that was all he cared about.

Tippi came awake slowly, knowing she was medicated by the lack of acute pain. Also the floaty feeling in her body.

AJ sat in a chair next to her bed, refusing to get in his own bed and sleep. He wanted to hear from her lips that she was okay.

When her eyes fluttered opened, AJ was the first thing she saw. He looked so good, so alive, she started to cry.

"What's the matter, baby? Do you hurt? Do you want me to call the doctor?" He hit the call button on the bed.

"I was so worried about you," she slurred her words slightly because of the pain meds. "We have to find Jon and Elana. You have to go find them."

She was bruised and broken, wasn't wearing makeup and her hair needed to be washed. She was the most beautiful creature he'd ever seen. She was more worried about him, Jon, and Elana than herself. How had he gotten so lucky? He needed to tell her, but didn't know how to find the words.

"Call Jax. Find out how he can get you to Russia."

"I'm not leaving you alone."

"Did tonight teach you anything? I'm not cut out for your world. I can't just fly to Europe with you. I distract you. You distract me. I need to stay here and rebuild my work. You need to go do what you do."

She was sending him away. She didn't want him.

"Quit acting like I kicked your puppy," Tippi said.

"What?"

"Damn it you stupid man! Don't you know I love you?"

The world stopped. AJ didn't hear the heart monitor or the squeaking of shoes in the hallway.

"I love you." It felt so good to say it out loud.

AJ's heart wanted to burst and at the same time he was devastated. "Then why don't you want me here?"

"I swear, men say women are complicated, except it's

only because you make us that way." She closed her eyes, sighing.

When she opened her eyes, she pushed a button so the bed would raise. She noticed her cast. It was hot pink. AJ had written his name in black marker. That made her cry more.

"I want you here. But I want Elana and your friend Jon here, too. How are we going to have a regular relationship if you have to run off and save the world all the time?"

A regular relationship? What in the hell was a regular relationship? His eyes took on the look of a caged animal.

"I shouldn't have said regular. There is no such thing as a regular relationship, okay? What do I know about one either?" Tippi wiped at her tears.

Apparently he hadn't said that in his head like he thought.

"We can build a relationship together but we have to start without someone's life hanging over our heads."

AJ sighed. He wasn't ready to let her out of his sight. And, there was always going to be someone's life to save, somewhere else for him to go. Especially if Kimball stayed Deputy Director.

"I'm always going to be out of the country, Tippi. The CIA doesn't operate on American soil. How long are you going to wait around for me?"

Tippi opened and closed her mouth.

"Exactly."

The nurse came in and stopped any further conversation. "Excuse me, sir, you're going to need to move." She shut off the call light and checked Tippi's vitals.

"Now, you were out of it during the x-rays, dear," the older woman began. "We put the radiation vest over you during the procedure, but we always need to ask. Is there any chance you could be pregnant?"

Tippi opened her mouth. Closed it. Looked at AJ. His eyes were wide. Pregnant? Oh holy hell.

AJ stood, the chair made a clattering noise.

The nurse glanced back and forth between the two.

"Um, I don't think so?" Tippi said.

"We'll check since you're here."

The nurse made a notation on Tippi's chart then went into the hallway, shutting the door behind her.

AJ turned toward the door.

"Where are you going?"

"I have to leave. I need to go."

Pregnant. What in the hell was he going to do if Tippi was pregnant? He didn't know how to be a father. Kids? He couldn't have kids. Not with the job he did and the people he dealt with on an everyday basis. Pregnant? And she wanted a relationship. He had to find someone else to keep her safe. He couldn't stay here. He felt like the walls were closing in on him. His breathing picked up.

"What?" she said.

"To Europe, where you want me to go."

"I didn't mean right this minute!"

"When then? Huh, Tippi? What do you want from me?" He was getting hysterical.

"All of you." She wanted his love. She wanted his children. She wanted him.

"I can't give you all of me. Uncle Sam already has that." He leaned down and kissed her.

She wrapped her good arm around him. "Don't leave me, AJ," she said against his lips. She didn't just mean physically. He was shutting her out.

He pulled at the sling keeping his hand from being able to touch her. Threw it on the floor. He kissed her harder, jamming his hands into her hair. He kissed her goodbye and she knew it.

He turned and opened the door.

"I love you, you stupid man! When you figure out how to love me, you better come back damn you! Do you hear me? You better fucking come back to me, AJ Jensen!"

Tippi threw everything she could reach at the closed door as she sobbed and fought for breath. She stared with blurry eyes at the plastic pieces of the phone spinning like a top on the white tiled floor.

The two soldiers stationed outside the door pretended not to notice the tears in AJ's eyes when he addressed them. "That woman is now national security. I'll let the doctor and General know what's going on. No one gets to her, do you understand me? No one!"

AJ went in search of the doctor in charge. Being an Air Force hospital meant the staff knew when procedure had to be followed.

It took an hour for the doctor to set up a video conference with the Air Force General. At the last minute, AJ included the Director of the CIA, not Kimball. When AJ described the bio-weapons threat and what Tippi had created, there was silence.

"She has to be kept safe at all costs," AJ said, even though that was obvious.

The Director of the CIA stared at AJ over the video monitor. "Why didn't you include Deputy Director Kimball and where do you think you're going, Agent Jensen?"

"Sir, can I meet with you privately in half an hour?"

The Director waited a beat, then agreed.

AJ finished briefing everyone and left the hospital.

His hands trembled on the steering wheel as he drove to the office. There was an ache in his chest. He felt like he was leaving a piece of his heart behind.

Director Devlin was not happy with AJ's accusations.

"I think Kimball is dirty of something, sir. I think Jon Matthews and Elana Miller are the key to all of it. Please leave Deputy Director Kimball out of the loop until I can get back from Europe."

"You realize what you're saying could mean treason

charges against the Deputy Director."

"Yes, sir," AJ nodded.

"You also realize your career is on the line."

"Yes, sir."

"What about the woman?"

"Sir?" AJ asked.

"Kimball said weird things have been happening in her lab. Maybe she's the traitor."

AJ kept his anger in check. All he'd get for yelling at Devlin would be jail time and then he wouldn't be able to do anything for Tippi.

"If you look into it sir, you'll see she realized the samples had gone missing and asked tech to go over video footage. Footage that's been erased. She doesn't have that type of clearance."

"I will check into it. If I think she's guilty, I'll have her arrested."

"One week, sir. I'll be back in one week with everything you need. Keep men on her at all times so she's safe."

"Oh, I'll keep men on her. So she doesn't skip town."

AJ calmed himself again.

"Go," the Director dismissed him.

Out in the hallway, AJ tested the mobility of his right arm. Still not at full capacity, but he didn't hurt as much since he'd had everything checked out and gotten new stitches and meds. It had been almost a week since he'd been shot. He'd had less time to heal in the past. He probably should have kept the sling.

Using his secure phone, AJ called Jax. "So, I didn't make your flight," he said when Jax answered.

AJ quickly explained the explosion and the one week timetable to find Jon, Elana, and proof Kimball was a lying, traitorous bastard.

"Do you ever do anything the easy way?"

"Jax, it's like you've forgotten how I work."

They set up a plan. AJ would be in Moscow the following evening by hitching a ride in a carrier similar to the one Elana and Pete had originally gone over in.

AJ went back to the hospital. He found a vase of flowers on a reception desk he was sure no one would miss. He hoped Tippi was sleeping because he wasn't going to be able to look into her tear filled eyes again.

He sat in the darkness of her room for an hour writing a letter he thought he'd never write. A letter he hoped would explain to her why he wasn't worthy of her love and why he didn't know how to love her in return.

When he was done, he tucked it under the vase, kissed her goodbye, and slipped from the room.

He had a plane to catch.

35

Train to Moscow

Jon didn't want to wake Elana, but he knew he had to. Her back still looked horrible. It was red, bruised, and raw. He'd kept her alive but he hadn't kept her safe. His plan of purchasing multiple tickets was going to buy some time, but he didn't know exactly how many men to expect when they arrived. He figured three to six would be waiting for them.

Elana was more than capable of holding her own when she was one hundred percent. Like this? He figured she could take down one, maybe two, and he'd have to take the rest.

The small windows in the berth were set up so people couldn't crawl out. If he had a glass cutter, he could make a hole. He could probably shoot the window, but he didn't have a silencer. They were going to have to blend in with the crowd.

Jon kissed her shoulder. "Wake up, Lana."

She groaned, but didn't open her eyes.

He wrapped his arm around her waist and put his leg over her thighs. "Wake up, honey. I have to go out into the main part of the train and I want you coherent."

She moved into his body, seeking the comfort and warmth. Jon smiled. He wished so many things. Wished for the first time in his life he wasn't a single-minded bastard who had to get the job done. He wanted to hide her away and forget his responsibilities.

"Lana, baby, wake up."

She finally moved and opened an eye. "Hi," she said.

"Hey. I'd ask how you're doing but that would be a stupid question."

Elana traced the scar on his stomach. "The same as you probably felt when this happened."

"That was my emotions getting in the way of things." He frowned.

She ran her hand over the scowl on his face. "Emotions bother you, don't they?"

"Only when they get in the way."

She sighed. She'd been dreaming about Jon. Dreaming about the man she wanted him to be and knew he couldn't. "I'm awake. Go do what you need to."

He stared at her for a moment then moved out of bed. She watched him dress and transform. He went from the man who had been taking care of her for two days to the agent she'd first met. His personas were like clothing changes. Did she even know the real Jon? Was there a real Jon anymore?

He didn't look at her as he stepped into the hallway. When the door clicked behind him, he took a moment to get himself in check. He had to get them disguises.

Switching his brain to work mode, he made his way down the isles. He pocketed a cell phone, two scarves, a man's hat, and a cane.

By the time he got back to their berth with breakfast, Elana had dressed in Talia's clothes and covered the worst of her bruises and cuts with makeup.

When she saw the scarves and cane she asked, "Old lady?"

"Yep. I figured you're already going to be moving slow and a little hunched. You can cover your hair and most of your face."

Elana looked down at Talia's stylish clothes.

"I'll get a shawl of some kind," Jon said.

He slipped back out while Elana went to work. She wrapped one of the scarves around her face until only her eyes were showing. She made wrinkles on her skin with the makeup from Jon's field kit.

He came back ten minutes later with a shawl and two pairs of reading glasses.

After they ate, Elana took more medicine. They had an hour until the train arrived in Moscow.

"What's the plan?" she asked.

"Mikhail will be expecting us to run the fastest way out. We're going to stay on the train in Moscow. From there, we're going to Minsk and then Warsaw. Once we're in Poland, I have a contact who can get us home."

"You make it sound so easy."

"As long as we can get out of Moscow, we should be fine. They'll check everyone. You'll be my elderly mother who doesn't travel well. They'll leave us alone."

Elana was dubious. She nodded at the phone. "Who are you going to call?"

"Michael and AJ. Let Michael know to stay in the U.S. and let AJ know to come get us in Warsaw."

Jon spent almost the remaining hour going through his calls from his answering service. There were messages from Michael, Kamielle, Julie, and even Tony, Michael's old partner. Julie threatened to skin him alive for missing Christmas. Then she broke into tears, hoping he was okay.

Was it time to pack things in? Jon watched Elana nap. Could he be like Michael and take a desk job? Maybe.

Finally, he got through the messages. It was time to call Michael.

"Hello," Kamielle's sleepy voice came on the line.

"Hi, love," Jon said.

Kami screamed in his ear. Then, "Where the hell are you? Are you okay? Can you talk? Do we need to use secret code words or something?"

Michael ripped the phone from her hands. "Jon? Is it really you?"

"Sure is, Mikey. I'm good. I'm coming home. I have Elana. We're not out of danger quite yet."

"Where do you need me?"

"I don't want you anywhere near this continent."

"Damn it, Jon. Where are you? I'll meet you. What do you need me to bring?"

Jon closed his eyes. He wanted AJ and Michael as backup so damn bad he could taste it. But he couldn't put his little brother at risk.

"Jon David Carter. You fucking tell me where you are right now. I'll be there as soon as I can."

Jon laughed. "Bossy. Okay, but think this through. I don't want you in danger. Lana said I'm going to be an uncle again. Is Julie popping out more brats or is it you and my beautiful Kami?"

"It's me! It's me!" Kami said. "We're having twins, Jon! Twins. In eight weeks. You better be here for their birth! You hear me?"

"You can't come here if Kami's having twins in two months," Jon said.

Elana had woken and was listening with interest.

"We'd be back in a week," Michael said. "Who do you want me to bring as backup? Tony?"

Jon closed his eyes. What he'd said to Elana was coming back to bite him in the ass. People he cared about were going to be in danger. Why couldn't it be a team of SEALs like the last time he'd been in a clusterfuck? He hadn't cared one way or another if one of them died. They knew it was their job.

A touch on his hand made him come back to reality.

Elana whispered, "I'm no help to you right now. You need good backup."

Against everything in him, Jon finally said, "Fine. You and Tony. I'm going to have you call my buddy AJ, too. I think he's already on his way here. I'll meet you in Warsaw. AJ will know where. Be careful."

"Don't worry about me, bro, take care of yourself and that woman. I can't wait to meet her."

After giving AJ's contact numbers, Jon hung up and sighed heavily. He shut off the phone and systematically took it apart just in case Mikhail had some way to track random calls to the United States. Being paranoid had kept Jon alive for many years.

"They'll be fine," Elana said, rubbing his shoulders.

"Our parents died about five years ago." Where in the hell had that come from? Jon never talked about his parents.

"Oh?" Elana said.

"It was a plane crash. They had been visiting Mikey and his fiance. Not too long after they died, Mikey's fiance was murdered."

Elana covered her mouth.

"When I went home to help Mikey take care of the murderer, I reminded him if you didn't care for people, you didn't have to feel when they died." Jon took her hand. "I tried not to care for people. It didn't work. I've wasted so many years hiding from my feelings. Does my family even know I love them?"

"Of course they do," Elana whispered. "Your brother is going to come half way around the world to help us. He understands your job and your life."

"But do Julie and the kids? They don't know anything about me."

"What do you want me to say?" Elana asked. "That you should quit?"

Jon didn't know what he wanted anymore. The thought

of Kamielle pregnant with Michael's children almost brought tears to his eyes. Was he going soft?

"We need to get ready," he said. "The team searching for us is going to be waiting when the train stops."

Elana shook her head sadly and fixed her costume.

Washington, DC

Ilia took off his gloves as he walked back to his car. The vials were safe in his jacket pocket. Kimball hadn't even tried to fight him while Ilia questioned him about anyone who may have known what was going on.

He claimed no one. Ilia hoped that was true. He was ready to go home and didn't want Mikhail to send him back to this awful country. With Kimball dead, his work was almost done.

He just had to find the doctor. Kimball had told him she was in the hospital, heavily guarded. Ilia didn't know if it would be worth trying.

Couldn't Mikhail's scientists recreate the formulas using the samples he had? Mikhail would never know Ilia hadn't tried to get to her. He better check how easy it would be to abduct her, just in case. The last thing he needed was one of the Novlaks upset with him.

Langley, Virginia

Dear Tippi,

I'm sitting here watching you sleep, wishing life were different. I know that's not fair to say and I'm sorry. I grew up believing there's no such thing as love. My dad ran out before I was born and my sisters and I spent our childhoods defending our bastard and Asian heritages. I don't want to bore you with my horrible upbringing. People shouldn't have kids that don't know how to love or raise them.

I'm scared. I've never said that in my entire life.

I've been shot, bombed, run missions in the biggest hellholes of the world and never had the fear I feel when I hold you in my arms or look in your eyes. Everything about you scares me. I don't know why. Well, maybe I do. I don't know what to do with your feelings for me. I do know I wouldn't be able to say this to your face which is why I'm putting it here. Although this could backfire because now you have it in writing. (I'm smiling even if you can't see)

Tippi, I can't do this.

I don't know how to be a boyfriend or in a relationship. I damn sure don't know how to be a husband or father. I don't know what love is. I don't know how to do anything but follow orders and kill bad guys.

Forget me.

Forget what you think we have because we don't.

I'm going to set up an account for you and our baby. You'll never want for anything.

You deserve better than I can give you.

AJ

Tippi crinkled the letter in her hand. It took everything she had to not rip it to shreds. Stupid man! She wasn't pregnant! That's why he'd run out of her room? He'd run out of there like the devil was on his heels because the nurse had asked if she could be pregnant? Seriously?

Tears fell and Tippi wiped them away angrily. How could someone who worked for the CIA be scared of a woman and a baby? A baby she didn't have.

"Big dumb jerk," she said.

"Ma'am?" One of the soldiers poked his head in.

Tippi wiped at her tears. "Yes?"

"Can I get you anything?"

Tippi tried to say no. All she could do was sob.

Washington, DC

AJ and Director Devlin stood outside Kimball's house.

"You were right," the Director said.

"I still can't believe the chicken-shit shot himself," AJ said. "It doesn't make any sense."

"His suicide note explained everything, Jensen. He felt bad. Hadn't meant for Marcus to die in the explosion. He was trying to clean up his mistakes and destroy all the vials."

"How could he not have meant for Marcus to die? The poor kid was duct-taped to a freakin' chair! It doesn't make any sense, Sir. I'm going to make sure Tip, uh, Dr. Aldridge is still under security."

Director Devlin watched AJ make his phone call. The kid was so transparent. Devlin couldn't believe AJ had actually left Tippi at he hospital. He was head over heels and didn't seem to know it.

Oh, well. Not his problem. He had way more important things to deal with. The media was going to have a field day with this story. Deputy Director of the CIA stealing bioweapons from their own lab. Explosion in said lab. Suicide. What a mess.

AJ spoke with lieutenant Frost, one of the men stationed outside Tippi's door. She was fine, awake, but upset about something. Had thrown some more stuff and was crying.

Probably because of him.

AJ got off the phone. He was going to go back to the hospital. To hell with this. He needed to be with Tippi.

Wanted to be with her. Maybe if he crawled and begged, she'd take him back.

He was getting in his car when his phone rang.

Blocked number.

"Hello," he said.

"AJ Jensen? We've never met. But you know my hard-headed brother."

"Is this Michael Carter?"

"Oh, good. I was hoping I wasn't going to have to go through convincing you Jon had a brother."

"I was in Chicago," AJ said.

"Okay. Didn't know that. Jon always works alone."

"He wanted you safe. Realized I could help."

"Well, I need your help this time. He finally called."

"Called? Jon called you?" AJ almost dropped his phone.

"He's on his way to Poland. Warsaw. Said you'd know where. Can you get us to Poland asap? I want to bring Antonio Medina, too."

AJ was having trouble processing the change of events. One minute his mind was in bed with Tippi, the next it was figuring out how to get to Poland.

"I had transport set up to London. If you can be in New York City, like now, I can get us anywhere you need. Is Jon okay? What about Elana?"

"You know Jon. No big details. Just said he was fine, had Elana, and is ready to come home."

AJ let out a breath. They were both alive. Jax's intel had been correct.

"I'm calling in some favors to get us to the east coast as quickly as possible."

"Call me as soon as you're in New York," AJ said.

They hung up and AJ mourned the chance of going to Tippi. He'd have to do it when he got back with Jon and Elana.

36

Moscow Train Stop

The hit team only had five people. They roughly checked all the young couples leaving the train and briskly walked up and down the isles of the cars.

Jon and Elana sat in plain sight. They both wore reading glasses and Elana looked forty years older. Jon had darkened his hair with shoe polish and stuffed his cheeks with cotton to look slightly overweight. The men didn't look twice. Mikhail either wasn't paying them enough or they were new.

Elana couldn't relax until the train started moving. Jon helped her back to bed where she stripped and he doctored her up again.

"We have two full days until we get to Poland. About a day to Minsk and then a day to Warsaw."

"Sounds like heaven," Elana sighed.

"I'm hoping you'll be rested enough and the worst of your wounds will be starting to heal."

Jon ran his hands over her arms.

"Make love to me," she whispered.

"I can't. I'll hurt you."

"I need you."

Jon couldn't deny her anything. Couldn't say no even when he knew it was wrong. He turned her on her side and scissored their legs together. He spent over ten minutes petting her body and rubbing her so she'd relax. Then he spent hours making them both forget she almost died.

Moscow, Russia

Mikhail's carefully constructed world was falling apart. None of the teams had found Jon and Elana at any of the five train stops. Where in the hell could they be?

Then Ilia had called and told him Kimball was dead. That part was good. Except the doctor was too closely guarded to kidnap. But, Ilia had the vials. If Mikhail's scientists could not figure out the formulas, he would go get the doctor himself when she was no longer under protection.

Mikhail was just getting ready to end the call with Ilia.

"Wait," Ilia said. "Kimball did try to bargain with some information in exchange for his life. He said Jon Matthews doesn't trust many people. There are only a few European safe houses he's ever used in the past."

"Where?" Mikhail said.

"Poland, Russia, and Italy."

"I will send men to all of them."

Minsk, Belarus

Jon woke when the train stopped in Minsk. He couldn't believe they'd stayed in the berth, only eating when they had to and making love every moment.

He still had a day with Elana. She slept in his arms. Her color was better and the bandages had quit bleeding through. The ugly red lines of the infection were going away. He only had, maybe, two days left of antibiotic and pain meds. The safe house would be stocked with whatever he'd need.

She was going to be okay.

Jon kissed her temple and snuggled back down. He could get used to this.

London, England

It was weird for AJ to shake hands with Michael Carter. He was a slightly smaller, nicer version of Jon.

"Great to meet you," AJ said to both men.

Tony Medina looked a little like Antonio Banderas.

The three of them could be the start of a bad joke: a white guy, a Mexican, and an Asian go into a bar with machine guns. . .

"We leave for Minsk in an hour," AJ said.

As they left the airport Tony asked, "Is anyone officially backing this mission?"

"The director of Jon's and my unit knows we're here. He doesn't want anything in the media. We have weapons and transport, but that's it. We get caught, we're on our own."

"We figured," Michael said.

"Thanks for calling me," AJ said. "Your damn brother has a bad habit of trying to do everything alone."

"I know," Michael agreed. "He didn't want me to come. I finally told him I was coming whether he wanted me to or not and it would be a whole lot faster if I knew where to find him."

"I'll have to remember that tactic next time," AJ said on a laugh.

Warsaw, Poland

Two wonderful days of healing, eating, and making love. Elana wished they could stay on the train forever. She was finally able to move without breaking the skin open on her back and Jon quit treating her like spun glass.

They were getting ready to leave the train in their disguises from before. There didn't appear to be a team waiting for them, but Jon was always careful.

Elana stepped out first. She was hunched over and had the scarves wrapped around her head. Jon held her arm and every once in a while spoke in German reminding her to watch her step and asking if she was okay. No one paid any attention as they got a car to take them into the city and to the safe house.

It wasn't until they were locked in the safe house that Jon pulled Elana into his arms. "We have to get that makeup off you. It's very strange to see your eyes in the face of an old woman."

"Maybe you're seeing the future," she said. "You know what I'm going to look like thirty or forty years from now."

Jon smiled. Maybe he could do this. Not willing to jinx it, he sidestepped her comment. "The only future I see is you and me in a real bed."

"I think that's a wonderful idea," she agreed.

After days of feeling so helpless, Elana was tired of Jon being gentle. Never knowing what the future would hold made her needy.

She tightened her arms around his neck, threading her fingers in his silky hair. When their lips met, Elana licked and sucked at him until he groaned. He pulled her against him and her stomach quivered. Angling her head to the side, their teeth bumped and the clicking noise acted as a trigger. She jumped, wrapping her legs around his waist.

Caught off guard, he stumbled a little. "Whoa, baby. Slow down."

"No. I'm tired of slow. I want hard and fast," she said between biting kisses. "Like the first time. I want the feel of you being rough and gentle at the same time. Knowing it's for us. No one else or their cameras."

He pulled her tighter against him and walked down the hall. He went to the bedroom with the king bed and attached bath; the room he stayed in whenever he was here. He was glad she wanted him hard and fast. After the last week, he wasn't sure he'd be able to do gentle anymore.

As much as he wanted to throw her down on the bed, he knew it wouldn't be good for her newly healed back. He sat down, gripping her hips, pulling her against his erection.

She bit his chin, then his neck. Without finesse, she ripped his shirt over his head and spread her hands on his warm chest.

"I still can't believe you want me. I'm so plain," she said, kissing him.

Jon carefully removed the button up shirt she was wearing. Since she couldn't put on a bra, he was instantly rewarded with her creamy skin.

"What are you talking about? Every time I look at you, I feel the same way." He was quickly losing his control. "You're beautiful and sexy. You've made me feel again."

She sighed as he nibbled a path from her ear down to a pink nipple. She arched her back as much as she could while he gripped her hips with bruising force.

She leaned forward to whisper in his ear, "I'm tired of making love on our sides and not being able to move."

"Well, baby. Your choices are bent over the couch in the living room or riding me on this bed." His nostrils flared.

"Can I have both?"

"You're going to be the death of me," Jon chuckled as he removed the rest of their clothes.

"Would this count as dying in the field?" she asked.

"I don't think so."

"Damn."

She pushed against his chest and he fell back.

"Come here, baby," Jon winked.

Elana slowly crawled over his body. She ran her tongue up his abs and circled a nipple.

"I want you to love me, Jon. Can you do that?"

"I haven't had a choice from the first moment I touched you. I'm always going to love you. Want to love you. Need to make love to you."

Tears pooled in Elana's eyes. Her breath caught. "Don't make promises you can't keep."

"Never," he said.

As she settled herself over him, she closed her eyes.

"Lana."

When she didn't open them, he gripped her hips to stop her from moving. Tears ran down her cheeks.

"Look at me, damn it."

She dropped her head to his chest, her warm heat cradling his cock.

He groaned. "What's wrong, baby?"

"I need you so bad. Need you with me and I can't—" she sobbed against his skin.

"It's okay, baby."

"No. It's not." She finally opened her eyes.

Without much effort, she lifted herself and he slid into her wet, warm heat.

"How is it possible," she said on a sigh, "that it feels better every time you slide into me? How can it get stronger? Make me shiver and feel complete and whole?"

Jon gripped her hips. She slammed down on him before he could answer.

"Slow, baby."

"I don't want slow. I want you to fuck me and make me forget. Make this feeling of dread go away."

He couldn't give her much, but he could help her forget.

37

The sound of a ringing phone woke Jon. He reached for his pistol.

"Who has this number?" Elana asked, pulling the sheet to her chest.

"AJ."

Jon grabbed the phone

"Carter?" Automatic gunfire sounded in the background.

"Who the hell is this?" Jon asked. It wasn't AJ.

"Sergeant Aden 'Jax' Jackson. I've worked with AJ in the past. I don't have time for pleasantries. We're pinned down. The transport dropped us off—shit! Medina! Get out of there!"

The line went dead.

"Goddammit!" Jon threw down the phone.

"What's wrong?" Elana asked.

"Put on tactical gear, gather up everything you can. We need to get to the air strip."

They dressed quickly in BDU's and Kevlar vests. Michael and AJ were being shot at. Was anyone injured?

Elana loaded the weapons. They didn't have much.

Jon hot-wired a motorcycle. Elana put the weapons bag on like a backpack and held on to him as he raced through the streets. He hoped the military transport had dropped them at the same place it had dropped him four years ago.

The airstrip looked deserted when they pulled up. It had been over twenty minutes since the phone call. They could tell there had been a firefight, but it wasn't happening now.

"You sneak to the hangar around front," Jon said. "I'll go in through the back."

They divided the guns and ammo between them. All they had were pistols and extra clips.

"Jon, we don't know how many friendlies there are. I don't even know what Tony or Michael look like."

"Try not to kill anyone I know." He smiled, the bastard.

"Thanks," she said as she put two pistols in the holsters on her thighs and two more on the vest harness.

Jon did the same.

"Remember. I'm taking you somewhere tropical when we get off this damn continent."

"I'm keeping you to that," she said. Using precious seconds, she grabbed him and kissed him. "I'm not one-hundred percent. Don't worry about me. I'll be moving a little slow. Keep yourself, your brother, and your friends safe first."

Jon looked like he was going to argue so she kissed him again and went toward the hanger, ignoring the bad feeling in her gut.

Jon noticed the jet on the runway. The stairs were down. Was the jet for them or was it whoever had been shooting at Michael? Jon ran for it.

Elana made it to the front. There were two dead bodies by the door. She recognized them from the Novlak mansion. Fuck. Mikhail was here.

She wished there had been headsets at the safe house. What kind of CIA safe house didn't have rocket launchers, machine guns, a tank or two, and communication headsets? She was going to change that when she got home.

The door was open a few inches so she peeked in,

ignoring the pain in her back. There were more bodies dressed like the Russians. Maybe she'd be able to tell who Michael and Tony were by their clothing.

When there was no movement she toed the door open. A shot slammed into the metal above her head and she rolled into the hangar. The shot triggered an avalanche of gunfire.

"Elana?"

She turned to see a man who looked like Jon.

"Michael?" she said.

Bullets peppered the boxes she was crouched behind.

"Where's Jon?" Michael asked.

"He's coming in the back."

"Shit."

AJ appeared out of nowhere. He grabbed Elana in a bear hug and she whimpered. When AJ pulled back, she grimaced.

"Torture session with Mikhail Novlak and his buddy Juan." She grinned. "Good times."

"I am so damn glad to see you! I missed you," AJ said. "Where's Jon?"

"He's near the jet," Michael said.

"Shit."

"You both said that. What's going on?" Elana asked.

"Mikhail is here. With a mini-army. We've taken out half of them. He's holed up on the jet."

The jet near the back of the hangar where Jon was coming in. No wonder they kept saying shit.

More gunfire sounded and Elana had her pistol on a blonde man running toward them.

"That's Jax. Don't shoot him," AJ said.

She recognized Jax. A dark-skinned man was covering his back as they ran.

"Tony?" she asked.

The men nodded.

Jax and Tony made it to the group.

"Elana," Jax said.

"Good to see you again, Sergeant."

"Wish it was under better circumstances. I'm sorry about your partner."

Elana nodded. At some point she was going to have to deal with Pete's death. Just not now.

"Okay, we'll have a reunion later," AJ said. "I'll hold down the hangar and cover your six. Michael, you and Tony take point. Jax and Elana you fan out."

From the bay doors, Elana saw Petrov and Juan shooting out the open door of the jet. She followed their gunfire to Jon behind empty crates. Those weren't going to hold back bullets.

"Michael!" Elana pointed to Jon then Petrov and Juan.

Michael nodded.

Jax and Elana made a run for Jon while Michael and Tony shot at the jet. The two men quickly went for cover back inside the plane.

"Damn it! What are you doing out here?" Jon asked as Elana and Jax slid in next to him.

"You're welcome," Elana said.

"Jax," Jackson introduced himself.

"Thanks. I'll buy you a beer if we get out of this."

"When," Elana corrected.

More shots fired from the hanger and two men ran out.

The sound of gunfire ripped through the air. Jon saw Tony fire then spin around and slam to the ground. Michael ran toward his old partner and then he, too, fell.

"No," Jon yelled as he stood.

He felt the impact of a round slam into his bullet proof vest. Out of nowhere, Lana barreled toward him. She hit him like a linebacker and they rolled on the tarmac.

"Are you okay?" she said.

"We have to get to Michael and Tony!"

Elana laid down cover fire as Jon worked his way

toward the men.

AJ was still pinned down in the hanger.

She checked her clips. All she had left was what was in her gun and one other.

Petrov poked his head out the jet and aimed at Jon. Elana shot him in the head. When Petrov's body fell from the door, she had a clear shot of Juan and put two rounds in his chest. His body fell.

She had a brief anti-climatic moment. She wanted Juan to feel the pain she'd felt. But then didn't that make her as bad as the 'bad guys'?

Jon saw the bodies fall from the jet out of the corner of his eyes. Elana was amazing and he needed to remember to tell her. He rolled to where Michael and Tony were then pulled them behind the crates.

"Mikey! Mikey! Talk to me!"

Elana ran over as Jon was frantically pulling at Michael's shirt to see if there was blood or if the rounds were stopped by his Kevlar.

"Quit. . . touching. . . me," Michael rasped. He tried to laugh and started to cough.

Jon laid his head on Michael's chest. "I thought I lost you, buddy."

"Doesn't anyone care about me?" Tony asked, feeling his own chest.

The sound of the jet firing up had Elana on her feet and running.

"Damn it, Elana!" Jon yelled.

Mikhail couldn't get away. Tippi would always be in danger if he did. Elana started shooting at the open door to the jet. Mikhail aimed his shotgun and hit Elana in the shoulder.

Half the spray went into the Kevlar, half embedded itself in her arm. She screamed, stumbling to the ground.

Jon was up and behind her when Mikhail came into

view ready to shoot again. Elana shot Mikhail in the knee. He fell from the steps and lay unmoving on the ground.

Jon slid next to Elana. "What in the hell were you doing?"

Elana grimaced. "He has to die or Tippi will never be safe."

Jon shook his head. "I don't care about Tippi; I care about you."

"Tough," she said. "I care about both of you." She grimaced. Blood ran down her arm and dripped off the tips of her fingers.

Mikhail groaned and Jon stood, pistol ready. He helped Elana up.

The shotgun lay at least ten feet from Mikhail.

They heard a few shots from the hangar. They turned, ready to fire, and AJ came out, arm bloody.

"You okay?" Jon yelled.

AJ nodded, rotating his shoulder. He holstered his pistol. When he looked back up, his blood ran cold as he saw Mikhail moving.

Jon watched, confused, as AJ started running toward them pointing. They couldn't hear what he was saying.

Elana turned. Mikhail was pulling a pistol. Pointing it at Jon.

The world seemed to move in slow motion. She ran toward Mikhail firing. She felt heat on her neck then she finished emptying her clip into Mikhail's lifeless body.

Jon watched, horrified, as Elana fell to her knees and dropped her pistol.

Blood. There was so much blood. She fell backward, ripping at the neck of her Kevlar vest.

Jon yelled and ran to her. He dropped to his knees so hard his teeth rattled. He put out his hands, but was afraid to touch her.

"Can't breathe," she said.

"I know, baby." Jon ripped off her shirt to see where the round hit.

It wasn't in the vest.

Blood started to pool under Elana's head.

"Mikey! Help me!" Jon didn't recognize the sound of his own voice. He'd never sounded this desperate. Crazed.

AJ reached them first. Jon refused to acknowledge the look on his face.

"Oh, holy hell," AJ breathed.

"Shut up and help me get her vest off. I think it ricocheted. Head wounds bleed like a son of a bitch."

It had to be a ricochet. The blood was from the shotgun wound on her arm. She'd be fine.

She coughed. Blood ran from the corner of her mouth and trickled from her nose.

Fuck. No.

AJ helped Jon open the vest.

It was bad.

Michael sucked in a breath as he and Tony came running up.

"Jon," Michael started.

Jon whipped his hand in a silencing motion. Michael dropped to the ground next to him.

They found the main flow of blood.

The bullet had hit her neck.

Jon used her shirt to try and stop the flow, but it was no use. Almost as soon as he placed the balled up fabric on her throat it was soaked in blood.

As the color slowly leached from Elana's face she looked at Jon. "Love you."

"Don't Lana! God dammit! Don't you fucking die!"

"Live. Live for me. Live for you. Kill the bad guys. Kill 'em all. Love you. Always."

"No! God damn you, God. No! Fucking No!"

Jon beat on the ground and screamed at the sky until

Michael and AJ pulled him from Elana's body.

Jon swung his arms blindly and hit AJ in the face and Michael in the stomach. Tony tried to intervene and took a kick to the knee that put him on the ground. Jax waited off to the side hoping he wasn't going to have to shoot anyone.

Jon crawled back to Elana. His hands were bloody from punching the pavement. Bloody from her.

He shook her shoulders. "Wake up, damn you! Wake up! I said wake up!"

Her head flopped from side to side, the last of her life dripping out.

Michael grabbed Jon from behind and pulled him back, holding him immobile almost in his lap. "She's gone, Jon. Let her go. She's gone."

They sat like that. Michael rocking his big brother while they both wept like children.

38

Langley, Virginia

Fifteen dead bodies.

Fourteen bad guys had been taken out. One CIA fatality was acceptable by SOP protocol.

It wasn't acceptable to Jon. His mind kept replaying the moment when AJ and been pointing behind them. How could he have taken the bullet instead of Elana? Why was she dead and he was alive?

Kill the bad guys? He'd kill them all just like she said. Until they killed him.

"Jon?" Michael asked. Michael had never been scared of his brother. The dead eyes looking at him now were that of a stranger. "Do you remember when Crystal was murdered? I survived that. You'll survive this. I found Kamielle and love again. So will you."

Jon shook his head.

"You will."

"No." Jon's voice sounded rusty. "I knew better. I ignored my own advice, hell, my own world. All it got me was empty. Elana," he choked. "Lana said I was like the Tin Man or the Grinch. She didn't know how right she was. My fucking heart trusted me and grew. Lot of good that did. I'm the Tin Man again. My heart is going in the ground with her."

Michael let it go. He'd felt like that when Crystal died. Jon would love again.

He had to.

Tippi hobbled up to the group of men. Her arm was in a sling and she was walking with a cane. The doctors hadn't wanted to release her for Elana's funeral. She'd gotten up and walked out anyway.

"I'm so sorry for your loss," she said quietly.

She couldn't believe Elana was dead. It wasn't real. She looked around at the other men and women attending the graveside service.

She turned to AJ. "Can we talk?"

He shook his head and turned to walk away.

"You want to do this in front of everyone? Here?"

He stopped, yet didn't turn around.

"Fine. I'm not pregnant. You're off the hook. Run away to whatever country you want, you big coward." Her voice started to get loud.

The men stared at AJ's back, then at Tippi.

She raised her cane like she was going to hit him with it and Tony stepped between them.

"Miss Aldridge, I'm Antonio Medina. Let's go sit down where you'll be more comfortable."

He took her to some seats up front and began talking about nothing until she stopped crying and took his hand.

"Thank you for not letting me make a scene at Elana's funeral." She wiped away some tears.

"If we were anywhere but here, I would have let you beat him with your cane. Held him down, even, so you could get in some good shots."

She smiled and gripped his hand more tightly as the minister began to talk. Tony didn't let go.

AJ ripped his eyes from Tippi and Tony. "We found the USB drive hidden in the vent in Tippi's bathroom."

Jon nodded.

"Pete did a few things right."

Jon's jaw tightened.

"We can prove Kimball was selling bioweapons and set you all up."

"We still have some loose ends," Jon finally said.

"I'll go with you back to St. Petersburg to get Enrique and Boris. Even with Mikhail dead, Tippi is still in danger. We never found the missing vials of biohazard material even though Kimball's 'suicide note' said they were destroyed."

"Saving the world," Michael said, "is going to get you two killed."

Jon couldn't handle it anymore.

"Give Kamielle a kiss for me," he said to Michael. "I won't be there for the babies being born."

He walked away.

"This is your fault," yelling followed Jon's back. "You're supposed to be the best. You couldn't keep her safe!" General Joseph Miller dropped to his knees next to Elana's coffin. He threw his arms over the top and cried.

Tippi broke into sobs and Tony pulled her into his embrace, muttering soothing nonsensical words.

AJ walked away. She'd be better off with someone like Tony. Someone who was always on American soil and could take care of her. He hadn't done a good job. And now Elana was dead. The look in Jon's eyes was enough to help AJ walk away. Tippi would be safer without him.

Michael and Jax stood silently through the services. How was Michael going to explain to Kamielle he'd lost Jon? She wouldn't understand him walking away from the family. Wouldn't understand his need for revenge.

Michael wondered if the men in Russia knew what hell they'd unleashed on themselves. Jon was single-minded when he took a job. Having his heart ripped out was going to make him even more ruthless and deadly.

Michael wiped away a tear as they lowered Elana's

coffin and fired the salute. General Miller took the flag and saluted with tears streaming down his face.

Was Michael going to be getting a flag for Jon in the near future? He closed his eyes and said a prayer to a God Jon had abandoned long ago.

Jon found himself at CIA Headquarters. He stood at the entrance staring at the stars carved in the wall for fallen agents.

There had been one hundred two stars.

Now there were one hundred three.

He put a hand over the newly etched star and lowered his head.

"Lana," he whispered, "you didn't deserve this. It should have been me. I will stop Boris Novlak. I will keep Tippi safe. I will kill every bad guy I can until my last breath."

He closed his eyes.

"I promise."

About the Author

As a teacher, Kyona is always writing stories and reading books for work and fun. Reading gives people an opportunity to relax and escape the pressures of everyday life.

Life is short; enjoy it any way you can.

No Regrets
Even If It Breaks Your Heart

Slow Fire Burn